DISCARD

Summer Long-a-coming

HARPER & ROW, PUBLISHERS, New York

Cambridge, Philadelphia, San Francisco, Washington

London, Mexico City, São Paulo, Singapore, Sydney

BARBARA FINKELSTEIN

Summer Long-a-coming

a novel

SUMMER LONG-A-COMING. Copyright © 1987 by
Barbara Finkelstein. All rights reserved. Printed in
the United States of America. No part of this
book may be used or reproduced in any manner
whatsoever without written permission except in
the case of brief quotations embodied in critical
articles and reviews. For information address
Harper & Row, Publishers, Inc., 10 East 53rd
Street, New York, N.Y. 10022. Published
simultaneously in Canada by Fitzhenry &
Whiteside Limited, Toronto.

FIRST EDITION

Designed by Ruth Bornschlegel

Copyedited by Marjorie Horvitz

Library of Congress Cataloging-in-Publication Data
   Finkelstein, Barbara, 1953–
     Summer long a coming.
     I. Title.
PS3556.I4825S9   1987   813'.54
86–45656
ISBN 0–06–015692–9

87 88 89 90 91 HC 10 9 8 7 6 5 4 3 2 1

Grateful acknowledgment to
Daniel Marlin, Mimi Naish, and Marcie Horowitz
for reading *Summer Long-a-coming*
in an earlier draft.

Dedicated to Carole Malkin

"Well, you are in a desolate condition, 'tis true, but pray remember, where are the rest of you? Did you not come eleven of you into the boat? Where are the ten? Why were not they saved and you lost? Why were you singled out? Is it better to be here, or there?" And then I pointed to the sea. All evils are to be considered with the good that is in them and with what worse attends them.

—DANIEL DEFOE, *Robinson Crusoe*

Book One

1

THE SUMMER I TURNED FIFTEEN, hornets infested the maple tree shading Bolero's doghouse. No creature—not the cicadas that chattered into the bark of weeping willows, not the seventeen-year locusts that chewed holes in sassafras, nor the spotted ticks that grew the size of filberts—had ever advanced upon Jake's Poultry Farm like those wide phalanxes of disciplined hornets. Our property on the outermost rim of the Jersey Pine Barrens was as trusting as a girl, and anyone with the inclination could have trespassed at will. The farm had no steel-mesh gates or wandering lines of fence posts. Except for the game hunters in hunting season, nearly everyone else heeded the weathered "No Trespassing" signs posted on trees throughout the woods. So it was exciting on that morning fifteen years ago to see those audacious bees ignore my mother and father's prohibitions for outsiders to keep away.

It was nine o'clock by the time I got downstairs, and as usual, the danger was already under control. Outside, my father was motioning to Charlie, the black farmhand who lived in the sagging annex to our house, to move the ladder away from the tree. Every wave of his four-fingered hand assumed that compliance would follow, but soon he began to alternate commands in English and Yiddish when his emphatic gesturing failed to make the point. As Charlie lifted the ladder, a fat blue vein inside his dark temple pulsated out of sync with his slow walk, and his eyes took in only the slope of his own cheeks. I thought of ways to distract Charlie, so he would trip or fumble the ladder. Then maybe my father would demand my participation, and I, too, could have a chance at heroism. But even though my parents often whispered to each other about Charlie's shaking hands and about the bottle of Cold Duck in his room, Charlie's arms held steady as he leaned the ladder against two wooden sawhorses.

With my father's spray of Black Flag insecticide, the hornets rose en masse from the head of the maple, as if the tree's hair had buzzed and stood on end. And then, one by one, thousands of hornets swooned downwards, hitting the ground practically dead. The yard chickens had long since huddled under the pear tree a safe distance away. But the cats saw potential sport as the hornets batted their transparent wings against pebbles and brown grass, and our mutt Bolero and his mother, Duchess, thinking they were in for a meal, rooted through the weeds. At once the animals felt the hornets' wrath. Cats dispersed in all directions and crouched under the truck and coop, pawing their faces to soothe the pain. The dogs, banking on human sympathy, whimpered and ran sidelong to my mother and my younger sister, Perel, now policing the driveway lest an egg or chicken customer drive off the highway quite literally into a hornets' nest.

For a while the hornets popped up and down, as if collectively hiccuping. As a last-ditch protest, one of the smallest dived into my father's face. Papa smacked his cheek hard and flung the hornet to the ground, killing it along with the others.

Farm children labor under a lot of myths. People think we grow up with an intuitive knowledge of harvests, seasons, the properties of water. The births of kittens and baby chicks supposedly teach us about regeneration; the slaughter of chickens, the predacious zest for survival. To herald our maturity,

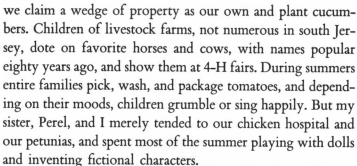

we claim a wedge of property as our own and plant cucumbers. Children of livestock farms, not numerous in south Jersey, dote on favorite horses and cows, with names popular eighty years ago, and show them at 4-H fairs. During summers entire families pick, wash, and package tomatoes, and depending on their moods, children grumble or sing happily. But my sister, Perel, and I merely tended to our chicken hospital and our petunias, and spent most of the summer playing with dolls and inventing fictional characters.

Mind you, the kids we knew at the regional high school were busily spending their summer vacations getting devirginized, smoking pot, and tripping for the first time. As removed as Long-a-coming was from city influences, a few of them were even grooming themselves to be flower children and understood politics well enough to distinguish between peace and war. But for Perel and me, summers meant a kind of quarantine. Of course we relied on *Time* and *The Today Show* to keep us in dim contact with the world outside Jake's Poultry Farm; and that's how we learned that revolutions, protestors, and burning cities competed for top billing in the world that mattered. Given—oh, given a lot of factors, but given mainly the demands of the chicken business, my life and Perel's resembled the little glass-domed winter scene my mother once bought me from the Long-a-coming Farmer's Market and Auction. Life inside that dome never changed, even if you turned it upside down to shake the snow and the glass grew hot in your hand. As a result, we never much stretched beyond the habits of childhood.

First, the dolls. None of them was in good shape, partly from overuse, partly from having had their plastic or cloth bodies wrapped with torn nylon stockings to simulate fashionable coiffures and bustlines. None of the dolls was Jewish, either, but usually Catholic orphans awaiting adoption in

Perel's bedroom. We could have practiced the piano down-stairs, could have read a book as my mother always encouraged us to do, could even have studied the different varieties of moss in the woods. Now and then, we did. But the fact is, Perel and I could not help ourselves, just as we couldn't help but domes-ticate kittens by locking them in chicken crates until they licked our fingers with gratitude. We simply took care not to perform any of our scenes in front of open windows where travelers on the Pike could see us.

The dozen voices of imaginary people were mainly Perel's creations. She was generous in seeing them as our joint effort, but my sister, not I, had the talent for parody, for exaggerating an element of a singer's style or the intonation of a gas station attendant's speech. One of her most cherished inventions was Luster, a redneck with a deranged Georgian leer. Another favorite was Pop, a calico kitten who passed the last days of his life slumped in the hole of a cinder block. Perel loved Pop for his insufferable agony, and outfitted him with a plaintive, cowed whine—a cross between a blond country-western croon and the earnest voice of a five-year-old child —and a sensitive heart that sympathized indiscriminately with victim and con artist alike.

I couldn't have been more than ten or eleven when we invented Sparsely and Saucer. We were convinced that "sparsely" and "saucer" were not genuine English words, but aberrations of Camden County language. To us they were nonsense syllables representing two hail-fellow-well-met south Jersey pals with voices like those of untrained opera baritones. We modeled them after Bill, the man who delivered the tanks of propane gas needed in the slaughterhouse. Bill was tall, wore a Poindexter crew cut even when the style had long passed out of popularity, spoke slowly, and prefaced most sentences with an "uh" that jiggled his Adam's apple. By our reckoning, Sparsely and Saucer were real Americans. They worshiped in the Long-a-coming Presbyterian Church Sunday mornings, bowled with their league Wednesday evenings, ate pancakes for breakfast, and participated in town meetings. They were respectful to women, whom they referred to as "honeys," because women were dizzy when it came to machinery and finance. Perel and I engaged them to Carnation and Anita, who suspected they were duds.

Our cast of characters also included literal renditions of people we knew, like Rodney MacDuff, our tall, emaciated, effeminate former piano teacher, who lived with his cousin in a white Civil War–era mansion in town, and who had tried, with varying degrees of success, to teach Perel and me some Beethoven. From him we picked up a laugh like a death rattle way down inside his throat, and the walk of a monstrously oversized praying mantis on its toes. And to illustrate anything exotic, Perel imitated the high school French teacher, whom we named Mrs. Barbarian. Mrs. Barbarian doused her hourglass figure with French cologne and consistently wore three items: a black dress, a red sweater nubbed with lint, and a gold bracelet. To amuse herself, Mrs. Barbarian frequently tittered, "Don't fight; just kill each other."

In retrospect, our time would have been better spent packaging sugar cookies and frozen fish fillets in Hammonton, or doing volunteer work at the Melody School for Emotionally Handicapped Children in Long-a-coming. Or if my parents had sold the farm and bought a guesthouse in Atlantic City, as they talked of doing, Perel and I might have spent that summer spinning cartwheels in front of Convention Hall. Or if my parents had enrolled Sheiye in a Brooklyn yeshiva, as they had occasionally threatened . . . In the past fifteen years I have considered a hundred ifs; as if all my concentration would grant me mastery over that summer.

7

What a laugh! I'm not much different from my mother and father after all. As a child, I could never tolerate their maniacal review of the past: What happened in 1942? Why did the Nazis send my father's family to such and such a camp as opposed to such and such a camp? (I could never remember the names.) And why did Papa only eat potatoes in July . . . until I would stomp out of the kitchen, furious with my parents, not the Nazis.

Now and then, I have thought that when my mother was pregnant with me, she replayed the images of her Polish-Yiddish youth in her mind so often that she transfused that endless, answerless style of investigation to the child sucking a thumb inside her. By the time I was six, I was already instructing myself to remember what I looked like at five; how I felt after I read my first book; who my teachers had been. Scraping my nails on the past, testing my foothold in the future, was habit with me by the time I was ten. All I needed was a personal holocaust to twirl around in my mind, and then I could carry my parents' obsessiveness with me into my generation. That's what my fifteenth summer gave me. And now it seems all I ever do is live in 1968.

A few days after the hornet incident, Perel and I took a walk to the woods. Neither one of us liked to go alone because of the dragsters and garden snakes. It always struck me as a little odd how scared we were of rural life. What did we expect to see in the fields and woods? Wild dogs, maybe, or another forest fire. Once, I remember, our whole family and Charlie drove out to Atsion Lake to watch the trees of the Wharton Tract burn down to charcoal. Fire engine companies from Long-a-coming, Loudon, Chesilhurt, and Elm drained half the cedar lake trying to extinguish the flames. Hundreds of local residents stood about transfixed, drinking beer and flirting with each other. For the first time in my memory, I saw my mother crying, as raccoons, field mice, chipmunks, opossums, weasels, all kinds of birds, and trees too, it seemed, straggled out of the woods on broken wings and singed paws. I felt confused because I knew my mother didn't even care much for cats and dogs.

Ruthlessness seeded the Long-a-coming woods. What looked like the calm rotation of seasons was actually the advance of pines throughout the field, choking the soil so that my father had to move his vegetable garden near the slaughter-house cesspool. Rural beauty, too, often seemed just one of nature's whimsies. The black-eyed Susans, which broke the green and brown monotony of south Jersey scrub with an arresting jumble of yellow every Memorial Day, were dead by July Fourth. And while the forests of the New World were fair game for rabbits and not runaway Polish Jews, an image of a stalked child accompanied me on my trips there. Little wonder I feared the Jersey Devil, a mischief-scheming creature, part bat, part kangaroo, that reputedly dominated the Pine Barrens.

Perel and I usually took Bolero along as our guardian. The three of us and Duchess had established a ritual: Seeing us head for the woods, Bolero skidded as far as the chain allowed, running all his weight into the leather collar around his neck, yelping desperately. Duchess lifted herself up heavily and whimpered, unsure if she was responding to danger or excitement. Bolero's mother was a canine octogenarian and so inert that she had won the right to stay unchained. Overcome by blindness and confusion, she flopped down in the driveway and napped. "Wanna go for a run, 'Lero?" Perel asked. It was my duty to restrain our mad dog while Perel undid the chain. Unleashed, Bolero crashed past our thighs and sped down the

9

path to the woods. "Okay, 'Lero," Perel shouted. "Take us for our run!" We were off behind him.

Once past the coops, Perel abruptly stood stock still, called Bolero, stuck out her hand like a traffic cop, and began swiveling her chubby hips. "Stop! In the name of love!" she warbled, in the honey-coated voice of a Motown singer. Perel curled her thin lips and batted her naturally long-lashed eyes behind her glasses as if they were leaden with mascara. "Sing it, sister!" I encouraged in my Sparsely and Saucer voice. Perel tapped her brow, shook her head up and down slowly, more like a rabbinic sage than a singer from a black girl group, and finished with, "Think it oh-over!"

"Haven't I been good to you?" chorused Pop, weakly.

The Motown singer repeated talmudically, "Think it oh-over!"

A horsefly buzzed around our ears, and we tore off towards the railroad tracks to outrun it. "Bzzz," went Perel, zigzagging the fly's route with her hand and landing on my nose. "Ow!" cried Sparsely, in his wounded-bear voice. "That hurts!"

Perel hung her head down like a child assessing how much to cry. She buckled the corners of her mouth, looked at me sideways, and pealed off a wail in Pop's voice. "Waaah! I'm sorry! Please forgive me. I'm just a little cat and I don't know any better!"

"If you'll be my *hantekh,* I'll forgive you," I said. Sometimes Perel and I pretended to be some inanimate object. To atone for being a fly, Perel had to let me dry my hands on her as if she were a hand towel.

"All right," Pop whined. I ran my hands across the dewy weeds and rubbed them on Perel's arm. When I touched her, her whole body became as stiff as Papa's wood chicken catcher.

We walked on until we got to the tracks, stopping every

few feet to whisk ticks off our sneakers and Bolero's paws, or to examine some purple weed we had never seen before. At the railroad tracks, a perpendicular path intersected the farm's. The right fork eventually led to Long Avenue, Long-a-coming's main street. Had we lived in town, we would have thought Long Avenue dull, with its Ambler's Grocery, Marnie's Five-and-Ten, the Freihoff School of Dance atop Humble's Supermarket, the fire hall, library, American Legion, Rodney MacDuff's mansion, the post office, First National Bank of Long-a-coming, and Strawb's clothing store for men. But because our visits to Long Avenue were limited to July Fourth to watch the local parade, or to Saturday evenings, when my father bought the *Philadelphia Inquirer,* all those commonplace buildings with their humdrum activities were as dramatic as uncharted tundra. The left fork continued on to a clearing in the woods and a power station made entirely from silver-gray steel and rubberized wire, like an ominous set of monkey bars. I was always a little surprised to see it in the woods, waiting with criminal patience for the destruction of the surrounding trees.

Bolero decided which direction we would take when he darted off towards the station. We followed the dog a few yards, when I noticed some sassafras leaves fall to the ground. Somebody was standing there in the woods, dressed in a white sailor's uniform, the sole of his shoe flat against a tree trunk. In spite of the dusty path, his outfit was spotless. The sun shone full in the guy's face as he shielded his brow with his forearm and met my stare. In that instant, his half-concealed face made me think it was my brother Sheiye, playing a trick on Perel and me. I squinted, and in the next second I thought he must be from some other era, maybe a decent boy come home from battling Japanese subs.

His decency notwithstanding, I immediately considered

the possibility that the sailor would murder us. How many times had my parents warned my sister, brother, and me that treachery lurks everywhere but in your own home? Most people, they implied, had a secret thirst to kill. A sailor on dry land—suspicious. I should have known, what with the blue sky as a decoy, that this ordinary day would end in death. Soon my blood and Perel's would spatter the sailor's whites. . . . Sheiye would be left an only child.

The sailor looked sullen, all right, but only because Perel and I had startled him. Suddenly, Bolero bounded up behind my sister and me and careened into my ankles. Affecting a blasé air, I bent down and patted Bolero's head. Life on a chain had dulled his senses, and he did not growl until the sailor cleared his throat and said, "I always was kinda scared of dogs." Bolero divined a threat in the sailor's voice and, frantic, raced back to the farm in a cloud of dust.

Bolero's betrayal dissolved my spellbound passivity, and I said softly to Perel, "Let's turn around and walk away, real normal-like." I figured that if we started running, we would frighten the sailor into attacking us. But he resumed his original pose, apparently indifferent to our presence. Perel and I sauntered off, and after a few steps, I had calmed down enough to be furious at Bolero. And soon I was furious at my predicament as a child on that farm. Bolero was no different from anyone else in my family. We were cowards, including my parents who settled on a south Jersey chicken farm and mined it with Orthodox Judaism, exploding little bombs of Sabbath and Passover, incapacitating their children so they couldn't function properly anywhere outside the farm. Hiding in the Polish woods from the Nazis, from Christians, and now hiding in America. A habit. All they know how to do is hide, and now that's all I know how to do.

Halfway back to the farm, Perel cried out, "Duck! A

car!" Occasionally, souped-up cars and motorcycles rumbled down the path from the Long-a-coming drag strip or from overgrown forest trails. But I knew it wasn't likely that a car should be coming from our house. Few local people disregarded the property rights of Jake's Poultry Farm, pulling off the White Horse Pike to use our driveway as a shortcut to the lovers' lane by the railroad tracks. In an instant, I saw our green flatbed truck lumbering towards us, carrying pails of chicken slop to the manure heap near the tracks. Perel and I jumped off the path and flagged it down as a startled rabbit hopped away to a protected clover patch. "I hope it's not Sheiye," Perel said, too distraught to hide behind one of her voices. Immediately, I insisted, "Not a word of that sailor to anyone, okay?" Drawing herself up like Rodney MacDuff, Perel wheezed, "Of caws not!" as if any intelligent person understood that the unpredictable does not tolerate discussion.

As the truck drew closer, Sheiye's face, rich with inscrutable connivance, floated above the steering wheel, bobbing in time with the toy bulldog's head that some butcher had long ago affixed to the rearview mirror. In the passenger's seat sat Charlie, his bloodshot eyes scanning the dry field and his brown arm on the window casing. Neither Charlie nor Sheiye altered his expression when they spotted Perel and me. I was sure they hadn't said a word to each other since they had gotten into the truck. Their silence, probably born out of incompatibility, seemed complicitous to me nonetheless.

Sheiye braked to a stop. "Can we get on?" I called to him through Charlie's window. Sheiye motioned with his hand to the back of the truck. "Only if you help us unload," he said. Spoiled as my sister and I were, we really did enjoy some farm chores, and only our lack of responsibility had made our offers to help so sporadic. We clambered onto the tires and over the sideboards and nestled between buckets of chicken guts. Sheiye started with a lurch, and Perel and I grabbed onto the cabin's metal backing. "Bastard," I muttered. I knocked on the rear window to get the men's attention. Sheiye looked at me through the rearview mirror and crimped his mouth so that indentations pocked his chin. Charlie turned his head a scant thirty degrees, the vein in his temple counting a beat for every whir of the truck's engine. I waved. Charlie's lips twitched and he smiled. Perel craned her neck, chewing on an imaginary rope of chicken gut like a cat, complete with gagging.

At the manure heap, Perel and I shoved the slop buckets to the edge of the truck bed, while Sheiye and Charlie overturned them. The heap, a misshapen tepee, rarely shrank below six feet; and even though many of the buckets were already teeming with newly born maggots by the time they were loaded on the truck, I still liked to watch the pile grow dense with feathers and multicolored innards. The manure glistened in the dead of midday.

As always, Sheiye dangled a chicken head before our eyes, sliding his voice up and down with a ghostly "ooooh!" "Stop flinging that ghastly chicken head around, you little twerp!" Perel groaned like Rodney MacDuff, exaggerating Rodney's limp wrist. I squinted at my brother and tried to deny the face I saw before me. It was the sailor's, then my brother's, then the sailor's, back and forth like those double-image postcards of Jesus sold in the Long-a-coming Farmer's Market and Auction. The picture of Sheiye menacing two girls with a chicken head awoke me to a realization: Any intimation of unmanliness rubbed against Sheiye's nerve. I understood why even back then. Our parents wouldn't let any of us date non-Jews, which meant we dated no one. While their dictum made Perel and me unpopular in school, it utterly desexed my brother. I was sure he would have hurled a bunch of chicken guts at us if Charlie hadn't been there. But we were all shy around Charlie, humbled into restraint by his blackness and averted eyes.

Charlie patted the tobacco pouch inside his shirt pocket and eyed Sheiye scraping muck off his boots. Even after eight years with us, Charlie was still a mystery. For example, a few minutes after the destruction of the hornets, I had sidled over to him where he stood with his back against the gray cinder blocks of the slaughterhouse. He was rolling himself a cigarette, an activity I loved to watch. Charlie's hand shook as he folded the pouch into his shirt pocket and lit the cigarette. I wanted to ask him if the hornets had scared him, if that's why his hand was shaking. Instead, curiosity shaped a non sequitur, and I asked, "Charlie, you married?"

Charlie shook his head slowly, his reserve impenetrable, and dragged on his cigarette. I guessed he was an "old bachelor," or an *alter bucher,* as my parents referred to him in Yiddish. But in Charlie, bachelorhood was the consequence of decision, not failure, and not, as little Pop would have sniffed, insecurity.

The buckets unloaded, the four of us settled back into the truck: Perel and I pressed against the backboard, peering through the cabin window to pester our brother; Charlie in the truck's cabin with Sheiye. My brother stared lazily at the ignition key, probably to prolong our contact with the smelly slop buckets. Charlie, perennially unmoved by the pastimes of the Szusters, merely glanced at my brother from the corner of his eye and patted his tobacco pouch. I had first seen that look of unconscious contemplation on Sheiye a day or two earlier, when I found Mama lecturing him about something—sex ethics, I assumed—in the kitchen. Sheiye looked cruel, and I believed he was humoring Mama for the moment but planned to debauch as many south Jersey maidens as he could lay his hands on when he started college in the fall.

15

Once the truck began moving and the drone of the engine provided cover, Perel nudged me and sang "My Secret" by the Platters, in a powerless, tuneless voice: " 'Nobody knows the thrills and the glows, the ebbs and the flows, whoa, I've got a secret—' " I shook my head to cut her off. "Not a word about that," I reminded her, nodding in the direction of the railroad tracks. "Oh, honey!" Saucer chided. "I know!"

Why was I so intent on keeping that episode a secret? I had the same reaction to the sailor as I had had to anti-Semitic insults from some boys at school. I never mentioned them to anyone, not to my parents and not even to Perel, in whom I had always confided. Why talk about something shameful? My parents were tight-lipped about the Nazis, and I was tight-lipped about my classmates. I puzzled over those comments time and time again, wondering what I had done to elicit them. I never laughed too loudly, rarely tattletaled, and used the word "nigger" once to accommodate my friends. I figured that if I passed my social studies tests and raved over the Beatles, no one could ever differentiate me from the rest of the group. When someone insulted me, I assumed I had slipped up. And now I had the notion that if Perel and I hadn't wandered to the railroad tracks, the sailor wouldn't exist. Or he would simply be a tiptop fellow hiking to the power station, returning later to his God-fearing Christian home on Auburn Avenue for Monday-night ham. My eyes turned innocence into depravity.

Perel and I smiled at each other, anticipating our favorite part of the ride. My brother (or father, when he drove) would always floor the gas pedal as he approached the weeping willow tree about four hundred feet from the house. My sister and I would stand up, hold on to the metal backing of the cabin, and feel the dizzying smack of the summer wind on our faces. The green and yellow arms of the tree drooped onto the windshield, completely obscuring the bend in the path, and we had to stoop not to get lashed by them. The test of bravery, however, was to hold out long enough to feel the first whip of the branch against an arm. That moment—just before the willows slapped the hood of the truck—more than any other on the farm, sent a flash of pleasure down my spine, where it rippled a few seconds against the bottom vertebrae.

But this time, after the bend, Sheiye didn't slow down. He was supposed to, as my father always did, fearing that one of us might be coming up the path. I remember Perel and I stood up again and yelled for Sheiye to watch for the cats and dogs in the driveway. Perel started pounding on the cabin window. Out of spite, it seemed, Sheiye wouldn't brake. I don't know what Charlie was thinking. He stared out his window, indifferent to the racket Perel and I made, brushing off dragonflies and chicken feathers that fluttered against his sweat-beaded forearm.

When Sheiye hit the brake, the truck was going at least forty miles an hour, which felt half again as fast on the rutted path. I know he had had enough time to see Duchess lying in the driveway where Perel, Bolero, and I had left her a half hour earlier. It wouldn't have taken much dexterity to avoid her, and he wouldn't have overturned the truck, as he claimed would have happened, if he had swerved. And why had the accelerator pedal never gotten stuck, as Sheiye swore was the case, when my father drove?

The right front tire rolled directly over Duchess's round body, and once the truck was upon her, Sheiye turned the steering wheel so that the vehicle's high chassis passed over her without another scratch. The truck did end up tipping slightly but caught its balance a few yards farther on. In my panic, I feared that Sheiye would gun the truck straight into the White Horse Pike and kill us all.

By the time my parents ran outside to determine the source of the noise, I had leapt off the truck to check Duchess, Perel was kicking at Sheiye's door, and Charlie was leaning against the black-patched fender, shaken, wiping his brow with a rumpled white handkerchief. Duchess jerked her hind legs several times and squealed like a baby pig. Her fat girth, previously clumped against her ribs after years of desultory old age, was now oozing out a hole near a dried-up nipple. I touched her side gently, hoping that through her pain Duchess would feel a love I had never really had for her. She could bear neither the additional pressure nor my insincerity. She stopped wriggling and died.

With Duchess dead at my feet, I could not imagine hating anyone more than I hated Sheiye. Perel scooped up loose pebbles from the ground and hurled them at him, while he parried her attack with a raised elbow. Despite his undeniable responsibility for Duchess's death, he would not tolerate our abuse, but improvised phony karate slaps to drive us away.

My parents, though shocked, looked relieved. After all, it was only Duchess, the old dog who got underfoot, and who forced customers to detour around her sleeping body. Neither Mama nor Papa was the type to ask "What happened?" when the obvious stared them in the face, so they made very little comment. Most important was the never-ending work of the farm. It required resourceful solutions, which Papa began dispatching at once. *"Hehr awf!"* Papa yelled at Sheiye, still assailing Perel. My father looked at Charlie, and I thought he might demand an explanation from him. But Charlie had been quick to separate himself from our family council, and had busied himself with rolling empty slop buckets off the truck bed.

"What're you gonna do about *him!*" Perel cried, throwing one last stone at Sheiye.

"Gey avek!" Papa warned Perel and me. "Beat it!" As Papa saw it, Duchess's death was a regrettable but trivial episode, no matter how it had come about. And with chickens waiting to be fed, now was no time to press for judgment. It was useless to argue. Perel and I stormed off to the house, screaming that nobody's parents were as unfair as ours. I did not fail to notice Mama's embarrassment as she contemplated some way to hide her children's latest brawl from Charlie.

Even before we reached the front door, I felt something steam up through my fury. It was a recollection of my mother responding to a question I had once asked: "What people do you hate?" "I don't hate people," she had answered. "I only hate murderers." How did that jibe with her present indifference to Duchess's death? Moreover, I knew my parents would not subject Sheiye's crime to scrutiny. Mama and Papa did not brood openly about alternatives; they did not suffer for hours on end before choosing a course of action. So I wondered if their dismissive attitude boiled down to a matter of necessity: Could Sheiye get away with murder because he was indispensable to the farm? Or was one more dead animal on a chicken farm a big to-do over nothing? I only knew that if Mama and Papa had wanted to punish Sheiye, they would have done it at once.

Our appeals to justice exhausted, Perel and I tore out of the kitchen, back to the driveway. Mama was taking dry laundry off the clothesline; Papa had stalked off to the left-field coop. Unbeknownst to us, Sheiye had parked the truck under the maple tree, dismantling the scene of the crime. Meanwhile, Charlie still labored at shoveling the dog's body into a bucket. As my sister and I ran past, I was struck by the blur of sweat from his armpit to his lower back. The absence of a like stain on his other side gave Charlie an asymmetrical look.

We heard Sheiye fiddling around with wrenches or screwdrivers in the coop feedroom, a place about which Perel and I were superstitious. A few years earlier, she, Sheiye, and I had sealed four live baby chicks in an empty Danish cookie tin, which we then abandoned on a rafter beam. A year or two later, when my sister and I worked up enough courage to open the tin, we found nothing inside, not even dust. Sheiye swore that he had never freed the baby chicks, and explained that bacteria had worn them down to nothing. "You and Perel killed them," he accused when we questioned him. Even though Sheiye had shared in our experiment, we accepted his accusation. I thought the feedroom was a fitting place for him to hide out, for now our brother could throw this old crime up in our faces.

"I hope you're looking for a shovel," Perel laid into Sheiye. "'Cause you're gonna bury Duchess."

"Sure you don't wanna do the honors, little girls?" Sheiye asked. "You have a knack for burying things, eh? I guess we're one for one now." He picked up a ratchet and flicked an index finger against the wheel.

"I didn't know we were in a contest," Perel snapped, the closest she would come to acknowledging the baby chicks.

Sheiye held the ratchet up to an eye, studying the tool as if it, not Duchess, were the reason for this confrontation. "Accidents happen," he said, giving the wheel another twirl. "But you little girls wouldn't know anything about accidents, would you?"

"Only turds know about accidents," I said. The fact is, Sheiye had reason on his side, tendentious though it was, and now only crude insults could bail Perel and me out.

"Well," Sheiye said, sure of victory, "I'll bury your dog for you. But you've gotta come along and watch."

Perel and I stared at Sheiye, speechless. By now I was less

repelled by Duchess's death than by Sheiye's attempt at intimacy. It always surfaced when least expected. As a rule, Sheiye picked fights with us—dragged us by our legs around the backyard, chucked rusted railroad ties at our heads. Inevitably, though, his overtures towards us turned friendly, and out of nowhere he suggested some outing together. This current one stunned me. Perel and I protested with some obligatory curses that Sheiye should burn in hell forever, but truthfully, his ultimatum was as tempting as a bribe. For one thing, Sheiye's willingness to bury Duchess was an implicit admission of his guilt; for another, we were curious about the burial of an animal in the earth.

Spade balanced on his shoulder, Sheiye ran up the dirt path to intercept Charlie, who walked slowly towards the manure heap, where Papa had ordered him to dump Duchess. Racing into the funeral procession from the field, Bolero frolicked around the slop bucket, undistressed by his mother's corpse.

Charlie turned back, and Sheiye, Perel, and I continued on to a weedy grove of trees beyond the left-field coop. Once we came to a stop, flies swarmed around Duchess's body. My sister and I swatted at them while Sheiye dug the grave. None of us spoke, not out of discomfort with each other or out of deference to Duchess, but because this unexpected gathering had a somber air of ceremony about it. When the hole was finished, I did not want to put the body in the ground. She'll get sandy, I thought, as if that mattered. I spied a torn page of the *National Enquirer* caught in some nettles, the lead story about a woman who had given birth to two hundred and fifty children. Before Sheiye dumped Duchess into the grave, I lined it with the newspaper. In a few days, I thought, I could dig her up and add more newspaper to stave off further decay. Oddly, by the time Sheiye packed the loose dirt down with his sneaker, I was thinking no longer about Duchess but of that erratic ray of sweat down Charlie's shirt.

That night, I stroked the land between my thighs to punish God. I didn't know why cruelty should reign in my family, but it did. That night, the world's evil was centered in Sheiye. We were a family of survivors—all of us, not just my parents. I viewed us as survivors of evil. That made us good, didn't it? But what was wrong with Sheiye? I saw the look in his eye in the rearview mirror when he floored the pedal. He was bedazzled; the possibility of someone else's death excited him. He was beckoning a repeat of my parents' past, but twenty-five years later, he wanted to play the role of executioner. I thought of him across the hall in his bedroom. I bet he slept well.

In the morning, I remembered a dream. My arm was draped around the pimply shoulders of a fat anti-Semite named Kurt Harvey. Though repelled by his obesity, all I wanted was to sink my fingers into the ply of his belly. Together we lived in the ramshackle doghouse of Rocky, long dead, where Sheiye had once spent the night for not helping my parents in the slaughterhouse. With Kurt Harvey, I was fearless, not because I ambled side by side with my enemy, but because I had been transformed: I had no concept of fear. To imitate cowardice, I pretended to hide behind the left-field coop, where oversized ants crawled beneath rocks and rats heavy with chicken flesh waddled over rotted lumber. Still asleep, I saw the white light of a crystal chandelier the size of a sputnik that Kurt Harvey had installed in our doghouse. When I woke up, I knew it would be a long time before I would ever see incandescence made tangible again.

2

THE DAYS FOLLOWING THE HORNET INVASION passed typically. On Tuesday, a farm labor transport bus broke down in front of our house, stalled half on the shoulder of the road, half in our driveway. The buses of migrant workers fascinated me: All of them were converted public school buses that had been out of commission a few years. It was common throughout the southern counties to come across the broken-down vehicles on the highway or on side roads, or parked alongside blueberry bogs and twin white Port-o-Sans. I don't think I ever saw more than one or two white faces in their windows. In the evening, as I watched the buses return to Philadelphia and Trenton, I expected to see the black figures, their hair covered with paisley kerchiefs, clapping their hands and singing gospel lyrics, as I had seen black people do on the Traveling Baptist and Gospel Mobile. Instead, the passengers either dozed or leaned their elbows on the window frames and let the stagnant heat and bus exhaust blow against their upturned sleeves.

As I sat on our front steps, I fixed on one figure among the passengers, all of them dressed in fruit-spattered work clothes, standing outside the bus and fanning themselves with handkerchiefs. He was of middling height, middle-aged, light-skinned, and wore a rumpled flannel shirt that must have itched as he picked. While many of the others looked down at the dry ground, this man was sullenly memorizing the layout of everything in view: the slaughterhouse to his right, our hulking gray and green shingled house across the driveway to the left, the three parallel chicken coops farther back, the fragile dogwood my father had watered and pruned for eighteen years, Bolero yapping, the rusted swing set behind the house, a cesspool behind the slaughterhouse and another near the Pike, the dusty white bus-stop shelter near the stalled bus, and the god-awful blanket airing on the clothesline.

His appraisal of our property completed, he began chewing his wad of bubble gum in slow, repeated chomps. Steeling himself into a single beam of arrogance, he blew a bubble that covered a good third of his face. And when the pink mess exploded on his nose and cheeks, I shook from my shoulders down to my waist, just as if I had heard a gunshot.

The bus driver thanked my mother for the bucket of water she had carried over to him. He nodded his head at the guy with the bubble gum, whom several passengers were now persuading to get back in the bus, and said, "That Draft ain't nothin' but a growed boy. Beautiful flowers," he added, admiring the lilac bush at the driveway entrance. He uncapped the radiator and I thought I heard him tell Draft to get back to his seat. Draft stuck out his tongue to clean off the gum and disappeared with the others into the bus.

The rest of the week was typical too. On Wednesday night I heard some clatter downstairs, followed by the pounding of my father's bare feet on the kitchen floor, and then his voice explaining to my mother, "Charlie. *Shiker.*" Drunk. The next morning an egg customer told us about the crash of a drag car into the stadium seats of the Long-a-coming drag strip. On Friday Russell's Funeral Parlor handled burial arrangements for the twenty-two-year-old dragster, just home from Vietnam. If the town was sad, I didn't know of it, because the Szusters had nothing to do with Long-a-coming.

Then came Shabbos. To my parents' outstretched arms,

Shabbos offered a bouquet of fruit and flowers from the World to Come, wrapped in a smell they compared to the cherry orchards in the Polish towns of their childhood. At the children's feet, Shabbos dropped a booty of shackles and laughed into our ears, "You're free to rest now." As far as Perel, Sheiye, and I were concerned, Shabbos overran Jake's Poultry Farm with a crew of trolls clutching at its shoulders, a regiment of dybbuks and golems assembled from a week's worth of bad dreams. Shabbos's trolls posted themselves in the driveway, policed the coops, and bound our fingers so that entertainment, whose expenditure of effort looked at times like work, was impossible. A dozen times a day I would ask my parents when Shabbos would be over, when the weekday routine could resume its hegemony. Invariably, my father would say, "Why do you want to chase her away? She just got here and will disappear all too soon." If Shabbos was a woman, all I had ever seen was a harridan waving a list of prohibitions in her hand.

Most of the morning passed as quickly as regular time, probably because Perel and I spent it on her bed, tickling each other and screaming our heads off. Later we ate potato chips and red cough drops for breakfast, and neutralized the queasiness in our bellies with a glass of milk. But by ten-thirty, Papa wanted us to pray, his son up in his own room, his daughters in the piano room. Though we had both independently decided we were atheists, Perel and I rarely faked our prayers. We sat on the piano bench with a single *siddur* between us, and chanted the Hebrew words we barely understood with the vague hope that something God-like would remember the Jews of Long-a-coming. Papa wanted us to *daven* for at least a half hour, but Perel and I had only learned enough prayers for ten minutes. To fill up the time we sang Passover songs, regardless of season, and sometimes whispered *Kaddish*, nervous that, in reciting the prayer for the dead, we were wooing the Angel of Death.

Beginning at noon, two of the trolls positioned themselves atop the number twelve on the kitchen wall clock, one clenching his fists round the hour hand, the other round the minute hand. You could almost hear a screech like train brakes as time slowed down against its will. My parents ate their usual twelve o'clock dinner—too early in the day and too un-American, I thought. After thanking God for the meal, Papa read the English and Yiddish papers and shortly took Mama and the Shabbos Queen into bed with him. By two-thirty, the trolls had slipped a little from their uppermost perch, unable to defy gravity forever. Their heels dug a bloodless gash into Shabbos's hip, from which Shabbos drew even more courage.

By afternoon I felt vanquished, and lay down on my bed to study the "Word Power" list in the *Reader's Digest.* Soon afterwards, when I practically could see Shabbos floating around my room in trillions of microscopic air droplets, I conceded defeat. In a mood halfway between drowsiness and pain, I filled up with pity—for a kitten's eye infection, a teenage boy's flat head, the way my father's body rocked slightly while he read the papers, and how my mother's lips spoke when she ate, reminding her that hunger also has a taste. The weekday could never have mastered me like this.

I barely recognized the Shabbos Brantzche, tempted to run free behind coops and brambles but rendered inert by childhood obedience. What was Shabbos, really, but a claustrophobic memory set upon me, citizen of a new world with too many tantalizing diversions? The weekday motored me towards adulthood and choice; Shabbos parked her charabanc alongside my parents' Chevy and tapped out a message on my forehead that I could never elude the past; that I wasn't traveling forward at all, but had gotten thrown back into the rubble of ancestral commitments.

Why did I want to resist Shabbos when I had never known another way to live? Shabbos, this queen of generational memory, wanted imperial dominion over me, wanted me to forget the circumstantial injuries that made up my own private memories. It's no wonder that I can remember stark events like death but few of the nuances that live for a moment in an exchange of glances and then disappear. I can't even remember if I liked the smell of cut grass or if it made me choke.

Despite my ambition to blot out Shabbos's influence, I always looked forward to the stories Mama told those afternoons. One of them, "The Dzatkele and the Babkele," was a fable she had heard as a child, and now Perel and I never tired of hearing it.

The Dzatkele and the Babkele lived in Poland. One day they had to visit another town for a few hours, and before they left they instructed their three children not to let anyone into the house, especially a mean bear who ate children. Sure enough, when the Dzatkele and the Babkele were gone, the children heard a knock at the door. "Who is it?" they all cried. "I'm a little orphan," a voice whined, "and I'm hungry. Please open the door and give me something to eat."

The children were moved by the orphan's sad voice. One child said, "It can't be the bear, because bears don't talk." And the other two agreed. But when the children opened the door, the bear fell upon one of them, a girl, and swallowed her up. The two others managed to hide in the *kutshament*, the tiny space between the oven and the kitchen wall.

When the parents returned, they found the bear rubbing his belly and moaning. The two children wriggled out from the *kutshament* and told their parents what had happened. The Dzatkele and the Babkele were angry that their children had disobeyed, but this was no time to scold. The Dzatkele grabbed a kitchen knife and he and the Babkele sliced the bear open. Out jumped their daughter! To punish the bear, the Dzatkele and the Babkele stitched pebbles inside his belly. Celebrating, the Dzatkele and the Babkele danced with the children around the groaning bear, and sang:

> *Shteyndelakh un beyndelakh*
> *Klingen in bo-akh!*
> *Brantzchele un Perele*
> *Geyen esn a goldene yo-akh.*

> Little stones and tiny bones
> Ring-a-ling! Your belly!
> Brantzchele and Perele
> Drink up the bad bear's golden jelly.

I could not articulate how or why, but "The Dzatkele and the Babkele" somehow struck me as a parable about the war, and consequently, Perel and I wanted to know how Mama had survived it.

"One time in winter," she told us, "I decided I had to find food for my brother. Of course I was hungry, but I imagined my brother must be even hungrier. I stood behind a building and watched a German patrol the street. It must have been an hour I stood there and shivered. Finally, I couldn't take it anymore, the cold or my hunger. I decided that whatever happens, I have to get my brother some bread. So without checking for the Nazi, I entered the street. And do you know, the Nazi was gone!"

"And you found the bread?" I asked Mama.

"Yes, I found the bread," she answered, ending the story.

Further probing brought no more information, and I concluded my mother had survived the war because of Polish manna.

On any given Shabbos, this is the only fact I ever heard about my mother's survival. Our questions about the war pushed this particular incident into the foreground of my mother's memory, where it stood before us like a prisoner who jostles the ranks of fellow prisoners as he steps forward for questioning. Did this episode represent the worst of her experiences? I had never heard any details at all about the deaths of my mother's or father's family and imagined, ridiculous as it sounds, that science fiction Nazis had beamed them to another planet. Maybe there really was nothing more to know about my parents' past, and their life of chickens and Orthodox ritual summed up who they were.

"What about Papa?" I sometimes persisted. "What happened to his family?" I could only ask about my father's past while he slept on Shabbos afternoon; probably I really didn't want to hear about it. Not from him, anyway.

"Shhh!" Mama whispered. Her brown eyes suddenly turned filmy, the way chickens' eyes do as their milky lids shutter for the night. *Please,* they begged, *no more questions. Don't upset Papa.* "But why doesn't he tell us?" I demanded. *"Vek eym nisht awf; er shluft,"* she whispered again. Don't wake him up; he's sleeping. Papa lay on the couch, his eyes closed and a copy of the *Jewish Daily Forward* on his chest. A snore, like the beginning of laughter, scraped the sides of his throat. Mama cocked her head to one side, wrinkled her brow, and pursed her lips as if she were about to say something in Polish. "A motortsicle," she said, in a language not quite English or Yiddish. Her little joke ended any further investigation.

To appease our disappointment, Mama offered to show us old photographs. She stored them in a leather bag, hidden in the top drawer of her clothing cabinet, as precious as Elijah's silver wine goblet wrapped in an old white panty and stored next to her diaphragm. The photographs it held—too sacred for the ordinary photograph album, which contained recent pictures of us playing with cats and chickens—were old, and without exception had been taken in Poland, Russia, and Austria. Each picture, yellowed and cracked, was of a person or a group of people. No buildings, no geography. More often than not, they were close-ups of a face. One of Mama's most intriguing descriptions was of a balding man who looked somewhere between twenty-five and forty: "This man returned to his family's town in Poland and took revenge on his Christian neighbors." Hardly anyone smiled, either because the circumstances of their lives at the moment were too dire or because the camera threatened to yank out their souls. In fact, so many faces looked on the verge of tears that I judged those few with smiles to be fakes. One such picture showed my mother at eighteen, after the war. Her black hair pulled back, a gold earring in her right ear, she stood in the crook of an enormous elm as if it were her home. She was beautiful. I couldn't imagine the woman who was my mother spontaneous enough to hoist herself up the side of a tree, and position herself, arms akimbo, between its branches. Her eyes and lips were stretched into a smile of victory.

The other picture was of my father. Unlike the crew cut he had worn ever since he became a chicken farmer, his hair in this picture was Stalin-thick and wavy. He was seated at a long table with another dozen or so men, all with coffee cups before them. My father's eyes were small and almond-shaped, like mine, and when he smiled, they slanted upwards. The narrow but deeply etched scar over his left eye exaggerated the Oriental slant, and like a third eyebrow cast a mix of cruelty and mischief across his brow. When the camera shutter blinked, he was looking askance at his neighbor, who might just have told a joke. I wondered if in the next second my father, who was not yet father to anyone, didn't burst out laughing. In his right hand he was holding a cigarette, a temporary stand-in for his amputated thumb. "How come Papa stopped smoking?" Perel and I asked my mother. "I wouldn't let him smoke," she said. Bemused, she added, "He gave it up because I didn't like it." Screwing up her features to the center of her face, she spat out, *"Feh!"* How unlike that slender *kresavetse* she was now, with a round belly fattened by bowls of sour cream and cucumbers.

"What happened to Papa's thumb?" I asked. "Did he lose it in the war?" My mother's face had just recomposed itself, when it fell once more into a grimace. *"Lomir redn fin shenere zakhn!"*—Let's talk about prettier matters!—said the woman who wore Playtex rubber gloves whenever she ripped the guts out of a freshly slaughtered chicken. She was already part of the photographs in her lap, moving her lips silently to respond to the pictures' questions. Somehow her preoccupation with the leather bag of European pictures left a look of indifference on her face, and I was annoyed with her for the hundredth time for not ever thinking about anything.

Shabbos ended and the new work week immediately reasserted itself with a long night of slaughter. It was always safe for Perel and me to offer our help in the slaughterhouse, because we knew our parents would reject it. They viewed the chicken business as their personal degradation, and believed it would be ruinous to subject their daughters to it. That night, though, I decided I wasn't going to sit in front of our black-and-white TV with its ever-fading picture. It was more than boredom that drove me to observe the activity that let Perel and me live like provincial nobility while everyone else on the farm suffered.

I got up from the brown and yellow flowered armchair and rubbed the back of my thigh where a loose spring had pressed against it. Keeping the kitchen door from slamming, I walked stealthily across the driveway so as not to rouse Bolero into a chorus of tenor barking.

Through the slaughterhouse window, dotted with tiny white flecks and smashed pellets of excrement, everyone's face looked like dripping candle wax, and their bodies like ornate candelabras. I watched my mother hand my father a newly dead chicken for plucking. Customers often commented on how young she looked, and though to me she had always appeared old and unstylish in her de-ribbed corduroy pants, I saw now for the first time what they meant. The paisley kerchief covering her black hair accentuated her round, pale face and smoothed out the delicate hairline wrinkles at the corner of each eye. Not much over five feet tall, she looked like a tubby girl who had wandered into a playground furnished with props of the slaughter trade instead of merry-go-rounds. Her gaze, too, was like a child's, oblivious to the existence of others. Innocence I had never noticed before washed over her brown pupils, and through the blurred window I saw how much Perel was her mother's daughter.

My brother said something that made my mother press her lips together in a blend of amusement and reproof, and elicited a dismissive wave of her hand. The vague look disappeared and, glowering at the scratches on her hands, Mama pulled on her yellow Playtex rubber gloves.

A beige, melting figure darted from the defeathering machine to the rusting barrels near the scale and then to the aluminum table where my mother disemboweled the slaughtered chickens. Craning backwards with difficulty, it pointed a four-fingered hand towards the twenty or so crates of live chickens piled near the barrels. That was my father. Just then he caught sight of me, my breath against the window having formed a round cloud the size of a cantaloupe. As my mother stooped under the table to arrange a new row of white plastic slop buckets, my father shook an index finger at me, and I could see him mouth the word *"Gedenk!" Gedenk* meant "Remember, I warned you, you're not supposed to be here," and was half threat, half joke. No matter, for he immediately focused his attention on the rubber prongs of the defeathering machine and seemed to forget about me entirely.

Knowing my mother would eventually spy me at the window and command me back to the house, I paid strict attention to everything before my eyes. *Remember what you see,* I thought. *Gedenk.* Yet now when I try to remember the slaughter, I mostly recall how runny the windows were, how streaked with the glue of water and chicken; how the naked light bulbs on the ceiling were haloed yellow in the fatty mist; how my underarms smelled like chicken soup. Sometimes when I walk through a train station tunnel I close my eyes and pretend that I am walking through the slaughterhouse, breathing in the propane fumes and the freshness of matted straw stuck to the chickens' feet. It didn't have the raw flesh stench of butchershops or the dishwater air exhaust of fast-food restaurants, but a sun-baked odor, cooled in the shade of a maple, a potpourri of intestines clogged with semidigested chicken feed, the choking perfume of pollen and weeds, and the gasoline waste from the Pike. It also held the smell of chickens clawing at human hands, squawking noiselessly, the sound of their terror muted by the machines and the flapping noise of a fan belt.

As I shifted my attention back to the barrels, another figure came into view. It was Mr. Berg, the *shoykhet,* whose blessing, Papa had told us, initiated every slaughter. The *shoykhet's* two lips, barely meeting each other, praised God's reign over the universe, and then clamped shut. From his apron pocket he took out a long razor that caught the light of the uncovered bulbs, and stropped it against a flint on his hip. Coarsened by the job, he reached for a fluffy white chicken, which Sheiye had pulled out of an open crate, yanked the chicken's neck backwards, and then slit its throat. With a thump, he stuffed the carcass, a red-feathered necklace now spreading down its front, into a funnel overhanging one of the rusted barrels. The *shoykhet* wiped the blade on his apron, returned it to his pocket, and took a drag from the cigarette he had laid on the scale. Breathing heavily from the humidity and his sixty-plus years, he would repeat this process until dawn. My father often widened his small eyes and remarked, *"M'zugt az Mister Berg iz a gelernter"*—People say Mr. Berg is a learned man—and I tried to imagine him as a young student with curly sidelocks, hunched over a nicked mahogany table in Warsaw, bleary-eyed over a purple-bound *Gemara* that smelled of tobacco and mildew. But even my father was stunned by the discrepancy between the Mr. Berg who split hairs over the *Khimish's* ten thousand interpretations with the Camden, New Jersey, community of rabbinic elders, and the Mr. Berg who grunted and wheezed and was so unattuned to the common amenities of daily life that he once transported a live chicken back to Camden on his shoulder.

After a minute or so, Mama finally saw me, and waved me away. I didn't move. She disappeared from view, and the next thing I knew, the slaughterhouse door swung open and she yelled, *"Gey arahn in shtib!"* Get back to the house! You would think we were in *Gone With the Wind,* and the slaughterhouse was Tara burning.

"Why?" I shouted back. "I want to watch."

"I don't want to pay doctors' bills for you! *Gey arahn in shtib!*"

"But, Mama!" I cried. "It's eighty-five degrees out here. How am I going to get sick?"

"You'll get sick!" Mama screamed again, unwilling to part with the explanation she had hit upon to mask the shame she felt for slaughtering chickens. Then, as if she had been waiting for any opportunity, well timed or not, to say what was on her mind, she hurled out, "Why can't you enjoy being a child? I'd have done anything for a normal childhood." I had the feeling that she had addressed the gray brick of the slaughterhouse, not me. Tensing my knees and leaning forward, I wanted to hiss, "I hate this place and I can't wait to leave." Instead, I sniffed, "There's a glob of blood on your cheek."

Waving her hand at me again, as if I were a troublesome mosquito, Mama dabbed at her cheek with a rumpled handkerchief and straightened the scarf on her head, preparing for battle. I regarded her command as the bullying prerogative of adulthood, a show, but I didn't want to test her conviction. As I ran across the driveway, I realized I was starving, my stomach burning with the same acid I felt after a fight with Sheiye.

No sooner had I pulled the kitchen screen door open and slammed it shut than it opened behind me. Afraid that I had angered my mother, I got ready to dash upstairs to my bedroom. But it was only Mr. Berg, tracking muck on the floor that my mother had waxed Friday morning. *"Zayt azoy gut,"* the *shoykhet* began, "a little gless of djoos."

I walked back into the kitchen and poured Mr. Berg his juice. When Perel and I weren't around, Mr. Berg knew how to help himself. But whenever a woman was within grunting distance, he requested her intervention. "Tenk you," he said, and threw back his head, drinking the juice in one gulp. He stroked his protruding belly to guard against indigestion, and set the empty glass down in midair. I could swear I saw Mr. Berg smile as he loosened his fingers around the glass, still under the thrall of destruction that work in the slaughterhouse spun around him. Despite his loyalty to the 613 commandments that Jews are supposed to obey, an anarchic unruliness had slipped through the net strung by Torah. I had observed similar quirks in my parents: my father with his insistence that the telephone receiver be replaced upside down; my mother with her compulsion to store used sanitary napkins under the bathroom clothes hamper until she could secretly burn them. Sometimes I attributed these irregularities to the Nazis, sometimes to God.

Of course the *shoykhet*'s glass dropped, though you would never have known from the bemused look on Mr. Berg's face that he was aware that glass at the mercy of gravity falls and breaks into quite a few jagged pieces. He rubbed the nicotine-stained beard on his cheek and blew air through his nose like a zebra. The *shoykhet* looked up at me and Perel—who had run into the kitchen at the sound of shattering—first with one eye, then with both. He chuckled, clearly waiting for me to say, "Don't worry, I'll clean it up." I did, and before the last splinter had been gathered up, he turned towards the door, kissed the tassels of his undergarment prayer shawl, and stepped up on his toes to kiss the *mezíze* nailed to the door-frame above his head. "Ah, gehrils!" Mr. Berg poked his head back in, coughed, and said, "Your mama says to go to sleep." Mindful of the juice, he nodded at the remaining broken glass on the floor and crossed the driveway to the slaughterhouse.

"And I thought he was thirsty," I sighed.

Rocking her hips in a semicircle, Perel began to shake her index finger at me reprovingly in slow motion. She pointed to the slaughterhouse with her head and warbled in a breathy voice, " 'Nothin' you can say can make me stay away from my guy!' "

" 'My guy!' " I echoed. I spread my arms wide around the invisible body of a fat man.

" 'No handsome face can ever take the place of my guy!' "

" 'My guy! My guy! My—' "

In Papa's half-stern, half-deprecatory Yiddish, Perel switched characters and admonished, *"A bisl derkherits,* Brantzchele, Perele, *nu?* How about a little respect?"

I lifted a wedge of sticky glass. Looking calmly at the droplets of yellow juice on the shards, I yielded to a memory of a long crescendo squeal of rubber tires on asphalt and the riot of tinkling windshield glass. The Pike collision had occurred one warm Shabbos afternoon before summer vacation began. Perel and I rushed into my parents' bedroom to get a clear view of someone else's tragedy. When we jumped onto the bed and stared out the window, Perel's mouth dropped open and her eyes stopped blinking. The entire front of a station wagon was crumpled and intermeshed with the wooden pole of a streetlamp.

"I'll call the police," I said, realizing that by using the telephone, I would be violating Shabbos in order to save a life. I rolled off the mattress and my knee buckled. I phoned the town police, and a woman's voice informed me that everything was already under control. By the time I got back to the window, a small crowd of highway commuters had parked their cars and gathered on the shoulder of the road. In the distance I heard the three short blasts from the firehouse announcing a highway accident to the citizens of Long-a-coming. Within a few seconds, the siren of the Long-a-coming ambulance wailed faintly in the distance and then boldly as it approached the wreck.

A local do-gooder was standing in the middle of the four-lane highway directing traffic. A major accident like this, where the driver or passengers were severely hurt, gave me a rare opportunity to see how other people lived: One man honked his horn, impatient to continue his Saturday afternoon cruising; another followed suit, starting a chain reaction. Mothers humored restless babies; peals of laughter erupted from several cars. A policeman listened to a voice on his CB radio, the message swallowed up by electrical static. Otherwise, life went on, barely recognizing the local tragedy.

It was time to ferry the sole victim to Kepler's Hospital, a few miles west in Sicklertown. A man dressed in a brown highway patrol uniform swept the sparkling, shattered windshield and headlights into a metal trough. The glass had turned the road into a brilliantly lit heaven—a firmament in reverse. It seemed a shame to throw it away.

The crowd parted to make way for the ambulance team. A man's voice rang out, "Careful now, her spinal cord's broken."

Perel and I looked at each other. "Her spinal cord?" I repeated. "What's that mean?" I questioned Perel as if she were a doctor, as if she were the older sister.

Soberly, Perel predicted, "She'll never walk again. There's nothing they can do for a torn spinal cord."

"How do you know?" I asked.

"I read it somewhere. It doesn't grow back together. She'll be paralyzed for life."

"Are you sure?" I asked. "Are you sure she'll be paralyzed for life?"

"I don't know," Perel said, appraising the depth of my dread. "Maybe there's an operation they can perform." Saucer tried to reassure me. "Science is making great strides every day, honey!"

Since I was willing to face the most upsetting circumstances, or at least I believed I was, why did Perel have to soften the bad news about that woman's spine? It's peculiar how in any of our interactions, each of us shifted from antagonizer to protector to denier. Two opposing positions always existed, waiting to be filled. I question how much belief either of us had in her own point of view, and to what degree we took sides simply to avoid the imbalance resulting from agreement. How much like my sister I was acting in this situation. . . .

Perel and I wrapped the *shoykhet*'s broken glass in an old Sunday *Inquirer* and threw it in the trash bucket. "We may as well honor our mother and father and go to sleep," Perel yawned.

"*A bisl derkherits,*" I said. Discomfited by the memory of my weakness, I flexed my biceps.

"Perel?" I wanted to tell my sister about my look into the slaughterhouse. But whatever sensation was uppermost in me—pity, embarrassment, disgust—precluded words. I think I can understand the motives of those primitive societies whose elites prohibit other members of the tribe from participating in certain secret rituals. Without an agreed-upon silence, mystery cannot flourish; and without mystery, domination is impossible. Without domination, we are all equal—all equally unremarkable. As it was, I had so little rapport with Mama and Papa that if I held my tongue, at least I would be in their inner circle for a while.

"G'night, Luster," I finally said to Perel, and we settled into our bedrooms at the opposite ends of the hall upstairs.

In my bed, I listened to the sound of traffic on the Pike. I lay on my stomach and looked up at the indigo summer sky spackled with stars and wondered why I wasn't the kind of person fascinated by the constellations. If I were, I wouldn't be so preoccupied with the frailties of humankind. If someone asked me to describe a feeling that has been with me all my life, I would say it was the feeling I had while lying upstairs in my room at the age of fifteen, listening to the approaching roar of a tractor-trailer's engine, and then holding the disappearing sound in my ears as long as possible, wondering at what point the sound disintegrated into nothingness; all the while reviewing my life and its shortage of adventure, its lack of destiny, and doubting that anything would ever happen to me. I felt like one of history's oversights. This, I decided, was what people outside Jake's Poultry Farm meant by loneliness.

As I drifted off to sleep, my body convulsed for a split second, as if I had fallen from a cliff, and tripped off a memory that had been close to the surface of my consciousness ever since the *shoykhet* dropped the glass and made me remember the car crash: "I have no sympathy for the parents at all." That's what Mrs. Barbarian, my French teacher in school, had said when she learned that a five-year-old girl was killed on the Pike near our farm. The girl and her two older brothers had been dodging the cars on the highway as a game one Sunday afternoon, until she ran straight into the door of a blue pickup truck gunning at fifty miles an hour. On impact, the girl was thrown twenty feet up in the air, and splatted face down on the gray asphalt. "I have no sympasee for zee parents at all," Mrs. Barbarian said. "It oo-as zair responsibility to keep an eye on zair children."

There are all kinds of war survivors. One was Mrs. Barbarian, whose entire response to the war was contained in the single memory of her mother, dead at the hands of an alleged quack doctor. The rest of the war she peeled away like segments of an orange, exposing the small, perfect face of misery, the face of an ideal French mother; a mother who would still be alive today if it weren't for a hundred ifs; a mother who kept constant watch over the young Barbarian, and primed her to be the decent Catholic Barbarian she was as a high school French teacher, with a heart as wide . . . as an orange seed. Yes, there are all kinds of survivors who treasure the pain of their own suffering, and think it the most precious of all possible torments. As well it may be. This is what I have learned about suffering: It erases more and more elements in the world not directly connected to it.

Unlike Mrs. Barbarian, I felt no desire to berate anybody in that family bound together for the rest of their lives by the boredom of three children on a Sunday afternoon fifteen years ago; and I only pity the mother and father who had long forgotten the reason why they ever got married, and who lost a daughter when they closed their eyes to the irreversibility of their lives for just a minute. But mostly I remember the two brothers who will wish for the rest of their lives that they had sat in church that Sunday, or visited their cousins, or been anyone but themselves when their sister landed smack on the double white line of the White Horse Pike.

3

❧ FOR A LONG TIME AFTER SHEIYE HIT DUCHESS neither Perel nor I said a civil word to him. Every time he walked past us, Sheiye would try a gambit like, "Interesting book, little girls?" not caring what kind of response he got, be it snicker or insult, as long as we acknowledged him. "Murderer!" Perel hissed at him, unwilling to forgive. *"Gott geht dir shtrufn!"* she cried— God's gonna punish you!—using one of the few Yiddish expressions we left untranslated. "Big college man's gonna live at home with Mommy and Daddy," I contributed, the sort of remark that usually elicited a sock to the shoulder. But now Sheiye held himself aloof, a master at pruning our rage when it threatened to exclude him from our lives permanently. This was, perhaps, his gift for clairvoyance.

Family lore held that Sheiye was born wrapped in a *zekl,* the birth cowl. The Viennese pediatrician who delivered him at Bindermichel, the Linz displaced persons camp, said that the intact *zekl* was a good omen, and Sheiye's life was bound to be lucky. As a child, I considered the possibility that my brother might be the Jews' Messiah, deliberately masquerading as the most unremarkable of south Jersey boys, outwitting everyone who thought him dim. I thought it prophetic that he should live in a town called Long-a-coming.

Sheiye did have talents. He drew caricatures of rabbis and of our pious *shoykhet,* and sketches of all kinds of duck-billed humanoids that slithered down the pages of his science fiction paperbacks, and of his bar mitzvah copy of the Hebrew Bible

too. Even his crabbed handwriting looked like amoebic creatures on spindly legs, all having resisted the instruction of a
grade school teacher. As soon as the caricature was drawn and
admired, Sheiye crumpled it up and threw it in the trash.
Sometimes he lit a match and watched the drawing burn down
to ash in a chipped glass plate.

My brother had musical ability too, maybe even more
than I, who was something of an idiot savant and could play
popular music on the piano by ear from the time I was twelve.
But he had no patience for written notation, which meant that,
in the long run, his own adolescent compositions were merely
spontaneous expressions of boredom or pain. As a result, he
played well what he knew, particularly the two rhythmic
pieces he had composed. But he never improved. Perhaps out
of frustration, Sheiye moved on to trombone, "a more suitable
instrument for a young boy, anyway," according to Rodney
MacDuff. Though our house had two floors, a cellar, and an
attic, neither wood nor brick could muffle the howl of Sheiye's
brass. Sheiye waited until Perel and I had sat down in the
living room to study or read before he began practicing in the
piano room. *"Hehr, nor! Er blust shoyn!"* Perel would say,
imitating my father's Yiddish. Listen to him! He's blowing!
Not content to play behind closed doors, Sheiye paraded into
the living room. He thrust out his hips, repeated the slides up
and down, and blew the spit that had collected in the loop onto
the floor. No amount of pleading with our parents to banish
him and the trombone to one of the coops helped. Sheiye was
the only son, and when we girls preyed on him, my parents
rushed to his defense.

After he set aside the instrument, Sheiye would sit himself down at the kitchen table and gorge. From the refrigerator
he took a twelve-ounce package of cheddar cheese and fed
himself mouthful by mouthful with a butter knife till he

finished every last bit of it. Next came the Shop-Rite challah. He gouged out the soft center of the bread and left the shell of brown crust in the plastic bag. To punctuate the meal, Sheiye downed the contents of an orange juice or milk carton. Sated, "like a drum," as the Yiddish expression goes, Sheiye returned the empty wrappers and waxed cartons to the refrigerator. Later I wondered: Maybe Sheiye, the potential Messiah, believed that if he returned the empty packages to the source, they would miraculously regenerate the food.

Beyond taunts, words failed Sheiye. At school this drawback left him flustered; at home he expressed his discontent with his fists. If Perel or I disobeyed his edict to get him a glass of water, Sheiye answered with a kick to our ribs. If the fool inside me begged for trouble—and it did out of sheer perversity—I would insult Sheiye for some past cruelty or for his poor school grades. At once he countered with an arm vise he had learned on the high school wrestling team. My shrill screaming only aggravated him further; relentlessness of any kind tested Sheiye's endurance. "Stop screaming and I'll let you go!" he commanded. But pride and lack of trust committed me to the fight, and I promised to spit in his face.

After one of our tussles, I would race upstairs to my room and seethe at my mirror image: "I hate Sheiye! I hate him! I hate him!" I think my hatred thrilled me. My body shook and my skin tingled; simultaneously, I felt hungry and renewed.

One time I hurled a wooden chair down the eleven steps at Sheiye after he threatened me with a can of Hawaiian Punch. Instantly, I was free from my life of routine: the unending days of egg sales; the *shoykhet*'s unvarying request for a *glayzl* juice; the disappointment the mail brought every morning; my unfulfilled wish for the Smothers Brothers to pull into our driveway, intrigued by the possibility of buying fresh eggs and poultry; the vigorous boredom with which day toppled into night. I envied the chair its journey, and felt a greater intimacy with it than with any person I had ever known. All at once, I stood outside my family and its continuous line of grieving ancestors, restrained for centuries by the maxim *"Lomir nisht zahn vi goyim"*: Let's not act like gentiles. I was no longer a Szuster. I was an animal. This was Sheiye's doing.

As young as I was, one thing was already clear: Love was a feeling that was receding deeper and deeper into my memory, associated with the image of my mother beaming down at me, her hair tucked under a red paisley kerchief, while I, her five-year-old daughter, sang "America the Beautiful." But mother love, like father love, was too subtle to sustain me, too whimsical, and not always apparent. Only this fraternal hatred, steady and plentiful, made me feel brilliantly alive, put me in the same league with suffering human beings like Mama and Papa. What, in fact, would prepare me for the suffering I sought? What would change me from a coward to a heroine? Would it be Duchess's death? I always organized the minutiae of my daily life along a kind of memory slide rule, with the repetitious habits of cleanliness and egg sales bunched up to the left of my mind, the outstanding embarrassments and rare visits off the farm spaced further and further apart to the right. I placed each of these incidents along my memory slide and sensed that none of them would do. None of them was horrible enough.

Mama told me now and again, with a hint of disapproval, that I could walk into any room and know in a flash what was going on. That quick thinking, I believed, grew out of my hatred for Sheiye. Without this hate to light my way, I would be "as any other man," like Samson without his hair. Mama also said that some people took longer than others to grow up. Her children were notoriously late bloomers, and maybe in another ten or fifteen years we would all love each other. I pictured myself at thirty, watching *The Merv Griffin Show* from my pink-canopied bed, curlers in my hair, a box of pralines on the quilt—my hatred long vanished and with it my intelligence. I had to hold fast to some of that hatred or lose my wits to maturity. So I avoided my brother and baited him too. And I wished till my legs trembled that Sheiye would die.

By mid-June, Sheiye guessed that our anger had already peaked. He marched into the living room, where Perel and I sat reading, and announced, "I'm going exploring. I'll count to ten. Decide if you're coming." I would never have believed that after only two weeks, I would feel nothing more than irritation towards Sheiye. It was finally habit that cemented our days together, not hysteria. By the time Sheiye had slowed down to nine and a half, Perel and I piped together, "All right! We'll come!"

And so it happened that Perel and I took a hike with a person we detested. Tacitly, Sheiye and I had established a truce, and it was understood from the moment that the three of us set out for the woods that he wouldn't attack us; in fact, should we encounter a dangerous human or animal, he would probably act as our protector. These moratoria in the endless conflict with my brother were so rare that, like the outbursts, they were exciting. Our occasional hikes signaled the only times I willfully yielded to Sheiye's intelligence. From his many Shabbos trips to the woods, he knew which paths led to Atsion, the drag strip, junk heaps, and gravel pits; and he could determine how many people had traipsed through the woods earlier that week.

Sheiye wasn't afraid of the woods the way Perel and I were, and he disregarded boundaries. So what if the land beyond the railroad tracks didn't belong to my parents? So what if he felt like rolling down the incline of our neighbor's wheat field? Sheiye feared only what he saw. A white rabbit in the flesh could send him scampering away in the opposite direction, but it didn't occur to him that another white rabbit might show up some other day in a completely different location. Likewise, he would frequently make himself scarce whenever my father began rounding up chickens for slaughter, hardened or oblivious to the punishment for such avoidance in the past. Sheiye acted as though he had no memory. I couldn't understand him: so timid among strangers, yet willing to risk his safety among trespassers and forest animals. What motivated him? Boredom with books? With Shabbos? Was he genuinely curious about nature? Or did he encounter anyone on his forays?

At the railroad tracks, Perel and I eyed each other collusively, half expecting to reencounter the sailor from a few weeks back. Sheiye was too preoccupied with his destination to notice our suspicious glances. "Wanna see something you've never seen before?" he asked us, uncharacteristically patient. "Once we get there, though, you've got to tell me something you never told anyone else. Something I don't know about."

Perel and I looked at each other and I shook my head up and down. We would barter our most private shame for a look at the world beyond the farm. Determined to levy my own ultimatum, I countered, "And you've gotta *tell* us something too." To my surprise, Sheiye complied without hesitation, as if he had been expecting this precondition, and the moment was so solemnly different from our usual hostility that I was sure we would all honor it.

The path we took led to Atsion, and the closer we got to the lake, the more junk we found strewn on the ground. Indignant, Sheiye called the litterers *vilde khayes* and *goyim,* who didn't know what respect for private property meant.

"It's not our property, anyway," I shrugged. "It's somebody's," he said, and kicked at a Coke bottle. Technically, I didn't believe in dumping helter-skelter, either, but junk fascinated me. Scattered under pines were tires with worn-down treads, blue-tinted soda bottles, crumpled bits of aluminum foil, fragments of forty-five rpm records, sneakers pocked with cigarette burns, a mattress with protruding coils, a car seat, a lamp with the light fixture hanging limp like a chicken's neck after slaughter. Dissatisfied with the banality, I looked about for something more precious, like jewelry. *Is all this what other people cherish?* I asked myself. I decided that the key to understanding Christian society must lie elsewhere.

A mile from Atsion, Sheiye led us deeper into the woods. If we listened closely, we could hear faint cries of children at the lake and the rumble of car engines at the drag strip. Sparrows and bluebirds dove through beams of sunlight illuminating the powder and damp of the forest floor. An occasional twig snapped, centering all sound in a break made by no visible animal. I loved sound created by distance and invisibility.

"Hey, what's that?" Perel asked in her Sparsely and Saucer voice.

"That's something I bet you little girls never saw before," Sheiye answered proudly.

True, I had never seen one firsthand, yet I immediately recognized a crude gallows in a hacked-out clearing. Built from poor-quality wood, the structure had not yet acquired the rotted appearance of weather-beaten lumber. Not much higher than six and a half feet, the gallows stood like an oversized Hebrew letter *bet,* and looked as substantial as the stick-figure gallows Perel and I drew when we played the word game Hangman. Whoever built it had strung a shoelace where rope would be ordinarily, a touch that underscored its feebleness. Sheiye was already tiptoeing on a rock, pretending to hang himself from the shoelace, when I asked, "Who built it?"

"It wasn't here last summer. Don't look too strong to me," he said, giving the supporting beam a kick.

"Watch it!" I yelled. "You might break it."

Pop chimed in, "But, Brantzche, someone could get hurt."

The longer we contemplated the gallows, the more emphatic its silence became. I began to get bored and suggested examining the dune buggy tracks at one of the gravel pits. In the ethereal voice of our dolls, Perel replied, "I'm spent. I must rest up before we continue," and sat down on a stool tethered to the supporting beam by a rusted link chain, elbows resting on her knees.

"Okay," said Sheiye. "I showed you something you never saw before. Honor your part of the bargain."

Perel and I looked at each other. "You're older," Perel stalled. "You tell."

"Yeah, but you tell stories better," I said.

"Just one of you tell it," Sheiye complained, impatient. "And it better not be idiotic." Regaining his earlier aplomb, he said, "I probably already know, anyway."

I'm not sure what Perel had in mind. As far as we were concerned, nothing happened in our lives worthy of being considered "secret." The only event that came close was our chance meeting with the sailor the day Sheiye ran over Duchess, and that's what I offered.

"That's not much," Sheiye challenged, disappointed. "Are you sure he didn't do anything to you?"

"Like what?" Perel asked.

"Like did he touch you?"

"That's ridiculous," I said, though that, of course, had

been my fear exactly when Perel and I first saw the sailor.

"You shouldn't walk around here alone," Sheiye scolded.

"You do," said Perel, scratching the stool with a pointed stick.

"Hey, little girl!" Sheiye yelled. "You're gonna ruin that chair."

"Why should you care?" I asked, and suddenly guessed the reason for his concern. "You built this, Sheiye, didn't you?" I accused. "You act like it's yours."

Sheiye, enigmatic, only smiled and stroked the gallows tenderly.

"Tell us your secret," I demanded. "You promised."

"Well, it's time you little girls learned that all females have babies," Sheiye snorted.

"And how 'bout if I don't want one," I said.

Sheiye answered, "You'll have one anyway. Once you're twenty-five, all girls get pregnant whether they want to or not."

Perel's wide eyes blinked with incomprehension, brown as acorns among the rustling oaks.

"You owe us a better one than that," I complained, confident by now that my education in Family Living class was accurate enough. "It's something about this, isn't it?" I said, nodding at the gallows.

Sheiye broke a long, dead branch off a rotting log and began stripping its bark. I gathered he was prolonging our get-together in the woods, and this information about procreation was a way of clearing his throat for some more significant matter. "This would make a pretty decent walking stick," he said.

"Yeah, and this'll teach us to trust you," I replied, strategically peeved.

"Don't rush me! I'm getting to it!" Sheiye bent his knees

and held the stick horizontal. He stood frozen for a few seconds, a disciplined samurai. When he shifted the stick upright, resting it on his shoulder like a rifle, Perel began making impatient clucking noises. "Maybe I'll end up killing someone in Vietnam," he said, marching in place.

"You gotta take good aim to shoot from Glassboro State Teachers College," I said, emphasizing "State" and "Teachers." Sheiye had avoided the draft only by getting accepted by the local low-status school.

"If you don't tell us something like you promised," Perel said, fed up, "I'm going back." It wasn't Perel's nature to issue warnings and double warnings; she announced a decision only with the utmost conviction.

"Okay, okay," Sheiye answered. Kicking at the fallen log sporadically as he spoke, he asked, "You know about Mama and Papa, don't you?"

"How could you not know about them?" Perel groaned. "All they ever talk about is the war and the chicken business."

"Yeah, but did you know they were tortured during the war?"

"Oh, come on," I said. "If they were tortured, they'd be dead."

"Mama told me Papa was tortured," Sheiye insisted.

Perel had already formulated an explanation. "Mama talks to you just to get you to help in the coops." Whenever work in the slaughterhouse ended early, my mother often sat up in my brother's room speaking with him, as she had the day before Sheiye killed Duchess. I half expected him to drop the torture riff and confess that he had gotten a Christian girl pregnant.

"You're making this up," Perel said, testy now, and scratched at the stool's underside.

"I didn't ask you to believe me," Sheiye said. "But that's

the truth." Making the sign of the Star of David over his T-shirt, Sheiye added, "I swear. *Mugn duvid.*"

"Who tortured him?" I asked. I hardened my voice with disbelief, but I had no doubt that Sheiye was telling the truth. We didn't make *mugn duvids* lightly. "The Nazis?"

"Yeah, some Germans and Ukrainians. In a slave labor camp."

"Papa wasn't in any camp," I said, trying to trip Sheiye up. "He doesn't have a number on his arm. Didn't they give them numbers?"

"Mama says it was before they started with the numbers. And besides, Papa was in a slave labor camp, not Auschwitz."

"Did you tell anyone at school?" I asked.

"You think I'm crazy?" Sheiye said. "You better not say anything at school or you'll never hear the end of it. Perel, you understand?"

Perel scoffed, "Why should I repeat stuff that isn't true?"

Sheiye warned, "Think what you like, but keep your mouth shut. I tell you, you'll never hear the end of it."

As I pondered how to provoke Sheiye into recanting his story, Perel jabbed her stick around the bottom of the stool's seat and asked, "Hey, what's this?" She stood up, tipped the chair over, and squinted her eyes behind her thick glasses. "There's a letter etched into the wood," Perel said.

I joined her and read off, *"D."* I turned to Sheiye. "If you built this, why'd you sign a *D?"*

"To throw off the police, just in case they ever came back here." He smirked.

Perel rolled her eyes. "The only people who come back here are weirdos. This place gives me the creeps. Brantzche, let's go back."

When I made a move towards her, Sheiye lurched forward and blocked me.

"I can't very well let you little girls go back by yourselves, can I? Why don't we go for a swim first?" he suggested.

" 'Cause it's Shabbos," I said, "and if we come back with
tans, Mama and Papa will kill us. See you around." Perel and
I took one last look at the gallows and headed to the path.

Still carrying his walking stick, Sheiye followed behind.
"Better not say anything about what I told you or I'll tell
about that sailor," he warned us again. "Not about the gallows
and not about the war."

"Oh, shut up about the war," Perel said. I could see how
she had already hidden Sheiye's information like a precious
possession she would have trouble locating when she wanted
it in the future.

The three of us began to walk back to the farm, not
stopping to look at flowers or snakes. Our truce with Sheiye
was over. "Okay, dogs, back to your kennel!" he ordered,
gently prodding our ankles with his walking stick. He would
have kept it up the whole trip had Perel not screamed so loudly
that the crows abandoned their nests. Sheiye compromised. He
kept calling us dogs, but changed the stick into a rifle, aiming
only at the weeds and sky.

4

꿈 TOWARDS THE END OF JUNE, Lalke and Mendl Decher
came to the farm and occupied the spare bedroom on the
second floor. Lalke was a third or fourth cousin to my father,
his closest living relative, but sufficiently distant so as not to
pollute our lineage with her misguided taste in men. Lalke and
Mendl had sold their blue jeans stall at the Long-a-coming
Farmer's Market and Auction a few months earlier, and having
lived out the lease on their apartment in Pleasantville, near the
south Jersey shore, were now preparing to ship themselves and
their Country Squire station wagon to Israel, which, as Lalke
said, was the only place for a Jew to live.

Lalke and Mendl were the two largest Jews I ever saw,
looming tall and wide over the dollhouse Szusters. I imagined
them as a pair of walking salt and pepper shakers, fit for
Goliath's table, or as larger-than-life-scale figures in a natural
history museum. They weren't simply tall; their bones, muscles, coloring, angles, and curves were lost inside dunes of fat.
Their elbows and knees were dimpled, their chins terraced into
three pouches. Our house was inadequate to withstand Lalke
and Mendl's long strides and heavy-footed plodding to the
bathroom in the middle of the night to gargle, and contained
them as a glass bottle contains a model ship. A child resulting
from the union of these two behemoths could only be something as remarkable as the Jersey Devil, but the only child
Lalke ever had was with a first husband before the war. A
Polish teenager with celebration in his yelp had hurled the

child into the air and shot it dead along with its father in a kind of target practice.

From my earliest childhood days, Lalke and Mendl visited us every Sunday evening when the Auction work week ended. They bought Perel, Sheiye, and me Wrigley's chewing gum and hexagons of dark chocolate. With my parents they dined on onions, sardines, and rye bread. Lalke's eyes invariably moistened when she beamed down at Perel and me sitting together, thigh to thigh, in the same armchair, watching *The Ed Sullivan Show*. "Do you know how much your mama and papa love you kids? Do you know what your parents went through?" she asked us in accented English. Our answer was always the same uncomfortable grin and an unspoken prayer to leave us alone. Mendl would position himself between the TV and my sister and me, his simian arms akimbo like those of the Jolly Green Giant. In his half-English, half-Yiddish baritone, he thundered, "Ah, you little monkelach!" He uncrossed his arms only to perform along with Ed Sullivan's comedy routines, particularly ones involving Topo Gigio, the talking Italian mouse, until Lalke summoned him back to the kitchen to discuss business and the war with the adults. Crestfallen, that's how Mendl faced his wife.

Like Sheiye, Mendl had a number of unusual talents. He improvised polkas and ballads on his ever-present accordion; he spoke fluent Yiddish, English, Polish, Russian, Ukrainian, and German, and knew enough Hungarian, Spanish, and Hebrew, as he put it, *"tsi flirteven"*—to flirt with the ladies. I assumed this facility with languages constituted a kind of streetwise genius, a genius that had enabled him to survive the war. But aside from these musical and linguistic gifts, Mendl was a bungler. Nothing demonstrated this more convincingly than his talent to wring misfortune out of a placid five seconds. He would walk past a perfectly sturdy table and suddenly its wooden leg would crack. He would lay his mitts on you for a kiss and accidentally slam you in the ribs. A car ride with Mendl at the wheel was best spent in reestablished dialogue with a personal God; in his most attentive moments, Mendl drove with one hand on the steering wheel while the other skoaled wild toasting gestures across the expanse of the front seat. His recklessness stemmed, perhaps, from the half gratitude, half resentment he felt towards Lalke, for her business acumen and his parasitic reliance on it.

Mendl, I observed, shrugged off all concern for personal safety and, as a result, endangered us. I remember one case in point three summers before Lalke and Mendl stayed with us. Lalke was sitting in the kitchen, a blue denim apron shielding her voluminous skirt and blouse, complaining about a Puerto Rican couple who had teamed up to steal a shipment of denim caps. Mendl stood in the doorway between the kitchen and living room and gurgled at an Italian trapeze act on *The Ed Sullivan Show.* "O solo mio! Tra-la-la-la-la!" Mendl boomed. He roared at his prankishness and at the embarrassment on my face and Perel's. I looked into the kitchen and caught my father's eye. He snorted his throaty laugh as if to explain that sometimes adults are children. Lalke yelled, "Hey you, *komiker!* Hey you, lover boy! Get your sexy body in here! *A shlak zol dekh trefn! Kim aher!"*

"Sure! Sure! Sure! Sure!" Mendl answered. "Sure" was the latest expression he had picked up at the Auction. Mendl delighted in rolling the English *r* behind his lower teeth, and with each new "Sure," the muscles of his face arched into a new clownish contortion. "In a minute!" he called to Lalke. Imitating one of the Italians tiptoeing daintily across a high wire, he bent down to avoid the low-hanging chandelier that my parents had bought at the Long-a-coming Lighting Supply Store. Mendl pretended to lose his balance and totter. "Ah, you little monkelach!" he bellowed, and before she knew what had happened, Mendl scooped Perel out of the chair and into his bearish arms.

Against the backdrop of the TV trapeze act and a Strauss waltz, Mendl floated the nine-year-old Perel through the air. "She flies troo de air wit duh gradets of ease! Ha! Ha! Ha!" he syncopated with a howl. Perel's eyes turned from brown to black with terror. Her chubby body involuntarily turned rigid, and she strained her head as far from Mendl's lips as possible. When our eyes met, she wordlessly begged me to wrench her free of this madman. In the midst of Mendl's footwork, he bounced Perel's head into the fake brass cone of the chandelier.

The bump Perel received scared her less than the realization that Mendl was truly a danger, and she started to wail. Mendl stopped singing, my mother jumped out of her chair in the kitchen, and a forlorn look of apology filled Mendl's eyes. Perel tore free of Mendl and threw herself around Mama's waist like a five-year-old. Mama stroked her daughter's head, and couldn't contain her anger at Mendl. *"Farvus firste zekh uhp vi a kind!"* Why do you act like a child! she jabbed under her breath.

By now Lalke had heaved herself out of the kitchen seat to investigate the turmoil in the living room. "Whas going on in here?" she asked with a little laugh, assuming that Perel and I had attacked each other over seating rights, or that Sheiye was starting up with us again. When she looked at her husband she understood immediately the source of the problem and cursed, *"Ay, Gey kebenye matre!"*—a half-Yiddish, half-Russian oath that meant something like, "Go lie where your mother lies," which in Mendl's case suggested Auschwitz. *"Antshildik zekh!"* Apologize!

Papa, meanwhile, continued to add dollops of sour cream

to the fresh strawberries he and Mama had picked after slaughtering chickens that day. He glanced through the kitchen door, saw that no blood had been spilled, and decided to let us fools thrash out a conclusion, content to learn later from Mama secondhand what had transpired. In one of his well-considered commentaries, he addressed us all: *"Kinder,* Ed Sullivan *volt zekh gesheymt!* Children, Ed Sullivan would be ashamed! Do you know his wife is a Jew?"

What puzzled me about Mendl was his expression whenever his wife chided him, or whenever my father insisted Mendl had read someone's character all wrong. It was the same glaze of chastisement you see in the round brown eyes of a dog who has trampled through a well-tended flower garden. I remember at least one occasion when that confused look covered Mendl's own brown eyes with something like the rubbery translucent veil separating the white of an egg from its shell.

The incident, which happened a few weeks before his residency with us, grew out of an argument about *The Ed Sullivan Show.*

Sheiye hated *Ed Sullivan.* He preferred *The F.B.I.,* with its dragnet episodes of interstate embezzlement schemes and foreign spies intent on toppling the American government. On that particular summer Sunday evening, Sheiye strode down the stairs from his room, headed directly for the TV, and switched the station Perel and I had been watching.

"What do you think you're doing?" I yelled. "Jesus Christ! You don't even ask permission!"

"According to the Bible, the man is superior to the girl," Sheiye said coolly. "I don't need a little girl's permission."

"Put Ed Sullivan back on, scholar," I said dryly.

"Brantzche," Perel whispered. "Don't say Jesus Christ!"

But Perel was absolutely on my side and ready for fisticuffs. She stopped inspecting her strands of brown hair and jumped up from the floor, where she had been sitting to cool off. Sheiye's hand held fast to the TV dial, and he blocked the screen with his thick waist. "Move!" Perel grunted.

"You better go play with your dolls if you know what's good for you, little girl," Sheiye said.

"You have no right to barge in here while we're watching TV," Perel huffed. "Go back upstairs and squeeze your pimples."

That was the instigation for Sheiye's first blow—and Sheiye's first blow beckoned Perel's return kick. "Who do you think you're kicking?" Sheiye barked, now giving vent to the acid brew forever simmering inside him.

"The last I looked, John Lennon didn't have pimples, so it can't be him!" Perel flung back, preparing to launch another kick at his shins.

Sheiye grabbed Perel's foot and raised it as high as it would go. "Let go of my foot, strawberry patch!" Perel screamed.

"We'll see who's a strawberry patch!" Sheiye blustered. He shoved his face, covered with a sheath of acne scars, into Perel's, holding her leg all the while. To her discredit, Perel started screaming in earnest, for we both knew that screaming only incensed Sheiye. In fact, Sheiye's sole victory as a high school wrestler had come after his opponent shouted in an attempt to distract him. "First the bastard screamed at me, and then he ripped a hole in my T-shirt," Sheiye had gloated. "That was the final straw. I had him pinned in three moves." Now Perel's cries unnerved Sheiye; when Perel's mouth was open, Sheiye spat into it. Perel looked as if she had bitten into a piece of putrid meat. She didn't dare swallow or say another word lest Sheiye's saliva roll down her gullet.

"Taste good, little girl?" Sheiye laughed.

Perel spat Sheiye's saliva back at him, and it landed on his mouth.

"Right in the kisser!" I cheered.

"Who said anything about kissing?" Sheiye said. "If kissing's what you want, little girl, kissing's what you'll get!" And he dove towards Perel's lips.

This time when Perel started screaming, she turned her head to the side. Not content with spitting at Perel's neck, Sheiye pushed her against the TV. Weary of the domestic quarrel, the TV whined, and a tiny white dot sucked its image towards the center of the screen, making it disappear like the powder cleanser that concentrated a household's dirt into a pinpoint and whisked it away inside a white tornado.

When the audio spiraled down into a steady low buzz, the four adults in the kitchen, who had been reconstructing the war's chronology, bustled into the living room. First came Mama, her cheeks bulging with challah; behind her followed Lalke and Mendl; last came Papa, whose appearance at all warned that his patience had finally been challenged, and that as a result he could rationalize any unpleasant consequences. This moment was always the pivotal point in any of our intersibling battles. Whose side would Mama and Papa take? Their son disappointed them; he preferred go-carts to *Gemara*. A scene like this could provide an opportunity to take a potshot at Sheiye's failures. Or Mama and Papa might feel responsible for their son's academic limitations, in which case they would rage at Perel and me for highlighting them. Oftentimes the causes of our conflicts were irrelevant. What mattered most was our parents' momentary disposition towards each of their children, and the point at which they had been interrupted in their war chronology.

This time they took their cue from Mendl. He was

genuinely shocked by the sister-brother hostilities; this evening was the first time ever he had viewed them outright. His eyes widened, and he swallowed with effort. You could see the fantasy that Mendl had cultivated about our family disintegrate into horror at Sheiye's bullying. *"Farvus nemste eym nisht tsen* a psychiatrist?" Why don't you take him to a psychiatrist? Mendl asked. His jaw dropped. "A boy his age shouldn't act like this."

Towering above, Lalke reminded us, as she always did, "Do you kids know what your parents have been through?"

My mother was ashamed that outsiders had witnessed our bellicose intimacy. She sighed, "We should have enrolled him in a yeshiva. We have friends in Brooklyn . . ."

"Makh zekh nisht narish," Papa said, opting for the sympathy stance. In Papa's eyes, ganging up against a petty mischief-maker was an act of cowardice. "He'll outgrow it," he reasoned.

"He's already eighteen years old," I protested.

"An eighteen-year-old is barely out of diapers," Papa said. "The only thing an eighteen-year-old boy can do is beat you up, and that's what Sheiye did."

Sheiye smirked, but Papa turned towards him and said, *"Ti mir a toyve 'n trug zekh up."* Do me a favor and beat it. That was Papa's way of democratically expressing his displeasure with all of us. Perel, meanwhile, had already pressed herself against the wall, just in case Papa held her responsible for disrupting the evening's peace.

Sheiye had been counting on a victory, and disappointment lodged in a tic under his eye. "You all make me sick, sick, sick!" he said angrily. He headed out into the night.

My mother blanched. "Where are you going? It's dark outside!"

"I'm obeying my father," Sheiye said, enunciating each word. With his chin thrust forward, he added, *"Yekh trug zekh up."*

At such moments, I could never predict my father's reaction. He would raise his eyes not quite heavenward but lower, more likely to the bathroom upstairs. You might debate whether he was about to smile or begin raging. His thin lips, shiny with sweat and supplication, seemed uncertain how to respond to the present situation. If anything, they looked about to question God's sanity in parceling out such a bad lot of children to him, especially in light of everything he had already suffered. With a look that said God's wisdom is not often apparent, Papa returned to the kitchen, the neutral zone.

Perel was satisfied with Papa's judgment. She said through the screen window, "Yeah, Queero, take a walk."

"Kinder, please!" Mama pleaded. "A brother and sister should love each other. *Alevay!* If only I could have my brother near me now!"

"Mama, you and your brother love each other so much that you're here and he's in Israel," I said.

More exhausted from fighting with us than from working in the slaughterhouse, Mama concluded, *"Luz mekh tsi-ri."* Let me be. She returned to Lalke, back in the kitchen, to my father, and the sardines. I had the feeling she wanted to whip something more caustic at me but decided that silence was wiser. Immediately I regretted my nastiness, but knew my behavior wouldn't alter much in the future. This, I realized, was the attitude my father described when he said, "Children: That's their nature," just as he would say when a chicken scratched him, "Chickens: That's their nature."

Mendl, his eyes bright with undeserved guilt, was so distraught by the recent episode that he walked outside with his accordion, settled himself and the wheezing instrument on the bench behind the house, and played "Moscow Nights" to the fireflies and mosquitoes. I looked through the kitchen window to see him, and possibly Sheiye too. Against the silhouettes of the three chicken coops, Mendl swayed slowly from side to side. When the accordion expanded, Mendl leaned back to encourage the flow of air; when he closed it up, he nearly collapsed over it, proprietary, hugging the sound to his massive chest. The squat, wide box instrument was made in Mendl's image like a son, a friend who understood him when no one else did. He went on playing lullabies and folk melodies, dotting his meaty fingers gracefully on the Chinese-checker pattern of the accordion, consoling himself for Sheiye's behavior as if he himself had spat on Perel and broken the TV. When the stars cordoned off the streak of clouds in the black sky, Lalke stole up behind her husband and cushioned her pillowy arms around him.

As the move to Israel drew closer, Mendl became giddy. He danced across the kitchen floor, singing to Perel and me in the living room, "I'm going to be a *halutz!* I'm going to be a pioneer! Watch out, you Arabs! Oh, sure! I'm gonna get you!" He pantomimed loading a machine gun and took aim at Lalke's head. "Very funny, buster," she said in English, and returned to a Bashevis Singer story in the *Jewish Daily Forward*.

Lalke's silent concentration just then was atypical. For the most part, the seriousness of her current plan did not sow a pensive attitude in her, and she still talked up a storm. I discovered how easy it was to muffle the Yiddish language into gibberish. I did not want to listen to Lalke or my parents; all their thoughts were stuck, glued like feathers to the revolving cylinder of a slaughtering machine. If I wasn't careful, this language would transmit their ugly obsession to me and de-range me as it had deranged them. Yiddish, with its strictures and death tallies, was a poison. Nobody healthy, nobody care-free, spoke it. I panicked that so much Yiddish had already seeped into my consciousness and wondered if I could possibly achieve total illiteracy in it. After all, my father claimed that the Polish language visited such unbearable memories on him that he had obliterated it from his mind.

My program for amnesia was not successful. In spite of my intentions, I, and Perel, could not help but understand one of the adults' more pragmatic discussions: To whom would Lalke and Mendl sell their white '62 Cadillac?

Mendl wanted it to go to someone at the Auction, a Puerto Rican woman with hoop earrings and red lipstick. My father tried to persuade Mendl rather to sell it to a man named Lonik, a war survivor, who delivered eggs to grocery stores and farmers' markets throughout south Jersey. Lonik had re-cently had a run of bad luck: His wife had changed the lock on their front door and demanded that he never cross the threshold again or she would have him arrested for trespassing. The title deed was in the wife's name, and Lonik had no recourse but to obey. At least Lonik's children stuck by him. He said that the children had always wanted a Cadillac, and to reward their loyalty he would buy one for them. In the course of the story, Lalke dabbed her eyes with the corner of her skirt and agreed that Lonik should get the car.

"Mendl," my father said, as if to a child. "If you can help a fellow Jew, why not do it?" Shaking his head to clear away pictures of past adversity, he added, "You remember how much the *goyim* helped us. . . ."

"But I promised," Mendl persisted stubbornly. "She's my friend."

Mama and Papa stared at each other in amazement. The concept of friendship bewildered them. Adults didn't have friends; they had a husband or a wife. Lalke stood up to reach for a toothpick in the dish cabinet, sat down again, and began picking at her teeth. "You'll be better rid of such 'friends,'" she winced. "I've put up with your 'friends' long enough."

"She cares more about me than you do," Mendl said, defending himself in a battle he knew was already lost.

Sensing her advantage, Lalke continued, "That's right; I have put up with your 'friends' long enough and now it's my turn to throw some weight around." Turning towards my father, Lalke said, "Get in touch with this righteous Lonik and tell him the car is his for four hundred dollars." She underscored her resolution with a spontaneous burst of sympathy: *"Got zol eym up-hitn!"* God protect him, poor soul!

"Okay, sister," Mendl said in English. "You win this one, but you're not gonna make me sell the guns."

"The guns?" my mother echoed. She focused alternately on each face at the table. "What guns?"

Lalke may have been a big-mouth, but she also possessed a candor that could momentarily humble her. Embarrassed, she stated simply, "He has guns. A pistol and a rifle. He target-practices in Pleasantville with the *shvartse* and Puerto Ricans he meets at the Auction."

"And now you're gonna ruin my life by taking me to Israel," Mendl shouted. "The least you can do is let me protect you from the Arabs."

My mother: "A Jew should own guns? For pleasure?" Stunned, she sat forward, and her elbow jostled a glass of iced tea. A line of light-brown liquid streamed down its side and onto the tablecloth.

"Now you know what I've put up with all these years," Lalke lamented. "Other women . . . *shvartse* . . . Puerto Ricans . . . guns. Mendl doesn't care about his own kind. He never did." Facing her husband, Lalke said bitterly, "A Judenrat bum! That's what you were and that's what you still are!"

"My friends are all better than you!" Mendl fumed. The impending isolation, which life in Israel threatened, threw Mendl into a panic, and he cried, "The Jews—the Jews are scum! I'm not going to Israel and that's that!"

"Yeah, yeah, sure, that's that, lover boy," Lalke said. "That's that and you'll do as I say or end up a fat bum on the street. Then we'll see where your friends are!"

Simultaneously, my mother and father demanded, "Mendl, you have to sell the guns."

"They're my guns," he said.

Whereupon Mama, Papa, and Lalke began discussing the issue among themselves. In a hushed voice, Mama said, "Lalke, if you don't sell them now, you'll have trouble in Israel. Who knows what he's capable of doing?"

"Who are any of you to tell me what to do?" Mendl cried. That bright, guilty look returned to his eyes and suddenly Mendl understood: He had nothing in common with Lalke or the Szusters! Mendl belonged in south Jersey, at the Auction, on the Boardwalk, at the gun club, with people who accepted him. What good were the Jews? They were choking him. In a rage, he burst out, "I'm taking both guns with me and I'm gonna kill as many Jews as I can!" And with a rebelliousness as much impotent as fierce, Mendl picked up Mama's glass of tea and hurled it to the floor.

From my vantage point in the living room, I saw Mama's lips part, about to order him to clean up the mess. But she was too afraid and wouldn't look Mendl in the eye. Perel began splitting strands of her hair, and torn between eavesdropping and hiding, she compromised by taking off her glasses to handicap at least one of her senses. Papa looked in at me and burst out laughing, maybe to assure me that Mendl was only temporarily acting flooey and there wasn't anything to worry about.

Mendl flew out of the kitchen door, this time without his accordion. I wondered how long he could entertain himself solely with his anger. The accordion would have kept him occupied indefinitely.

With Mendl out of earshot, Mama looked earnestly at Lalke, now on her knees collecting the broken glass, and said, "He's a maniac! Why didn't you ever tell me? Lalke, you have to get a divorce. You're still young enough to find another man in Israel. Divorce Mendl in Israel. The government will take care of him. You've done your share."

"I can't divorce him," Lalke said. "He needs me. Who'll take care of him the way I do?"

"Lalke, do you know Mendl propositioned me once at the Auction? He set up a mattress behind a curtain and expected me to—to do you know what!"

I tried to catch Perel's eye, but her face was now completely curtained by her long, brown, splitting hair.

"Promise me you'll get a divorce," Mama begged. *"Er iz meshige!"*

Unable to surrender this picture of Mendl as a lunatic, Mama looked at no one in particular and suddenly announced her revelation: "He doesn't have a brain. He's just an inflated piece of meat that you have to feed every day." Mama puffed out her cheeks to underline the point.

Lalke looked tired. Her admission of shame after so many years of secrecy carved out a lull in this interfamily battle, and with her only soldier gone AWOL, the major general admitted defeat. Her shoulders sagged and her blue-winged glasses slid down her hefty nose. She shook her head sadly. "I can't put him out in the street like a dog. He wasn't this bad in the beginning. I swear he wasn't. The war made him go a little off his rocker, being a policeman for the Nazis and everything, but I thought that in time, with someone to take care of him, he would recover his senses. I just didn't know."

Lalke wrapped the pieces of broken glass in an *Inquirer* and threw the bundle in the garbage. Mama started to continue her imprecations, but Lalke cut her off. She looked squarely at my parents and said, *"Vi volt gekent zahn andersh, az Hitler, yimakh shemoy, iz dokh geveyn der shadkhn?"* What do you expect, with Hitler—God damn him!—as our matchmaker?

The three sat in a kind of silent memorial to the war dead, until Mendl finally walked through the screen door, determination in his eyes. "If I have to go to Israel, I'll kill the Jews," he said. As Mendl passed Mama, he kicked at her chair. "You're so smart you tell yourself when to bleed! You hear me!" he yelled, on a rampage against all manifestations of female intelligence. He thudded past Perel and me, up the stairs to the guest room. Perel's glasses forded the river of hair covering her face. She still refused to look at me and studied the grating on the window fan, as if it mattered more than anything else.

"I'll kill you! I'll break your neck!" Mama screamed. "I'll kill you if you talk to me again!"

Papa laughed at Mama's hysteria and told her not to talk *narishkeyt*.

As far as I know, Mendl never killed anyone, either Arab or Jew, though rumor has it that he was arrested once for wielding a sawed-off pipe through Ramat Gan. And Lalke never divorced him, though she had ended up promising my mother she would.

I guess it takes a person like Lalke Decher to understand endurance. Only someone who has married out of penance or pity, or out of physical love, long past, can believe that loyalty must override expedience. And so Lalke has always tried to reunite me with my parents, convinced by the example of her own life that no man should put asunder what God hath wrought. If not for Lalke, I might have either glorified or excoriated Mama and Papa. But she alone has kept my parents life-sized for me; she has shown me that their flaws were often honeycombed with goodness. It is thanks to Lalke that I received a brown mailer last summer containing cassette tapes and a note in misspelled English: "I always taut you kits shud no wat your parents wet troo. It is not to lat for this taps to do som god."

Lalke, for the first time I did not shrug off that silly, worn phrase of yours. For the first time I saw you as a canny mediator, not just as a fool who married the wrong man. I suppose a woman who has lived nearly forty years with "an inflated piece of meat" works around obstacles.

Every few weeks I listen to those tapes the way observant Jews listen to their rabbi's sermon on Shabbos. I pore over the stories and their possible interpretations, flicking on fast forward and reverse, just as yeshiva boys burn their eyes out over *Pirke Avot*. In case my parents think my soul abandoned my body and that the Szusters and the farm are only remote oddities to me, I designate you, Lalke, as intermediary to tell them it isn't true. Tell them this kid wants to understand what we went through.

5

November 17, 1979
Tel Aviv, Israel
Rukhl Sussman Szuster, as told to Yaffa Simontov
Collected and edited for the World War II Jewish
Survivors' Archive at Yad Vashem

My father was Riven Sussman and my mother was Frieda
Cosak. We were five children; six, if you count Leah Fayge,
who died when I was quite young. I barely remember her. The
eldest was Leyve, then Royse, then Aaron, then me, then
Perele. All the children were born in Kritnetse, in the *Gubernia
Wolinska*. In Polish, Kritnetse is Kritnice Nadbugim—Kritnice by the Bug River. When my father was born there,
Kritnice belonged to Russia, not Poland. My mother was born
in Zamość.

We weren't rich but, honestly, we were a satisfied family.
The children were good students and we loved each other. One
month before the war broke out, the Russians drafted Leyve.
We heard rumors that the Germans had captured and killed
him, though no one ever told us for sure if he was dead. We
always believed that somehow he survived because he lived in
our hearts. Then in 1939 World War II broke out and trouble
became our lot.

First, Poland was split in two. Germany claimed the west
side of the Bug. Russia claimed the east. Russia mandated the
area as their border and a potential war front. I was a child.

All I knew was that I would learn a new language. Then in 1940 the Russians relocated us one hundred kilometers away in a hamlet called Ludvikov.

Our mother died there. She had been sick for years. Once, I remember, I found her in the kitchen in a dead faint. I was scared and threw a pot of cold water on her. Maybe she was having a stroke. The water helped, but she was never very strong after that.

Life went on. We went to the Russian school and adapted to our new lives. Then, in 1941, Germany attacked Russia and occupied the whole Ludvikov vicinity. The Germans began issuing anti-Jewish decrees. Then one day we heard a *geshray* and *geveyn* from a family we knew called Katz. The *goyim* killed Avram Katz, his wife, and two young sons. They burned his house to the ground. Three daughters, who happened not to be home, were spared.

The Jews got together and formed a guard watch lest the Germans kill more of us.

By spring of 1942, we had already fled Ludvikov, sought shelter in the Seleskes, where my parents used to rent orchards, and returned to Kritnetse, for lack of a better choice. My father collected straw and bits and pieces of wood and built a *buda* on our old property. A *buda* is . . . before the war people built shacks near the orchards they rented. It looked like a doghouse. After the summer harvest, you dismantled the *buda* and went home.

Scattered chunks of brick lay where our house used to stand, the last remains of our oven. We gathered the bricks and my father made a crude hot plate. "This is the best place for us," my father said. We felt good in that *buda,* indescribably good. Every corner, every spot, was home.

Our luck lasted until May 25, 1942.

Gestapo had by now already come to Kritnetse, and had begun rounding up Jewish children for slave labor. My father was terrified that the Gestapo would snatch up Royse, fifteen years old, and Aaron, eighteen. He begged a neighbor, a *goy* named Leonti Cybulski, to take my sister and brother in. Cybulski agreed. Royse and Aaron would work for him and they could sleep in his stable.

Every day the Gestapo demanded something from the Jews. One time they wanted meat, one time they wanted eggs; one time they wanted money, one time they wanted gold. Two days after Shavuos, the Gestapo commanded the Jews to buy a calf. The Jews dredged up a few groschen among them- selves and bought the Germans a calf. *M'hot gerisn shticker.* Blood from a stone, that's what the Germans wanted.

May 24, 1942, Royse returned and said, "I don't want to wallow in Cybulski's hay. I want to stay with my family. Whatever happens to you will happen to me too." Despite arguments from my father, Royse refused to go back to Cybulski. Aaron stayed, though.

May 25 before dawn, my father heard an uproar from town. He lifted his head and said to Royse, "Go into town and see what's going on. Maybe we'll have to escape today."

Royse got dressed and went into town. When she re- turned, she told *der tate,* "People say the Gestapo will march through town at noon. They might shoot. But you have time. Go back to sleep." Royse went back to sleep.

After a few minutes my father sat up and said, "Rukhl, *gey avek fin dahnet.* Get away from here. The less you are home, the better."

I didn't know where to go. I knew only the Jewish section of Kritnetse. My father insisted I go to the *goye* who sells lima beans and bring some home for lunch.

I wanted to cry and say I wouldn't go. But to disobey my father—such a thing wasn't possible. I looked at my father and sisters and something choked in my throat. But I didn't protest. My father gave me directions to the *goye*'s place and I got ready to leave.

Perele sat up and said, "Rukhl, take me with you. If you don't, you'll come back and find us all dead. They'll kill me!"

I didn't understand what my little sister meant. What she described was lunacy, a *vildkeyt*. How could I believe that when I left, I would have no one to come home to? Her heart, *nebekh*, sensed she would be killed.

Perele asked me to sew a button onto her undershirt. While sewing I said, "I can't take you with me. It's cold, it's dawn. I won't be long. I'll bring the lima beans. We'll be together soon. You'll see."

As I left the *buda*, my father called me back. He led me to a tree and said, "Your mother's gold necklace, her gold earrings and wristwatch, are hidden under this tree. If you come back and don't find us here, help yourself with this. At least you'll be able to buy bread."

I still couldn't grasp what my father meant. Why show me? Why not show my sister? I looked because I was told to look, and then I left.

I walked through the Bombegasse. And I see how everyone in the whole shtetl is running. One is carrying a pillow, one is carrying children. But what this running signified, I didn't know. If I had understood a little more . . . if I had been older . . . if I had had more or less common sense . . . I would have run back home and told my father to run too. Or I would have returned and not had time to save myself.

Everyone ran, so I ran too. Before I knew it, I outran everyone and found myself outside the Jewish section.

I got to the home of the *goye* who sold lima beans. I knocked on the door. The *goye* asked who's there and I told her. She opened a window and said, "Wait a couple minutes. My husband is sleeping and has to get dressed. He'll open the door and you can come inside."

Through the window the *goye* asked me how my father was, how the whole family was. I said everyone is fine. Her husband opened the door and I heard shooting from town.

At the same time, I saw my cousin, my uncle Haynochl's daughter Miral. Miral was running, pulling her hair and crying. My head started spinning, and then the whole world started spinning. I cried to Miral, "What happened?" Miral said, "Rukhl, you have no one left. They killed everybody." When she told me that, I started crying that I have no one left.

The *goye* with the lima beans said, "Wait here. I'll find out what's going on."

I waited and watched the *goyim* riding horses and bicycles, all headed for town, where you could hear people screaming and crying.

The *goye* returned and said, "Rukhl, it's true. They killed all the Jews in town. Run!"

When she said "run," I asked where to.

The *goye* said, "Take off your shoes. It'll be easier to run. And take off your coat too."

I took off my shoes and coat and began running. I ran through fields, through meadows, through puddles. I didn't know where I was running. The cold slashed through the soles of my feet.

I caught up with a girl named Khanke Kleiner. Both of us ran past the house of another *goye*. I forget her name. This *goye* held a Jewish child in her arms, Malkale, the daughter of Ksil Schmaltz and his wife Khava, neighbors of ours. The *goye* begged us to take the child. "Have pity on me," the *goye* said. "Take away this Jewish child or they'll kill me too!"

Miral and I knew that if we took Malkale, we would get caught. At least with the *goye,* the child had a chance. We kept running until we came to a crossroads. Miral said, "Rukhl, would you take a look! There's Aaron!"

I lifted my eyes and sure enough, I saw Aaron. Immediately I assumed that all the others were alive too. Aaron knew I had been with our father and sisters, so he assumed they were alive too. I told him my story and he told me his:

Aaron said that when he was in Cybulski's hay, he heard bloodcurdling cries, and he heard our sisters screaming. He looked out from Cybulski's stable and saw that the Germans and the Ukrainian collaborators encircled the shtetl. They gathered together all the Jews and led them to a bunker left over by the Russians. The Germans commanded small groups of Jews to enter the bunker. Then they shot them. The process continued until the Germans killed everyone off. Aaron wanted to run to the bunker so he could die too. But Cybulski grabbed hold of my brother and punched him, and refused to let Aaron leave the stable. Cybulski gave Aaron a horse bridle and reins. He told Aaron to run to the woods with them. If *goyim* saw Aaron with a bridle, they would assume he was a *goy.*

Aaron carried the bridle and reins for a while and then threw them away, where he couldn't remember. It was in his mind, as it was in mine, to run to the Seleskes.

We talked and cried, talked and cried, and didn't notice we had left Mirale behind.

Who should we run into now but the same Ukrainians who helped the Germans kill off the Jews? From one of the other roads, they saw us running.

They caught up with us and yelled, *"Stój!"* Stop!

Aaron said to me, "You escape. I'll let them catch me. You'll survive and remember us all." I said, "I don't want to live alone. You escape. You'll survive and remember us all." While we were bickering which one of us should escape and survive, the Ukrainians aimed their rifles at us.

The Ukrainians said, "Ho! You're carrying food to the Russian partisans. Spies! You're under arrest!"

A group of young Ukrainians led us to the *posterunek,* the police station. They beat Aaron. They commanded him to run. I knew that if Aaron ran, the Ukrainians would shoot. They would say Aaron tried to escape. When they socked Aaron with their rifles, I blocked the blows and received them. I wouldn't let Aaron run.

They led us to the Polish police in a place called Cztezeric. Inside the police station, we heard Miral's voice. The Ukrainians had caught her too. We eavesdropped. The Polish police asked her where she was going. She said she was looking for work. The police asked us if we knew Miral and we said yes. Is she looking for work? they asked. We said yes. So the three of us were detained.

After positioning the rifles against our noses and asking us to smell the bullets, they said they were going to kill us.

They decided to take us back to Kritnetse. If the Judenrat could prove that we were not spies, we could live. The Judenrat, you know, was a Jewish council, a stooge council created by the Nazis to do their bidding. We knew the Judenrat didn't even exist anymore.

On the way to Kritnetse, the Ukrainians beat us again. One of them couldn't have been more than seventeen. Aaron said his name was Panas and he knew him from school.

As we traveled to Kritnetse, the Ukrainians rounded up more Jews. Two were orphan boys, one eight, the other ten.

The Ukrainians shot at one and killed him. I saw this with my own eyes. They also caught a woman with seven small children. I think her name was Peshke Leder. Her eldest daughter was Miriam, next Sureh, and I don't remember the others. The youngest was seven weeks old. Her husband's name was Yossl. He was dead.

The Ukrainians were beside themselves. What a fiesta! They threw us into a cellar of a Jew, now dead, by the name of Yankol. The cellar was covered with mold.

Goyim came to stare at us. We pleaded with them to save us. Nothing helped. Cybulski came by and promised to see what he could do.

All night *goyim* threw wood and stones into the cellar windows. They screamed, "*Żydy!* We're gonna kill you!" They were thrilled they had run into such good luck.

What could we do? We lay in the moldy cellar for two days, the door above us bolted shut and blocked so we couldn't possibly escape.

Built into the wall was a cubbyhole. My cousin, Miral, a big girl, stuffed herself into it. Don't ask me how she scrunched herself up to fit. Miral said, "This is where I'll hide." Who knows what she was thinking. There was no hiding place. We saw that death was near.

The Ukrainians finally led us outside and began debating with each other what to do with us.

One of the policemen guarding us was Panas. Aaron begged Panas, "Don't look and let us escape." Panas said, "I can't do that. My job is to keep an eye on you. Times are different now. We've got to kill you."

The Poles and Ukrainians had a big discussion about where to kill us. They couldn't take us to the bunker. It was already overflowing with dead bodies and blood. Someone suggested the river, but the Poles needed the river for their daily affairs.

One of the Poles was the *deshatnyik,* a local politician. This *deshatnyik* was one man with an ounce of humanity. He said, "If I tell you not to kill them, you won't listen anyway. Do what you will, but I won't kill people." He left.

The Ukrainians took us back to the police station in Cztezeric. Along the way they picked up more Jews.

Panas said he wanted to release me. He pointed to an old woman in a house and said, "That's my grandmother. She'll hide you." I said, "Release my brother and I'll go to your grandmother." He said, "I only want to save you." Your brother has to die, he says, but me he wants to save. I said, "If you kill my brother, I have no reason to live. Life with you and your grandmother is no life."

Near Cztezeric, Panas began beating me and said, "It's too late now. Even if I wanted to, I couldn't let you go."

In Cztezeric the police lined us up outside and said, "Time's up!" We Jews stood shoulder to shoulder facing the police. I reached for Aaron's hand so dying wouldn't be so hard. The police hit our hands.

At the last minute—just as the policemen took aim—three jeeps with seven German soldiers pulled up to the police station. These were ordinary soldiers, not Gestapo, and they were in their sixties at least. Their job was to collect eggs, milk, butter, sour cream, from the Poles for the Gestapo. They took a gander at us—fifteen of us children. The soldiers asked the Ukrainians, "What's going on here? What are you doing with these children?"

The Ukrainians exulted. "These are *Juden! Żydy!* We're going to blast them away!"

A German said, "Take them back to the police station. I'll decide the rest."

Back to the police station. The Germans ordered us into a room one at a time and asked, "Why were you running? The Ukrainians say you are spies and you carried food to the Russian partisans."

As the questioning progressed, the German soldiers realized they were dealing with children, the youngest seven weeks old. They asked if we were hungry. We said, "We don't want anything from you. Let us go!"

The Germans tapped their feet on the floor and screamed, *"Haben Sie Hunger oder nein?"*

We got scared and said yes, we have *Hunger,* we'll eat.

They said we would have food any minute. And sure enough, they brought bread, hard-boiled eggs, milk, and even a little sugar for the baby.

We had food, and now we wanted freedom. We begged to leave. The Germans said they couldn't release us. They said they would go to Ludmar,* a town larger than Kritnetse, and ask their *Gebietskomisar,* their commanding officer, what to do with us. Whatever the *Gebietskomisar* said, they would do. The Germans left and we stayed in the cellar.

In the morning the Ukrainians moved us to another room. They sang us a death lullaby. "Kiss life goodbye," they sang. "Your time is long overdue."

The room had an open window. My brother said he was going to jump and run away. I always had my work cut out with Aaron. "Who jumps from a second-story window without breaking his legs?" I asked. "You'll be a cripple."

While we talked, we noticed a short, fat German riding a Rover, a bicycle. He was driving straight towards us. When Aaron saw him, he said, *"Kinder,* this German has come to save us."

*Vladimir-Volinskii.

The short, fat German came into the building and blurted out, "Where are the *Juden?*"

Oh! The Ukrainians were living it up. The *Juden? T'hoste!* Here they are. *Farvus nisht?* Why not?

The short, fat German learned our history and said, "*Kinder,* I'm letting you go. But don't dawdle. Hide!"

Where to hide, we ourselves didn't know.

No sooner were the words out of the short, fat German's mouth when I yanked Aaron by the arm and said, "Let's get out of here." With my yank, Aaron and I were the first out the door.

Outside, a Ukrainian guard stood watch. He gave Aaron a kick. In disbelief, Aaron asked, "Why did you kick me?" I yanked Aaron's hand again and said, "Take that kick and let's go. Thank God you're still alive, and run."

Overwhelmed with joy, Aaron shouted to everyone he saw, "*Puścili nas!* They let us go!" We passed a barefoot woman with fat legs carrying a knapsack full of hay. Aaron goes up to her and says *Puścili nas.* The *goye* doesn't understand what *puścili* and yes *puścili.* She couldn't have cared less if a Jew was killed or set free. I saw, as always, what a job it was to pull Aaron away from danger. I said, "Let her alone and run."

Running, we decided to go back to Kritnetse. Maybe someone did survive. Maybe our sisters . . . maybe our father . . . maybe they escaped at the last minute.

Every person we approached in Kritnetse said, "Go away. We're afraid. We don't want to keep you here."

No father. No sisters. Killed on the twenty-fifth day of May, two days after Shavuos, 1942. Two weeks later, after begging *goy* to *goy* in Kritnetse—where some people were better than others and gave us a piece of bread and some milk; but sleeping, we had to sleep outside in a pile of straw or in a garden, and some Poles wanted to begrudge us even this and yelled, "Get out, *Żydy!* They're killing you and you deserve it"—at wit's end, we returned to the Seleskes and began our saga with Leszek.

6

November 19, 1979
Tel Aviv, Israel
Yankl Khaim Szuster, as told to Yaffa Simontov
Collected and edited for the World War II Jewish
Survivors' Archive at Yad Vashem

My three younger sisters were blond enough to pass for Christian. One day in June 1940, they followed behind a Christian mob to the cemetery and watched as Nazis murdered a family of Uchan Jews. From that day on, whenever the Gestapo marched through Uchan, I hid. Hiding and running became my policy.

For as long as I can remember, I was plotting how to leave Poland. I always intended to make it to Palestine or America, and like most of my friends, I belonged to one of the Zionist youth groups. I knew there was no future for a Jew in Poland. But I was a young boy with no money, my father's only son, by his second wife. I stayed in Poland.

Shortly after the massacre in the cemetery, the Germans ordered us to the center of town. They told us to travel light, instructing us to bring only bedding and nightclothes. Dozens of wagons stood ready to carry us "east." Amidst the Germans' bullhorns and guns, their brown uniforms and whistles, my mother, father, older sister Brantzche, three younger sisters, and I piled into a wagon with several other families. For nearly two days we traveled in the horse-drawn wagons, eating what little food my mother and sisters carried with them. At the end of two days we came to a train station.

My mother was scared. She and my father whispered to each other, back and forth, for an hour. People were running and bumping into each other, and in the confusion, my mother and the four girls jumped from the wagon and escaped from the station. My father told me they planned to return to Uchan. But after a day, my mother and sisters returned to the train station. The children had cried that they were tired and hungry, and couldn't make the five miles home.

Maybe ten minutes after my mother and the girls returned, half a dozen empty trains pulled into the station. The Gestapo began chasing us and barking orders like dogs. *Männer rechts! Frauen links!* Men to the right! Women to the left! The Jews were crying and screaming and praying. It was a terrible sound and I will never forget it as long as I live.

The Gestapo beat us with their rifle butts and ordered the men to load the Jews' suitcases and knapsacks into one car. That took the better part of one day. Meanwhile, the train full of women and children pulled away, and I never saw my mother and sisters again.

For three days my father and I rode in an unlit train car that stank from urine, excrement, and vomit. Among a hundred men, we didn't have a cup of water. We knew it was day by the splinter of light filtering through the door, and we knew the train's direction by the signposts we left behind.

On the afternoon of the third day the train creaked to a halt. The doors flung open and I was blinded by the daylight. Before the dog-faced Germans came into focus, I heard again the terrible sounds of Jewish men crying and praying. When the air hit my nostrils, I realized that the train also smelled of rotting flesh. In front of us stood the uniformed Germans, their eyes and rifles aimed at our faces. They didn't waste a second and began smacking us with the rifle butts and calling us "filthy Jews." I don't know how I managed it, but as I jumped from the train, I twisted my body to avoid the blow of the butt, and I was the only one unscathed.

A freshly painted wooden sign informed us we had come to Staw, a slave labor camp near Chelm. The Germans and their Ukrainian helpers kept barking like dogs. It was impossible to understand what they were saying, even if you knew German. If you didn't understand, a *pstenk* with the rifle butt.

They kept us naked for four days, and June in Poland is still not very warm. This was a special torment for the religious men, who covered their genitals with their hands. Their greatest shame was discovering naked women in the camp too.

At the end of the first week, the Germans gave us cheap prison clothing. They set us to work digging irrigation ditches.

The first time I escaped from Staw, a German caught me and dragged me back to the camp. I almost died three times that day.

First, the German wanted to drown me. He commanded half a dozen Jews, two of them my cousins, to bind my hands and feet and throw me into a trench full of sewage. I kept pleading that the only reason I tried to run away was because I hadn't gotten my bread ration that morning, and once I found bread outside the camp, I had every intention of returning. Staw was like my home, I said. My father lived there. How could I leave him? The Germans asked the Jews if I was telling the truth. No one contradicted me. An older Jew even offered me his bread ration.

A Ukrainian guard walked up to us and asked what was going on. The German said I had tried to escape and the

Ukrainian offered to settle my case with a gun. I swore up and down that I had no intention of escaping, and anyone in the camp would vouch for my honesty and work habits. Then the Ukrainian began kicking me and pounding me with his rifle butt. My hands and feet are tied, so I can't do anything but swear I was only hungry.

The Ukrainian drags me away from the Jews, beating and kicking all the while. Now and then he relents and asks me in a kindhearted voice to tell him the truth, I can trust him, he won't hurt me. When I repeat my story, he beats me again. The Ukrainian points to a tree and says, "Take a good look because that's where you're going to hang." So he orders the Jews to make a noose and put it around my neck. And I keep protesting that I didn't escape, I would never leave my father in a thousand years.

The same German who wanted to drown me runs up to the Ukrainian with a piece of paper in his hand. He tells the Ukrainian to take the noose from my neck; he has a decree from his superior to give me another chance. It's true, the German says, the Jew was hungry and wandered outside the camp to find bread. The two of them untie my wrists and ankles and drag me back to the barracks.

The next morning my body was swollen and marked head to toe with tremendous yellow and black bruises. My head was hot and my skin drenched in sweat. Every time I inhaled, I thought I had breathed my last. I heard my father crying as he nursed my wounds. The pain was so bad I didn't care if I died.

My cousins pulled me to my feet and carried me out to the ditches. Someone stuck a shovel in my hands and I started digging.

※

In a few weeks I recovered and was ready to try again. My father stole a pair of shears from a toolshed, cut a hole in the wire fence, and returned the shears. He told me where he made the cut and casually I inspected the site. I told my cousin Reuven that I was escaping that night and asked him to come with me. "Tonight isn't good for me," he said, like he had plans to study Talmud or who knows what. I asked Yosl, a boy from my town, if he wanted to escape, and he was game.

You see, it was easy to break out of the camp. The problem was staying free. I tore the wire open and crawled through with barely a scratch. Yosl wasn't so lucky. He caught his ass on a piece of wire and I could barely keep from laughing. I had to piss on the wound to stop the blood.

I had spent three months in the work camp. I promised myself I would never return there alive.

Yosl and I returned to Uchan. I learned that my half-brother Avram was dead. How could that be? He had been hiding at the home of some Poles, and in a few months time a perfectly healthy twenty-five-year-old man was dead. I asked some of the remaining Jews in Uchan what happened. A distant cousin of mine named Shosha said she heard the Poles talk about poisoning Avram. They didn't want to shoot him, they didn't want to set him free, so they compromised with poison in his food.

One day as Yosl and I are hiding in a Pole's barn, in walks my father. I can only attribute our reunion to extrasensory perception. Both of us knew somehow that this Pole's barn would be the place to meet up with each other. My father and I had decided nothing in advance, and we assumed we saw the last of each other at Staw. We fell on each other's shoulders and I told him about Avram.

My father and I were together sixteen days. A sixteen-year-old Pole discovered my father in the barn while Yosl and I were out looking for food. We returned and found my father groaning and his nose bleeding. Parts of his beard lay in clumps on his coat. He was in a fever and could barely recognize me.

He begged me to find him water. I said I couldn't. If I left the barn now, the Poles who did this to my father would be on the lookout for me. I would get caught and that would be the end of us. My father said what a rotten son I was. *I* would be responsible for his death, not the Pole. What could I say to that? I told Yosl to hide and I would look for water.

No surprise, the Poles caught me. They dragged my father and me to a truck and bound my hands and feet. They didn't have to tie up my father because he was in no condition to move a finger.

I don't know where they were taking us, maybe to Staw, maybe to Gestapo headquarters, maybe to the woods. None of the Poles bothered to guard us. In fact, not one of them carried arms. They knew the Jews were a docile people, more inclined to turn the other cheek than come to blows. They knew that a shrimpy Pole could intimidate a big, muscular Jew.

While the Poles in the truck were devising how to kill us, my father untied my ankles and hands. I jumped off the truck and ran back down the road. Either before or after my father declared, "Hear O Israel, the Lord Our God, the Lord is One"—the prayer on a dying Jew's lips—I know that he pleaded with God to spare his son's life.

I ran straight into a Pole. He must have seen me jump off the truck. He yelled at me to follow him to the police. For the first time in my life, I socked a Christian in the jaw, and made a break for the woods.

After the war I saw the German from Staw on a public bus. He was the same German who wanted to drown me first and then got me a reprieve. I wanted to point my finger at him and shout that he was a Nazi. I wanted to report him as a criminal, but I was scared. As far as I could see, I was the only Jew on the bus, and I was afraid the *goyim* would kill me sooner than turn over one of their own. In a sweat, I got off the bus at the next stop.

7

ON THE MORNING OF JULY 4, 1968, low gray clouds separated us from the sun like a celestial *mekhitse*, the barrier in an Orthodox synagogue that divides the male worshipers from the female while allowing each side a guarded glance at the other. Such weather was unusual for a south Jersey morning: Thunder, lightning, and rain typically began in early afternoon, hoping to steal their way unnoticed into the bluest part of the day. Then the jackhammer noise of cicadas and grasshoppers went dead and in their place a deep purring rolled into the sky from the middle of the Atlantic Ocean.

With the morose clouds low overhead, Perel, Papa, and I waited on the lawn of the Long-a-coming American Legion for the July Fourth Day parade to begin. ("I'm gonna rain, I swear I'm gonna rain," Perel said in the voice of threatening rain.) As always, I was eager to get off the farm and gape at the transformed languor of town life. But there was an obstacle to my pleasure on this trip: Papa. I felt an unwanted intimacy with my father, the result of having watched for years his head nodding as he read the *Jewish Daily Forward*, his thumbless hand cup his balls as he dozed, his thumbless hand force an enema up Perel's constipated ass years earlier; of having memorized the malnutrition tuber scars on his razored nape. I had watched his wretched figure, embalmed in *talis* and *tfilin*, rock back and forth in prayer, engaged in a monologue to God, his grief silent at all costs. How could I appear in public with my father's private habits spliced into my eyes? Suffering ought to be a reclusive matter. Watching Papa think his tortured thoughts in public embarrassed me to the point of humiliation. He observed Long-a-coming's goings-on without comment, seeing other people's ceremonies as casual distractions with no greater significance than what met the eye. Yankl Szuster believed only in the invisible: Anything tangible was illusory. His grief was more real than a ten-year-old poppy queen waving her hand from a red and white crepe float.

Observing Perel's reactions to Long-a-coming was less painful to me because she had less of a past. Perel and I had never known other quarters and couldn't compare the anticlimax of our present lives to the disaster of the past. I noticed Perel start a bit as she recognized Kathy and Karla Russell, twin daughters of Willy Russell, the alleged grand dragon of the south Jersey Ku Klux Klan. Kathy and Karla were easily the skinniest people in south Jersey, maybe in the whole state. Their rib cages were bony against the unfashionable jerseys they wore all summer long. Heightening their wraithlike appearance was an oily cob of towheaded hair atop each head. For an occasion as special as July Fourth, the twins had curled the wispy strands into tight ringlets that showcased their masculine Adam's apples.

As we looked on, a twin tickled the other's armpit. One of creation's most unsettling sights was the twins laughing. It's not that their laughter looked satanic, as you would expect from the daughters of a Klan dragon. Exactly the opposite. The twins appeared fragile, martyred by their father's hatred; one extra giggle would return them to dust. They rarely talked to me or Perel or to anyone else. Kathy and Karla reminded me of the two kitten runts under our sole pear tree, animals plagued with scabrous eye infections that left them weak and emaciated. You can imagine how ostracized such physically unappealing girls were in high school.

Perel, my father, and I lined up with the other townspeople along Long Avenue. I darted my eyes from Papa to Perel so often, studying them, that Papa asked if I was sun sick. He looked up to the darkening sky and predicted the temperature drop that would accompany the rain. Papa had no idea what disturbed me. The demands of Jake's Poultry Farm afforded him no leisure to ponder the developments of his children's characters, no time to notice how one bit her nails, how another split her hair, how another's eyes twitched as a precursor to rage. Like love, intimacy isn't necessarily reciprocated. To fend off my discomfort, I asked Papa if he had enjoyed parades as a boy.

"It wasn't exactly a parade," Papa said in English, careful not to offend the populace with a foreign language. "It was a funeral procession in honor of General Pilsudski."

"Who?" Perel asked.

"Shpeyter," Papa said. Later. His reversion to Yiddish meant the story had something to do with anti-Semites and would likely invoke his loathing for Poland's semipagan Christianity. To satisfy our curiosity and delude Long-a-coming, he added in English, "You outgrow your childhood enthusiasms." I looked at Perel and she rubbed her eye, centering all her attention on an imaginary mote, embarrassed. The people of Long-a-coming hadn't outgrown their childhood enthusiasms. They played softball on Saturdays. They shot deer in hunting season. Did my father's theory mean I would stop playing piano? Stop loving Perel? Papa pressed his thin lips together, and the pragmatic fix of his eyes dissolved for a moment. Some memory had prompted a maxim in his mind, but he was reluctant to share it with children too young to appreciate it.

"That's impossible," I said. Papa raised his eyebrows and shrugged.

The parade was the usual fare: marching band, Boy Scout troop, limping veterans, Lions Club, Ladies Auxiliary, police force, and fire squad. While the spectacle was the kind of activity I would usually appreciate—observation without participation—I felt uneasy, and then disappointed because I wasn't thrilled to be off the farm. The townspeople elbowed each other for a front-line view, excited to see their children and bridge partners caparisoned in the garb of heroism, an opportunity that day-to-day Long-a-coming rarely offered. The more their eyes narrowed with sentimentality, the more isolated I felt, and I was compelled to place my hand on my breast to mask my faithlessness. Perel pecked her nose into my arm and said she was the dove from the Dove for Dishes TV commercial. She tucked her hands under her armpits and exercised her elbows to take flight. Perhaps it was then that I realized Perel couldn't communicate with me in anything but cartoon voices, hiding behind them as she had once hidden behind her hair to escape Mendl's tantrum.

This year the speech in front of the American Legion was a eulogy for "one of our fallen American boys in Vietnam." The fallen boy's name was Something Vasquez, who as I recalled used to live in Hammonton. I didn't know why Long-a-coming valued this corpse, or how Hammonton had relinquished it. It struck me as odd that the Long-a-coming town council, which had once voted to evict a black family from town, had now acquired a dead Puerto Rican to bury under the new Vietnam plaque.

A young policeman stood at either side of former Sergeant Grant Fitting, a bulky, red-faced World War II veteran officiating on the Legion porch "in a dedication to honor, pride, and patriotism." The policeman on the left looked familiar to me, and his handsome, tanned face made my stomach muscles flutter. I hoped to catch his eye, but his gaze spun to the single-propeller plane parked on the lawn.

The crowd's buzzing died away. Grant Fitting, Former, as Perel called him, began talking about Something Vasquez and how Something took his place alongside the fighters for democracy of the two world wars. A short gray-haired woman with a snowman figure stood nearby, weeping into a rumpled handkerchief, surrounded by a coterie of Puerto Ricans who cosseted her trembling shoulders and wiped their own tears away.

Now the veteran stomped his foot and shouted something about cowardly doves in Congress and on the streets of our American cities. "Dove? Did I hear someone call my name?" Perel whispered. Dazed by the zeal of a man who had lost no family during the war, Papa watched the speaker seethe, while Perel flexed the fingers of each hand into wings and waved them at her sides. When I saw the scar over Papa's left eye arch, I was so overcome with prohibited laughter I couldn't speak. Perel continued chirping and I began to count the seconds between the rumbles of distant thunder and lightning to get hold of myself. At the sound of tittering, we turned around and saw four teenaged boys in frayed shorts and dirt-stained T-shirts stooped on the ground, making picking motions. *What was funny about that?* I wondered. Some of the grieving Puerto Ricans looked over their shoulders to locate the source of disrespect. Their survey stopped at Perel and me; drunk on family intimacy liberated in a public place, we appeared to be in collusion with the boys. I realized then that they were mimicking Puerto Rican blueberry pickers. Perel's eyes met the Vasquezes' and she flapped her arms all the harder, mired in the mockery she didn't share.

Arms raised to pacify the disgruntled Vasquezes, Grant

Fitting rasped that anyone who died in the service of American democracy, be they black or white, brown or yellow, Christian or Jew, male or female, deserved the highest honors due a hero; and without toleration for one another's differences, the country would go to hell in a handbasket. The crowd eyed the boys uncritically and applauded.

"*Der nahr shtipt*," Papa said under his breath, meaning the rebuke for Perel and me. But he wasn't angry; he wasn't exasperated. *Der nahr shtipt* literally means "the fool pushes," and that, Papa surmised, was the root of our problem: The fool who resided deep inside us burst the carapace of our will, booting us towards frivolous urges ill-timed for serious occasion. Papa saw no point in punishing the fool, and announced with a shrug that he was driving back to the farm. We could stay at the parade if we promised to take cover when it rained. *Der nahr* may have *shtipt,* Perel told Papa, but we were certainly sober enough to get out of the rain.

Papa wasn't gone five minutes when Kathy and Karla Russell waved at Perel and me. Like two TV antennae on stilts, the twins straggled towards us. Perel whispered, "Let's pretend we don't see them," and, feeling for my hand, tugged me towards Long Avenue. We inched our way through patriots, now singing "God Bless America," and then froze in our tracks. Kathy, or maybe it was Karla, tapped Perel on the left shoulder, and the other tapped me on the right. Neither Perel nor I could then have guessed that the twins were dying, each held hostage by a collapsing aorta, and by a father's wrath which their fragile hearts literally could not withstand. No, we couldn't have known they were dying, but illness spoke directly to our own pretensions to immortality, driving us into a posture hostile to the carriers of disease. Perel and I didn't know, yet we understood and denied. Kathy and Karla didn't know, yet understood and accepted. Perel and I smiled hello, pitying and aghast.

Shyly, Karla said to Perel, "The school principal is reading the Bible at the cemetery. Can you come?" Perel shrank behind me a foot and answered in a small voice, "We have to beat the storm." But the twins appeared not to have heard her, and while one extended my sister a finger, skinny and knobbed as Hansel's twig, the other steered me by the elbow. I felt Perel's hand fall from mine. Though I didn't want to stand uncomfortably in the Long-a-coming cemetery and listen to a Bible reading, I didn't resist the rhythm of the crowd, and threw myself into a break in the parade line. In two seconds the float bearing the poppy queen caught up with the convertible Plymouth chauffeuring World War I veterans too feeble to walk, and now made crossing impossible. Safely across the street, I turned to look for my sister. A number of thirteen-year-old girls with curly brown hair and dimpled knees were scattered among the spectators, but none of them was Perel. I picked up a fallen red crepe poppy and scanned the crowd again. Like a crossed-eyes illusion, a twin appeared on either side of me. "I can't find Perel," I explained, frightened that I had provoked cataclysm at Perel's expense. "Don't worry," they said. "She'll show up at the cemetery. That's where everyone is going."

Perel did not show up at the cemetery. I should have offered some excuse to the twins and gone to look for her. But I couldn't resist that persistent, dooming hope that something might happen; for I had begun to suspect that history was a mirage that only others saw.

The sky grew darker and the thunder more bilious overhead. Each twin edged closer to me. The school principal tugged at his collar and necktie and settled an atlas-sized Bible on a reading stand. In an appropriately basso profundo voice, he strained for a revisionist similarity between the American war for independence and the battle of Jericho: "And it shall come to pass, that when they make a long blast with the ram's horn, and when ye hear the sound of the trumpet, all the people shall shout with a great shout; and the wall of the city shall fall down flat, and the people shall ascend every man straight before him." Throughout, I imagined that one of the marching Lions or firemen had dragooned Perel into the alleyway behind the five-and-ten and stabbed her to death with a Legionnaire's rifle butt. I thought: *If anything does happen to me, it won't be history; it will be some piddling incident that runs amok and exposes my cowardice.*

To rattle me further, the two young policemen previously flanking Grant Fitting, Former, now stationed themselves on either side of the principal. Despite the low-hanging clouds, the weather was still warm, and the handsome, dark-haired policeman wiped his brow with a pocket handkerchief. That's when I remembered him, or the memory he awoke in me.

It was 1962 or '63, at some holiday Bible reading in the cemetery. Vaguely, I remembered all three Szuster children waving miniature cloth American flags and marveling at the dates from the 1800s chiseled into the headstones. Perel chatted with Maureen Gare, a friend who had once played hooky from school to read *The Pilgrim's Progress*. Sheiye prowled between the headstones collecting discarded flags. I, as usual, believed that only aberration—either some unpredictable expression of romance or some witless subversion—would give the day meaning, and I scoured the cemetery for signs of it. No sooner did I notice a tall, slender teenager than a group of his friends teamed up to shoot a spray of black fountain pen ink into his face. The boy, dressed in a white T-shirt and blue denim overalls, sat down in the shade of a tombstone. With a white handkerchief, he wiped the ink from his brow in long, patient strokes, shaking his head good-naturedly. Every time I thought of the boy, covered with black ink, cleaning his face with the white handkerchief and smiling at the spattered cloth, my stomach muscles contracted. I honestly didn't know if I was enchanted or repelled. That boy and that cop, I could swear they were one and the same man.

The first drops of rain tapped the maple leaves as the principal ended his sermon with advice to seek haven from the storm with our families. "I have to find my sister," I told the twins. "I can't go home without her."

Kathy chided Karla (or vice versa) for letting Perel out of her sight: "I took Brenda's hand, you were supposed to take Pearl's." Living in the sway of their father's reputation, the twins were moved by his power if not by his philosophy, and assumed that the Russells shaped events more than they really could have. By consensus, they offered to enlist their family station wagon to patrol Long Avenue in search of Perel.

I couldn't have hoped for a better opportunity to indulge my lust for catastrophe: a ride in the pouring rain through Long-a-coming in Willy Russell's station wagon. Lots of people said the Klan met at Russell's Funeral Parlor on the corner of Long Avenue and Almond's Folly Road. The funeral parlor was one of Long-a-coming's most modern-looking buildings, constructed in the fifties from pink and silver brick. Its chips of granite and quartz outsparkled the white, box-shaped pants factory catercorner on Almond's Folly Road and the gray railroad-car diner several hundred yards away. Freshly painted beige sashes ribboned the few windows like arms crossed on a boastful chest. The funeral parlor was so much more imposing than any other building in Long-a-coming—an air of smug immortality in its ever-contemporary look—that I wouldn't have been surprised had the townspeople looked forward to dying. The Russells lived in the same building where the family conducted business. As time passed and the funeral parlor prospered, they added a wing to the house, and then a rectangular swimming pool, and finally a green tennis court, a stone's throw from the black ghetto called West Long-a-coming.

I had no choice but to accept the twins' hospitality, because now the storm broke full force, pelting our bare arms and faces with rain. Truly off guard, I felt myself spirited away, a twin at either elbow, towards the cemetery entrance, where the Russell car waited.

"Hoo-ee!" Willy Russell cried, the last one in the station wagon. Without looking at anyone, he stripped off his T-shirt and wrung the rainwater out over his head. In a roughhousing mood, he wrung another few drops over his skinny daughters' towheaded curls. "Guaranteed to put hair on your chest!" he guffawed. The twins squealed with delight and turned to share their joy with me. "Get it, missus?" he asked. "Hair on our daughters' chests—"

Russell turned around. Not only did he see his timid, sulking wife, pressed against the door in hopes of falling out or hiding as best she could from her obstreperous husband, and holding her youngest child, an infant boy, tightly in her lap; he also saw me.

"I got my fingers in a lot of pies," he taunted, "but I ain't got a one in the adoption business. Who are you!"

Kathy piped, "This is Brenda Szuster, Daddy. Karla lost Brenda's sister." She launched a volley of nose tweaks, followed by air blows into her sister's ear. The child in his mother's arms whined. The mother made farting noises on the child's neck to humor him.

"Chee, Eileen, you goddamn got Kurt-boy riled," Russell said. The twins laughed.

Eileen Russell ventured a few words into Kurt-boy's teary cheek. "You're not helping," she said in a thick Tennessee accent. "None of yous is helping." She pulled her tiny ally to her breast and offered him a square of melting Hershey.

One twin cracked an egg on top of the other's head, running her hands down her sister's neck to simulate the dripping yolk and white. "Eileen, didn't I tell you to lay off?" said Willy Russell in a mimicking southern accent. The twins stifled their ghoulish laughter. Most likely Willy Russell had earned Kathy and Karla's loyalty by turning their mother into a whipping post without ever laying a hand on her.

Russell started up the car and turned on the windshield wipers. This man, who had named his children for the initials of his favorite acronym, looked at me in the rearview mirror and told me to wipe the back window. "Everyone pulls their own weight around here. Aye, my little bitches?" Slowing to a stop at the railroad tracks, Russell bared his yellow teeth like a wild dog's and pretended to gnaw Kathy's and Karla's flesh to pieces. If their father's language offended them, his ruffian playfulness absolved him. I couldn't understand their adoration for him and their contempt for their mother: How had he turned the children against her?

I was about to wipe the window with my salvaged red crepe poppy, ready to sacrifice what I loved at the command of someone I hated, when Eileen Russell fished for a tissue in her purse and handed it to me. I cleared the condensation away. She smiled at me and, looking at the rain, apologized: "My husband . . ."

"Now to find the wandering Jew," Willy Russell said.

The twins didn't laugh. Girls as hideously lean as Kathy and Karla Russell were too obsessed with their own deficiencies to believe that religion or color was a credible impairment.

Perhaps their antipathy towards their mother siphoned off their hatred for outsiders.

Bored with insulting his family, Russell tuned in an all-news radio station. Dispassionately, the news announcer read an up-to-date tally of Vietnam war dead. Willy Russell was listening but didn't comment.

The twins suddenly looked at each other and began blinking their eyes in simulation of the red-flashing train barrier signals. They begged their father to wait for the train so they could count the cars. Terrific. Russell looked at his wife through the rearview mirror and said meaningfully, "I can wait." Eileen Russell buried her head in her son's limp shoulder, squeezing him so hard he whined in his sleep.

The barrier arms bowed to each other, and the first cars clattered past. The twins began counting in a singsong. I thought that if I stared hard enough I could conjure Perel out of thin air, but all I saw was a bedraggled old man with a nicotine-stained beard sitting on the cement steps of Marnie's Five-and-Ten.

"Looks pretty deserted," Russell said.

"What's deserted mean?" a twin asked.

Willy Russell threw back his head and pretended to gobble a bunch of grapes. He gulped, then said, "It means there ain't nothin' in sight."

I imagined Perel's decomposing bones lying behind the store, stray cats licking at the remains of her chubby flesh. Thunder would shout Joshua's great shout, and the walls of rain would flatten her into the ground.

"Maybe your sister already walked home?" Eileen Russell comforted.

"Wandered, not walked," her husband corrected. He peered through the windshield wipers, feigning interest in the lettering on a flatbed car.

Eileen Russell sighed.

Willy Russell sighed falsetto, and his daughters rocked with laughter. Vindictively, he located his wife in the rearview mirror and drawled, "Don't you sigh at me, hooker." Another ten minutes with the Russells and I was sure to unearth the arrangement they had struck with each other to endure their conjugal hatred.

The caboose rolled past, the barrier arms lifted, and Willy Russell put the car in gear. As if threatening to ditch me right then and there, he grumbled, "I ain't doing me or no one else no favor chauffeuring a rich man's daughter around. I got better things to do."

But in five minutes, he made a right-hand turn into the driveway of Jake's Poultry Farm. I had dreaded the continued search for Perel, but dreaded even more the sight of our gray-shingled house. I loathed Willy Russell, yet I was afraid to go home and face my parents.

My mother was standing in the rickety vestibule, watching the rain and waiting for me. Eileen Russell rolled down her window and called out, "We were looking for your daughter. Did she get home all right?" She breathed easily, somehow knowing that Perel had gotten home before the storm, confident that no misery could sprout around her greater than her own.

"Tenk you, tenk you," Mama said, bending slightly at the waist. "Tenk you for brinkink Brenda home. Yes, Pearl got vorried about deh storm and valked home by herself. A little vet, but aw-kay. Tenk you!"

With Perel safely accounted for, I was reluctant to leave the car, nervous that Mama might hit me in front of the Russells. But as I entered the vestibule, she only shook her head and said, "Perel locked herself in her room and won't talk to you." She opened the screen door for me. "I'll never trust you with Perel again."

Willy Russell pulled around the leaning pole in the middle of the driveway and headed for the Pike. The twins sat with their arms draped across each other's bony shoulders, staring robotically through the windshield. Without warning, the car shifted into reverse, and the passengers, taken unawares, jolted forward in response. Mama opened the screen door a smidgen and waited to quote egg or chicken prices. After half an hour in Russell's presence, I was braced for worse. He whispered something to the twins, who wrinkled their skeletal brows. The one closer to the door slapped her large-knuckled hand over the lock button protectively, and I thought I detected a shadow of protest in her almost instinctive action. And then, impatient, Willy Russell reached across his two daughters and rolled down the passenger-side window. Crushing his daughters up against the door, he shouted to Mama and me, "Heppy Hannukah!" and laughed. First Mama looked confused, but in the next second, anger replaced that deferential smile she habitually wore for the egg customers. She opened the door wide and shook her fist at the muddy gash in the driveway that the tires of the station wagon had dug into the earth.

"*A sheynem dank,*" Mama said to me, closing the door to the rain. Thanks a lot. She shook her head to clear Willy Russell's insult from her memory. She didn't live in south Jersey to put up with that kind of nonsense.

I knocked on Perel's bedroom door, and as Mama had warned, she refused to answer. "Perel, I have something for you," I pleaded. "Really, I do. You don't have to see me if you don't want, but at least come get your gift." Laying the red crepe poppy on the floor, a skimpy bouquet of apology, fakery, and love, I walked to my room, stood in the doorway, and waited for Perel's curiosity to get the better of her.

Quietly, Perel emerged from her room and saw the flower lying at her feet.

"I'm sorry, Perel," I said, craning my head forward. "I'll never leave you like that again."

Perel smiled and braided the green wire stem of the poppy into her hair. Her forgiveness was so sudden and absolute that I felt both immense relief and disappointment at being denied a battle. "I promise, really, I'll never do it again," I swore, trying to prolong our conflict while ensuring that the rift had been soldered.

We bounded down the stairs holding hands and sailed past my baffled mother at the kitchen sink, and my father spreading old *Philadelphia Inquirer*s on the floor to brush Stop-Rust on the egg-candling box. We skipped—my God, we skipped happily to the field, the sun once more overhead, and I hadn't realized how happy I was until today—and we watched the remaining acre of yellow black-eyed Susans nod in the early summer breeze, rustling amens in memoriam to their own short-lived season.

8

THAT EVENING AT SEVEN O'CLOCK, Perel and I tramped through the field down a well-trod path to the Assumption Parish School and the nuns' houses. As dusk fell, we positioned ourselves behind a tall sassafras to watch the Annual July Fourth Long-a-coming Assumption School Carnival. Our experience at the parade earlier that day tempered our enthusiasm for Long-a-coming's celebrations, but even the awesome Russell twins couldn't cow us into forgoing one of the town's major events.

In the center of the school playground stood a Ferris wheel ringed with red, yellow, and blue light bulbs. Balloons popped; plastic guns took aim at indestructible plastic ducks; parents handed children stuffed animals; pink bushes of cotton candy eclipsed the faces of toddlers. Freckle-faced boys chased whirling merry-go-rounds and yelped as they hurtled down a greased sliding board. I would have liked to cavort about the playground too, but I was deathly scared of a second rendezvous with Willy Russell, whose contempt for Roman Catholics would not stop him from having fun.

Perel nudged me. "Is it my imagination or is that Queero?" she asked. "There, in front of that red and silver booth, with a sandwich in his hand. See?"

The brown curly hair, the sloping nose, the wide mouth and thick lips belonged unmistakably to Sheiye. He hadn't told anyone where he was going, and no question about it, my parents had no reason to assume their son was milling through the crowd at the Assumption Parish. I marveled at Sheiye's boldness, given added weight by the unkosher sandwich he had bitten into.

Perel and I settled deeper into the woods to get a view less obstructed by sassafras leaves. Sheiye, we observed, walked from booth to booth, savoring his food, not talking to anyone. After a few minutes of aimless wandering, he stepped up to a proscenium screen painted white to simulate tufts of clouds and green along the bottom to suggest a field. Inside the proscenium alcove stood a set of card tables holding soft drinks and a cotton candy machine. Manning this concession was a thin, light-skinned black man dressed in a blue and white checkered shirt and denim overalls. On his head perched a red-white-and-blue-striped top hat with white stars circling its brim. He appeared to be the only black person at the carnival. Whenever someone requested a soda or a cone of cotton candy, he clasped his hands together and bowed deeply from the waist.

I recognized him. It wasn't hard to remember from where, since I saw so few faces that summer. When his customers walked away with their purchases, he dropped his servile manner, and the sneer on his face disappeared. He reached into his shirt pocket, unwound a piece of foil, popped something into his mouth, and started chewing vigorously. I had suspected that he was the same man from the broken-down farm labor transport bus disabled near our driveway earlier that summer, and when I heard the dim backfire of his bubble gum, I was certain.

Perel said she recalled the bus driver but didn't recognize this Uncle Tomming Uncle Sam. "You don't remember that his name is Something Draft or Draft Something?" I asked her.

"Brantzche," she replied, "how do you expect me to remember the name of every pathetic creep that graces my path?"

We watched Sheiye saunter from booth to booth, stopping to handle belt buckles, paperbacks, hammers, and painted plaster figurines of deer and the Virgin Mary. Every few seconds he disappeared from sight as he investigated the various displays. My eye muscles strained to keep him in view. Among the carnival-goers, Sheiye no longer had the diplomatic immunity from the world's prosecution that the farm offered, and I persuaded myself that as long as I could see him, he would remain safe. Sheiye, however, didn't act threatened, but walked among the parents and their children like a nondiscriminating Messiah come to bless the righteous and the wicked.

Once again I was stung by a paradox. The sight of an egg customer sent Sheiye hiding, too shy to carry on a simple conversation about the weather or his future plans. Yet there he was on alien ground, at ease in a foreign culture on the farm's periphery. What gave him the courage to cross the farm's borders? Partly, I realized, it was Sheiye's money; my parents paid him wages for his work in the slaughterhouse. How long had he planned on attending the carnival? It wasn't an event he could boast about to anyone in the family.

Sheiye reappeared from behind a booth wearing a hat, a Confederate Union Jack cap, blue-gray with two crisscrossing bands stitched on its front. At the time I didn't know what the hat represented, but I comprehended its message: Only the most belligerent white boys at school wore them to the football pep rallies, and the very presence of one of the hats could incite a rumble between black and white. I let out a low whistle, and Perel pressed her glasses tightly against the bridge of her nose. "Are you sure that's Sheiye?" she asked. That was my sister, all right. Any unpleasant bit of information and she was prepared to junk her vision.

Not far from Draft's booth stood a cluster of fun-house mirrors. Sheiye positioned himself in front of one that stretched his muscular frame into that of a fragile stickman. Evidently disturbed by the wan image, he hurried away to a mirror that padded his shoulders with humps as thick as a camel's. He adjusted the hat over an eye and, arms akimbo, admired himself.

A tall, angular man with a hoop of keys attached to his belt loop approached Sheiye and slapped him good-naturedly on the back. Sheiye looked up at this lean giant, not sure whether he should return the grin or recoil. Another smile and chummy slap on the back decided Sheiye in favor of friendship. He moved aside a few inches and made room for the man with the keys. The latter flexed his biceps and fired an invisible machine gun at the mirror's two inflated images. Sheiye did the same. Keys jingling at his waist, the man leaned into Sheiye's ear and whispered something. My brother shook his head up and down and together they headed towards another booth, surrounded by bright photographer's bulbs.

The lights lit up the face of the stranger first, and I started as I recognized him as the protagonist in a recent Long-a-coming scandal. Jack Millington was a local celebrity, you might say, twenty-six years old and first cousin to Willy Russell. He was the subject of an *Independent Record* story headlined "Coroner Accused of Rape," a lengthy article detailing his involvement with a half-Jewish Klan infiltrator and her subsequent accusation that Millington and his best friend raped her at the Lodgeway Motel. It was a messy story, with no conclusive evidence of Jack Millington's guilt and Annette Berliner's innocence, and if anything, it made Millington look like the hapless victim of a confused girl.

Perel said she had never heard of Millington. My sister pressed her glasses against her nose again and read the sign above the booth: "Kwik Pix, thirty cents."

Millington motioned to Sheiye and the photographer, a pimply teenager dressed in white overalls, to wait a second. He ran off towards the parking lot behind the Assumption Parish while the photographer considered Sheiye from a variety of angles. I waited for Perel to jump up and say she had had enough. But she kept her eyes fixed on the photographer's stage lights and the actors before us. The disbelieving look on her face was the same she wore that day in the woods when Sheiye told us that twenty-five-year-old women get pregnant whether they want to or not.

Millington headed back towards Sheiye with exaggerated stealth, the keys tinkling with each step. The silver trigger of the rifle he held glinted like a fallen star in the dusk. The merry-go-round kept circling; its riders kept squealing; but the only sound I heard was the thwacking of metal keys against Millington's hip. I wanted to scream, "Sheiye, run!" Ever since I had laid eyes on the carnival, I sensed danger. People moved about without any purpose but to enjoy themselves. Books shared tables with artificial flowers, balloons, and chocolates. Objects with no direct relationship to one another all shared the same moment under the same corner of sky. The farm and its activities had little in common with that kind of chaos. And now, because he had been won over by these helter-skelter amusements, my brother was going to get his head blown off. Millington handed him the rifle and cupped his palm around the keys gently. Sheiye cocked the hat over his eye cowboy-style and rested the butt on his shoulder.

"Hoo-ee!" shouted Millington, splitting the silence I feared presaged my brother's imminent death. Sheiye smirked as the photographer aimed the camera at him and snapped the picture.

Those *hoo-ee*s have always sounded like a declaration of victory to me, victory that ballyhoos the subjugation of the loser. The rebel yell congratulates the foreclosure of conscience: It's a call to deny contemplation. Of course the charm of the *hoo-ee* depends on the well-timed toss of a Johnny Reb cap high in the air, or the wringing out of a rain-soaked shirt over one's own head. But the appeal exists only for those who elevate immediate expression over deliberation—hardly the hallmark of a Szuster. *Hoo-ee* is the triumph of all that is unsympathetic and godless in a human being. Maybe that's why it caught the attention of a young priest talking to a small group of parishioners not far from Sheiye.

With his hands raised in half surrender, the priest excused himself and approached the happy trio. His black pants and shirt were pieces of the darkening summer night come to subdue the wild glow of the photographer's lights. His arms hung at his sides, garishly white, almost lost in the glare of the bulbs. The priest said a few words and Sheiye lowered his eyes. Nothing but his lips moved when he spoke, not his hands, not his feet; there wasn't even a humid breeze to tussle the cowlick at the back of his head. Sheiye held the rifle out to Millington. Staring the priest down, Millington mumbled something, but his irritation was no match for the priest's conviction on his own turf. Millington headed off to his car, grasping the rifle at its middle. Fingering the keys with his free hand as a parishioner might finger rosary beads for solace, Millington looked as if he were heading home after an unsuccessful day shooting at quail.

Hoping to demilitarize the carnival completely, the priest turned now to Sheiye. A few more words from the priest, an extended hand, and Sheiye doffed the Confederate hat. The priest's eyes roved across the carnival grounds, waiting with studied patience for Sheiye to reveal the guilty merchant. Sheiye pointed the hat at a booth. He sulked, scuffing his sneaker on the tarmac. The priest took the hat and, with Sheiye at his side, sought out the offending salesman. His head bowed, Sheiye had become an unwilling penitent.

A few seconds later, Sheiye reappeared, *sans* hat, *sans* priest. Alone, he seemed revivified. He turned this way and that, undecided about which amusement to pursue next. When his gaze settled upon its desired object, he gave his pants a yank at the waist and walked back towards the photographer. The pimply-faced boy was dimming some of the lights and shouting out, "Kwik Pix, thirty cents!" Sheiye tapped him on the shoulder gently. The two of them laughed and greeted each other as old friends. With great solemnity, as if he were purchasing an expensive stereo or a house, Sheiye slowly peeled off a single dollar bill from a cash wad. The photographer reached into his overalls pocket for the instant photo, laughed again, and handed it to Sheiye. Judging by the photographer's extra thump on Sheiye's back, I gathered that my brother had refused his change.

Studying the picture and walking, Sheiye looked up and found himself once more in front of Draft's booth. My brother opened his mouth in a wide circle and either hiccuped or burped, waiting until Draft finished serving a little girl her cotton candy. Solemnity gave way to meretriciousness and Sheiye flashed a dollar bill before the black man's face. Draft persisted in his subservient manner. Sheiye collected his change while clasping a cone of pink cotton candy to his mouth. I'm not sure, but I think Draft smiled. As other customers stepped forward to make their purchases, Sheiye watched them and

Draft's theatrics. A thunderclap couldn't have moved Sheiye then.

The creaking of a screen door distracted Perel and me. A nun dressed in a black habit had opened the back door of her single-story home to reveal a color TV tuned in to what looked like the evening news. The screen was a *toye-voye* of blue denim and khaki, and I could hear the blurry chant of antiwar slogans. Suddenly, a small mutt scampered down two stone steps and made straight for us, growling and barking in a high-pitched yap. The nun took heed of her little guardian's warning, walked onto the stoop, and scanned the woods in our direction. The mutt skulked towards us a few inches at a time. "Bolero should take lessons from him," Perel whispered.

"Scat!" the nun yelled at Perel and me, two weasels waiting for nightfall and crime. Frightened by the little dog's ferociousness, we tore down the path to our own gray house. As I ran, I glanced over my shoulder several times, to see Sheiye still laughing at Draft's masquerade. Only Jack Millington's surprise attack, in which he ripped off a clump of Sheiye's pink cotton candy, stopped my brother's laughter cold.

9

⚜ THE NEXT RELENTLESS SHABBOS found me impatient as ever with the lack of great drama in my life. I was relieved that my search for adventure had not ended after those unnerving episodes on July Fourth. Caution, as much a component of my nature as desire, had merely domesticated my curiosity and turned it back to the farm, at least temporarily. So, while my parents courted Shabbos in their bed and my brother created and destroyed gnomes on paper, Perel and I unlocked the door to Charlie's room and foraged among his possessions.

Like our cellar and attic, Charlie's room was new territory every time we set foot in it. Though nothing appeared any different since our last visit on his day off, we looked about with the expectation that this time we would see something we had overlooked before. What a place to search for excitement—a cot, a sink, a gas heater, and an aluminum table left little space for anything else in the room. Above the sink basin, beneath the girlie calendar, hung a glass shelf that held a drinking glass, a razor, and a shaving cream brush. The blue and red linoleum floor had been laid down years before my parents bought the farm, and it showed the scuffed, faded traces of neglect. Even though the room had been a later addition to the house, its walls were cracked and its lighting dim.

"He still hasn't washed out his sink," Perel said in her dismayed Pop voice. She ran her index finger around the basin and then held it up to me, the swirls of her fingerprints like a black-and-white woodcut. Mopping and laundering would not have alleviated the gloom much, for it stemmed from Charlie's inability or unwillingness to adopt this room as his home. But even if you displaced every last remnant of Charlie's essence, the room would remain what it was from the start: a testament to gloomy necessity. I thought of Charlie sitting on the annex steps, his work pants spattered with dots the color of dried sienna, his eyes red like the blood-damaged eggs we called bloodspots.

Perel and I busied ourselves with opening and closing the heater's flue, staring at the bustlines of daytime TV stars in the *Enquirer*s, and holding a magnifying glass up to each other's eyes. I decided to flip through a stack of comic books piled up near the annex door; Perel raised the magnifying glass Sherlock Holmes style, got down on her knees, and began inspecting the room. "I'm going to get to the bottom of this!" she wheezed à la Rodney MacDuff. She lay down on her side and peered under the cot.

The comic books did not belong to Charlie: We had come into them about five years earlier, from a butcher who thought they would interest the Szuster children. Most of them were old *Batman*s and *Superman*s, which interested Sheiye much more than Perel and me, so I rarely sifted through the box. My mother hated the comic books, fearing they would eventually damage our ability to concentrate on school-work, and she often threatened to burn them. If she had made good on her word by that Shabbos, I would never have come upon the folded news clipping secreted between the pages of the *Archie* in my hand.

The clipping was dated May 23, 1942, and had been printed on the front of the Senior, Alabama, *Courier*. At first I assumed that the butcher or one of his children had placed it inside the comic book and forgotten about it. But I was already so primed to uncover the hidden facts about Charlie's life that once I saw the date I suspected that the clipping did indeed belong to him.

"Hey, Perel!" I said, feeling perhaps for the first time that something was about to happen on the farm, that the mysteries packed into the walls of the house, the floor of the slaughter-house, the dirt in the field, were going to reveal themselves to me one by one. "Come and look at what I just found!" I began reading aloud from the clipping: "Senior, Alabama, May 23, 1942. In a surprise verdict today, the ten-man, two-woman jury in the Abalone County Courthouse found Charles Dixon not guilty of raping the daughter of a prominent Senior physician. . . ."

Still reclining on her side, Perel eased herself up on her elbow. I half noticed how wide her eyes were and how her lower jaw had dropped to pucker her lips like a doll's. In Mrs. Barbarian's voice, I cooed, "I sink oo-ee ahr on to some-sing beeg. Come here, Chew-girl, and take a look at zees!"

Placing the magnifying glass back on the heater, Perel stood up and announced, "This isn't right. What we're doing isn't right. This is Charlie's room and we shouldn't be here."

"Oh, honey! Come on!" Sparsely said. "You've looked through my diaries loads of times without my permission."

"Two wrongs don't make a right," Perel answered in her own quavering voice. Turning the doorknob, she looked around at me, and said, "You shouldn't be here, either. It's not right."

As a last effort to control Perel's exit, I called to her, "Come here, *hantekh!*"

Perel's full lips clenched into a single line, her nostrils flared like a colt's, and the brown of her eyes barricaded itself behind her lids. Nearly all that remained untouched were her cheeks, two boats anchored in the storm of her face. "You know, Brantzche," Perel said in a brittle tone, "you really are too bossy for your own good." And with a toss of her head, she left the room.

"But, Perel, I was only kidding," I called after her in Pop's supplicating voice. I was alone. Without my sister, whom I had always seen as a carbon copy of myself, I was alone in the world. Rebellion and nonconformity were the order of the day, yet the thought of being a discrete individual terrified me. Perel and I interpreted the events of the farm and the outside world together. We decided what interested us and what didn't. I didn't want to finish a discussion knowing we held two opposing opinions.

Yet if I didn't read the clipping immediately, my parents or Sheiye might find me snooping in Charlie's room. Or the clipping, folded in thirds, would disintegrate, and my excitement, temporary as all my pleasures were on the farm, would follow suit. As I have said, my memory is weak on so many scores, but much of that article stayed with me, as if I had something at stake in remembering it.

After three hours of deliberation, the Senior, Alabama, *Courier* recounted, the jury in the Abalone County Courthouse found Charles Dixon not guilty of raping a white woman. Ira Sagan, Charlie's lawyer, persuaded the all-white jury that Miss Alison McKwethy's relationship with her uncle's black hired hand was freely chosen and continued "without coercion" for nearly a year. The townspeople, it seems, were stunned not only because Miss McKwethy was white but also because her father was a prominent Senior physician. I actually recall one sentence from the article: "Miss McKwethy stared down at her lap, and this reporter thought he saw her bottom lip tremble."

I doubt I had ever read anything with such keen interest, almost expecting that each word, each letter, would divide and subdivide, like cells undergoing mitosis, and soon I would have a cellular mass of information about this man who had lived with us for eight years. I read the article again, and then another time and another time, but the yellowed newsprint refused to communicate anything more. Then a small piece of paper fluttered from my hand to the floor, drifting and spinning like a maple seed, prophetic. Age had dried out the Scotch tape that had attached a smaller clipping to the back of the main article. I picked it up and saw a passport-sized photograph of people in ankle-length white gowns, one behind the other in a haphazard line. When I had studied the picture, I saw that they actually stood in a T-shaped configuration, and while the wind had belled their white tunics, the bodies beneath suggested army recruits at strict attention. Some held placards, whose slogans were difficult to make out from the tiny photo dots. The only one I was sure about said "KKK is here to stay." Even at fifteen, I thought: *Highly original, but memorable nonetheless.* I didn't spend any more time lost in cynicism, and read the article. The figures in the picture were members of the Knights of White Brotherhood, some type of Klan sect. Fifteen of them had gathered in front of the Abalone County Courthouse to protest the verdict in McKwethy versus Dixon. When asked why they were demonstrating, a man inside a long, billowing sheet answered, "This nigger's gonna pay for this—and so will his Jew lawyer!"

I didn't know what to think. Was the Charles Dixon in these articles Charlie? Was he a criminal? Had this Knights of White Brotherhood "fixed" him? How did he end up in south Jersey? Why on earth had he hidden these articles in a place where someone could find them, and why had he saved them at all? Maybe Charlie figured he would never have another day of glory or infamy in his life, and he yielded to the undeniable pleasure of being newsworthy.

Were all these people mentioned in the articles still alive? If they were, they had to be about Charlie's age. Surely time had extinguished the fire of Charlie's supposed liaison with Alison McKwethy and the threats made by that voice inside the long, billowing sheet. But then, only people in south Jersey—"Americans," as Sparsely and Saucer defined them—measure time by clocks and calendars, marking its passage with funerals, birthdays, and wedding anniversaries. The twenty-three years between the end of the war and 1968 certainly hadn't eroded my parents' obsession with the deaths of their families an iota. Candling eggs and eating Sunday chicken roasts managed briefly to interrupt the steady rain of conversation about the war, and often I wondered why those activities succeeded where others, like TV movies and trips to Atlantic City, had failed. Certain people, I decided, would never learn how to live in the present, which meant to me that they would never learn how to live. Period. So was this Charlie's story too? Had he dug a hole for himself on this backditch farm so he could brood his life away?

I had to tell Perel. If I could get her to listen to me, she wouldn't condemn us for snooping in Charlie's room. We were investigating, not invading privacy. And who knows, our knowledge about Charlie might come in handy someday. My head spun as I stood up. I blamed the dizzy spell on hunger and the humid odor of tobacco in Charlie's room, not on the bleak suspicion that Perel wanted no part of Charlie's existence. Carefully, I refolded the clippings and inserted them back into the comic book, fully intending to return the following Shabbos to inspect them once more. I forced the *Archie* into its original spot at the bottom of the box.

I noticed that my underarms had started to smell. The

room was hot and stuffy, and I wasn't aware till then that the temperature outside must be near ninety-five. Standing in the middle of the room, I raised my elbows and blew cool air into my armpits. My luck, Sheiye and Bolero sauntered by outside and stared through the window. Sheiye's impetus to victory was often good fortune; most of his strengths, in fact, were due to chance—his height, his sex, his skill at trivia. As I met Sheiye's eye, it occurred to me for the first time that Charlie's windows had no curtains.

"Looks like you need a shave, little girl," he yelled, and sang the Rapid Shave ditty. Bolero barked once, and he and Sheiye sped towards the field path. Cords of repulsion knotted in my throat for the hundredth time that summer, and I tasted something like copper inside my cheeks. But I didn't dare provoke Sheiye for fear that my parents might hear me and catch me in Charlie's room, or that Sheiye himself would tattle. Where was he headed now? It didn't matter. I was making my own discoveries, and I would let Sheiye in on them in my own sweet time. Maybe. For now, I had the upper hand.

Upstairs, I knocked gently on Perel's bedroom door. She didn't answer. I heard the sheets rustle, and decided to let Pop act as intermediary: "Perel, can I come in?"

"I'm sleeping," a muffled voice complained. Even as a young child, Perel had taken her afternoon naps seriously. Sometimes, especially on Shabbos afternoons when I wanted her to walk with me or play Scrabble, I would get giddy, hoping that low-grade hysteria would seduce her into wakefulness. But my sister held fast to her silence. "Perel?" Pop whimpered, and I opened the door with a light push.

In spite of the heat, Perel's body was submerged from the neck down under the covers, and a floppy feather pillow hid her head. Usually when I found her sleeping like this, I removed the pillow, to find her temples wet with perspiration. I couldn't understand how she didn't suffocate. Still asleep, she would grope for the pillow and nuzzle her face back under it. "It's the light," Perel would say. "I can't stand to see any light when I'm sleeping."

"Perel!" I said to the lumpy pillow. "I have to tell you about Charlie. Wait'll you hear! I'm not sure, but—" Perel cut me off. It was rare that either one of us interrupted the beleaguered Pop. Abruptly, she lifted herself up on her elbow, just as she had done in Charlie's room. She eyed me as if I had been asleep for ten years and had forgotten that Perel Szuster's limits could not be breached. "I thought I told you I didn't want to hear about it," she said, and punctuated her annoyance with the same sentence in Yiddish: *"Kh'vil es nisht heyrn!"* She dove back under the pillow, and I thought I would suffocate.

Sometimes persistence is the confirmation of insensitivity, an unwillingness to accept the complicated motives that compel another person to stop listening, to resist discovery. I persisted in Pop's voice, as if Perel's response were nothing to take seriously. "But, Perel, if you'd only hear what I have to say!"

Perel had two options now. She could either scream at me, the way she did when she was disgusted with Sheiye, or she could train her anger to freeze at the back of her throat, demolishing my glibness with a few curt words. She chose the latter. Wasting as few words and as little energy as possible on my imbecility, Perel said in a level tone, "Brantzche, get out." With finality, she sandwiched her head in between two pillows.

Only a few minutes earlier, I had reveled in the solitariness of my great find. Now I was exiled to my bedroom along with it. My banishment made me remember an incident of nine years before. It was summer, and Perel was almost four.

She stood at my bedroom door brushing her teeth, while I lay propped in bed with *My Weekly Reader*. I insisted that she leave immediately and let me get on with the grown-up business of reading. Grinning, she kept on brushing her teeth. In a huff, I jumped off my bed and shoved her. The toothbrush knocked hard against the rear wall of her throat and blood began to trickle from her mouth down her chin.

Perel was sick for weeks. Mealtimes were the most unbearable, for she swallowed even the most finely strained food with difficulty. Faced with such a pathetic scene, my mother would fly at me and tear my hair, which she herself had braided the same morning. Her rage was capricious, and something as irrelevant as a hurricane report on the evening news would send her sweeping down on me with a flurry of blows. Sometimes my father had to hold her back. A tacit ban was placed on all conversation with me. And Perel was all but quarantined from my presence. Each night that summer I curled up in bed alone, abandoned, terrified by the shadows that loomed and shrank on the walls whenever cars and trucks passed by my window on the White Horse Pike. My mother's resentment eventually petered out into a succession of lesser grudges, though she still retailed a tithe of bitterness for me as a memento of her hatred. Until my fifteenth summer, my sixth had been the worst of my life; maybe that unfair rebuke was a nightmarish precursor of what was to come. Once again I was alone with my punishment, far away from any other human being.

That evening in the dull haven of my bedroom, I wrote down as best I could remember the details of the two articles and hid them in a tear in my mattress ticking. When I got to the comment about "Jew lawyer," my stomach turned. Even though Charles Dixon—never once referred to as "Mister"— had been in the most threatened position of all the characters in that drama, Ira Sagan's fate disturbed me too. Now the possibility that some harm had befallen him promised to keep me awake for hours. That goes to show the tribal straits of my sympathies.

I must have had a premonition that I wouldn't get a second chance to study the articles. The very next afternoon, I happened to look out the kitchen's back window and saw my mother and Perel sitting together on the bench, eating watermelon and talking. Perel caught sight of me and called out to ask if I wanted to take Bolero for a run. She made no reference to our spat the day before, treating it as a tussle over a chicken's wishbone. In a minute we were off, and I was overjoyed, stroking Perel's hair and pretending to lick her face.

A half hour later we returned, to see my mother walking towards the house, her back to us, and a fire blazing in the trash barrel, flaming tendrils poking through the surrounding mesh of chicken wire. Undulations of heat floated an ashy page of *Superman* in our direction. "Did you tell Mama anything?" I snapped at Perel. My sister's voice shook. "I didn't say a thing. I swear I didn't!" Perel's eyes grew wide and liquid as she maintained her innocence, and I knew she was lying. Oh, she probably didn't admit to trespassing in Charlie's room. More likely she had merely encouraged Mama to throw out the comic books because they provided a nesting ground for the field mice, or because Sheiye would read *Superman* instead of biology at Glassboro come fall. Most distressing of all was that Mama, a woman in her late thirties, would hearken to her twelve-year-old daughter's advice.

I could only eye my sister obtusely, stupefied by her dogmatic lack of curiosity. If only I had understood the logic of tracing a fear to its source, I might have questioned Perel about her precipitous flight from Charlie's room. But my badgering was inopportune now, and threatened to isolate Perel from me even more. Nonetheless, I was left alone to puzzle over the fact of yet more suffering in a town named Senior, only two days before my mother's father and two sisters were murdered by the Nazis.

10

DURING THE SIXTIES one of our favorite TV shows was *Lost in Space*. For three years the Robinson family hurtled through the cosmos in their Jupiter II spaceship, forced to abandon an overpopulated earth for the unknown Alpha Centauri. Faithful to TV reality, the Robinsons never argued with each other or with their robot, and all were unanimously united against the sinister Dr. Smith. The family's conflicts struck me as trivial. Fighting off vengeful humanoid carrots must have been manageable compared to learning a new planet's language, or to discerning the manners of a foreign galaxy. Perhaps the three children might enjoy life in exile, but how could the parents? They would always yearn for Earth. How could they placate their memories—the taste of cherries and potatoes, the sight of a child standing at a shaded crossroads, the excitement of an outing to the reed marshes. Dreams of home would trouble their sleep; afternoon reveries at the kitchen table would prompt the children to ask, "What are you thinking about?"

Jake's Poultry Farm, I often imagined, was something like the Jupiter II, and Long-a-coming one of the planets where the spaceship crash-landed. How long could the Szusters survive, untouched by the territory beyond the farm's borders? Didn't they want anything from that alien world—friendship, sports, a varied diet? The Szusters refused nourishment from the outside world, so naturally they began to devour each other.

Perel carried the family standard by harboring grudges. One afternoon, for example, she tore up the stairs in a huff after Mama told an egg customer that Perel looked like Sheiye. To my sister's mind, this meant she killed dogs for sport. Instead of protesting Mama's comparison, though, Perel refused to speak to anyone, including me; and in her rage, she taped a blunt razor blade to her bedroom door to announce her plans to kill herself.

That evening when the entire family had gathered to watch situation comedies on TV, my mother demanded an explanation of the "razor blade business." Perel scraped a sliver of yellow wax from her ear and rubbed it into the flowered slipcover. Staring into the TV screen as she began breaking off the split ends of her hair, she answered lazily that the razor blade was nobody's business but her own. Such snootiness more often styled my mode of communication with Mama and Papa, and when Mama looked over at me to see if I was prompting Perel, I responded with an exaggerated I-don't-know-what's-eating-her shrug.

Papa looked up from his *Jewish Daily Forward.* Querulousness had dulled Perel's blackish-brown eyes and drawn the corners of her full lips into an old woman's frown. Papa asked in a tone half sarcastic, half philosophical if Perel had had enough to eat that day. Perel announced she had no plans for ever eating again. Papa's eyes slanted jerkily, like two bees lifting off from a zinnia in Mama's flower garden. He shook a crease out of the newspaper and returned to his reading, wisely realizing that silence was the best treatment for *der nahr* that *shtipt.*

"Go take it off," Mama said.

Perel primped her curly hair like Betty Boop and pulled out a bobby pin. She laid it down on the arm of the chair.

"There, it's off," she said, without taking her eyes from the TV screen.

"Little girl is bucking for a beating," Sheiye warned, sprawled out on the floor. He gave a hyperbolic yawn and declared the next half hour of TV his.

Perel glowered down at Sheiye. With the TV light casting oval shadows under her eyes, she looked like a ghoulish football player. "It's a miracle!" she snickered. "I never heard a strawberry patch talk before!"

Sheiye ignored the insult that was stock abuse from his sisters, convinced that at any moment Perel would hang herself. Well acquainted with the road to my father's anger, Sheiye looked into Papa's fungal toenails, deformed since his days of frostbite in the Hrubieszów woods, to gauge the distance to outright fury.

Ignoring his crabby children, Papa read aloud from the *Forward* about a nineteen-year-old Polish refugee and her year-old baby, and how her husband loved them both and was willing to convert to Judaism. Papa looked up from the *tsaytung* and met Mama's eye with a face that said, *Here is a man who wants to be a Jew and our children want to be assholes.*

Had Mama sat alone with Perel, she would have murmured how people sometimes get "down in the dumps." She was acquiring English idioms and liked that expression. But with her authority openly challenged, she read the go-ahead in her husband's eye and prepared to teach Perel a lesson about the value of life.

"Perele," Mama began softly, a note of tense affection still in her voice. She used the diminutive form of my sister's name to give Perel time to disavow her nastiness. "Perele," Mama repeated. "I'm eskink you in plain effryday Inklish: Ket tuh razor blade and brink it to me."

"I already cut myself once," Perel said, holding up a perfectly unscathed index finger. "You wouldn't want me to cut myself again, would you?"

Mama arched forward in her chair. Perel snapped another split end, gloating at our mother's gullibility.

"Yeah, little girl," Sheiye said. He craned his neck to face Perel. "Why don't you cut yourself again?"

"Perel," Papa said, folding the *Forward* in half. "It's been a long day. Maybe you're tired. Why don't you go upstairs to sleep. Stop making us all crazy with your nonsense."

"Nonsense!" Perel exclaimed. Her frostiness turned to ice. "Any minute I'm going to commit suicide and all you tell me is *gey pufn!*"

Papa threw aside the *Forward*. His face was one unbroken plain of rage. An involuntary stomp of his foot had officially marked the onset of his wrath, which, like a Jewish holiday, began at nightfall and would continue until the next evening. My father was a man of unshakable faith. The murder of his family and his world hadn't challenged his belief in God. Three times a day he prayed from a worn brown *siddur*, no matter how pressed he was with the chickens. Shabbos mornings he read the Torah portion to himself. He blessed God's name before putting a crumb of bread in his mouth. He burned his fingernail parings because law commanded it. Jewish law and interpretation were instinct with him. But one unwritten tenet formed the foundation of my father's Judaism: Thou shalt not die out. There was no God-given commandment more elemental than that. If you rumbled with God's creation, *s'hot dir gefeylt a klepke*—you had a screw loose. If God willed it, Perel would have to live forever.

Papa shoved the heavy armchair with Perel still in it against the wall. Nothing could help her now, even if she begged for mercy. Papa had become iron-fisted and unappeasable. However he might smite his youngest child would be justified in the quest to teach her respect for survival. Stunned by her incorrigible arrogance, Papa yanked Perel out of the armchair and slapped her across the face. A splotch of red washed over the gray TV color in Perel's cheeks, and I instinctively covered my own face, feeling the sting of Papa's four-fingered hand.

"What did you say?" Papa yelled. "Repeat it!"

"I said I'm gonna commit suicide! And I don't need a razor blade! I can use a gun!" Perel looked more frightened of her own proposal than of Papa's abuse. "I can throw myself in front of a car!" she wailed.

Sheiye pressed the palms of his hands against the floor and forced himself up. "Don't say I didn't warn you, little girl," he said.

Before Sheiye could take a step, Papa dragged Perel by her chubby arm to the middle of the living room and slapped her again. The sound was like splitting timber. Mama sat on the edge of her seat, overtly supporting Papa's mete of punishment, and guarding her daughter too, lest an excess of damage be done. Uncomfortably, she commanded Papa, "Not her face," and my father began beating Perel's ass, the blows landing with such frequency and force that Perel's underwear was left in tatters around her thighs. Now that the violence had begun, there would be no end in sight. Sheiye no longer had the stomach to cheer Papa on and tried to pick his way through the family fracas to the stairs. Papa blocked him.

"Nobody's leaving!" Papa shouted. "This will teach you what happens when you want to commit suicide!"

Papa shook my shrieking sister by the forearm. "Still want to commit suicide?" he demanded.

"Just as soon as you let me go!" she cried, her words distorted by a bolus of mucus and tears in her throat.

Papa lifted Perel up under his arm like a burlap sack of chicken feed and stalked out through the porch to the White Horse Pike. I couldn't see how close to the highway he dragged her, or if any cars happened to pass by. I don't know if a car's oncoming headlights, accusatory as eyes, overcame Papa's inertia, or if Papa finally broke Perel's spirit, but I soon heard my sister wailing, "No! I don't want to commit suicide! I swear I don't!" Coming face to face with the Pike was more than Perel could bear. Now there was no question of pride or tolerance to pain. She stumbled back into the living room several strides ahead of Papa. Her face was smeared with dirt and snot, her shredded underwear exposed her lacerated ass, and her humiliation was public. Cured of her suicidal intentions, Perel ran upstairs to her bedroom, sobbing. Papa forbade that I follow her. I was relieved because I felt myself about to laugh uncontrollably. That fucking *nahr* was my master.

The morning after Perel's "suicide attempt," Sheiye locked himself in the bathroom. The previous night's drama might suggest that Papa's bloat of anger had driven Sheiye to cower among the faucets and enamel for safety. But the truth was, Sheiye usurped the bathroom every few weeks with no forewarning, no discernible reason but vengeance against his leisure-class sisters. At first no noise would issue from the room at the end of the hall. After a few minutes, the toilet would semiflush, flush completely, and recoup its energy with a gurgling-brook sound. Silence would follow, then running water, then the sound of the toilet lid hitting the seat, then more water. Yellow aluminum curtain rings would scratch against the matching rod as Sheiye adjusted the pink plastic curtains. These were the persnickety noises of an epicure sampling a smorgasbord of dazzling entertainments.

Perel, in no mood for further reproof, rapped on the

bathroom door. "Yoo hoo, Queero," she said. "Hurry it up in there."

"I'm surprised the little girl can get off her *tukhes* this morning," Sheiye answered, his voice filtering through the crack between door and woodwork. "Isn't that sweet ass of yours black and blue?"

"Hey, Sheiye," I cut in. "Don't forget to wipe the seat."

"Brantzche, don't you know that normal guys lift the seat up?" Perel spoke into the crack so that Sheiye had to feel her breath. The notion that Sheiye couldn't meet a criterion for normalcy made him jiggle the doorknob violently.

"I suggest you go outside—"

"I suggest you go outside," Perel mimicked.

"—and wipe that sweet ass of yours with *bletlakh*," Sheiye ended, confident that Perel wouldn't report his insult. Perel and I had asked Mama how she wiped herself in the woods during the war. Mama said she had had to pick *bletlakh* —large leaves—to do the job. Apparently, Sheiye had heard the same story.

Perel slapped the door with her open palm, almost as self-punishment for believing she could trust Sheiye to avoid unmentionable subjects. "You're disgusting, Queero," she said.

Every five minutes Sheiye, Perel, and I resumed our positions, he leaning on his side of the bathroom door, Perel and I on ours. The more we insulted Sheiye, the more he baited us. I think our contempt titillated Sheiye's yearning for a woman, frustrated by our parents' fiat that he date those nonexistent Jews. Our repulsion washed over Sheiye like water in his bath and gave him a point of contact with the female sex.

"Brantzche, I can see your flat chest through your pajamas." Sheiye whistled. "You oughta use Perel's baby fat to pad your tits."

"I'll save some for your face," Perel shot back. "It's so twisted out of shape, you need it more than Brantzche."

"Queero, if you don't get outa the bathroom in three minutes, I'm calling Papa," I threatened, his insult having pulled out all the stops from my antagonism.

"Go ahead," he replied. "See whose side he's on." Here Sheiye had an edge on us. On ordinary days Papa could quickly judge Sheiye as a ne'er-do-well with no talent for books or religious observance. But on days of slaughter, he was Sheiye's advocate, heralding him as the only child in the family with any real value. Perel and I he eyed much as laborers have eyed daughters of ease for centuries: with resentment and self-reproach for supporting our indolence.

"He doesn't pick the same victim two days in a row," I said, not sure what Papa might do.

"Bethidth," Perel lisped, dishing up her cruelest barb, "they're *thekht*ing today and they need your manly athith-tanth."

Sheiye rattled the door and unlatched the lock. "I'll give you some manly assistance!" he yelled. Perel and I ran to her bedroom and locked the door. But Sheiye had no intention of relinquishing his claim. He pounded his foot three times to simulate pursuit, playing at the ogreish stereotype Perel and I had assigned him. We had no recourse now but to appeal to a higher authority.

"I'm not going downstairs until Mama and Papa leave," Perel whispered.

I wanted to ask Perel if she was all right. But I felt the *nahr* start to *shtip*, even in one of the cartoon voices. Instead, I said, "Perel, you have to go downstairs sooner or later. Act like you don't care."

"They're sickening." She rubbed her stomach and pretended to vomit. Neither one of us looked the other in the eye,

Perel because humiliation would start her bawling, me because I should have taken the blows with her.

"I'm hungry and I've gotta piss," I complained. "We have to make them kick Queero out."

"I predict one of his marathons," Perel said. She bounded over to the bureau mirror, positioned her face an inch from it, and popped imaginary pimples. "Hi, my name is Queero," she brayed. Perel stuck out her jaw to create an underbite and flexed her bottom lip. "See how misshapen my face is from years of squishing? Wee-wee-weet!"

"M'tur nisht makhn khoyzik!" I said, echoing one of Papa's aphorisms. Don't mimic! Frequently, when Perel and I spoke in our voices, Papa raised his hand as if to belt us. Sometimes he did. He hit us for our own good, he said. If we made *khoyzik,* we would end up becoming one of our bizarre characters.

Perel and I donned shorts and sleeveless blouses. I walked down the stairs first, compulsively counting off B-R-A-N-S-Z-U-S-T-E-R for the eleven steps I took. Perel followed behind, an orgulous gaze directed through the front porch windows facing the White Horse Pike. At the bottom of the staircase we encountered two Szuster trademarks. One was our black telephone placed on the TV with the receiver turned upside down in its cradle, so that it looked like a squat, obese, plastic creature carrying a dead child belly up in its two dwarfish arms. The other was the sound of our parents reinventing the war in the kitchen. Mama said something about 1941. Papa corrected, No, it wasn't '41, it had to be '42, because so-and-so was already dead. Neither Perel nor I addressed them when we entered the kitchen. I sat down at the table and flipped to a photo in the new *Time* magazine of a Vietnamese woman, her face screwed into a permanent wail, her skinny arms raised high above her head to present a dead, immolated baby as evidence to the camera. Perel fixed herself a bowl of Cheerios.

"Where's the good morning?" Papa bellowed. He leaned his head back and pursed his lips, trying to capture the huffy style of Perel's anger. Could this be the same man who had released a torment of blows and invective against his daughter the night before? He behaved as if we had all hugged one another good night and waltzed off to bed, like the family in *Make Room for Daddy*. Chuckling, Papa asked us how we liked the telephone. He was pleased with himself for having startled our expectation that everyday objects should conform to their recognizable outlines.

"Uh-uh! At the table!" Papa commanded, reviving the voice of order. Attempting a final rebellion in the face of sure defeat, Perel had begun to carry her bowl of Cheerios into the living room. For a second, she faced the mutely grieving telephone and deliberated the consequences of defiance. Sullenly Perel sat down at the table, treating the three feet between our parents and herself as if it were three miles. She spooned the Cheerios to her mouth and said nothing.

"Perel," I asked, "how can you eat before you piss?" Addressing Mama and Papa, I said, "I have to piss, and Sheiye won't let us in the bathroom."

"Ask him nicely and he'll let you," Mama replied, licking a mound of sour cream off a tablespoon. Shaking her head, she pined, "If only I had had the luxury of a bathroom when my brother and I hid together. I would have let Aaron stay there all day if he wanted." I found it hard to accept Mama's loving submission. In her war stories, Mama had always implied that Aaron was a tad slow-witted and had survived because of her pity. Though the Szuster children had never met Uncle Aaron, he had come to symbolize all that is torporous and uncomely in a human being. In fact, we sometimes provoked Sheiye by calling him an "Aaron." But Mama saw nothing inconsistent in this newly invented, unqualified love for her brother. She preached, in effect, that she had no murky psychology to undermine her family devotion, only love dispensed with parity to everyone related to her. Her own children, she charged, suffered openly from sibling rivalry. But in Europe, who had ever heard of such a thing?

"I hope your bladder was stronger than Brantzche's," Perel sniped through the Cheerios.

Papa warmed his hands on his coffee cup. "Today of all days you have to tear each other to bits?" he chided, and nodded towards the gas range.

On the asbestos heat pad sat a short, wide-mouthed glass filled with hard white wax. A yellow-blue flame flickered an inch above the rim. It was a *yurtsaht* glass, a memorial candle used to commemorate the anniversary of a death. We had a cabinet full of empty *yurtsaht* glasses, enough to hold dozens of drinks at a banquet. To me, *yurtsaht* represented yet another Jewish holiday whose celebration was whimsical and whose meaning was indecipherable. I would not have been surprised to learn that no one else on earth knew a thing about this candle, and assumed that my father had designed a new holiday to remind us that we were Jews.

"And what's this about?" I asked.

"I want you and Perel to *daven* today," Papa said. Gone was the imperious command. The man who had dragged his suicidal daughter to the Pike the night before now gave a capitulatory shrug. He turned his gaze to the cloudy swirls in his coffee cup, as if looking for the vestiges of his maniacal rage there.

My father's sadness caught me off guard. I resented my middling responses—sympathy and embarrassment. The last thing I wanted was to see Papa, this monster, shrink into a human being.

Suddenly, Mama was more concerned about the bathroom than about Papa's *yurtsaht*. She anticipated our questions about the candle and rose to Papa's defense. He willingly forfeited his claim to manhood for a second and became a boy remembering a nightmare. What an anomaly: Here was my father, stocky, arm muscles poised to lift chicken crates and shift transmission gears, now perceived by my soft-bellied mother as defenseless, vulnerable to the curiosity of children. Papa's severed thumb, puckered like a chicken's ass, rested on the rim of his coffee cup. He looked out the kitchen window to the slaughterhouse. A single word about the *yurtsaht* candle had had enough power to enfeeble him.

"Sheiye is in the bathroom," Mama said. She stood up abruptly. "Let's see what we can do."

"Twenty-eight years ago today, the Nazis gassed my mother and four sisters," Papa said. He set down the coffee cup. I thought how in a movie Papa's hands would have trembled, but in real life they were steady.

"And?" I asked.

Papa looked me in the eye. "There is no and," he said. He rubbed the stumpy thumb against his cheek.

"Okay," Mama said quickly. "I'm not going upstairs alone."

Perel took her empty cereal bowl to the sink and turned the water on full strength, no doubt to drown out all conversation.

"Just let it there, Perele," Mama said. "I'll do it later." Washing dishes, Mama believed, would unduly ruin our once-in-a-lifetime childhood, but a beating—someday we would thank her for it.

"That's it? That's the explanation?" I asked. "I want an explanation."

"The explanation is that I want you and Perel to *daven!*"

Papa shouted, jerking back in his chair. I had long braced for the day when Papa's veins would come flying out of his head like a bouquet of *tfilin*.

"I don't understand," I said. "How do you know it was today? Did you have a calendar?"

We heard the honk of a car horn as an egg customer drove up in a rusted white station wagon. "Yankl, *nem* care," Mama said in her half-English, half-Yiddish dialect. She murmured, *"Got tsi danken!"* Thank God!

"Rukhl," Papa said, getting up. "Tell Sheiye I need him in the coop in an hour. Charlie too." Before Papa walked out the screen door, he turned to Perel and me and resumed his Mount Sinai style of oration: *"Daven!"* What a relief: I preferred his imperforate suit of mail to the chink in his armor.

Mama's eyes were moist with the pleading look she wore Shabbos afternoons when we examined the photographs from Europe. Lest I ask another question, she suggested going upstairs, in speech so clipped it seemed she was reading from a script. Perel left the cereal bowl unwashed and headed for the screen door.

"Whereya going?" I asked in one of our panoply of voices. My sister turned around and peeled off two napkins from the white napkin holder on the kitchen table. They were, I knew, makeshift toilet paper.

" 'e's gonna be oled up there all doi," she said like Paul McCartney. "Aye c'n feel it in me bones." Perel rolled her eyes, and I knew her joviality was forced.

"At least come up with me," I pleaded. "If it's only me, he won't get out."

"I don't feel like fighting with him," Perel said in her natural voice. She picked up the Scholastic Book Club edition of *Wuthering Heights* lying on top of the *Jewish Daily Forward* and nestled it inside her armpit. The *Forward* fell to the floor.

Perel stepped on it as she crossed the door without saying another word. Mama sighed as she stooped to retrieve the Yiddish newspaper.

The please-no-more-questions dew had evaporated from my mother's eyes. Her lips, moist from a breakfast of cucumbers and sour cream, were still pressed together. Mama's facial expressions had always been centered in her mouth. When she ate, for example, you saw that her lips had known hunger. Whereas I was a fastidious eater, separating meat from fat, potatoes from string beans, my mother indiscriminately combined chicken flesh with pickles, oily yellow skin with challah soaked in puddles of gravy, bone marrow with ginger ale. Only splinters lay on Mama's plate after a meal.

Mama and I trudged upstairs as if we were scaling Mount Everest. B-R-A-N S-Z-U-S-T-E-R, I counted off to myself again. A line of sweat trickled down the side of Mama's face. She forced air through her parted lips and said in her rolled *r* English, "Terrible." I didn't know if she meant the heat, which she detested, the battle between her children, or the mission to evict Sheiye from the bathroom. I was too intent on the line of sweat to ask what she meant. Admiring the labor that produced this perspiration, I sometimes dabbed water on my temples and hoped that my mimicry would finally change me into a suffering being like Mama.

"Sheiyele," Mama said, tapping gently at the bathroom door. *"Dus iz di mame."* This is your mother.

"No kidding! How ya doin', Mama? Long time no hear from!" Some water splashed. Sheiye was in the tub.

"Sheiyele, when do you think you'll be out?" The diplomatic approach, but spoken in the cadence of the Mourner's *Kaddish.*

"Gee, I don't know. I have this pain in my back. I'm trying to soak it away."

"You've been in there all morning, Queero," I scoffed. "You oughta get out before you shrivel up."

"I appreciate your concern, Brantzche, sister of the flat chest, but don't worry about me. Why don'tcha go outside and kiss your sister's boo-boo?"

"Sheiye, Papa needs you in half an hour," Mama said. No more diminutive. A good sign. "If you don't help, *s'vet zahn tsuris*"—there's going to be trouble.

"Gee, Mama, I'd really like to help you both out," Sheiye said. His body squealed against the enamel. "But it's this pain, see. It limits my activities."

"If you don't get out, I'm gonna piss in your room," I warned.

"You just try that, little girl, and I'll break your ass."

"Kinder! Kinder!" Mama cried. "What would you do if you had no parents and you had to live together in the woods?"

Mama raised this question now and again, praying that when push came to shove, her children would realize that they really did love each other. But the thought of surviving a war alone with my brother was horrifying. I stared into the bathroom door, long in need of a paint job, and saw no other option. Looking at my mother point-blank, I said, "I'd rather be dead than live in the woods with Queero." As Mama's face registered the unflinching cruelty of my statement, I pondered how miserable I would be if persecuted by the Nazis *and* Sheiye. Certainly I would need a box of tissues to muffle my sobs. My brother interrupted my musings.

"Mama, do you have your period? Are you tripping on LSD? I'd send Brantzche to the Nazis before I'd spend a single night with her."

"Sheiye, if I have to send Papa up, he'll break down the door," Mama said in a voice sharp as paprika. "And I won't stand in his way." Knowing my mother, she was more distressed by Sheiye's reference to her period than to the Nazis. She had never even spoken the word "period" to me.

"You did a great job of raising your only son," I accused Mama. "Eighteen years old! Who can believe it?"

"*Fardreyt zekh ayere eygene kep!*" Mama said. Drive yourselves crazy! She dismissed Sheiye and me with an exasperated wave of the hand, turned, and headed downstairs, still embarrassed about her period.

I told Sheiye he would be sorry if he didn't beat it. "What'll a pipsqueak like you do?" he asked. To emphasize his contumely, Sheiye farted underwater.

Waving white napkin semaphores at Perel, reading *Wuthering Heights* in a lawn chair, I ran off behind the middle coop to do my business. Crouching, I nearly lost balance as I shied my thong away from my water's path. Near my foot, I noticed, lay an earthworm, all but a fraction of its tubular body covered by soil. Steadying myself, I pulled the worm by its rear and stretched it like a rubber band. With a twig I cut it in two, leaving one half writhing in the dirt and the other on the urine-soaked napkin. Sheiye had taught me that an injured earthworm regenerates, so I rationalized my cruelty as resurrectional.

Still feeling like Mama in Poland, I side-skipped back to Perel and reminded her that we had to *daven*. She settled a blade of grass in her book and said, "After what they did to me last night, I'm supposed to pray for their parents?"

My sister and I decided to fake *daven*ing, an uncomfortable decision, but one which we justified in light of the thrashing Perel had had to endure. In the piano room, we sat listening to Bolero bark desperately under the maple tree. Ordinarily, the piano bench was our pew and the door to the kitchen our view to the east, to Jerusalem. To spite Papa, we faced west. But the authority of my father's dictum paralyzed our bitterness. In addition, I saw, I had underestimated Perel's desire for penitence. If I turned the pages too quickly, she pressed down her hand on my index finger. I think she was looking for a way to forgive Mama and Papa, just as we had sought to forgive Sheiye after he ran down Duchess. When you are cornered in a family you didn't choose, you balance anger and forgiveness, or else perish. Though I understood this, I still resented Perel's benevolence. I looked down at the Hebrew letters, contorted on the white page like fallen soldiers, and wondered why my life, barely begun, had already implicated me in the crimes of the world.

11

November 17, 1979, and December 1, 1979
Tel Aviv, Israel
Rukhl Sussman Szuster, as told to Yaffa Simontov
Collected and edited for the World War II Jewish
Survivors' Archive at Yad Vashem

After the Gestapo murdered our father and two sisters, Aaron and I returned to the Seleskes. Our parents used to rent cherry orchards from the Christian owners there, so maybe people would remember us kindly. If no one helped us in the Seleskes, we were as good as dead. Certainly no stranger would risk his life for just any Jew.

In Vierov near the Seleskes, a Christian woman named Handka and her husband Andrej took me in. I was thirteen years old, not very big, but I made myself useful in their house and vegetable gardens. Meanwhile, Aaron found shelter and work with a man named Leszek. My brother was already eighteen and strong enough to harvest, plow, and tend livestock.

So I stayed with Handka and Aaron stayed with Leszek until September 1942. Then the Nazis started to gather the Jews of the Ludmar ghetto, a few miles from the Seleskes. The Nazis dug long graves, marched the Jews to a forest named Pytilin, lined them up, and shot them to death. At the same time, the Nazis ordered all Jewish children to turn themselves over to Gestapo headquarters. Any Christian sheltering Jewish children should now turn them in too. You see, there was no food in the ghetto, so quite a few Ludmar Jews had arranged for Polish peasants to take care of their children. Well, the Nazis had the Poles round these children up. They killed them.

One day as I was weeding Handka's garden, I heard the tall grass rustle. Handka walked towards me with a loaf of bread in her arms. She stood before me and said, "Rukhl, Pani Leszek told me you've got to turn yourself in." She said the Jewish children had to congregate at the home of a rich *goy* named, uh, his name was, yes, Kustetski. From there the children would be carted away to Pytivna, to their deaths.

Handka looked at me. Or I should say she looked at my coat, my linen skirt, and shoes. She had loaned them to me when I first came to her house. Handka sized me up and said, "Rukhl, tomorrow you'll be dead. But until then you need something to eat. Here, take this loaf of bread. But the jacket, take it off. You don't need it anymore. I'd like the skirt too, but I can't very well send you away naked. The jacket, please."

Brokenhearted, I took off Handka's jacket and handed it to her. I thought: *The jacket goes to Life and I go to Death.* I felt the deepest connection with that jacket, and it was difficult to part with it. But I did. Handka offered me the loaf of bread.

As I was staring at the bread in my hands, Handka said, "Leszek said to take the paths through the forest and field to Pani Kustetski's house. Leszek will wait for you in the clearing." Handka's words wakened the sleeping hope inside me. I did as she said. At dusk I headed towards Kustetski's house along the forest and field paths. Sure enough, Leszek was waiting for me.

You see, Leszek was the *soltys,* the mayor of three villages, and the villagers obeyed him. I was afraid, but I thought if anyone can help me, he can.

Leszek told me to follow him. I did. He led me to a barn near his brother-in-law's house. Hide behind the furthermost bale of hay, he said, and no matter what, no matter who enters the barn, I shouldn't say a word. So I asked Leszek, "What about my brother? What about Aaron?" Leszek said he was sparing Aaron too.

One more instruction: "When I come in here and make a noise like 'Hoo! Hoo!' " Leszek said, "then come out."

I did as Leszek told me. I hid behind the furthermost bale of hay and didn't make a sound. In all his brilliance, Leszek announced to his family that if they happened to see someone in the barn, they shouldn't throw him out. Well, when the relatives heard that someone was hiding in the barn, of course they became curious and began inspecting. They yelled and whistled and turned bales of hay upside down. But it never occurred to them to check the bale in the rear. I didn't breathe. Night came and Leszek's relatives gave up their search.

A few hours later, Leszek opened the door. "Hoo! Hoo!" he cried, and I crept out from under the bale of hay. He said we were going to his house now. But I couldn't walk side by side with him on the main road. I was to take a roundabout route through the fields to his house. When I got there, I was to look for the garden where the lilies grew. There among the lilies I would find my brother.

As I approached the road near Leszek's house, I heard the cries and pleas of Jewish children. They were packed into wagons, some adults too, and each one knew they were riding to their deaths. I crawled through the autumn lilies, saw my brother and felt overjoyed. I heard the wheels of the wagon clatter as they drove over the dirt road.

Leszek stooped down under the lilies. "Listen, children," he began. "You don't have to worry anymore. I'll take care of you. But I want you to promise one thing: Promise you'll be my children. You, Aaron, will marry my daughter Galina.

You, Rukhl, will marry my son—" I don't remember the son's name just now. It'll come to me.

Aaron and I agreed. So we slept in Leszek's barn at night and hid in the forest during the day. Every morning Leszek brought breakfast out to us in the barn, and twice each day sent food to us in the forest with his son or daughter.

This arrangement proved to be too troublesome for Leszek. Maybe he had figured that the Nazis would disappear in a few weeks, the war would be over, and Aaron and I would become his children-in-law. But looks like there were still plenty of Jews to kill and the Nazis had no intention of leaving. After a month, Leszek said to us, "There's no end in sight to all this killing. You've got to leave."

Then he changed his mind again. "Children, don't go to the forest today," Leszek told us. "Stay in the barn. Don't let anyone see you. I'll bring your food as usual."

Aaron and I understood something was afoot. We didn't know what, but something. Well, this is the explanation:

Not far from us in the Seleskes, two Jewish families lay in hiding. One man was called Pinkhus Diamond. With him was a wife and two children. The second was called Kaddish Karsch. He also had a wife . . . no, I'm making a mistake. His wife, pregnant, had already been killed. Kaddish was in hiding with his parents. Anyway. Leszek knew that these and other Jews would be killed the very day he warned Aaron and me to stay in the barn.

In the morning Aaron and I awoke to hear shouts and tires screeching. We peered through a crack in the barn walls and saw something like a feast at Leszek's house. Ukrainian police arrive in jeeps, and they're running here and there, as if they're engaged in the most important sort of business. By afternoon, not a leaf trembled in the cold air. Leszek entered the barn and let us know what happened.

"The Jews are dead," Leszek said.

We understood very well what happened. Leszek knew in advance that the Germans and their Ukrainian helpers planned to kill the Jews. He knew and didn't warn the Jews to escape.

Leszek was one of the biggest *banditn*. He turned in hundreds of Jewish children to the Gestapo, knowing full well what their fate would be. But Aaron and I, we were destined to live. Yet how could one of the biggest *banditn* have saved us?

The next day Aaron and I learned that a few of those unfortunate Jews had, in fact, escaped. Pinkhus Diamond and Kaddish Karsch survived. Two sisters, Dvoyre and Tsila, plus a married woman named Peshke too. It just so happened that these five had left their hiding places earlier to beg for bread from some sympathetic *goyim*. When the Germans and Ukrainians attacked, the five of them weren't there. Peshke heard the screams of her husband and two children and began to run towards them. But Dvoyre and Tsila held Peshke back, covering her mouth with their hands. Peshke lives in Canada today.

After the massacre, Leszek approached Aaron and me again. Like a father, he called us children. He said, "Listen, children, I can't keep you anymore. Don't show your faces again in any village under my jurisdiction. Because if I run into either one of you, I'll have to turn you over to the Gestapo."

Leszek wasn't joking. Once Aaron and I left the barn, he set about on a campaign to find us. And if he couldn't actually kill us, he meant to make our lives as miserable as possible. One of the biggest *banditn!* Leszek knocked on the doors of all the *goyishe* houses in his precinct and warned the residents: "Whoever hides a Jew or knows of a Jew's existence will be killed and his property burned to the ground." We had to hide now from the very man who had saved our lives.

Oh! The son's name was Boris.

What could we do now? We had no shoes, no clothing, and the weather got colder and colder.

Aaron and I decided to go to Kritnetse. Right before the Nazis came to our town, Aaron and my sister Royse were staying with a family named Cybulski. At the Cybulskis, Royse had left a good pair of boots and Aaron a pair of shoes. We decided to visit Cybulski under cover of darkness and ask him to return both pairs of shoes.

One night that week, we headed for Cybulski's house and took a path leading to a village called Puzof. We knew the path well. Or so we thought. The longer we walked, the deeper and deeper we stumbled into a forest. There was neither village nor house in sight. Somehow we had lost our bearings. For hours Aaron and I blundered around those woods. Finally, we retraced our footsteps and returned before dawn broke. Through a hole in the wall, Aaron and I studied the path we took and couldn't understand where we went wrong.

Two nights later I announced that I was going to try my luck alone. Aaron begged me not to go. For sure the *goyim* would catch me and kill me. But I was convinced that Aaron needed shoes more than I did. I felt positive his feet were colder than mine. I had no mirror to see my own pitiful face, and could only see Aaron's suffering. So I started down the path, and this time it was the right one.

I knocked on Cybulski's door. I said it's Rukhl Sussman and pleaded with them to return Royse's boots and Aaron's shoes. Without any argument, they handed me my sister's boots. As for Aaron's shoes, Cybulski stammered that a Russian soldier, an escaped prisoner, had begged him for shoes. That excuse was supposed to keep Aaron's feet warm.

I tucked Royse's boots under my arm. I couldn't return without shoes for my brother. What should I do?

Not far from Cybulski's property was the Jewish cemetery. My father's parents were buried there, and so was my older sister, Leah Fayge, who died at eighteen. Back home people used to say that the dead rise up from their graves at midnight. I figured I'll go to the cemetery, lie down on a grave, wait for the dead to arise, and ask them what to do. I kept my eyes open and waited.

But where on this earth have the dead arisen? No ghost sought me out. All was quiet. The *goyim* slept snugly in their beds, well fed, warm. Not me. I sat wide awake, hungry, cold. Well, I saw my goal was futile so I set off down the path back to my brother.

Wouldn't you know I got lost? I knocked on the door of a house. Dogs barked at me. But I was lucky. In the middle of the night somebody woke up and showed me the way back to the path. He even asked me whose daughter I was and gave me a piece of bread. It was my good luck to stay alive.

By the time I reached the Seleskes, it really was daylight and I was afraid to pass through Leszek's territory. Until nightfall I hid inside a small grove of trees, worried that someone might see me huddled behind the bare branches.

When I found my brother that evening, he was crying. Aaron said that as soon as I left, he heard a gunshot, and thought the Gestapo killed me. If I was dead, Aaron said, he didn't want to live without me. He was prepared to turn himself over to the Germans. You can imagine how thrilled he was to see me. Plus I had brought him a piece of bread. But no shoes.

We were desperate. The first snow of the winter already

lay on the ground. Finally, we decided whatever will be will be: We'll see Leszek and beg him for clothing.

Leszek's wife looked at Aaron and took pity. He was barefoot. She gave him a coat, the sleeves of a jacket, and a pair of old galoshes. I bound Aaron's feet with the sleeves and he stuck them into the galoshes. Leszek's wife threw a piece of bread into the bargain.

Aaron stuck his hands into the coat pockets. He felt something. Inside were half a dozen yellow ID patches and a tailor's tape measure. Leszek had stolen the coat from a murdered Jew.

I returned to the Seleskes once after the war. Alone. The Russian Army had drafted Aaron. Aaron and I decided that after the war, I would wait for him or a letter from him in the Seleskes. So who do I see when I get back? I see Leszek's wife. And she's crying to me how the Ukrainians murdered her son Cheroza; and she's saying how she prays for the day when Aaron returns safe and sound so he can marry her Galina. You can wait till hell freezes over, I thought to myself. I said nothing.

Years later, I learned that Leszek died in jail, probably tortured to death by the Russians. When an old friend passed through the Seleskes to see if he could retrieve his belongings (which he couldn't), he ran into Leszek's wife. She begged him to help her husband get out of jail. And she explained how her husband had saved the lives of so many Jews, particularly his friends Rukhl and Aaron Sussman.

I thank God that Leszek got his due for being such a rotten person.

12

November 17, 1979, and December 1, 1979
Tel Aviv, Israel
Yankl Khaim Szuster, as told to Yaffa Simontov
Collected and edited for the World War II Jewish
Survivors' Archive at Yad Vashem

In Uchan lived a man named Yoshke, who imitated people. He twitched his mouth to imitate people's smiles and narrowed his nostrils to imitate their anger. He neighed like a horse to mimic laughter and mooed like an unmilked cow to make a cartoon of their misery. *Khoyzik gemakht,* that's what he did. He made fun of people. It got to the point where Yoshke could no longer hold a conversation in his natural voice. His face looked like a horse's hoof, it froze into such a horrible twist. I think Yoshke didn't know who he was anymore. When he laughed, people were embarrassed for him. "It's only the *meshigener khoyzik makher.*" It's just the idiot clown. Thanks to Yoshke, I was careful never to imitate another person's habits and never to covet another person's charms. I would rather know that I am wholly myself, even if I am nothing more than the sum total of all my weaknesses. Better that than to look like the wisest man's nightmare.

I think I was ten when my sister Sorale died. She was lying in bed, recovering from a cold. My sister Brantzche— I can't remember if she was older or younger than me— Brantzche brought Sorale a bowl of hot soup. My mother had just ladled it from the boiling iron pot into the bowl, so the soup was scalding hot. When Brantzche handed Sorale the bowl, the soup sloshed over the rim. You know that when something is hot, you can't hold on to it. So Sorale threw her hands up in the air, or maybe she stuck her finger in her mouth. Well, boiling soup splashed everywhere. It soaked through Sorale's nightclothes and burnt her skin. She suffered for a few days from fever and then died. I don't remember the funeral; I don't remember sitting *shive*. I don't know if there was trouble between Brantzche and my mother. Who knows? Maybe when the Nazis came for my mother and sisters and took them to Sobibor, my mother thought God was punishing her for Sorale's death. All I remember is that life went on.

When the Poles told me the Nazis had finally killed my father, all I could think of was my stomach. I hadn't eaten for maybe ten days. So you ask me how did I feel when I learned my father was dead. I felt hungry. The Poles offered me some vodka. I can't drink your vodka, I said. Vodka is for happy occasions, not for funerals. I'll take some soup if you have it.

No, I didn't lose my thumb in the *arbeitslager*. It happened earlier, when I was ten, eleven years old. I was helping my uncle and his sons thresh grain. My job was to push the wheat into the opening of a threshing machine. The machine looked something like a meat grinder, with a pipe to receive the wheat and blades to twirl out the grain. One time I shoved the wheat into the pipe and pushed against the rotating blades with my thumb. When I yanked my right thumb out, blood was gushing everywhere, onto the threshing machine, onto the grain, the wheat, onto my pants. I don't remember feeling pain. One of my cousins vomited. We didn't have doctors, and we certainly didn't have anesthesia. It wasn't like today. So my uncle and my father too, I think, led me into the barn and chopped off half my thumb with an ax. They had to do it or else I would have died from gangrene. I was delirious and in fever for days. Before the war, that was the worst thing that happened to me.

The scar over my left eye also comes from a childhood accident. My cousins and I were washing a horse. I was in charge of the horse's *tukhes,* lucky me. I thought I was doing the horse a favor grooming him, and I expected the horse to understand this. A horse's body is sensitive and I must have touched him in the wrong spot. So what does he do? He kicks me. I'm lucky he didn't back up and squash me to death. I learned never to stand behind a horse. Unfortunately, sometimes in life you learn a lesson and never get another chance to apply it.

But the bullet wound in the upper corner of my right back, that is thanks to the Nazis. I was in the woods hiding when I felt something sharp sting my front shoulder. Before I had a chance to clasp my hand to my chest, I felt something fly right through my back. It was the bullet from the Nazi's gun, ripping through my body. You know what the Jews say: We don't believe in miracles; we depend on them.

My youngest sister was afraid of people. I think a man with a long beard and a black coat had poured water on Mindele once, on purpose or by mistake, I don't know, and that's what scared her. Friend or stranger, it didn't matter. When someone knocked at our door, Mindele bit her fingernails and pressed her face into the wall. A frown scared her; so did a kind word. My father said Mindele would outgrow her fear. He sang *nigunim* to God and asked the rabbis to pray for her. But months passed and my sister was still afraid.

One Shabbos when my father was in *shil,* my mother took Mindele to see a psychic. I went with them. If my father had known, he would have tanned our hides. Not only was it Shabbos but the psychic was a *goy;* not only was he a *goy* but we sought his advice; not only did we seek his advice but we paid for it with groschen on Shabbos. The three of us climbed a flight of stairs and entered a dark apartment with red drapes.

I don't remember much about the psychic. He had thinning black hair and pimple scars on his cheeks. He wore a black top hat inside the apartment. That was strange for a *goy,* I thought. *Goyim* go bareheaded inside buildings. I wondered if he was really a Jew. But working on Shabbos in a Christian town? I was confused.

The psychic asked Mindele a few questions. She hid behind my mother's back and clapped her hands over her eyes. He asked my mother how long Mindele had been like this and what had kicked off her fear. My mother said she didn't know. The psychic said some abracadabra, advised my mother to drop two egg whites into a glass and stare at them. Mindele was supposed to sit with her back to the eggs. My mother paid him and we left.

At home my mother did as the psychic instructed. She stared into the egg whites and saw the faces of three beardless men. Mindele looked at the faces and started crying. By the end of the week, though, her phobia was gone.

In the summertime, my parents rented an orchard from a wealthy owner. Mostly we picked plums. Later we dried them in an oven made by placing heated logs in trenches. The trick was to keep the logs red hot without starting a fire. Other people ruined a day's haul of apples or plums. Not my mother.

She was an expert at drying plums, and no one ever heard of a fire in our section of the orchard.

Our only means of transporting the dried plums was our backs. One afternoon my father walked along a road on the way home with a sack of dried plums saddled on his back. He looked up from his path and, lo and behold, he saw a pony grazing in the middle of the field. The law in Poland stated that if you found a stray horse or cow, you could claim it as your own. My father all but danced for joy. He would sell the pony and make enough money to live on for, who knows, maybe a year.

My father shifted the sack of plums from one shoulder to the other and walked towards the pony. It was brown, healthy, with firm legs, and its neighing flew away with the wind. With his free hand, *der tate* touched the pony's thigh, and his hand went through it. The pony whinnied and trotted into an open field. My father chased after him, shaking dried plums through an opening in the sack. He caught up with him in time to see the pony vanish before his eyes.

Well, my father knew a hallucination when he saw one. He looked around to see where he was. The sky was blue but the air was misty, like it was full of tears. His neck was covered with sweat and the sack of plums slid down his side. My father began saying *T'hilim,* Psalms. He didn't know if he was in the presence of the Divine or the Satanic. *Der tate* gathered up the sack and ran from the field, dropping more plums. At home he explained his small cache by saying he had gotten hungry along the way. For days we laughed behind his back whenever he used the outhouse.

I think my father avoided that field all his days. A year passed before he told anyone, including my mother, about the vanishing pony.

13

MY MOTHER LEANED OVER the oak bureau in her bedroom and stared into the mirror. She fixed her mouth into a stiff smile and smeared deep-red lipstick onto it. Umming her lips together, Mama replaced the lipstick cover and dropped the tube into her black vinyl pocketbook. She blotted her mouth on a white handkerchief and offered it, according to her ritual, to Perel. My sister was mesmerized by the reddish silhouette staining the cloth, and she studied it the way a doctor studies an X-ray. "Red lipstick is old-fashioned," Perel observed. "Nowadays women wear light pink and white." Mama dabbed the corner of her mouth with an index finger and said, "Maybe someday I'll change." She had no intention of frosting her lips, but spoke with gentle indifference so that her daughter would not lose hope.

Eyes still on the mirror, Mama stood up straight and rubbed her round shoulders. The bra pinched, and her flesh poured over the elastic straps like challah dough over the brim of a baking pan. "Brantzchele," she said. "Can you loosen the clasp in the back?" I always waited for that question. Sometimes Perel and I fought over this privilege. Touching Mama's body, I pretended my own was ample and pliant, instead of bony. I undid the bra and latched the hook into another metal clasp, wishing that every day was as exciting as that Thursday afternoon in August. Each week Mama and Papa drove the truck fifteen miles to Buena Vista to buy eggs wholesale, a sideline to the main slaughterhouse business. And that's when I felt happy.

The idea of leaving the farm made Mama festive too. She backed away from the mirror, stumbling on the throw rug like a little girl on a snagged jump rope. Sprawled across the double bed lay a purple-flowered cotton dress, the one she rotated with a blue-flowered shirtwaist for her trips to Buena Vista. Mama leaned over the bed and stroked the dress with her fingertips, as if waking a sleeping child. She smoothed the creases, flattened the collar, and picked motes of lint from the hem. Once she had slipped into the dress, Mama continued pressing out wrinkles, baffled and charmed by the feminine self that emerged with a change of clothes. She opened the door to the oak closet, reached into the bottom shelf, and pulled out a pair of bone-colored low-heeled shoes. Stepping into them, she swayed left and right, admiring the effect in the mirror. But vanity was for Americans with a future, not for a thirty-nine-year-old woman with eight years of schooling. Mama raised her eyebrows and blinked, minimizing the pride in her new appearance. In spite of herself, though, her mood had lightened, and changing from farm pants to a traveling dress was like lighting candles Friday night: The ordinary work week put on royal garb and became Shabbos.

As Mama sprayed a can of Clairol at her short black hair and breathed in the mist, Papa's voice boomed from the kitchen: "Rukhl! Socks! I need a pair of socks!" We heard Papa's feet pad towards the bedroom. *"M'tur nisht arahn-kimen!"* I cried. "Entry forbidden!" Mama squatted on the floor, hiking her skirt up at the knee, and opened the bottom bureau drawer. As she withdrew a pair of black socks rolled into a ball, she bobbed her head and echoed merrily, *"M'tur nisht arahn-kimen! Du-o zenen nor fro-en!"* Perel stood up and blocked the entrance to the bedroom, a sign that she had forgiven Papa for beating her. Papa shouted, "You should always treat *di mame* like this. She's a queen and you're her court!" *This is how a family should act,* I thought: the members sparring with each other kindly, concerned for each other's happiness, nosing each other into the outside world.

I rarely saw Mama and Papa this defenseless. Those Thursday afternoons when they left the farm behind gave me reason to celebrate and cringe, just as I did on our occasional trips to Atsion Lake. There, among south Jersey's factory workers and farm laborers, my parents seemed to enjoy themselves in spite of some vague, unspoken vow not to. Mama believed that bounding into the water was unhealthy, whereupon Sheiye disobeyed her advice by leaping immediately into the lake. Papa gave one of his snoring laughs. Disturbed by my parents' atypical calm, I looked away at the black and Puerto Rican kids playing tag in the water. I wasn't used to relaxing with Papa and Mama. Besides, having a good time with them was inconsistent. I would let down my guard, for what? So that when we got back to the farm Papa could yell at me for tramping through the coops without permission?

"Let's go in," Papa said in English, convinced that his children couldn't understand Yiddish in a non-Jewish setting. He stood up and peeled off his work pants, to reveal loose-fitting bathing trunks—a dead giveaway of his outmoded European fashion habits. In the water, Papa floated on his back, the only "stroke" he knew. The cavorting of nearby swimmers chopped the water and waves splashed up to his nose. Determined not to touch bottom, Papa shut his eyes, sealed his lips, and flailed his arms. I thought for sure he would drown. "I'm getting out," I announced. I couldn't bear to see him so earnestly taking advantage of his rare leisure, soaking the masterful ogre out of his body and conjuring up the boy who cared less for competence than for fun—a likable chap.

At the blanket, Mama handed me some quarters to buy ice cream. Papa protested that the food was technically un-kosher, but Mama couldn't resist. She requested a "sendovich," and I imagined Perel and me returning from the concession stand with a tiny Russian dressed in a cossack uniform. I shuffled back to our blanket with three ice cream sandwiches, drawing the pink bath towel around my shoulders to make me feel like Miss America. As Mama pulled off the waxy wrapper, she licked the melting ice cream from the sides, smacking her lips and jauntily rocking her head from left to right. Her lips lay under a veil of ice cream the way her skin lay under the sun, happy and grateful. "You should never bite directly into ice cream," Mama cautioned, breaking off pieces of chocolate wafer and sneaking them past her savoring lips. "You can get sick." This wasn't a lecture so much as homage to her own mother's wisdom.

And then the far-off, preoccupied expression came over Mama's face, and on the blanket sat a woman I didn't know. Hunched over, licking ice cream, Mama shielded her large breasts, protecting an inner homunculus that kept its own counsel. She gazed into the disappearing ice cream, her head nodding thoughtfully in agreement with some silent discourse. I asked as I always did, "What are you thinking about?" Back came the "nothing" that kept me from communing with that embryo of memory which still recalled a Ukrainian nationalist melody or the time little Rukhele climbed an apple tree and inadvertently peed on her mother's head. I tried to fathom how this woman, now buoyant with memory, could possibly be the same woman who sped dreamlessly through life on Jake's Poultry Farm.

"Rukhl, *gib zekh a shokl!*" Papa now commanded from the living room. That meant get a move on, but literally translated as "give yourself a shake." Perel jumped up and down in front of the doorless bedroom archway and flopped her arms and neck about. "I'm gibbing myself a shukl," she said. Papa peered through the archway and yanked up his zipper. *"Nu,"* he said, raising his eyebrows at Perel. *"M'tur nisht makhn khoyzik."* Perel said, "Okay," and proceeded to repeat her pantomime. Papa jolted back his head like a chicken startled by thunder, but there was no need for us to worry. Thursday afternoons were like Simchas Torah, the holiday when you are encouraged to parody rabbinical intellect: Papa's admonition not to mimic mocked his own strictures.

Excited by the imminence of her departure, Mama didn't know what to do first. She blinked her eyes a few times at Perel and made a cartoonish grin, implying that Papa was just joking, but you never knew, so don't push him too far. Mama tightened the purple-flowered belt around her waist, primped her stiff black hair, folded a white handkerchief alongside the Israeli airmail letters in the black vinyl pocketbook, admired her rear in the mirror, and gave one last look at her lips. "I'm comink!" she sang, displaying her membership in her children's English-speaking world. She hung the pocketbook on her half-bent arm and waited for her two daughters to escort her to the front door. Perel and I linked an arm through each of Mama's and steered her through the kitchen. Papa honked the horn lightly. "I'm comink!" she repeated, as enthusiastic as if she were meeting a long-lost relative at the Philadelphia airport. We showered our mother with kisses, like the March sisters in *Little Women,* and waved goodbye at the truck until it was a green speck on the White Horse Pike headed east.

In spite of our camaraderie in the bedroom, I was anxious to bid good riddance to my parents. With them gone, I could breathe. Yet the aura of impending doom that hovered continuously around Mama and Papa made me worry that they would receive a phone call in Buena Vista from the Polish government, recalling them to their *shtetlakh*. But what was I thinking? I was shipping them back to a concentration camp. I would never see them again. I would be an orphan, surviving on frozen chickens from the slaughterhouse walk-in freezer, collecting buckets of rainwater in case the pipes got blocked, inviting friends instead of imaginary voices into the house. Perel and I returned to my parents' bedroom, where the smell of hair spray still lingered. My sister stood behind me and wrapped her arms around my waist. "Carnation, alone at last," she said in Saucer's gruff voice. I looked into Mama's bureau mirror and pretended Perel was the boy in the cemetery July Fourth years ago.

"Lesbian sisters!" Sheiye said. He leaned against the white woodwork of the arch, the very spot where I saw a square-headed monster loom at me when I was five, and burped a series of eighth notes out of his trombone. Now my brother rested the instrument on his shoulder and leveled his head with the monster's. I closed my eyes, praying Sheiye would vanish in that standard puff of smoke. A few seconds later I opened them, to see Sheiye now standing at the foot of the bed, playing some nebulous jazz tune whose chaotic melody demanded first short staccato thrusts of the brass and then long, braying advances and retreats. He made it through half a dozen measures and blew accumulated spit out of a release valve onto the bedroom floor.

"Get away!" Perel screamed, and volleyed *Wuthering Heights* into his knees. Sheiye hopped backwards, boomeranging his rump out of harm's way. He tramped down on the paperback and shuffleboarded it under the bed with his sneaker.

"I could make mincemeat out of you!" Sheiye yelled. He scrunched his lips against the mouthpiece and conducted the slide up and down. As Perel attempted to thwack Sheiye's trombone with her bare hands, he backed off a foot and shot spit out the brass proboscis onto Perel's bare legs. She walloped the trombone with a hairbrush, and when Sheiye again blew into the instrument, a wheezing sound like air in an empty cough drop box rasped through the tube. Repeatedly, Sheiye flippered the valve to expel his spit. It trickled onto the floor, but the trombone's thin, diarrhetic sound did not improve. In a flash, Sheiye leaned it against the oak closet and began slap-fighting Perel, who made clipped, operatic shrieks like an air-raid alert. Twisting her arm hard, he said, "There's no one to hear you! No mommy or daddy to cry to!"

I pounded on Sheiye's head with a pillow. He grabbed at it with his free hand and clapped it over Perel's head. "Now see what you made me do?" Sheiye said in a soft Peter Lorre voice. "It's your fault if your little sister suffocates to death, Brantzche." Perel was kicking and screaming under the pillow, mussing Mama's neatly made-up sheets and bedspread. Between Perel's wriggling and my pushing, we managed to topple Sheiye onto the floor, which only infuriated him more. He reached for his trombone and jabbed it at Perel's stomach. I think he would have punched us black and blue if the honk of a car horn hadn't interrupted our boxing match.

"Papa said you have to sell eggs," I lied, so disgusted with Sheiye that I placed this burden of egg sales on him.

"Don't you princesses ever do a stitch of work around here?" Sheiye asked, narrowing his eyes. Was that the bone he had to pick with us?

"Papa says you're a coward," Perel seethed. "You hafta sell eggs 'cause you took up the bathroom all day."

"Well, I've been in my room sleeping, so how'm I supposed to know who comes for eggs?" He hurly-burlied up the stairs to his bedroom and locked the door. The horn sounded two more times. I had hoped that by now the customer would have driven away.

"Brantzche, please go," Perel said. "He made my face all red." Perel was in no shape to face a customer, certainly, but the real truth is that we were all afraid of outsiders. They made jokes; a lot of them talked like they had just moved up from Virginia; they left their engines running and fumigated the kitchen with car exhaust; they discussed their parents' cancer; sometimes they asked if I liked being Jewish. Mostly, no one wanted anything but three dozen eggs, but my perpetual state of second-guessing put me on edge.

When I saw the scowling face in the dusty purple '59 Plymouth, I expected a reprimand for taking too long. Summoning up my courage, I approached the car and looked in through the open driver's window. A middle-aged black woman with graying hair and a neck like a turkey's drummed her fingers impatiently on the steering wheel. "Can I help you?" I asked. My voice cracked, and I realized I was afraid of her. It was plain to me that I was scared because she was black and cantankerous—though black alone scared me enough. Several years before when my parents were away buying eggs wholesale, a tall black man on his way from Atlantic City to Philadelphia, a man with a lot of people in his Cadillac, had pulled into the driveway, walked straight into the house in his long, gray pants and white marching shoes, and asked Perel and me questions about eggs and when my parents would be home. He stood near the kitchen screen door for a good ten minutes. We tried to act casual, Perel and I, but the man saw we were scared out of our wits. I think he enjoyed watching us writhe. And now the black woman knew I was afraid, which gave her the faith to snarl at me.

"You know, darlin'," the woman said into my eyes, "that

sun is too high in the sky for me to sit here waitin' for you to mosey on out." I looked down where the glass window sank into the hollow of the car door. If I stared there long enough the customer might think I was mentally ill, and realize she was wasting her time chiding me.

"I want three dozen medium eggs," the woman said, looking up at me with one eye shut, and speaking as if I were the daughter of a sister she had hated since childhood. She was nobody to me, yet her anger fanned out like a peacock's tail and shadowed me. And for some reason, I felt she had a right to berate me, and I couldn't understand why. I turned towards the house, my eyes never once meeting hers. "And don't sneak in any cracked eggs," she called after me.

"Bitchy, bitchy," I muttered to myself. I lifted three dozen boxed eggs from the cool cellar floor and mounted the rickety wooden stairs up to the kitchen. *It's one thing for parents to insult you,* I kept thinking; *it's quite another to humble yourself before a sun-stroked old biddy.*

Returning with the three dozen eggs, I heard the creak of Charlie's peeling white door a few feet away and watched Charlie sit down on the annex steps. Bumblebees hovered over the hollyhocks, and Bolero began barking. I remember noticing a white handkerchief crumpled inside the same shirt pocket where Charlie kept his rolling tobacco, and I remember how he flapped it listlessly against his damp face. I opened the screen door with my thigh and positioned myself before the driver's open window. I waited for the woman to take the eggs, but she was not interested in accommodating me. She lifted each box one at a time, spreading them out on the floor of the passenger side. I wanted her to ask the price. But her scowl suggested that she had come to an important conclusion in life: She did not need to know anything from white people. Nor would she make herself vulnerable to a child with a wavering voice. I recognized this as a strategy and momentarily felt sorry for her. A mixture of pity and fear withering my self-confidence, I mustered up the last drops of aplomb and said, "That's eighty-nine cents, miss." Without a word, she handed me a dollar and I returned to the house for change.

Why don't three dozen medium eggs cost a dollar? I grumbled to myself. A nice round figure and I wouldn't have to face the Plymouth again. But eighty-nine cents was a given, the way oxygen in air is a given. There was nothing to do but hand that wretch eleven cents.

I walked reluctantly to the car and gave the woman her change. The penny dropped into the center of her palm. But the dime rolled like a wheel along her index finger and was sucked into the vortex of her lap. I could swear she had let the coin fall on purpose.

"Whatsa matter?" she snapped, closing one eye again. " 'Fraid the color's gonna rub off?"

My mistake was to hang my head, ashamed, tacitly confessing my villainy before her—and Charlie, still sitting on the annex steps. Maybe I *was* afraid to touch her hand. While the rest of my generation sang about reaching out in the darkness, I thought grazing a stranger's skin was an inappropriate act of intimacy. It was one of those small contacts that shocked me.

No defense, no alibi shaped itself in my head. I stood at the car window, the accused, waiting for the judge to pass sentence. I thought I would shit in my pants.

"How'd you like it if I told your mother, huh?" She was relentless. "I bet she don't wanna know you afraid of black skin."

No, don't tell my mother. She'll blame me for your fears. I hope I had enough pride to say nothing, but I don't remember. All I know is that I was a Milquetoast. This woman had pulled into the driveway prepared for a fight, and now she bared her fangs in the face of my timidity. I should have barreled out of that house and crooned, "And how are you today," the way Papa did. I should have smiled, done anything but act my sullen, shy self with the customers. But I didn't. All I could do was contract diseases like bitterness and longing. I wondered if Sheiye's prejudices would be passed to me like a flu.

The black woman moved her hand to the gear shift. "Go on now! Shoo!" she commanded. To my shame, I heard the aluminum screech of a window sash from above and saw Sheiye's head sink back into his room. To complete my humiliation, Charlie stuffed the handkerchief back in his shirt pocket and disappeared into the shabby annex.

Bolero barked at the car now making a U-turn in our driveway. All I could think was that Mama and Papa had failed. This black woman was exactly what my parents had tried to shield me from. Anger, blind accusation—these belonged to Europe, not to south Jersey. And if I told Mama and Papa about this interchange, what would they have said? "Brantzchele, *mach zich nisht narish!*" Don't be ridiculous! Or, *"Biz tsi der khasene veste shoyn hubn gegat fargesn!"* By your wedding day, you will have forgotten all about it! What would such minimizing responses suggest? That I cower from every personal vendetta, philosophy, and social upheaval that rushed into the farm in my parents' absence? True, Mama and Papa had hidden from Nazis—successfully; but of what use was hiding to me in Long-a-coming 1968?

The car waited for an opening in the White Horse Pike traffic and edged onto the road to West Long-a-coming, the township's enclave of blacks. The next thing I knew, I was sitting on a lawn chair, dazed, trying to understand how that scene had unfurled around me. I was mortified that Sheiye and Charlie had witnessed it. Miserably, I hoped that the woman would wrap herself around a utility pole.

While I was brooding in the backyard, hating the black lady and dreading Sheiye's inevitable ridicule, I reached one conclusion which the Peace generation had not been able to teach me: Thereafter, when I would wait on customers, I would press their change firmly into their palms.

Forced up through the center of my rage was a single memory of West Long-a-coming.

When white people talked about the black ghetto, they lowered their voices. The little town was built off Almond's Folly Road, named for the road engineer who wanted to dig a route starting from Highway 165 to the old Long-a-coming Glassworks three miles north but, due to lack of funds, only made it halfway. The walls of West Long-a-coming homes were papered with photographs of sons gone off to join the service, wedding pictures, inspirational messages, glossies of John F. Kennedy and Martin Luther King, Jr., and Jesus Christ in all his anguished poses. Parked in front of every third shingleless house was one car at least five years older than any in Long-a-coming. No matter what the season, children wearing black-and-white Keds and cut-off pants played in the driveways and quieted German shepherds. The older children walked slowly along Almond's Folly Road on their way to high school, raising their foreheads in hopes of hitching a ride each time a car passed. The only thing that interested white people about West Long-a-coming was scandal. Once, for example, an egg customer had told Mama about a mother who had instructed her daughter how to use a diaphragm.

Mama had pulled into a dusty West Long-a-coming

driveway and parked the blue Chevy. The dirt lawn was a playground of dismembered household appliances. The guts of a fan lay spilled out near the shell of a refrigerator. A toilet bowl sprouted weeds. Half a dozen patchwork-colored cars were sprawled on their backs like gigantic dead crickets. "Stay in the car," Mama had said to us in English. That was the first time I noticed that Mama's English sounded an octave higher than her Yiddish.

Attached to an opening in the house was a car door. Out poked two wooden crutches, then a leg, then a fistful of finger stumps like a bunch of eggs cut from a slaughtered hen. The only intact organ was an elliptical smile around a black man's gums. Otherwise, an entire leg gone. An arm gone. Fingers gone. Earlobe gone. Toes deformed as Papa's Shabbos afternoon walnuts pushed through the black man's torn sneakers. Where the leg had been he wore a long, thin tapering cane, the kind black amputees wore on the *Ted Mack Original Amateur Hour* for a tap-dancing routine. The summer sun lassoed a ray around the aluminum peg.

"My eggs! They're here!" he said, lumbering down the steps. "Are these your little girls? Hello in there, darlin's!" I was too scared to say anything. Perel and I avoided catching each other's eye. I looked at Mama for a cue, but she treated the man in her usual overly polite way. Mama opened the back door, bent down, and picked up three flats of eggs. She carried them past the car door into the house. I stared at the door to make sure Mama would exit in one piece.

It was all over in a minute. As we pulled out of the driveway, dust swirling from under the tires, Mama looked at Perel and me through the rearview mirror and said in middle-C Yiddish, "I just wanted to teach you a lesson. Now you'll know everyone isn't as happy as you."

The creaking springs of a truck chassis announced Mama and Papa's return from Buena Vista. As it drew nearer, the green truck, last seen as a speck on the Long-a-coming horizon, began to fill up the driveway and block the slaughterhouse from view. I stood at the living room window and held up my palm, trying to blot out the truck from the landscape. Mama waved at me with a polishing motion. She had seen me and thought I was waving hello.

The truck's engine was still knocking when Papa swung open his door and began carting egg flats into the cellar. He called for "Chahlie" to help. Charlie walked through the annex door as he always did, slowly, leaning more heavily into his left foot than his right. For Papa, the outing to Buena Vista had meant business as usual, and he began to issue a set of directives on how to unload eggs with maximal success.

For Mama, Buena Vista had been an excursion to a new land. She lined up bushels of potatoes, peaches, mushrooms, apples, and cherries on the kitchen floor, and gleefully recounted to us how she had climbed up trees to pick the fruit. I remember once having watched my mother in a pick-it-yourself orchard. Her eyes filled with tears, more from hay fever than from sentiment, and she became that woman, that stranger with my mother's name, who remembered a life before her children were born. In the evening, she doodled a picture of a square house planted in the middle of a broccoli-topped grove of circle-bearing trees.

The culmination of those Thursday evenings was the corn. Papa lugged a bushel of Jersey corn to a pit of vegetable peelings along the driveway, into which Perel and I shucked the green husks. We cleaned the worms from the corn's yellow skeins, draped the silk through our hair, and pretended we were Rapunzel. Now and then I have thought that life would have been happier had Papa bought a vegetable farm in 1950 instead of a slaughterhouse.

After we carried the corn to the house, I grabbed Mama by the waist and kissed her cheek, partly from gratitude, partly from remorse for all my ill will. "Vell, vell, my darlink," she said, ossifying *w*'s, rolling *r*'s, clunking *g*'s. She taught me the tango while the smell of corn and butter filled the kitchen and living room. We begged Mama to tell us where she had learned to dance. Remembering, she said she forgot. Perel and I wanted Papa to dance too. He propelled his arms a few times, and for all the world he looked like he would shoot through the roof. When Perel complained, "You have to move your feet," he stomped heavily, an American Indian praying for rain. "That's not dancing," Perel said. Papa shrugged and promised to take lessons someday, a project as likely as his conversion to Zen Buddhism.

An hour later, Mama, Papa, Perel, and I were sitting in the living room with plates of buttered corn, watching some New York City cops slug it out with antiwar protesters on TV. Sheiye stood in the middle of the staircase, unsure if the program was worth sitting down for, and gaped at the blood, staining tourniquets and blue jeans dark gray on our black-and-white screen. We returned to the kitchen for third and fourth helpings, the news special ended, and the situation comedies reclaimed their time slots. "The revolution of black folk is come, ay, Brantzch?" Sheiye said, brushing against my ankle on the way to the piano room. I said nothing and didn't complain about his piano playing for fear he would tell my parents about my brush with black skin.

Fortunately, Perel was well engrossed in a self-instruction guide for beginning knitters and had fallen back on her habit of tuning Sheiye out. As I picked corn kernels from my teeth, I thought how safe from war and protest I was on the farm. All the major events of the outside world—the Tet offensive in January, the assassinations of Martin Luther King and Robert Kennedy in the spring—these were someone else's nightmares, and as such, lacked the personal horror that my dreams custom-tailored for me. Nonetheless, the angry black woman had bored her way into Jake's Poultry Farm like a carpenter ant. Without Mama and Papa standing guard at their posts, the world was always ready to invade, to sting and bludgeon. What none of us ever figured, though, was that trouble just as often bores from within.

An hour or so before nightfall, Perel, Bolero, and I trotted to the railroad tracks. My sister and I were afraid the woods had harvested some new derelict, but our allergy to boredom made caution intolerable. We persisted in viewing Bolero as our protector. Like many a native-born American, we were positive thinkers: We chucked out empirical evidence of Bolero's unreliability for the sake of a lark.

Perel huddled against the embankment and listened to the tracks for an oncoming train. Sheiye had taught us that. Sure enough, Perel heard a dim rumbling in the steel. In the western distance a yellow pinpoint of light glowed brighter and brighter, and we jumped off the rails and watched the train chug towards us. Maybe this time it would have a passenger coach, and we would see who traveled between Philadelphia and Atlantic City. But the night trains almost always carried freight, raw materials and finished products, about as interesting to us as chickens. This one was at least fifty cars long. As usual, I kept my eyes open for the sight that would transform my life. But only rust-colored cabins and flatbeds labeled *Erie-Lackawanna* and *Baltimore and Ohio* creaked by, delivering lumber and steel to south Jersey's fiberglass and trailer assembly plants. That bulb of yellow light flickered, an eye with tunnel vision, blind to Long-a-coming and its residents. As the front of the train pulled towards town, the engineer pressed the train whistle.

"That's an American sound," I said. "You know what I mean?"

"Yeah," Perel agreed. "It makes me feel like we're on an outdated TV show, like *The Andy Griffith Show*. In Mayberry."

"And when we get home, Aunt Bee is gonna have pancakes and syrup piping hot on the table," I said.

"At night we'll eat Jiffy Pop," Perel nodded. "Mom will go to the PTA meeting and Dad will play bridge with his pals at the American Legion. They'll talk about where they were stationed during the war."

"My boyfriend Skip will want to take me to the Long-a-coming Drive-In Theater. That'll make me feel swell."

"You can double with Planet-Top and me," Perel said. "Planet-Top is perfection in human form."

"We'll have to be home by nine o'clock," I said. "Dad has to be up by six to get to the office in Philly on time."

"What'll Mom do all day?" Perel asked.

"Oh, bake gingerbread. She'll be a mom," I said.

"What about Sheiye?" Perel whispered. Sheiye didn't belong in our remodeled world.

"You mean our kind brother, Steve? He'll nickname us 'Freckles' and 'Junebug' and slip us Hershey's chocolate when Mom's not looking."

"But neither one of us has freckles." Perel laughed.

"We'll have freckles. But only when we're young. When we grow up, we'll look like Tuesday Weld."

Perel lifted her head to the sky in mock inspiration. "People will see a picture of us—the Shuster family, spelled with an *h,* not a *z*—on a billboard, right on the White Horse Pike. We'll be drinking Pepsi."

"We'll belong to a generation," I said. The train whistle blew again. "If we really want to fit in, Saucer, we'll have to drop acid. And we'll have to go to protest marches in the rain. We'll have to sleep in tents outside the Washington Monument and breathe Mace."

"I can handle the Mace," Perel said, "but I don't know about the rest."

"You gotta keep up with the times, Sauce, if you're gonna be a real American. A rrreal Yenkee, like Mendl used to say."

"Freckles," Perel said, putting an arm around my waist and patting Bolero's head. "We have a bright future ahead of us. We're Americans."

The caboose clattered on the rails, spewing coal chips from the tracks over the embankment. A lone man wearing a gray-and-white-striped jumpsuit, a matching cap, and electrician's gloves waved at us. He had no determinate age, no identity other than "caboose man"; and Perel and I were simply two anonymous country girls with a mutt. We returned his wave. How much more American a tableau could you dream up?

In Mama's Polish-Yiddish accent, Perel said, "He don't rrreally know ve're not hundert pehr-tsent, you know, Amerrrican."

"Hit's awk-kay," I said. "Chust prrretend."

We waited for Long-a-coming to blacken the train's hind red lights, and then Perel, Bolero, and I walked back to the house and to our futures.

14

December 8, 1979
Tel Aviv, Israel
Rukhl Sussman Szuster, as told to Yaffa Simontov
Collected and edited for the World War II Jewish
Survivors' Archive at Yad Vashem

The Polish partisans tolerated skilled Jews. One partisan did Aaron a favor and took him on as a shoemaker. Pinkhus Diamond became the adjutant to the *porucznik* Biale, head commander of the partisan unit. Byale advised the rest of us thirty Jews to scatter ourselves to the four winds.

If I left the partisan-controlled village for a Ukrainian-controlled village, I was a dead duck. The Ukrainians would say I was a Pole and kill me. So Dvoyre, her sister Tsila, and I stole into the house of a farmer named Franciszek. He was a Pole but insane. He kept a bull and she-horse in his house, separated from his living quarters by a gray curtain. No partisans bothered Franciszek because he was too crazy to help them.

One day the partisans shot down a low-flying German plane. The plane landed in a muddy ditch. When the Poles ran up to inspect it, they found the pilot dead, his feet poking out the cockpit door. The Poles pulled off the pilot's boots and called for a celebration, that's how thrilled they were to shoot down a German plane.

Apparently, the German had had enough time to warn

his commanders where his plane had been shot down. Before long the Germans sent more planes and bombed the village. Houses and streets caught fire and burned.

A few days earlier the Jews had dug a trench under Franciszek's house and covered it with a long piece of lumber. If the Germans bombed the village, we would seek shelter in the trenches.

When the bombing started, I was the first one in. Everyone else piled in behind me. There wasn't room for another soul.

I heard one Jew, Itche, come running. He could only fit his head into the trench. The Jews yelled, "Itche, they'll see you!"

Itche said, *"A kapure der hintn, abi der kop zol lebn!"* I'll scapegoat my ass for the sake of my head!

When I heard that I began choking with laughter. Between my laughing and inhaling the smoke from a burning house, I almost suffocated to death. *Der nahr hot mir geshtipt.*

Everyone crawled out of the trench, I last, of course. Most ran to the woods. I remember that I had a loaf of bread in the house so I went to retrieve it. I helped myself to one of Franciszek's pots too.

On my way to the woods, I saw the *goyim* running. Mothers led their children and the children tripped on their heels, crying, "Mama, wait for me!"

I was overjoyed to see this picture. I thought, "Run! Get a taste of my life. When I had to run, you were comfortable in your homes and laughed at me. Run, *goyim!*"

The Poles attacked a troop of Germans and took them prisoner. They penned them in a barn. One side of the barn held milk cows, the other the two hundred arrested Germans.

The Polish partisans were fed up with the Jews. They had

already accused us of being filthy *Żydy* who ate up Polish food. But I approached the Poles and volunteered to milk the cows. One of them found a pail and handed it to me.

Into the barn I walked, swinging my pail. I wasted no time and grabbed whatever lay on the floor—straw, dried manure, wood chips—and threw it at the German prisoners. I cried, "I am a *Jude. Warum haben Sie kaput gemacht meinen Vater, meine Schwester? Warum machen Sie kaput alle Juden?"* Why have you destroyed my father, my sisters? Why have you destroyed the Jews?

A German answered quietly, *"Wir sind unschuldig. Wir machen gar nichts."* They said we're not guilty; we did nothing.

When the guard outside heard me screaming and saw chunks of wood fly through the air, he chased me out. I lost an opportunity to get milk.

One day a local chief of police named Tadeuzc summoned me to the police station. He asked, "Can you knit children's sweaters and socks?" I said yes even though I couldn't. But what about wool, I asked. Tadeuzc said the Poles would steal sheep from the Ukrainians. Could I shear sheep, he wanted to know. Yes, I said. I had never touched a sheep before in my life, but I figured by tomorrow I would run for my life and never have to shear sheep or knit sweaters.

Outside the police station sat a young guy holding a canteen in his hands. With a knife he was scraping off the name and identification number that every military issue canteen bore.

The *sheygits* says to me, *"Parszywa Żyduwko!"* Dirty Jewess! On any other day I could have swallowed my pride and said nothing. But that day the insult burned me. Why? Because now when the German bombed the village, he didn't ask who was a Jew and who a Pole. A bomb could drop and kill this *sheygits* before it killed me. A Pole no longer had reason to call me *parszywa Żyduwko*. This time I wouldn't write off the insult to plain stupidity.

I wanted to settle scores with him. I said, "I'm going to teach you a lesson."

He snickered, "What can you do to me?"

I said, "I'm going to take that canteen from you."

"You can't. It's mine."

"It's about to be mine," I said.

I was an embittered girl and cried at the drop of a hat in those days. I stood up, walked straight back to the chief of police, and knocked on his door.

I sobbed, "I left my canteen on the steps and the boy outside stole it from me. My name is still on it and he's scraping it off with a knife."

Since I was now commissioned by the chief of police to knit his children sweaters and socks, I stirred his sympathy. Plus, he had an investment to protect.

Tadeuzc told the guard, "Call the boy in!" The boy walked in, holding the canteen in both hands. Tadeuzc asked the boy, "Why did you steal her canteen?"

The boy protested, "I didn't! It's mine!"

I said, "It's mine! That's why I'm crying. Look. My name used to be right here!" I pointed at the crisscrossed scratches on the canteen.

The chief of police examined the scratched area and ordered, "Give it back to her. Now!"

The boy got scared and pushed the canteen into my hands. Concerned with more strategic matters, Tadeuzc told us both to leave.

Outside, I told the boy, "See, I taught you a lesson." He was afraid to tangle with me now and held his tongue.

I kept the canteen as a souvenir until after I joined the

Russian partisans. They made me throw it away because it made too much noise.

Our only hope was to locate the Russian partisans. Unfortunately, we met the Ukrainian *Banderowcy* first. By day they spoke to us kindly. By nightfall, when they learned we were Jews, they yelled, *"Żydy!* We're going to kill you." I understood Ukrainian and told the other Jews we had to escape.

Day and night we walked, until we encountered the Russian partisans and their commander, a man in his late thirties named Yosef. He was kind to the Jews. He told us everyone could slice off flesh from a slaughtered cow and roast it. We only had to take care not to cause smoke or we would give away our position to the Germans. The Russians had sacks of flour too, and we baked *pletslekh,* flat onion breads.

Yosef decreed an advance to the front. Only adults strong enough to carry rifles could move with the partisans. I was always the smallest and youngest, so Yosef said I had to stay behind at the partisan hospital in the woods. I would get weak or fall asleep, he said. I said I didn't want to stay at any hospital. I wanted to go with the others. I promised not to fall asleep, swearing to keep pace at the head of a column, just let me go. I wore Yosef down and he consented to let me come.

Late one afternoon we came to a clearing in the woods. It had rained all day and the ground was wet. For shelter, everyone had to build themselves a *buda,* a shack better described as a doghouse. Meanwhile, some partisans had started a bonfire to dry ourselves and our clothing. Leisurely, I dried my shoes, figuring that Aaron would make arrangements for my *buda.*

I returned to the clearing, dry and warm, and saw Aaron crawling into a *buda* he had built for himself and his friend Kaddish Karsch. Yosef saw my problem. He set off to gather grass and branches and built me a *buda*.

When I was ready to sleep, Yosef took off one of the two jackets he always wore and laid it under my head. He also covered me with a blanket he had used as a saddle for his horse. As we approached the front, he let the horse go free but kept the blanket.

In the middle of the night, as the rain penetrated the *buda*, and I was so tired I could barely move, I felt Yosef stroke my face. I expected him to choke me to death. I was too scared to say a thing. But Yosef only tucked the blanket more tightly around me.

The next day we were starving. I no longer had food stowed in my knapsack. Two days before, someone had pilfered my bread from under my pillow as I slept. The day before that, Yosef had found us potatoes. We were nearly finished boiling them when the order came to move on at once. The Germans had learned our whereabouts and we didn't have a spare second to pack the potatoes. I can't tell you how hard it was to leave on an empty stomach with the aroma of potatoes in my nostrils.

Yosef had some crumbs in his pockets and fed them to me. He always went out of his way to take care of the Jews. We had our suspicions that Yosef was a Jew and asked him directly if he was. He smiled but never said one way or the other.

Some of the Russian partisans were anti-Semites. They would taunt us with *"Żydy!* We're going to kill you!" I shivered that the Russians should disappoint us too.

Mud. The ground was mud. A lone person could never walk through it. You needed clusters of people to carry the stumbling ones out of it.

I was hobbling through the mud alone. I had gotten separated from Aaron, who marched up front with the rifle carriers. Behind me trudged Yosef, his boots making sucking and slurping noises as he struggled along. Whenever I found myself in a tight spot, Yosef bailed me out. And because Yosef was the commander, he moved at the head of the group and dragged me along with him.

We reached drier ground and then the Turia River. Stationed beyond the Turia was the Red Army. Yosef said we had to cross a bridge to meet the Russians. But the bridge was all but burned to splinters. Only a long piece of charred wood remained.

Yosef said, "I'll lead the way and you hold on to my belt. When I step with my right foot, you step with yours. When I step with my left, do the same. And whatever happens, don't look down. Keep your eyes straight ahead and don't totter. If you lose your balance, we'll both fall down and drown."

I took the greatest care not to look down or totter, and we crossed the Turia on that burnt ledge of wood.

We came upon a burnt-out village. Only one house still stood. To the right of the building were stacked bales of hay. People peered out from under them.

The partisans had agreed that one rifle blast signified "Get ready." Two meant "Prepare to fire," and three meant "Shoot!" As we neared the burnt house, I heard one shot. *Raboyne shel oylem,* I thought. This is it. In another second came the second and third shots.

Deafening gunfire followed, with commands to go left, right, straight ahead. Shots flew from every direction.

I began crying, "Now I don't have my brother!" I told

Yosef I was running for cover under the bales of hay where the other people hid. But these people began firing at us. They were Germans.

All around me, the sound of bullets. I hopped over bodies that fell in my path. Several people yelled, "Retreat!" No one knew whose commands to obey.

I saw people hurling themselves under the house. Wrenching free of Yosef's hand, I hurled myself with the rest of them. In a split second, scores of bodies, living or dead, I don't know which, landed on top of me. In another second my breath would fail me and I would be dead too.

Yosef searched for my hand and pulled me out. "You'll suffocate to death!" he yelled.

He said, "Now we have nowhere to go but straight ahead."

Straight ahead meant up a steep hill. At the summit waited the Red Army. The problem now was poor communication between the army and the partisans. Thinking we were Germans, the Red Army began shooting at us. The Germans understood the gunfire was meant for them and returned fire. Yosef and I were caught in the middle.

Running and crying about Aaron's safety, I realized we had been forced to a wide body of water. I watched people run headlong into the water and drown. Either shot down or exhausted, no one was making it across alive.

Leaping over wounded partisans begging for doctors and nurses, I say to myself, "If I step into this water, I'll drown too." And I'm yelling at myself, "All you had to do was wait at the partisan hospital. The Russians would have found us and set us free. Why did you have to get mixed up with the partisans and lose your brother too?"

Bullets whizzed around me. I lifted my arm and a bullet flew under it. Others whooshed past my eyes and ears like wind. Soon I stopped hearing the sound of bullets as they raced around me. If one had hit me, I am sure I wouldn't have felt a thing.

As I stand and watch the water with dread, I see a young partisan, no more than twenty, undress himself and roll his clothes into a knapsack. He ties the pack around his shoulder and heaves the rifle into the water. "Let it sink to the bottom," he says out loud, "but the Germans won't touch it." The boy jumps into the water and a bullet hits him square in the jaw.

From the corner of my left eye, I think I see people fording the river. I said to Yosef, "Let's follow them and try to make it across." Ice still lined parts of the river. It was April 24, 1944.

Yosef said, "First I'll knock the rifle butt into the ground. Then I'll grab hold of it and you do the same. When I tell you, grasp my belt and don't let go."

I did as Yosef told me. I held on tight to his belt and never felt the river bottom. Before we got to the other side, Yosef told me to cut my heel into the riverbank to gain a foothold. We crawled out of the river and saw dawn break.

Few people had made it across. I said to Yosef, "I'm not leaving. Here I lost my brother, and here I'll lose myself."

I sat down on a fallen tree log, talked to myself and cried. Yosef sat down and listened to me. All of a sudden he says, "Look who's here!"

I look up and it's Aaron! Tall, skinny, and wet! And carrying his rifle over his shoulder. I was overjoyed! I jumped up and asked, "Aaron, you're not wounded? You're whole?"

Aaron said, "If there's no blood, I'm not wounded."

We still had to trek through a burnt-out forest seeded with unexploded mines.

Yosef said, "I'll go first. Plant your feet in the exact spot where I plant mine. If I step on a mine, I'll be blown up, not you."

Aaron and I followed Yosef at a snail's pace and left the Turia behind. We arrived at a road and saw truckloads of Russian soldiers headed for the front. When they spied us, they waved and shouted, "Welcome, comrades!"

That struck me as funny. Earlier, the partisans had called us filthy Jews and now we were comrades.

I thought, *What's going on?* For a minute my head spun and I forgot that I had been captive under the Germans and had hidden in barns and forests for two years. Now I was free and able to come and go at will. I asked myself, "But where is everyone? Where is my father, my sisters? If I'm here, where are they?"

My reality reclaimed me: I was free and they were dead.

We received an order to make haste. The Germans were overpowering the Russians. After all we had been through, we still had thirty kilometers to go.

Hungry and exhausted, we ran those thirty kilometers, away from the war, away from the Nazi occupation, deeper into Russia.

Overhead flew German planes, showering us with leaflets that exhorted the Russians not to believe anything the Jews said; the Jews' stories were pure propaganda. If the Russians surrendered, they would be treated well. They need only carry a canteen, a spoon, and a dish for victuals.

As we walked and read those leaflets, we jumped out of our skins with rage.

15

December 8, 1979
Tel Aviv, Israel
Yankl Khaim Szuster, as told to Yaffa Simontov
Collected and edited for the World War II Jewish
Survivors' Archive at Yad Vashem

If you want stories, you are better off talking to my wife. She likes to tell them, and she knows how. Me, I don't like tape recorders. I would rather you just sit and listen and trust your memory to remember only what's important.

The main thing you want to know is how I survived. Did I have some special wisdom, a strong faith, some good friends among the Poles. It's like this: Say you have a farmer who discovers an infestation of ants on his property. The farmer begins to exterminate the ants with pesticide, and most of them he kills. But some ants, of course, develop an immunity to the spray and manage to escape. Maybe they even have time to start breeding. The farmer, meanwhile, buys an improved pesticide, sprays the ants again, and kills even more of them. But he will never kill the whole population. It's impossible. One ant runs fast, another happens to be away on a food-getting excursion, and yet another learns to live with the drop of pesticide on its back. Well, there you have the story of the Jews. We could have been one billion like the Chinese, but we were the ants and the rest of the world was the farmer.

You ask me why I believe in God, how I can still *daven* to Him three times a day in light of the senseless destruction of my family. You know, you can start out at point "A" and head off in twenty-five different directions. You can wander down strange roads for years, but eventually you have to come back to who you were—to who you are. I believe in God because I have no one else to believe in.

The first thing a human being has to accept is that he understands nothing. Do you know why we exist on this earth? Perhaps other worlds preceded ours, worlds with their own long histories and annihilation. Maybe the world we live in is a shadow world of the ones already destroyed, worlds strong and permanent in their day, and when they crumbled, their echoes created us, primitive people. How do you know we're not just atomic fallout from another world's nuclear blast?

The way I see it, you have two choices: You can say, "All I know is what I see; no God would allow a world like this to exist, and I don't believe"; or you can say, "I don't understand anything; I don't understand God's intentions, yet I believe there are reasons for our existence which are beyond our comprehension." I am a simple man, so I look to the wisdom of far more learned men than I. The Jews have a whole body of laws and customs, and we have a long history, all testifying that God exists, even though He defies human understanding. My mother and father were Jews and I don't know how to be anything else. I choose the second position because I am a Jew.

When I was a boy I loved two things: soccer and fishing. I could play ball and nothing else for hours. And fishing—forget it! My father literally used to drag me away from a neighbor's fish pond. The pond belonged to a Jew, but you still had to pay to take fish and we couldn't afford to pay. Well, if a father says not to do something, of course you do it. I couldn't help myself, that's how much I loved fishing.

But after the war, I lost the desire for the activities I had loved as a boy. I don't know how to explain it. Did I feel guilty, you ask. No, it wasn't that. It's just that what gave me joy in a former context gave me pain in a new one. A normal person tries to avoid pain, so I withdrew from my former pleasures.

One time my favorite cousin, Zalman, marched into our house and told me my sister Brantzche stuffed her brassiere. He ran out of the house before I could give him what-for. I caught up with him and gave him a good thrashing, and reminded him that Brantzche took a "D" cup. I wouldn't talk to him again until he apologized to me a month later.

General Pilsudski tried to liberalize the laws in Poland to include Jews in government, the army, and business. When he died, the Jews in Hrubieszów mourned. His funeral procession, or maybe it was an official commemoration march, passed through Uchan and stopped at the church. Zalman and I sneaked into the church and watched the mourners lighting candles by the altar, and making the sign of the cross as they kneeled. If my father had known we were inside a Catholic church, he would have beaten the living daylights out of me.

No, I don't think about the war every day. Maybe some people do, but not me. I am sure I would go crazy if I thought of my parents and my sisters, and of everything that happened to me in the slave labor camp and in the woods. I let my nightmares do the thinking for me.

One husband and wife I knew had been hiding in the woods with me for a year and a half. They were confident that they could hide as long as necessary. I remember their daughter, a thirteen-year-old scholar who could quote Torah by heart. Their self-confidence caught them off guard. One day some Poles found them in the woods and shot them dead.

It wasn't until the 1960s that I realized that my mother and sisters were cremated at Sobibor. The Sobibor death camp was only ten or twenty kilometers from the Staw work camp, and from what I have read, that was the only place their train could have gone.

Yosl, the boy who escaped with me from Staw, stayed alive until one year after liberation by the Russian Army. He had this idea that he could return to Uchan, do some kind of business, and live among his Polish neighbors. I begged him to leave Uchan. I told him about my cousin who had lived in Argentina before the war, returned to Poland to be with her sister, and was killed by the Poles *after* liberation. Yosl, who had saved his own skin on so many other occasions, now decided the time wasn't right for him to leave Uchan. Some Poles decided for him and beat him to death.

My father was a cantor. Here, look at this picture. I carried it with me the whole time I was in hiding. That's the Ten Commandments above the Torah's ark, and that's my father in the front wearing a *talis*. See how most of the other men are lost inside their beards, or inside their hunched postures, or they are just blurs in the picture. What stands out? My father: His eyes are the center of attraction. Seventeen other men and one little girl, and all you see is my father. Really, he was a charismatic personality. When he sang a *nig'n*, the women fainted. Especially when he sang a wedding *nig'n* he had composed. Women cried and fainted.

When I was in hiding, I used to listen to the wind whistle through the hulls of wheat. It was like listening to an orchestra of flutes. And when I lay very calm, I heard the beginning notes of a *nig'n*. I copied I don't know how many *nigunim* from the sound of wind through wheat. The wheat was never mine to eat, but its magic belonged only to me. I sang the *nigunim* to my father's soul, always with me in hiding. Unfortunately, I don't remember any of the melodies today.

16

ONLY ONE THING DISTINGUISHED Thursday, August 22, from any other summer morning: The truck kept stalling. It whined through first gear and petered out at second with an asthmatic wheeze. Although Sheiye got it to run after lifting the hood and jiggling some red wires around, Papa was nervous and around ten o'clock drove the truck over to Earl Whitaker's auto body shop in Long-a-coming. Sheiye followed behind in the blue Chevy, and forty-five minutes later the two Szuster men pulled into the driveway, Papa in the driver's seat.

Perel and I galloped from Bolero's doghouse up the cement steps of the house; there wasn't much else going on, and even an out-of-commission truck could ignite a spark of excitement in our lives. Whitaker couldn't promise to finish the repairs before five o'clock, and that was only if he got to it right away. What about Buena Vista? Mama and Papa would take the Chevy. They would cart home fewer eggs and hope customers would postpone their Labor Day egg-buying until the following week. Around five o'clock Sheiye could call Whitaker, walk into town, and drive the truck home.

The humidity that day was oppressive. Perel and I sat behind the house on lawn chairs, she reading *Tess of the D'Urbervilles* while I thumbed through *Time*. Every so often we honked our character voices at each other. Across the driveway, Sheiye tinkered with a semifunctional cement blade sharpener. Bolero barked at him for a reassuring pat on the head.

186

Charlie, sweat streaming down his temples, cleaned the slaughtering machines, rolled himself a cigarette, and returned to his interrupted game of solitaire. Customers in search of fresh eggs blasted their car horns and left car engines running, forcing Mama to inhale the exhaust. Papa sped about in perpetual motion, feeding chickens in the coops, pulling weeds from his vegetable garden, talking on the phone to butchers, and reading the *Forward,* the *Philadelphia Inquirer,* the local *Independent Record,* and *Reader's Digest.*

At four o'clock, Mama pranced about the bedroom, getting dressed for her outing. That was the last day she wore the cotton dress with blue flowers. As she applied her red lipstick, she mentioned a dream she had had the night before, something about an airplane. She was always dreaming about airplanes and fish. "What's the dream mean?" Perel and I asked. The interpretation never varied: "Or we'll get some good news or we'll have a visitor," Mama said.

As Mama walked through the kitchen, Perel petted her shoulder and purred into her ear. Mama's silent, pressed lips intimated she found the purring inappropriate for a girl almost thirteen years old, but she meowed back just the same. Perel proffered her cheek to Papa, demanding a kiss even if no one else got one. "Papa, your kisses are as wet as Bolero's," she complained. Papa feigned shock. "A dog? A father kisses like a dog? *A broch tsi mahne yurn! A bisl derkherits!*" A curse on my middle years! A little respect! He was still acting the role of the wounded party when he sat down behind the Chevy steering wheel and drove off.

Emboldened by Mama and Papa's departure, Sheiye insisted that Perel or I call Whitaker—otherwise, he wouldn't fetch the truck. This time it wasn't a question of a just division of tasks. Sheiye's sporadic adventures off the farm notwithstanding, a few words like "Hello, this is Steve Szuster; how are you; I'd like to know if my truck is fixed" presented an insurmountable obstacle to him. The phrases got jammed behind a shy smile and melted in the heat of a crimson blush.

Confronting us in the living room, Sheiye incited the traditional kicking and screaming. He pinned my arm, chicken-wing style, against my back and said he wouldn't let go unless I promised to call Whitaker. I screamed that I could care less if the truck was fixed or not, and he could call Whitaker himself. "Princess!" Sheiye grumbled, and cranked my arm up a notch. When Perel suggested that Sheiye drive the truck off a cliff, he lunged at her throat. "You're choking me, you ugly bastard!" she cried. Afraid that Sheiye might shove Perel into the TV, I kicked him in the ass. That only strengthened his resolve and he tightened—or pretended to tighten—his grip on Perel's neck.

"Call Whitaker, Brantzche, or I won't let go!" Sheiye threatened. Before I could respond, Perel socked him in the knee, and as he doubled over in pain, she kicked him in the other. Perel and I dashed outside, hoping that the Pike traffic would inhibit Sheiye's violence.

Who should we see pull into the driveway but Earl Whitaker. The brakes on Whitaker's peeling blue Ford pickup squealed over the ruts in the driveway, and his eyes strained through his ever-smudged horn-rimmed glasses in anticipation of larger craters. Next to him sat his tubby, raven-haired ten-year-old daughter, on seat's edge, peering from behind matching horn-rims past the bug-spattered windshield. She always widened her eyes when she visited the farm, expecting, like me, perhaps, to behold something wondrous. Whitaker honked twice as Sheiye tore down the steps behind us.

"Hey there, young man!" Whitaker called to Sheiye. "Thought you might 'preciate a lift." Looking at the three

Szuster children stopped in midchase, Whitaker said, "Too hot for tag, anyway, eh?"

The western sun highlighted the sweat on Whitaker's upper lip and chin. Whitaker was a small, wiry man with black frizzy hair inherited from his Italian mother. That wiry quality promised a peppery spirit, but Whitaker never quite sprang into action. At the prospect of opening the truck door, for example, he furrowed his brow, pouring total concentration into the notion. He adored his Dionysian-looking fifteen-year-old son and his overweight daughter. I never heard him say a harsh word to either child. I would have envied the Whitakers if they weren't so poor and simpleminded. As it was, their love for each other and their assumption about the Szusters' happiness played on my nerves.

"Hop in next to Angela," Whitaker encouraged. "When she hears I'm going to Jake's, she jumps in 'longside me and starts hollerin', 'The egg farm! The egg farm!' Ain't that right, cutie?" Whitaker's hand glanced against Angela's cheek, and the girl twisted on the seat with pleasure.

"Thanks, Mr. Whitaker," Sheiye mumbled. "I'll climb on back. It'll be less crowded and cooler out here."

"Suit yourself, handsome," said Whitaker, a little disturbed, I thought, by Sheiye's rebuff. To Perel and me, Whitaker shouted, "Man the home front, girls!" Angela waved at us and smiled, thankful to have glimpsed Jake's Poultry Farm, the barking dog, the yard chickens, and Jake's two daughters. A real farm. "Your brother will be back safe and sound in no time," Whitaker said.

"Oh, no rush, Mr. Whitaker," Perel offered.

The Ford pickup made a loop around the driveway and putt-putted its way onto the White Horse Pike. Sheiye flicked a boogie from his nose as farewell.

Invigorated by Sheiye's absence, Perel and I acted out skits with dolls, created bizarre characters, and played children's games—all this while our peers debated the benefits of withdrawal over condoms. Perel and I could seesaw on a makeshift plank and fulcrum for an hour without getting bored, restrained only by the possibility that someone from school might catch us being children instead of hip teenagers. We now hit upon a brilliant idea. We could play hide-'n'-seek. The worst anyone could accuse us of was walking around the driveway looking for something.

We defined our game boundaries and took turns as hider and seeker. After half an hour or so, I said, "Isn't this getting dull, Perel? I mean, how can you read *Tess* and enjoy hide-'n'-seek too?"

"What do you mean?" she asked ingenuously. "I like both."

"You're so smart," I said.

"Well, so are you, Brantzche. You read," Perel said.

"Yeah, I read, but you devour. I mean, I'm just a few years past Nancy Drew, and here you are, not even thirteen, reading Scholastic Book Classics. If books were chocolate, you'd be a blimp."

"I am a blimp," she said, eyeing her belly mournfully. "I'm a ybab taf."

"A what?"

"Baby fat spelled backwards," Perel said. "And you're a gab fo senob."

"Gab fo senob," I repeated. "Bag of bones. Really, Perel, am I that skinny?" She looked at me and sighed. "Oh, I guess I am on the lean side. I'll probably never get married. Men like women with big groodies, and all I got are goose bumps. I bet you won't have that problem in a couple of years."

"I'll go on a diet and find out my boobs are just baby

fat too," she said. Perel suggested working off our regret in another round of the game. She wanted to hide. *What if I had hidden?*

I hopscotched to the front of the house and counted to ten. Perel had said she would be somewhere between the back of the house and Bolero's doghouse. I first checked the doghouse. You never knew; she might risk Bolero's fleas and hair balls for the sake of a good laugh. I looked in and found only Bolero, whose hope for a run was now aroused.

"Give me a hint!" I yelled. "Ha-ha!" I said to Bolero, scratching his ear. "Get it, a *hint?*" I thought my Yiddish-English pun clever. "A *hint* is a dog, 'Lero. Did you know that?"

"Hey, Perel!" I shouted, spinning around in the driveway. "Dju hear what I said? I asked Bolero to give me a *hint*. Get it?"

While I pivoted on my heel, scanning the yard, I saw something move under a blanket near the bench in back of the house. It was obviously Perel lying flat on her stomach. I moved towards her slowly on tiptoe, hoping to trick her into divulging her position.

Halfway to the blanket, I saw Sheiye in the green truck. I saw him. I remember that much. Instead of using the driveway, he cut through the backyard, as Papa occasionally did to make a run through the westbound traffic. I hated when they used that route: I mean, you could be sitting out back reading, and all of a sudden you would see a car or truck barreling towards you. Papa, at least, drove slowly.

I saw Sheiye's head arched between the steering wheel and the dashboard, his lower jaw thrust out Cro-Magnon style. He pretended to aim straight at me. He always pulled that crap. We always complained, but he kept his *shtik* up. The point is, Sheiye saw me. My brother saw me waving my hands, warning him to drive away from the blanket. I admit, I didn't call out Perel's name. I tried, but my tongue was lead. I opened my mouth to scream and heard a frail, alto note deep in my throat, drowned out by the crack of Perel's body under Sheiye's wheels. The last thing I remember is the butcher's gift, the dog with the wobbly head, thrashing its snout again and again into the windshield.

17

SHEIYE'S PREHISTORIC JAW COLLAPSED into a modern-day gape. The truck's engine whined with the familiar broken noise as my brother braked to a stop near Bolero's doghouse. I didn't know how to participate anymore in my own life. I didn't cry or shriek, though both seemed fitting responses. I think I was trembling. I looked across the driveway at the blanket and saw that Perel's blood had spattered the cotton cloth, our makeshift seesaw, the grass. Everything was quiet except for Bolero's barking. And was I crazy, I thought his yips had become almost verbal, as if all along canine understanding had warned him of just such an ending. I turned to Sheiye sitting in the truck, his head slumped over the steering wheel. He was batting his forehead against the windshield like the toy dog's. He knew. Get out and fix the mess you made! No words. Just the sound of blood in my ears, like a heart pounding in a movie. Perel *had* to be unhurt. Any second now she would spring up and say in Saucer's voice, "Hey, Queero! What're ya tryin' to do, kill me?" We would gather stones from the driveway and hurl them at Sheiye, even though Perel believed you altered the earth's geology by the needless shifting of so much as a pebble.

Bolero continued his howling as the annex door swung open. I watched Charlie standing in the doorway, rubbing his eyes in the light. Please be Samson, I begged. Punish the evildoers. . . . and I wished myself in Perel's place. The walls of Jake's Poultry Farm did not crumble. Charlie surveyed the driveway and observed Sheiye's battering skull, Bolero's entangled leash, and my skinny body rooted to the ground. He craned his neck around the backyard, reorienting himself to the farm he seemed to forget whenever he closed his eyes. I prayed Charlie would see something different than what I saw. Maybe he was drunk, and would think it was 1960: He would scoop Perel onto his knees the way he did when we were children and his color meant nothing to us. But Charlie apparently saw the same blood-soaked blanket I saw and retreated to his room. The next thing I remember, I was in the slaughterhouse dialing the Long-a-coming police. In first aid class we were told to dial the police in an emergency, not the ambulance squad. The ambulance squad would only tell you to call the police and you would waste precious time. Vaguely, I wondered if the Long-a-coming police had earned the reputation their name suggested.

"My brother . . . ran over my sister . . . with a truck," I said into the receiver. *And the dish ran away with the spoon,* my kindergarten teacher sang in my ear.

"A toy truck or a real truck?" the female voice asked. None of this was real, and it wasn't happening to me. It was happening to someone else, a girl my age, a frightened doppelgänger, who had been asked to play Brantzche Szuster for an episode of *The Twilight Zone.* Absurdly, I answered, "A real truck." The voice requested information, my name, age, address, directions to the farm. You would think Jake's Poultry Farm had only just materialized out of thin air, and that the Szusters hadn't lived in Long-a-coming for eighteen years. Through the phone I heard the emergency siren and then its resounding wail across our neighbor's wheat field. Now the whole town knew calamity had upset the boring peace of Long-a-coming.

"My sister's hurt bad," I said. I was startled by the calm tone of my voice. If I got upset, the police wouldn't come. They would think I was a prankster and would ignore me. The woman's voice replied, "Okay, dear. Somebody already called this in." Her receiver clicked in my ear, and I yelled into the buzzing phone, "Wait! That's impossible! You don't understand! Nobody's here except me!" Air pumped my heart, blood circulated through my lungs. How could I still be alive? Perel would bleed to death. Everything was beyond my control.

The nonsense you think of in a crisis. I remembered those moments of silent meditation in fourth grade after the government banned prayer, and how I begged God to get me through the day without crying. That minute I couldn't cry even though I wanted to. A knock at the slaughterhouse screen door. "Hello? Anybody there?" I looked through the screen mesh and faced a young woman with slightly slanted eyes and a blond Prince Valiant haircut. Why couldn't *she* be under the blanket instead of Perel?

"My name's Lucy," she said, (or Linda; I don't remember). She waved two fingers at me. "I was driving by on the Pike and my daughter, uh, she saw what happened." The woman opened the door and touched my arm. "Is he all right? I called an ambulance. That man in the truck—is he related to you?" Lucy babbled on and on in a thick Philly accent: "folks . . . telephone . . . you live here alone . . . blankets . . . gauze . . ." How could anyone have seen what happened? Who was the "he" she mentioned? I wanted to ask, but curiosity was inappropriate now. In fact, it seemed to me what it had always seemed to Perel: forbidden. I didn't want to go outside. I didn't want this stranger's solicitude or her advice. And I was afraid of the police. Was I a criminal? Was Sheiye?

I dreaded Mama and Papa. God, I wished they would crash on the way home. But I needed them to set things right, to make everything safe again. I had to find Sheiye, that bastard.

I stepped past Lucy and wandered to the truck. The tread on the rear right-hand tire was splotched with blood and flecked with something yellow. I thought, *When Perel comes downstairs*—What was I thinking? I forced myself to look across the driveway. Charlie was propping his pillow under Perel's head and drawing his dingy blanket up to her neck. I saw Perel's brown hair; maybe it was Charlie's arm. Charlie flapped out his yellowed handkerchief and the cellophane tobacco pouch landed on Perel's face. He picked it up, smeared the blood against his pants, and stuffed the valued pouch into his pocket. Slowly, he wiped Perel's forehead. Black Jesus, heal my sister and I'll believe as the people of Long-a-coming.

I looked into the truck. It was empty.

Sheiye was still missing when the cops pulled up with an entourage of curiosity hounds. In no time, the driveway looked as merry as the Assumption Parish on July Fourth. Teenagers admired one another's souped-up jalopies, and acquaintances promised to meet later for a game of Bingo. A few people circled Perel and Charlie, demanding that everyone (but themselves) "stand back and give her some air." The sidelines spectators wrinkled their noses and refused to approach Perel's body. One of them—a boy named Mario, who had distinguished himself in junior high school by smoking cigarettes on the school bus—said loudly to the blond, flat-headed son of a chicken customer, "This is as close as I get to blood!" You and me both, his friend agreed. Mario added, "We used to buy chickens here, but we don't anymore." Us neither, said the blond. I didn't understand what chickens had to do with my sister, but I knew what the boys intended by this vicious non sequitur. I hated and envied them: dallying critics of pain and freshly dressed poultry, with an option to remain indifferent.

"Who lives here?" a blue-suited cop called out. I heard a volley of "she does and he does" from the townspeople as they pointed at me and Charlie. Lucy ushered me to a tall policeman with a "This way, honey; it'll be all right; just tell the policeman what happened." God help me, I felt extraneous, a walk-on. This wasn't even my tragedy. The people of Long-a-coming belonged in south Jersey. I didn't. They had every right to be on Jake's Poultry Farm, but I was a resident intruder. Now I saw that neither I nor Perel nor Charlie counted for much in our misery. Hadn't I learned that from the many accidents I had witnessed on the Pike?

I looked into the policeman's eyes. He was handsome in a dark, clichéd way: wavy black hair, hazel eyes, and pearly white teeth. While Perel lay dying and Charlie, not I, tended her wounds, I became hypnotized by the young policeman's parted lips, the perspiration rolling from his forehead into his eyes. I recognized the face, the jaw sharpened by age, the hair slightly longer to suit the fashion of the day. He was the boy I had seen years ago in the cemetery, grown up now with slender hips, a ghost come to claim me but finding my sister instead, the same policeman I saw at the July Fourth parade. I felt myself fix on him as my savior.

"Officer Lemons here," he said, nodding his head up and down. He was probably no more than twenty or twenty-one, yet to my fifteen-year-old mind, those few years' difference between us invested him with wisdom and finesse. He smiled down at me and asked my name. "Brenda," I answered, and the sound of my English name in Yiddish-speaking territory enhanced my feeling that nothing was really happening to me, Brantzche, but to a stranger named Brenda.

"Can you tell me what happened, Brenda?" Lemons asked. I thought, *This guy's gonna be chief of the New Jersey State Police one day. He's smooth and knows how to pretend kindness.* All those years I had lavished attention on the image of that dark boy in the cemetery—and now I felt irritation mix with my attraction for him. He was a fake. And I was disgusting. My sister was dying, and I wanted Officer Lemons to fall in love with me.

"We were playing hide-'n'-seek," I began. A little girl playing games, that's how he would regard me. From the corner of my eye, I saw a line of blood snake alongside the blanket. My lust was impertinent, and I felt ashamed. "Is she all right?" I asked Officer Lemons, and though I was desperate to hear him say yes, I felt I was posturing.

Without actually looking, I realized Charlie was pulling his blanket over Perel's head. "What are you doing? She'll suffocate!" I cried. Charlie looked at a ladybug or tick or something in the grass. He patted the tobacco pouch and headed back to his room. Lucy put her arm around my shoulders and soothed me with a "There, there, now." The red sun in the west shone through Lucy's hair and her blondness appalled me. Perel gone? Dead? But no one really tried to save her. What about mouth-to-mouth resuscitation? How about cardiopulmonary rescue?

"Did you see?" a man cried, and coughed into his hand. "Her guts. They're in her mouth."

I didn't want to listen anymore. I wanted to walk away, but I was afraid to disobey the cop. *The crowd is going to stone me,* I thought, *just like in "The Lottery."* Just because I happened to draw the wrong lot. What the hell happened? Life was supposed to get better for the Szusters: for my parents, who had suffered enough for one lifetime; and for their children, who were supposed to vindicate the crimes of the past by being happy. History wasn't finished abusing us.

"You were playing hide-'n'-seek. And?" Officer Lemons waited for me to continue. He touched my elbow and directed me to his car. "Too many people," he whispered to a fellow cop. The townspeople followed us like chicken hawks, plaguing me with a dozen "How did it happens." Lemons said, "Just give us a couple of minutes alone, folks." Yeah, and tonight you can all gossip about those weird, self-destructive Jews over a beer and a hand of rummy.

Lemons opened his door and motioned me around to the other side. He didn't even open the door for me. Sitting in the police car, listening to the CB static, I told Lemons how Sheiye plowed through the lawn, but I couldn't admit he ignored my signal. "He didn't know Perel was under there," I said. "It was an accident. It's not his fault." I protected Sheiye from the police as I had years ago from my mother when he threw a rusted bolt at my face. I loathed my brother, but I couldn't damn his moral recklessness before this angular, Christian face. My stomach turned, and I didn't know if I was revolted by Sheiye's act of murder or by my attraction to Officer Lemons's dark complexion.

"Where is Steve now?" Lemons asked.

Had I told him my brother's name? I didn't remember. "I knew your brother from All-State Orchestra," Lemons explained. "Myself, I played trumpet in high school. Nice guy, Steve. A little on the shy side. Steve's a bone player, isn't he?"

"I don't know where he is," I said.

"You don't know where he is," Lemons echoed, pondering some precedent, perhaps, in his short career to guide him now. A glimmer of compassion flickered in his eyes and he patted my wrist.

But then his professional glaze resurfaced and Officer Lemons wanted to know where my parents were and when I expected them home. My parents. Maybe at that moment my mother was sitting in the car, singing a Yiddish melody, one she remembered from her youth or learned from the *Bagels and Lox Show* on Sunday-morning Philadelphia radio. Maybe Papa was bellowing along, running her off key. Maybe they had stopped by a roadside vegetable market, Papa sampling a ripe watermelon that he couldn't resist buying, and Mama daydreaming about a row of petunias in her mother's flower garden. Papa mentioned some financial matter and together they had worried about the extra hundred chickens they had slaughtered without the security of a negotiated order.

"They'll be home six-thirty, seven," I finally answered.

Lemons detected the mournful sound of my voice and said, "Poor kid. It ain't gonna be easy for you."

Don't pity me, I heard Perel sing in Dion's 1950s voice. "Or Steve," I said. Why did I include him? I was hating him with all my strength.

"Speak of the devil," Lemons said. He opened his door and got out. Sheiye was coming down the path with a walking stick in his hand. The Jersey Devil with his pitchfork. How apt. And how unfortunate that I never asked the cop about that morning in the cemetery when he looked like a raccoon and ever since became the dark face that guided my hand at night.

As Sheiye limped into lawful society the townspeople collectively nudged one another and pointed at him. As they strode towards my brother, two policemen motioned the crowd with upraised hands to stay where they were. I didn't know if I was allowed out of the police car. Would they take Sheiye and me in as accused killers? The CB made unintelligible grunts about the "Szuster farm" and "westbound side of the White Horse Pike," and I cocked my ear to it to hear what was happening in my backyard. I watched Sheiye. He was standing near the truck with the two cops and Lemons, gesticulating as he spoke. How could he attempt to make sense of anything? The police finally couldn't restrain the townspeople from swarming around him; nor could they blockade the driveway from passersby, attracted by the flash of police lights. What a moment for my brother, who hid in his bedroom at the very sight of an egg customer. I wanted the crowd to lynch him.

Officer Lemons had stood silently alongside his two police buddies. I guess he preferred his own limelight, because he soon turned and walked back towards me. A sensitive individual, I thought, I hoped, coming to comfort the frail, suffering Brenda. Lemons rested his forearm on the open window of the car door. "Honey, you don't have to sit inside and boil," he said. I was irritated by his nonspecific "honey" but did what he commanded, simply because I did not know the next move.

I walked around to the driver's side. Lemons looked past me to the slaughterhouse and said, "Your brother claims you didn't signal him."

"I did!" But I held back from calling Sheiye a liar. I didn't want to be accountable for Sheiye's life behind bars and could not bring myself to incriminate him. "He didn't see me, but I waved at him. I know I did!" Lemons's lack of interest in me didn't frustrate my attraction, but his lack of faith in me did. "Okay, honey, okay," Lemons said. "Let's go talk to him."

"I don't want to talk to him," I said. Until then my mind and limbs were sluggish, but Lemons's suggestion broke the spell. He backed off a bit. "You don't have to talk," he said. "You can stay here or in the car, if you want."

As a group, the townspeople were less threatening than

they had been as individuals, but I still couldn't face them. Yet I couldn't stay in the car, either, with the CB crackling indecipherably. As I opened the door, that kid Mario and his blond pal approached me and asked point-blank, "Szuster, how did it happen?" I didn't answer them or anyone else. Lamely, I wondered if I could turn Mario in for illegally smoking on a school bus. Maybe there was no statute of limitations for a petty crime committed five years earlier. That's what happens on Judgment Day: Everyone else's guilt seems puny compared to your own. I had nothing on Mario.

When I found myself patting Bolero, I realized that only seconds before I had been wandering around the driveway in circles. I stood over the zinnias in Mama's flower garden, watching yellow jackets and bumblebees flit from flower to flower. I yanked at the semihorizontal cellar door to make sure it was locked. I looked at the yellow Jersey license plates on the cars in the driveway and tried to make out pronounceable words. I was hoping for a sign from God, understanding full well that my prayerful search confirmed just how utterly diminished my circumstances were.

I headed for the middle coop to hear God's voice, figuring that if a divine presence were concentrated anywhere on the farm, it would be there. Every Sukkos my father built a *sukkah* onto the coop's southern wall to commemorate the temporary dwellings of the Jews in exile from Israel. It was worth a try. I pressed my forehead against the cinder block. My brow hurt from the prickly surface, but that was necessary. God wouldn't notice me if I weren't in obvious pain. A rustle in the grass. Two tiny frogs leapfrogged around my ankles, ignorant of the peril my feet threatened. My faith had never been more tensile, or more puerile: I fully expected to see my sister break through the crowd and shout at me, "That war a close one, Luster!"

I spun around to see the police, medics, and townspeople thirty feet away, still scurrying around Perel's body. The madness before my eyes remained unaltered except for one detail: I saw Charlie's head rocking to and fro, framed by the annex window. With one hand he tucked a bottle of Cold Duck between his lips; with the other he pressed against the glass. Charlie's brown fingers, webbed on the windowpane, obliterated God from my sight.

Lucy spied me by the coop and hurried towards me, dragging her daughter, with her. Holding the squirming girl by the wrist, she gazed into my eyes and said, "You'll be better off in the long run if you look at her now. It'll help you forget."

I opened my mouth to tell her to leave me alone. But her daughter, still wriggling inside her mother's grasp, made me stop short. The child's hands were screwed into her wrists at a 180-degree angle, twisted into useless petals of flesh and bone. Her deformity reminded me of chickens afflicted with Newcastle disease, their necks perpetually contorted upwards, forced to contemplate the heavens till the day they died.

Maybe Lucy had accepted her own grief by staring it down every day, or maybe she was simply a harbinger of self-encounter philosophy. Whatever the case, all I wanted was to be anywhere else in the world. I knew this was the suffering I had envied my parents for, and for half an irrational second, I felt relieved that the waiting was over. But when I recovered my bearings, I knew I had gotten tragedy instead of destiny. For I had expected to view apocalypse without crumpling under its fallout. Up until that moment, my parents' tales of survival had done little more than fuel my self-emancipation fantasies of entrapment and escape. At best, staying alive was a question of odds, of monitoring the whereabouts of a predator, and sidestepping it in the nick of time. With Perel gone, I had the sickening realization that survival meant coming out the victor by chance, not by destiny or individual cunning. The Szusters were merely like the other creatures on the farm —chickens, earthworms, dogs—who, on suspending their vigilance for a second, succumbed to a greater, more confident power.

I felt something smack my elbow. It was the little girl's hand. She jumped up and down, delighted to have caught me off guard. I was surprised that she could make my skin smart.

"Heather! I want you to apologize to this poor lady," Lucy said. I felt like an eight-year-old, an orphan, a classmate of Heather's, and her mother was breaking up one of our fights. "Why did you do that?" the woman asked, puzzled by her daughter's unaccountable blow. Lucy touched my arm, and I recoiled. "A love pat," she chuckled. "Children are so violent. I reckon she'll outgrow it."

I looked over Lucy's shoulder at the weak smile on Sheiye's face and thought that Heather would become more herself as she got older, and occasionally that meant wantonly disregarding all self-restraint in the pursuit of love.

18

🌿 ONE MONTH LATER, Mama was still sobbing. Her despair was static, like the woe of female comic strip characters who boo-hoo from frame to frame. She couldn't control herself; recovery meant forgetting, and that was a sin against Perel's memory. Mama had practiced this sort of devotion towards her own dead family for over twenty-five years, so her reflex for grief was well tuned.

Perel's death became the new holocaust in the Szuster family—or, more accurately, it extended the old one. After *shive* week, my parents began brooding over the events leading up to the accident, just as they had previously racked their memory over prewar Kritnetse and Uchan. They cursed the truck's breakdown, blamed themselves for making the trip to Buena Vista on Thursday instead of Friday morning, argued over who was more guilty, Sheiye or me. I was dumbfounded by the picayune things that obsessed Mama and Papa. For example, when they pulled into the driveway that day, a medic was wrapping Sheiye's foot with an Ace bandage. Not that Sheiye was seriously injured, but the medics wanted to feel useful since they couldn't do anything for Perel. What Mama and Papa remember, though, was me clutching none other than Rodney MacDuff, the *real* Rodney MacDuff, our former piano teacher. I had heard a familiar rasping voice saying, "Oh my, oh my," again and again, the way it did when we mauled "Für Elise." And exultant that Rodney MacDuff's voice was Perel doing her Rodney MacDuff imitation, I turned, saw him, and threw myself around his bony ribs. I didn't want Rodney MacDuff's consolation; he came for the thrill, the way everyone else did. I wanted Perel, and for that second, he was Perel. I tried to explain this to Mama and Papa, but they insisted that Perel's death gave me an excuse to "smooch" with a *sheygits.* I never rigorously contested their condemnation. Although they didn't understand that it is sometimes easier to touch the less desirable of two men, the fact is, they had my number. They just didn't get the right man.

Papa, meanwhile, berated me for acting like a *luftmensch* — an "airhead," in modern jargon. One of the cops, not Lemons, asked me to find Perel's birth certificate. I don't know why he needed it, but I was so afraid I was a criminal, I did what I was told. I opened the screen door to the kitchen and came upon my father. He was standing in a semistaggered position, supporting himself with one hand against the kitchen table, *daven*ing from his *siddur.* He was crying, a muscular man with a baseball cap on his head, spit and tears on his cheek and chin. Depend on the *nahr* to *shtip.* I smiled. "They want Perel's birth certificate," I said, and concentrated my will on the corners of my mouth to keep from laughing. My father took a swing at my face and cried, *"Vus hoste getin?"* What did you do? I ducked in time. He hated me for being alive. Or maybe he had lost the wrong daughter. *"Aroys!"* he shouted, and came after me the way he chased escaped chickens. I ran to the field where Perel and I had once buried a dead kitten aboveground in a plastic bag to keep it from decomposing. A few hours later, after the cops and townspeople had left, Papa sent Charlie to fetch me. I don't remember if Charlie was drunk because I didn't look at him once. After *shive,* Papa harped on the irony that I wanted Perel's birth certificate when she was dead. *Herst, aza mishigas!*

Papa never lifted a finger against me after that, and

neither did Mama. Physical abuse made sense to them only as long as they believed it could even a score, and that, obviously, was impossible. Moreover, my parents were afraid of Sheiye and me, two murderers belatedly penitent; and they did not even want to touch us in passing. Perel's death only proved that their children didn't compensate for the murders of the previous generation but, rather, reenacted them.

An inquest might have pinpointed blame, but there wasn't any. My parents pleaded with the police to forgo an investigation, and declined the family counseling that a county hospital offered. The only visitor they agreed to see was the rabbi from the Conservative synagogue in Camden where Perel, Sheiye, and I had attended Hebrew school, and even he came only once or twice. With the world and their children deemed blood vandals, Mama and Papa commandeered the right to interpret Perel's death.

Mornings after slaughter were unbearable. *"Di host zekh git ungefresn bam shive-zitsn! Khazer!"*—You really fed your face at *shive!* Pig!—Mama railed at me one morning before I left for school. I don't know how she could see through her flood of tears during *shive,* but our eyes met once while I tried to eat a bagel and lox. What a fluke she caught me when she did: My belly was ravenous, but I couldn't get the food down. I could chew twenty times before swallowing and feel the food start to come up again. I could ignore the hunger by day, but not by night; often I would sleep for only two hours and then wake up shaking. If I went downstairs to the kitchen, I would disturb my parents. I finally stashed a box of Manische-witz Tam Tams behind my bed and munched on the dry crackers late into the night.

Ironically, it was the Day of Rest that especially tormented my parents. Mama and Papa's weekday insights tumbled around the Shabbos Queen's white lace ankles, and together they examined the week's obsessive brooding. The Shabbos Queen tried her best to replace my parents' hysteria with sadness, but they weren't ready for reflective grief. I would lie on Perel's bed and listen to their voices groan, shush, and grumble. Sobs and repeated cries for "Perele" were interspersed among the muffled words. If I dared come downstairs, my mother greeted me with, "You were jealous of Perel, weren't you?" I would demand, "Are you accusing me of doing Perel in on purpose?" Silence. In disgust, Papa commanded me to *daven*. *"Oy, hosti bagangn a nivayre! Got zol dir nor moykhl zahn!"* he said. You commited such a sin! I only hope God forgives you!

Why did they presume I could have prevented the accident? I didn't drive the truck. I didn't set Perel up to die. I was only a witness. On Shabbos I refused to look at the *siddur,* but continued the echoing monologues to the cavern inside me that I suspected was God or my soul. The sound of Perel's name on my parents' lips damned me, and I damned myself. Though I tried not to listen, sometimes I heard God's damnation too.

Sheiye spent every Shabbos locked in his room. He could have stayed at Glassboro State, where he had now started college, but he came home weekends. I tried to imagine him resting his elbows on his mattress, his chin in both hands, staring out the window at the truck. A hardback calculus textbook was open to page ten. Sheiye might try to work, but Perel's face, round and scornful one minute, twisted into a chicken's squawk the next, inevitably pushed derivatives from his mind. My brother reached for the Bible, arbitrarily opened it to some page, lost faith, and turned to a paperback on UFOs in Oregon. If Sheiye had ever considered the possibility that he was responsible for Perel's death, he never let on to Mama, Papa, me, or anyone else. He strode out of his room, belt undone, socks stretched half off his feet, his sloppiness a defiant sign that he need not dress respectfully during mourning because he didn't have a death on his head.

I think Rosh Hashanah coincided with Shabbos that September. Maybe not. Maybe the grimness of the Jewish New Year only reminded me of Shabbos. Traditionally, Papa and Sheiye prayed in Camden with Mr. Berg, the *shoykhet.* For years Papa had hustled himself and his son off to the Orthodox synagogue every Rosh Hashanah and Yom Kippur, claiming the field of atonement as male territory. No amount of pleading from Perel or me ever gained us admission to "Papa's *shil.*" Instead we were enrolled part time in the Conservative synagogue's Hebrew school for the ostensible reason that it was closer to the farm. It was—by two miles. That year, though, Mama refused to be alone, which meant with me. So Sheiye *daven*ed upstairs in his room, assuming he wasn't faking; Mama *daven*ed in the living room, mixing her prayers with lamentations for Perel's soul; Papa paced the kitchen wrapped in his yellowing *talis,* dabbing tears with the fringes; and I sat on the piano bench where Perel and I had prayed on holidays and *Shabbosim* since childhood. Privately, each one of us read in Hebrew and English Sarah's command to Abraham: "Cast out this bondwoman and her son: for the son of this bondwoman shall not be heir with my son, even with Isaac." And we read of the "he-goat for a sin offering, to make atonement for you"; and about the sorrowful Hannah, whose womb the Lord had shut up. On the day of communal repentance, the Szusters had never been more atomized.

After I searched the *machzor* for words of forgiveness, I decided to head to Perel's room; sometimes I thought I still detected her smell on the sheets. I got by Papa, who faced the slaughterhouse while he prayed, but as I passed Mama in the living room, she asked, "Where do you think you're going?" Her eyes, usually darkened by fatigue or reminiscence, were pink like a rabbit's. A white handkerchief was hidden under her *machzor,* wrinkled by the weight of God's word and Mama's despair. She wore a long-sleeved navy-blue polyester dress with no ornamentation, not even the gold bracelet she stored next to Elijah's silver wine cup and her diaphragm. The curtained windows and dark green of the abundant houseplants struggled to engulf Mama in their shadows; but her skin against the room and the dark fabric was lambent. I had felt this same mixture of rage and pity towards her thousands of times before. I turned my eyes away. "I'm going upstairs," I said.

"We're eating in half an hour," Mama said. Lost was the look of the hunted. Mama made the announcement as if she were issuing a military mobilization. I lifted my foot to the first step. "Afterwards we're walking to the field," and her voice cracked. My family had made a custom of walking to the railroad tracks on holidays when Papa couldn't make it to Camden, and 1968 would be no exception.

"I'm not going," I said.

"Yes you are!" Mama sobbed into the handkerchief. Her fingers fumbled through the *machzor,* seeking the prayer for the dead. Upstairs, I opened the door to Perel's room. Without thinking, I touched the rip in my blouse, the symbol of mourning I had to wear for a few more days. Perel's presence lingered in her room, the field, and the woods, and those places gave me leave to cry. Elsewhere—the rest of the house, school, the slaughterhouse—I held back. By September, I knew my misery stemmed as much from my imprisonment among the ever-judging Szusters as from the loss of my sister.

אָ

Shabbos and religious holidays were the only days we all ate together. My parents insisted on it. The five Szusters had never enjoyed a convivial atmosphere at mealtime, what with Sheiye's rant about Messiahs from outer space and Mama's overdone pot roast. But the reduction in our numbers turned routine squabbling into combat. Mama and Papa defended themselves behind one fortress, Sheiye behind his, I behind mine. Those meals disabused me of the idea that people seek each other's company for reasons of pleasure. Amazed, I watched Mama, Papa, Sheiye, and myself lob rounds of condemnation at one another, fighting with a spirit of determination I have never since reexperienced. It reminded me of the times Sheiye beat me up, and our mutual hatred made me tingle. And always on my mind was the unasked question: "How would Mama and Papa be reacting if *I* had been under the blanket?"

Papa sat in Charlie's corner seat; Mama nearest the stove; Sheiye and I across from each other. Mama served the chicken soup, with torn chunks of challah sinking to the bottom of the bowl. Even though I was starving, I knew merely by looking at it that I could never finish it. Avoiding the food, I got up to wash my hands at the sink and swayed with hunger. Seated again, I couldn't eat. "You gave me too much," I complained.

"You're eating Perel's portion too," Mama said.

"Give it to Sheiye," I retorted. I hadn't looked Sheiye in the eye for a week.

"I'm sure Perel would want you to have it," Sheiye said.

"You don't know anything about what she'd want." I looked at the soggy challah disintegrating in the hot, oily broth. Why couldn't Mama let us decide what we wanted to do with our challah?

Papa backed Mama. "Don't give her anything else until she finishes."

"Hey, that's hardly a threat in this house," Sheiye said.

"Don't make like we agree on anything, Sheiye," I said. "I never want to be on the same side of the fence as you."

"Don't worry, Brantzche. We're not."

Mama started to cry. Squinting his eyes at us, Papa asked, "Why do you have to keep upsetting *di mame?*" He examined a wedge of homemade pickle. Papa loved bottling his garden cucumbers, but now he wrinkled his nose at the slice on his fork. I wondered if he questioned whether the small joys of living would ever compensate for the destruction that had tailed him from Uchan to Long-a-coming. It had all been reckless destruction, as if God had faltered in His capacity to distinguish between the wrongdoers and the blameless.

Mama leaned away from the pots on the gas range and blew her nose. She forked pieces of boiled chicken and carrots onto five plates.

Sheiye said, "Tell us what to do to make Mama stop crying. We'll do it."

"Speak for yourself," I said.

"You've always been bitter!" Mama sniffled. "That's why you've always been skinny." She dropped a chicken wing next to a thigh on my plate, hoping perhaps that a gain in weight, however temporary, would fatten my resentment into confession. And, as part of her new ritual, she placed a plate with a small chicken wing on it where Perel used to sit.

"You'd be bitter in my position too," I said.

"Skinny too," Sheiye mumbled.

"*Di mame* is in a worse position," Papa said. "Do you know what it means for a mother to lose a child?" Mama cupped her forehead in her hand. The simple truth of Papa's words momentarily left her tearless.

"*Di mame* is in the worst position," Sheiye agreed.

"You're just guessing how rotten people feel because you don't feel anything yourself," I said.

The three of them had advanced to the boiled chicken while I was still working on the soup. I pictured myself in the kitchen ten years thence, staring into a moldy bowl.

"Brantzche," Papa said. *"Ven veste shoyn vern a laht?"* When are you going to be a *mensh?*

"When you believe me."

Sheiye slammed down his fork. "Mama and Papa don't believe liars!"

"Don't think I can't see what you're doing!" I yelled across the table. "Go ahead. Get mad every time you hear the truth. It doesn't change the fact that you were driving the truck!"

"And it doesn't change the fact that you didn't signal!"

"I signaled. I signaled! I signaled," I said. I pushed the soup away from me. "That's the truth, and you can do whatever you want with it."

"Sometime when we're alone," said Sheiye, "I'll tell you what I'll do with it."

"A vort keygn a vort," Papa said, shaking his head. Word against word. *"Kinder,* it's Rosh Hashanah."

I know Papa meant to signify a beginning, however doubtful. But his sigh suggested an epitaph for the Szuster family. Papa tore off a piece of challah, but his nine-fingered grip was momentarily weak, and the bread landed on the fifth, untouched plate of chicken. He tugged at the twisted loaf again and succeeded. Spreading a few drops of honey on it, he chanted in Ashkenazic Hebrew, "Blessed art Thou O Lord Our God, King of the Universe, Who bestoweth upon us the sweetness of Thy new year." Papa widened his small eyes and stared at the bottle of Manischewitz wine. He ate his challah, handed Mama and Sheiye theirs, and placed a small portion alongside Perel's plate. Even though I hadn't finished my soup, Papa passed me the fifth piece. I wondered which had predated which, my bitterness or my skinniness.

Mama took the lead to the railroad tracks, kicking dust up into the hem of her dress. She was breathing quickly, undermined by the small steps that detained her purpose. Beneath her jacket she clasped something to her stomach, as if the pressure on that item would keep her guts from spilling to the ground. Pausing by a tall pine tree, its upper half long withered from a bolt of lightning, Mama stooped and withdrew a cellophane packet from under her jacket. Inside the cellophane was the piece of chicken from Perel's ghost plate. She must have already ritualized these offerings: several bug-chewed pieces of plastic and some chicken bones lay scattered about. She propped the chicken on a rock nearby and started crying. Papa walked ahead and asked God the value of human suffering. Sheiye put his arm around Mama's shoulders, but she shook it off. A breeze blew through the top of the tree and tiny dried twigs rained down on us. I pulled my sweater closer to my body, driving hunger deeper into my spine. I hadn't made much headway with my food, and now Perel's chicken looked appetizing. We walked on to the woods, single file.

I always expect some sign of recognition from places revisited. But the steel power station grinned imbecilically into the sun's face, oblivious to the four Szusters at its base. A generator inside the station's bowels tripped on, humming noisily, and I covered my ears at the sound of a heart wound in the wrong direction.

What could my mother have been thinking? That she had not yet laundered Perel's clothing for storage, that her husband's first major purchase in their new country was twenty-three acres of land in Long-a-coming, New Jersey, bought without her knowledge; that together they built a slaughterhouse with their own hands. Mama's eyes fluttered as the afterimage of the power station cast gray bars across her family's faces. My ears were still covered when Mama fainted dead away, striking her husband's cheek before she hit the ground.

Papa and Sheiye roused her with exhortations in Yiddish and a few light smacks to her face. As she came to, she shielded her eyes, either from the glare of the power station or from her unwilling return to consciousness. "It's better where I was," she moaned.

I followed behind the two men as they escorted Mama back to the house. I was so afraid of her tidal grief that I walked a good twenty paces behind, wondering what Sparsely and Saucer would make of all this. When I stopped at the sound of a train whistle, Mama halted, and the three of them waited for me to catch up.

I wanted them all to disappear, especially Mama. For the thousandth time since Perel's death, I saw my mother doubled over and dry-heaving *Raboyne shel oylem,* God in Heaven, into her palms, as she and Papa made their way past me and Rodney MacDuff; and then blood all over Mama's blue-flowered dress. Maybe if I had kissed Mama on that Rosh Hashanah, things would be different today. But I realized that once I caressed her, I would be locked into a ritual of offering solace to her the rest of my life. I said, "I wish I were on that train right now."

Sheiye said "little girl" and shook his head. Papa clenched his thumbless fist and dug it into his side. Mama shrank away from me, pressing into the two men's chests, as if she could catch my insensitivity like a germ. Papa said, "Brantzche, when it's time to leave the farm, we'll let you know."

19

BY NOVEMBER, THERE WERE DAYS when I couldn't believe that Perel had ever been alive. Every morning I woke with the sense that I had been cheated, and in that moment before total consciousness, I couldn't remember why. Fully awake, I would whisper Perel's name into the sheets again and again to reassert her presence, but I only ended up with a string of nonsense syllables. To make my sister real, I tried to impose some connecting logic on a series of sequential but unrelated events, mapping out the decisive moments of her childhood: her bout with chicken pox, which had left two small scars on her left temple; the night she bit down on a charm bracelet and caught the clasp in her gums; the time I shoved a toothbrush down her throat. While no one of these clues to Perel's fate was telling in and of itself, I believed they all combined to presage her ultimate fate. Superstitiously, I concluded that the warning signs had been many and literal, and I had simply ignored them.

In searching for some persuasive explanation for Perel's death, I considered, of course, Sheiye. For him, I could not conjure up a history of sympathetic details. I could not remember his childhood illnesses, his telltale scars, not even one outburst of tears. I decided that he had had no use for those gratuitous impressions of everyday life which so engaged my attention; they had eluded him, for he concentrated his imagination on one objective only: violence. Convinced of the infallibility of my conclusion, I hated Sheiye more than ever.

But beneath this rage festered the belief that my brother and I were bound to each other, and in the past, Sheiye had taken pains to ensure our intimacy. That thought, more than any other, sickened me. I did not want to learn one more secret from him; I did not even care any longer to hear his confession of guilt. Desperately, I wanted to cut every last tie with him. And that's when I remembered the gallows and the bond Sheiye had established there between him, Perel, and me.

The first Shabbos in November, I wrapped myself in one of Perel's old jackets and got a book of matches from Charlie's room. I expected the room to look dramatically different because Perel was dead, but it was as it had been: the nicotine-stained playing cards in petrified red-and-black solitaire, the tabloids that smelled of tobacco, the girlie calendar, with the brown arm of November's Indian-feathered model draped around a snowman. I stuffed the matches into a hole in the jacket lining, shut the door, and put Charlie out of my mind.

Peeking into the open archway of my parents' bedroom, I found Mama and Papa clutching each other, eyes half open, their double bed anchoring them to the port of Shabbos. The sound of cars on the Pike, honking their horns to celebrate the latest win of the high school football team, had lulled them into fitful sleep, but just then a dragster squealing his wheels jolted Mama from the few minutes of peace she had wrested from the unceasing drone of memory. She whispered to Papa to check on me. "Brantzche!" Papa shouted from the bed. I tiptoed into the living room and said I was reading. Lately, Papa had taken to calling out my name like a drill sergeant whenever I was home. If he didn't find me upstairs, he would stomp outside and chastise me with a sharp *"Arahn in shtib!"* Get inside! If he found me in the kitchen, he would demand to know why I hadn't answered. *"Aroys fin shtib!"*—Get out! —he'd order. His arbitrariness fueled my resentment, but deep down I believed I was getting my just deserts for never having honored my mother and father.

Outside, Bolero started barking when he saw me. Ever since the accident, he had been barking more, if only because he hadn't gotten off his leash much. I stroked his coat, pleading with him not to frighten the turkeys in the pen on the other side of the coop, explaining that he had to stay put because it was hunting season and he could get shot in the woods. In a state of near-panic, I ran down the path until I couldn't hear Bolero anymore; I turned around several times to make sure no one was following me. Out of breath, I swore aloud to God that if He granted me communication with Perel, I would believe in Him. If I had to undergo some trial, like touching a snake, or to perform a miracle, like teaching Bolero to talk, fine, I would do it. I waited for a response, but all I heard was gunshot from the woods and a rustle in the weeds as spent bullet shells hit the ground. I realized that a bullet could easily knock into my brain and kill me. A *kleynikeyt,* a trifle, compared to facing my parents every day till I graduated from high school. Besides, I prided myself on not being afraid. Racing to the gallows, I thought that if Perel's death had accomplished nothing else, at least I would never feel fright again. Anything less than death didn't deserve a shudder.

Several false turns brought me to the brown cedar rivulets of Atsion Lake. I had walked too far into the woods. I retraced my steps for a mile, meeting two or three hunters along the way who scolded me for not wearing red or orange clothing. One middle-aged man with deep furrows in his brow said he had already taken aim at my gray jacket when he realized a girl, not a doe, stood in his rifle's bull's-eye. Fingers shaking, he handed me a red-and-white-striped kerchief from his back pants pocket and begged me to go home. I covered my hair with the kerchief, tied the ends together under my chin, and thanked him.

I had missed the gallows by a few feet—and no wonder, for as I came upon it, it looked different. Hung trussed to the crossbar was a deer, shotgunned and still bleeding from a bullet hole through the heart. Involuntarily, I cried out, deceived by preconception, for I saw that the gallows itself was no real gallows, but rather a rack on which to secure captured game. For the life of me, I couldn't remember if this was the same structure Sheiye had shown Perel and me, or if it had since been tampered with to disguise its malicious purpose. In the four months that had passed, the wood had served as a sounding board for the mundane obscenities of local hikers. A jagged, three-inch-high FUCK YOU was etched into the base, and NIGER COCK into the spine. The stool was still chained to the bottom joint, and was stained brown in places by the rusty links. I thought of Perel sitting on the stool not so long ago, listening to Sheiye's story about Papa. With the dead deer swinging ever so slightly behind me, I sat down and started crying.

In the near distance, empty bullet shells pinged through the air. My pounding heart informed me that I was a fool to be sitting here in the thick of hunting season. My newly found courage was an illusion. For better or worse, I was still alive, and that meant being afraid. If only I had brought a transistor radio with me. The hunters might be annoyed that I was frightening game away, but at least they wouldn't shoot me by mistake. I didn't know what to do. I thought I should abandon my original plan. The dead animal's skin gave off a smell like the inside of our window-locked Chevy on a hot summer day; and the carcass was too heavy for me to untie, even if I had had the stomach to do it. But I remembered our meeting at this site, and all that had happened since, and stubbornly decided to do what I came for.

I reached inside my jacket for the matchbook and started singing "Heat Wave" at the top of my lungs. " 'It's like a heat wave, burnin' in my heart' "; and to commemorate the perversity of Perel's humor, I translated it into Yiddish: *"Hits khvalye! S'brent bey mir in hartsn!"* Crying, I stood up and kicked the gallows at the lowest joint.

"That's all you have to say is 'Fuck you'? Well, fuck you too!" I cried. I charged at the joint, kicking a dozen times. My toes were smarting, but the gallows, groaning with the weight of the deer, didn't even splinter. I brought my eye an inch from the wood. The intensity of Perel's objection to the gallows made me associate it with her, her instinctive rejection of violence. As I talked to the gallows and inspected it, I realized I was trying to wriggle out of my decision to burn it, still mesmerized by the first impression it had made on me.

Calmer now, I backed away and said "Fuck you" again. I struck a match, and the wind blew it out. Sheltering it with my palm, I struck another one and lit a twig. I pressed the burning end gently against the frayed shoelace noose until it caught fire, but a rusted hook blocked the flame from spreading to the wood, and the shoelace ash floated away in the wind.

I looked at the NIGER COCK on the gallows' spine and pronounced "Nigger." I used that word once when I was thirteen: "Why'd you leave me behind with all the niggers?" I had asked Alexandra, the daughter of a fruit grower. She had walked away with some friends, leaving me to tag a bevy of black girls arguing about an unfair goal in our soccer game.

I lit another twig and held it against the seam where crossbar and spine met. As the wood began to smolder, the wind stole an ember from the twig and planted it in the humus.

I stomped on the ground where I thought the ember had landed and returned to the business at hand. But the wood had stopped smoking; my efforts had resulted in only a charcoal bruise. A quarter of my matches were gone. Better to dismantle the gallows and burn it piecemeal. Stuffing the matchbook into the jacket lining, I took my place alongside the deer's bleeding chest, raised my arms, jumped, and hooked my gloved fingers around the crossbar. My thigh brushed against the deer's body, tearing at the bullet wound and unstanching the flow of blood. The left side of my pants was streaked red now, as if brushed with a hasty first coat of paint, and I twisted myself clear of the animal. The wood at the topmost joint cracked from the additional weight and movement; a few furious kicks to tighten my grip, and the crossbar broke off in my hands. I felt the deer's double hooves in my ribs as the carcass and I thudded to the cold ground.

"Lucky you didn't get a hoof up your *tukhes,* little girl!"

Revolted by my contact with the deer and alarmed by the male voice, I choked on a scream. The hunters with their rifles hadn't scared me as much as seeing Sheiye.

"What the fuck are you doing here, Queero?" I said. Scrambling to my feet, I dusted leaves and twigs from my pants and jacket. Deer blood smeared my gloves. "Don't you go to college or something?"

"Inspiring little gallows, eh, crybaby? I see it taught you a new word."

"Gotta run home to Mama every weekend. She's not too bonkers to wash your Fruit of the Looms and fix her usual overcooked delicacies, eh, baby?" Two brown rabbits scampered into their lairs, and I realized I was shouting.

Sheiye sniffed the air and looked down at the fallen deer. "You didn't say you were planning a barbecue. On Shabbos, yet. The folks would love to hear that."

"They don't hear anything these days, in case you haven't noticed," I said.

"Oh, no? They hear me." Sheiye rubbed his bare hand along the deer's crumpled body, avoiding the ravaged chest. "So you finally figured out the reason for your precious gallows, eh, little girl. I really had you going there for a while, didn't I?"

"You're just such a good liar," I said. Motioning to the graffiti, I added, "But I thought for sure you could spell better than that. Did you write this before or after you killed Perel?"

Sheiye took a step towards me. His face was red from the cold air, but now a carmine color inflamed his neck and earlobes. He pulled the woolen flaps out of his hat and pressed them against his ears. "You better cut the shit, little girl, if you know what's good for you," he said. "I'm sick of your lies."

"Lies? You can't stomach the truth, Queero. Well, stomach this: Perel stuck her head out, and you ran her over on purpose."

"You know what I'm beginning to think, Brantzchele, dear? Little miss innocent!" Sheiye bent down and picked up a handful of dried leaves. He flung them at me. I shadowboxed so fiercely I heard my shoulder socket creak.

"Cut it out, you jerk!" I shrieked.

"I'm beginning to think little miss innocent wanted Perel dead. Yeah, that's right. You didn't signal. I never saw you signal."

I lifted my head up like a chicken gobbling rainwater and screamed into the sky, "You arrre a fucking liiiar!" A quail hopped from behind a nearby oak and sped down an animal trail.

In a falsely consoling voice, Sheiye said, "Now, now, dearie. You were jealous of her."

"*You* were jealous of *us. You* felt left out. She couldn't stand you."

"You were jealous 'cause she was smarter," Sheiye said.

"Tell me about it. I was proud of her brains. She could've been anything she wanted. But you put an end to that."

"Yeah, prettier too. Turn you upside down and she could have used you for a floor mop."

"She was not prettier than me." The words jetted out of my mouth as if they were flying to the moon. Come back! Don't land in Sheiye's ears! Yes, Perel was smart, even when she turned her back on curiosity. But I wanted a compensation prize—my thinness, my long, straight blond hair, my blue eyes.

Sheiye said, "Excellent. Dig your own grave, little girl. You were jealous and you're happy she's out of the picture. Now you can be the smart one *and* the pretty one." Sheiye swung an invisible baseball bat and watched the invisible ball fly somewhere out over Atsion Lake. "Victory by default," he said.

"Is that what you came here to tell me, you fuck?" I kicked against the dismembered gallows and then aimed at Sheiye's crotch. He blocked me with his hip and grabbed my foot.

"Whoa, little girl!" Sheiye pushed me into a pine tree, and I landed on my rump. The needles poked my face and I felt my skin tear. Pulling off my glove, I touched my cheek: no blood; just a perforated line of skin flecks I would explain in school as a cat scratch. Sheiye dragged me away from the tree. As I heaved myself upright he flung my hand against my chest. "Personally, little girl, I don't give a flying fuck what you're doing here. *Der tate* sent me to bring you back."

I stooped to retrieve my glove. "Well, tell your father

I'm too far gone, and there's no bringing me back. And do me a favor. Save your brilliant analyses for your guilty conscience." I wiped my nose with my sleeve. The scratch on my cheek burned. Bracing for another attack, I said, "I'll always know you ran over Perel just like you ran over Duchess. Fact: Perel stuck her head out. Fact: I signaled." Neither Sheiye nor I dared compromise. The compromiser would only acknowledge his guilt.

Sheiye lifted a foot on top of the crossbar, lying broken in a pile of leaves. "And I'll tell you something too, Brantzche, and hear me well."

"You're an asshole," I said.

"You can call me whatever you like from now till doomsday, but, sister, you're the one in a sinking boat, not me."

I sat down on the stool and began humming "Heat Wave."

"And do you know why, Brantzchele? Because it don't matter whose fault it is that Perel's dead. Yeah, that's the truth, and that's what you'll never learn. See your gallows? I swear on your *tsehakte* gallows that in one year, Mama and Papa will believe every word of whatever I tell them. You know why? Because they know I love them, and that's all that matters now. That's to my benefit. I love them and you don't. You're all eaten through inside, like termites chewed holes in your heart. I'm no brain, Brantzche, but I can guarantee I'm right."

" 'Can't keep from cryin'. You're tearin' me apart,' " I sang, curling my lips the way Perel used to.

"As for you, Brantzche," Sheiye prophesied, leaning forward at the waist, "you, you're gonna be a whore. A Jew whore. Mark my words."

I pinched my nostrils together and honked. "Lucky for me, queers like you have no use for whores, *yidn* or *goyim*."

Sheiye scooped up a stick and belted me across the arm.

"You can dish it out, but you can't take it, huh, shit-head!" I sprang up from the stool. "Come on! Hit me with your best shot! Knock me off, too!"

Sheiye hurled the stick into my ankles, but I jumped over it. Angry that he had missed, he began slap-fighting me. I tried to predict his next moves, but rage distorted my counterattack, and his wrestling expertise undid me. In two seconds, Sheiye was sitting on my stomach and had my arms pinned behind my back. When I began to scream, he tore the red-and-white-striped kerchief off my head and tried to stuff it in my mouth. My nose was so glopped with tears and mucus, I still didn't smell smoke.

Then a command issued from only ten feet away, spoken in the voice of stoic pity: "All right, that's enough now." Sheiye scrambled off me, clobbering me with his hiking boots, and I stumbled up after him. Facing us were two orange-clad hunters, one middle-aged, the other young, probably his son. For several seconds, nobody uttered a word, and it was difficult to say who was the most embarrassed. I suspected that the hunters were locals and had guessed who we were; for neither one chided us about the deer. The boy, sucking in his lower lip, was scared, his rifle at the ready, it seemed, in self-defense. As the father addressed us, he turned his son's gun barrel to the ground.

"I reckon your folks'll be kinda worried on account of this being hunting season," he said.

"We're sorry about your rack," Sheiye said, and I cringed at his willing share in the blame. "I'll have it fixed for you next week."

"It's nothin'," the man said, painfully sorry for the slanders he had overheard. He shifted uncomfortably, and with a perplexed frown, sniffed the air. Suddenly, without warning, the leaves and underbrush were ablaze. Yellow and blue flames were consuming the humus surrounding the gallows and groping for more solid nourishment. The dismantled lumber of the gallows undulated behind the waves of heat and I thought I smelled the propylene stench of burning animal flesh. The hunters, apparently, had not witnessed my efforts to burn their rack, and were unreservedly shocked, as if Sheiye and I had participated in witchcraft as well as in senseless recrimination. With a gamesman's experienced reflexes, the older man pulled me clear of the flames, warned me in a gentle, almost dreamy voice to stay back, and joined Sheiye and the boy, frantically beating the fire with their jackets. Fortunately, the ground beneath the pine and leaf cover was slightly damp, and in a few minutes Sheiye and the hunters had extinguished the blaze.

Sheiye put on his coat. "Why'dja do it?" he asked me, willing to implicate himself in my vandalism but not in my arson.

"You're big on the accusations today," I grumbled. But I was too humiliated to rebuke Sheiye in front of strangers and said no more.

"What if you had been alone, Brantzche," Sheiye persisted. "Christ Almighty, what would you have done?"

"I didn't set any fire!" My voice squeaked from shyness and fear. I was terrified now of being found out. If Sheiye believed I lied about the fire, he would say I was lying about Perel's death too.

Still saddened by our squabbling, despite the ruination I had nearly caused, the hunter urged us again to go home. His son was crouched over the deer's body, stroking one of its stiffening legs compassionately as if Sheiye and I were responsible for the animal's death.

"At least let me help you with the deer," Sheiye said apologetically. I had never seen him so ingratiating with strangers, and I wondered if he was trying to assert his man-on-the-street normalcy to me.

"All right, you're on," the man said. He had worry lines on his forehead like Chet Huntley on the evening news.

He and Sheiye hoisted the deer onto their backs and shoulders, staggering under its weight, while the son transported the rifles. The boy, about my age, looked at me long and dolefully, as if to complain that people like me—people who did not contemplate the consequences of their whims—caused all the trouble in the world. I tried to memorize his face, but all I remember is the lint in his orange wool cap.

I didn't wait for Sheiye to return from the hunter's truck, parked five hundred feet away on the main path, before heading back to the farm. In a short time, though, he caught up with me, nudging the back of my sneaker with his foot so that I had to restrain myself from hitting him and beginning our combat all over again.

20

EVERY YEAR, IN THE SECOND WEEK of January, the Long-a-coming American Legion presented a Citizenship Award to a "recent deserving high school graduate who has shown achievement in civic affairs." One day late in December, Sheiye got a letter from the American Legion informing him that this year the award was his. The form letter cited Sheiye's "contribution to the high school marching band and wrestling team." Don't ask me what these distinctions had to do with civic achievement. Maybe some patriot had witnessed my torpor that day in August and decided that "the little Szuster girl" had contributed her share of negligence to Perel's death, and "the Szuster boy" had been a victim of circumstance. For all I know, Long-a-coming wanted to show its sympathy to my whole family.

The second Saturday of 1969 arrived. After Shabbos, Papa and the *shoykhet* set up for a late night of slaughter, while Mama, Sheiye, and I drove into Long-a-coming. I hadn't wanted to go, but Papa, his eyes liquid and tyrannical with grief, commanded that the family stay together. Although I knew that an event at the American Legion was my chance to see how "real people" spent the weekend, I had no appetite for it. Surely, the Legionnaires and their wives would whisper when the Szusters walked in; they would count the months since the accident; they would pin blame; they would recall what had been foremost in their minds: that we were Jews.

Meanwhile, the Szusters would have to affect a display of family unity that didn't exist.

The only comment during the trip came from Mama, sitting at the wheel. "Who would think that in America you get an award for murder?" she asked. Sheiye told her to watch the road. I prayed I would turn eighteen in two seconds so I could leave the Szusters forever. Mama held back her tears lest she drive us all into a Ford pickup, which, despite her torment, she was not prepared to do.

At the Legion Hall, a busty young girl with braces on her teeth led us to a long banquet table. As I sat down, I caught the paper tablecloth on the sleeve of my blouse and then knocked over a glass pitcher with my elbow. I stood by, deeply embarrassed, as water droplets beaded on a dish of butter patties. A middle-aged woman with teased gray hair and a potbelly smiled at me and reassured, "Don't worry, there's more where that came from." Mama couldn't restrain herself. Submissive as a geisha girl, she faced the woman and said, "I'm sorry. My daughter should be more careful."

I waited for Mama to break down, but she didn't. I would have liked to glower at her, threatening to bare the family divisions, but the sight of her among men who had fought patriotically against the Nazis lopped the feet off my anger. Mama was out of place here, dressed in a three-quarter-length coat with a rabbit fur collar; her short black hair curled with bobby pins and sprayed into helmet steeliness with Clairol; her white gloves that the Christian ladies wore only to church. Her accent exposed her—and me—as outsiders. Mama spoke with nodding deference, acknowledging almost mournfully that the Legionnaires and the Szusters were two different species. Her use of English instead of Yiddish proved that the people of Long-a-coming would never be her confidants, and that she and they had never shared a common enemy. I felt as I always did with Mama in public: She and I were in on a secret, but I didn't know what it was.

And some demon, my brother. He sat on the other side of Mama, half his shirt collar crumpled inside his suit jacket, his black shoes patent with too much shine, and the flustered grin of a nine-year-old on his lips. Sheiye tracked his eyes up and down the long table at the variety of foods never seen in our house: potato salad, cole slaw, sliced ham tiled with mosaics of olive and pimiento, lightly browned dinner rolls. A reverend made a benediction over the American Legion and blessed the meal. A blond crew-cut boy stared at Sheiye open-mouthed and dropped his gaze when he realized I was watching. Sheiye whispered to Mama, "Are the rolls kosher?"

Mama's lips parted and then met as she scanned the diners, intent on Schlitz and liverwurst. Her gaze landed on me, and I looked away. Why should she get my sympathy, only to abuse me at home with her mourning? When Mama turned back to Sheiye, she sighed. It was somebody's fault that her children had always been bunglers. For years Mama had racked her brain to see if she had been to blame. After the accident, there was no question: The unholy influences on us derived either from Long-a-coming or from a congenital mental imbalance over which she and Papa had no control.

Every three minutes Mama checked her gold watch. She knew that, just then, Papa was struggling with chicken wire in the coop, with only Mr. Berg to help. And here she sat surrounded by the townspeople reminiscing about infantry units and GI Bills. The VFW president—the same Grant Fitting, Former—clinked a metal knife against a glass and called the meeting to order. He and the attendees discussed old business. Sheiye and I gorged on the rolls. I don't know what was in those rolls, but nothing since Perel's death had tasted so delicious. Mama's cheek flamed.

First on the list of new business was the American Citizenship Award. Thank God Fitting said nothing about the "Szuster tragedy." Mama looked at her watch and bit her lip. Already nine-thirty. What if Papa had strained his back heaving chickens into the crates piled on . . . on the truck? Why hadn't they sold the truck? She had begged Papa to, but they couldn't afford a new one. Mama's eyes teared, and she dabbed them with the index finger of her white glove just as the VFW president announced the winner of this year's award. People applauded and looked in our direction, to see Mama lachrymal with pride for her only son. Neither Mama nor I clapped.

Sheiye walked down an aisle formed by two banquet tables, chewing rapidly on his dinner roll so that he could offer his thanks to the Citizenship Award committee. Grant Fitting, Former, held up the parchment award and read the few words of praise, speaking slowly, overenunciating as small-town leaders do to fatten a thin ceremony. With his left hand Fitting offered Sheiye the rolled-up parchment; with his right he shook Sheiye's extended left hand. Sheiye had been instructed to practice extending his right hand for a handshake and his left for the award, but his coordination faltered. The committee had also suggested that Sheiye prepare a short speech of gratitude. In that moment, I could not hate Sheiye the way I had hated him for the past four months, and, in fact, felt sorry for him. He couldn't play the game. He was who he was, a monster with individuality. Turning at the podium to face the audience, Sheiye managed a thank you, I am honored to receive the Citizenship Award. The microphone screed and, purpose in his step, Sheiye headed back to his seat, fingering his lapels in unconscious mimicry of bombast—behavior that could have suggested either self-mockery or pride; both possibilities made me pity my brother all the more. Award in hand, Sheiye pulled out his chair and sat down.

Mama laughed. People applauded a mother's self-conscious pleasure as she shook her head and laughed—or so it seemed from an onlooker's standpoint. I soon realized that Mama hadn't laughed at all, but had sung an agonized arpeggio, each note a cry against the futility of her life. It was the same sound she had made nine years earlier when Perel couldn't swallow her food because I had rammed a toothbrush down her throat. That caterwaul had started in a key of compassion and ended with Mama pulling and pulling my hair. I had expected a hug of forgiveness.

Mama stood up and her chair made a scraping noise on the floor. The guests at our table stopped talking, prepared to hear her make a speech on behalf of her inarticulate son. Instead, she lifted her coat from the back of the seat and offered her apologies to her neighbors for so abrupt an exit. My husband, she explained, is waiting for me in the coop. Taking note of Mama's leavetaking, Sheiye reached for one last dinner roll. Mama got wise to him and whispered a warning in Yiddish: *"Luz es tsi-ri!"* Let it alone! Sheiye looked at his arm and then darted a glance at me, hoping I hadn't detected his loss of control, hoping I wouldn't remember when I had seen that look before.

"Now people will say I don't give you enough to eat!" Mama fumed in the car. "I don't feed my murderous children!" She hated when someone caught a glimpse of our lives, of the loyal covenant between parents and children degenerating into betrayed promises. She and Papa had worked hard to convince outsiders of our devotion to each other, and one dinner roll had threatened to unveil us as impostors.

川

By the following Shabbos, Mama and Papa had stopped criticizing Sheiye. One week the American Legion recognizes Sheiye's civic achievement, and the next Mama and Papa are docile. Perhaps, despite their anger, my parents had been impressed by the hoopla centering on Sheiye, which, mysteriously, had redeemed him. Maybe Sheiye's hunger for the dinner rolls softened Mama's store of pathos, and she saw her son as no more than an unruly babe, spilling milk bottles and offing younger sisters in his instinctive quest to satisfy the hunger only mother love could assuage. Maybe Papa read somewhere in the Torah that parents must excuse the transgression of an only son or risk the routing of male lineage. Or did Sheiye's positive thinking already accomplish his prophecy that in time he would win Mama and Papa over?

A few weeks after the award ceremony, Papa offered to buy Sheiye a used car. This way Sheiye wouldn't have to live in the Glassboro town house he rented during the week, and could commute from Long-a-coming. My parents promised not to enlist Sheiye's help in the slaughterhouse if it interfered with his studies. They promised not to blast *The Today Show* over the noise of the Pike every morning at seven. Implicit in their proposal was that they would button their lips about Perel.

Instinctively, I saw through their intentions: All would be well if Sheiye obeyed. Mama and Papa longed for the authority they had rescinded with the onset of their grief. If they forgave one child and stayed mad at the other, they could still mourn the third. They would bribe Sheiye back into the family without betraying Perel. But someone had to stay unforgiven.

On Washington's Birthday, I knew Sheiye had won. I spent most of the day off from school lying on Perel's bed, staring up at the white ceiling. At noon footsteps sounded on the stairs, and I tried to guess if they belonged to Papa or Mama. Two taps sounded at the door, the first louder than the second. The door opened, and I saw the dark circles under Mama's eyes.

"Why do you have to stay in here?" Mama asked in a frail voice.

"It's warmer," I said. "I'm moving in."

"It's Perele's room," Mama said.

"I'll use it until she comes back."

Mama pulled the ever-present white handkerchief out from her pants pocket. I picked up my French grammar book and closed my eyes at the thought of Mrs. Barbarian. When I opened my eyes, I expected to see Mama crying, excluding me from the magnitude of her sorrow. Instead, she had stuffed the handkerchief back into her pocket, and her eyes were now wide with an urgent plan. She licked her lower lip and said, "I want you to vacuum the house."

"This is something new," I said.

"Starting with Sheiye's room," Mama said.

"That'll be the day."

"Everyone has to work, Brantzche. Sheiye helps Papa, you have to help me."

"No, no. You can't change horses in midstream. What about my childhood? How can I enjoy the pleasures of my childhood if I'm vacuuming Sheiye's room?"

Mama retrieved the handkerchief and blew her nose. "Your childhood is over," she said.

I could have pushed Mama aside and locked myself in Perel's room; I could have rolled her up into a tiny ball and thrown her across time and the ocean into the Poland of 1942, as I had done hundreds of times before dropping off to sleep. But I gave in. She scared me, the way she did when she drove Perel and me to West Long-a-coming to "teach us a lesson," or when she gathered table scraps to feed a dead daughter. I preferred the mother who, vanquished, left me to indict myself for the crime of unhappiness. I didn't want to see a forty-year-old woman tear open the window, smash through the storm glass, and jump into a patch of frozen zinnias.

Mama watched as I vacuumed, directing the work like a foreman on a construction site. Sheiye's room stank of stale ginger ale and farted-up bedsheets, and I said so.

"In that case, you'll wash the sheets too, little girl." Sheiye stood next to Mama, his arm looped around her shoulders. I flicked the on-off switch shut with my foot and the plastic hose and nozzle dropped to the floor. I tried to elbow my way past Sheiye and my mother. Mama snapped, "You're not finished."

"Don't worry, Mama," Sheiye said. "I'll finish. We can't let the princess exhaust herself."

The bedlam in my heart had blocked out Sheiye's prediction that he would regain my parents' love. I hadn't given that prediction much credence and didn't observe Sheiye as he proceeded to make it a fact. All I know is that Perel's death made me shrink further and further away from my family, as if prolonged contact with the Szusters would suck me into their millennia-long victimization. Sheiye, on the other hand, would not abandon the accident, yet the focus of his attention was not Perel. That would have meant watching himself bear down on the truck's accelerator, tense his jaw, and rock in the truck's seat as the rubber tires hugged his sister to death. It would have meant imagining the person Perel might have become and where her questions would have led her. It would have meant loathing himself. But since Sheiye viewed himself and his crime remorselessly, in the third person, he made Mama and Papa's suffering the focus of Perel's death. This is the process my parents called admission of guilt. Or love. Or being a good son. They forgave Sheiye. They believed his version of that August day.

Disgusted, I decided to go downstairs to the piano, for the monotony of Hanon's scales managed to numb my unhappiness. I closed the door to Perel's room and walked down the stairs. Sheiye poked his head out of his room. "And God looked down and said, 'All is good,' eh, Brantzche?" Sheiye smiled and tapped the on-off switch with his foot. The monotonous scream of the vacuum cleaner resumed and drowned out whatever Mama was saying to her son. From the stairs, I looked up and saw Mama's crossed ankles as she sat on Sheiye's bed, her suede Hush Puppies coarsened by years of slaughterhouse muck.

21

🌿 THE MOOD OF THE SZUSTER HOUSEHOLD finally lightened when Papa announced that the family would emigrate to Israel. This decision to move did not stem from ideological commitment or the search for spiritual renewal; it stemmed from defeat. In 1948, as thousands of Jewish refugees swarmed into Israel, they visited their pain and indignation upon every corner of the country's geography; and in less than two years, Israel looked like the continuation of World War II. When my parents disembarked in New York in 1950, America promised to be a land of no memory. Now, with Perel's grotesque death, the United States, too, swaggered before them with the weight of unwanted memory, taunting them that America had only been a temporary resting place. In Israel, the losses of the past might be pervasive, but viewed from a distance, at least they were diffuse. Remembering there would be less personal, more endurable.

I refused to go with them. We fought—or I should say, I ranted every evening after school that I wasn't going, and Mama, in the tone she used to quote egg prices to customers, told me that, yes, I was. Once, I remember, Papa withdrew to the bedroom, where he lay on his back reading the *Jewish Daily Forward,* but every now and then he yelled in a hoarse voice that when parents made a decision, a child obeyed. "I'm not a child anymore," I said. "Ask Mama." Mama folded her hands and looked down at the living room floor, long in need of retiling, and now never to get it. "That was something else," she said.

I blew my breath against the cold kitchen window and wrote BRENDA on it with an index finger. The letters were backwards and looked Cyrillic. "Sheiye doesn't have to go," I said.

"Sheiye's a man," Papa called out. "He can take care of things."

"We can see how well he's taken care of things," I said.

Mama got up from her chair and walked to the window. With the side of her hand, she erased my name. "Brantzche, go to sleep," she ordered.

"I mean it," I vowed on my way to Perel's room. "I'm not going."

I had nothing against Israel. I assumed that someday I would visit. But I resented the idea of my parents uprooting me from the site of Perel's death. I wondered if I had become the kind of Jew who had resumed living among the Poles after the war instead of striking out for a new ghostless country—the kind of Jew my parents had always criticized. Yet I had this eerie sense that without Perel, I wouldn't exist anymore. Thousands of times our eyes had met and assured each other of our own superior communication. We had frolicked in a community of creatures with gruelly voices, and with the co-god of that creation now dead, no one else would bother with Sparsely and Saucer's dense garrulity or tolerate Mrs. Barbarian's peremptory opinions.

But I had a more pressing reason for my obstinacy. Before I left Long-a-coming, I wanted to understand the nature of my love for Perel. I might have ignored Sheiye's accusation of jealousy had my mother not reached the same conclusion. To be sure, envy was a component of my love;

though I had never felt intellectually inferior to my sister, I had never once outperformed her in school. What Mama and Sheiye perceived as jealousy was, in fact, ambivalence, and their accusation led me to contemplate it.

I had believed that Perel and I were identical, a belief borne out many times when we uttered the same thought simultaneously. Whenever she exhibited some trait, I expected it to show up in me. Yet Perel displayed one particular characteristic which I thoroughly disdained. Although I had never admitted it, I couldn't stand her inclination to hide. And I never really knew what precipitated that response in her. Why had she stormed out of Charlie's room that Shabbos and retreated to her bed? Why had she never explained the razor blade episode? And what was that flirtation with suicide anyway but one more attempt to hide? I could see hiding from my parents: They were quick to dismiss all our yearnings as childhood fancies. But why hide from me, except that I unwittingly threatened to expose her to something she didn't want to see?

I considered two possibilities: first, if Perel and I had not been identical, could I have loved her as her own person, with her own failings; and second, if we had been identical, would Perel's fearfulness and lack of curiosity eventually show up in me, leading me to a like end? The fact is, I had already observed this cringing reflex in myself in regard to the egg customers, and more seriously in regard to my father's past.

For years I had looked forward to the day when I would turn my back on the isolation of Jake's Poultry Farm. But now, with Perel's blood a part of the soil, I was tied to Long-a-coming body and soul. Worse, I thought I had no choice anymore to pursue one fate over another, for I felt myself closing off from all the adventures and discoveries I had once desired. And the more I pondered my reservations, the more I dreamed I didn't signal.

The prospect of moving to Israel raised some practical issues, as well. What would happen to the farm? Would my parents sell it? Would Sheiye live there? Could I? By 1969, no one would be likely to buy a subsistence chicken farm. Who but some desperado would want to be the proud owner of a slaughterhouse? We had heard countless tales of chicken farmers in Toms River, Lakewood, Vineland, and the smaller Jersey towns selling their property to housing tract developers and MacDonalds; even though the farms themselves were going backrupt, the land beneath them had stupendous potential for profit. Now, at the thought of never seeing Jake's Poultry Farm again, I felt our hulking gray house grow arms and embrace me. I wanted to leave; that much hadn't changed. But in due time I wanted to return. Someday I wanted to look at the farm with less prejudiced eyes. I also entertained the sentimental notion of leading my future child by the hand through the coops and slaughterhouse, describing the life of dead Aunt Perel and me.

For the next three months Jake's Poultry Farm took on the air of a transit camp. My parents shuttled back and forth between Long-a-coming and Camden to arrange for passports; Papa spoke on the telephone three or four times a day with prospective real estate developers, discussing deals which, to my relief, all fell through; Mama laundered sheets and old clothing and packaged them in brown meat paper for the Goodwill drop-off in front of Humble's Supermarket; and for several weekends, Sheiye helped Charlie collect the industrial-sized fans, chicken feeders, and incubators from two of the three coops and store them in the slaughterhouse until they could be sold. Still, none of these preparations seemed real to me. For a decade, my parents had talked of visiting Aaron in Israel, and their "Israeli trip" had become a standing joke with Perel and me. Yet soon, horribly enough, I saw that their voyage—and possibly mine—would come to pass, for by June, the El Al flight confirmations lay conspicuously on the kitchen table.

With my transplantation to Israel looming in the near future, insult and silence became the standard of my life. In fine Szuster tradition, I locked myself in Perel's room and hid. In fine Brantzche tradition, I stroked myself to sleep. Time and again, I made it plain that I would run away from home before moving to Israel. In a nasty mood, I promised that I would sell myself into prostitution rather than leave the United States, and would live in the woods if I had to. My parents had done it, and I could too. Dropping out of high school, surviving in the woods behind the Assumption Parish, and resenting my fate would put meaning in my life, the way slaughter had put meaning in my parents' lives. Better still, it would drive away my doubts about loving Perel.

One other matter was unresolved: What would happen to Charlie?

My father had bought him a radio that Christmas, and Charlie spent the winter toasting by the brown gas heater, playing solitaire and listening to KYW News. I occasionally caught sight of him when Mama opened his door to tell him Campbell's Soup and bologna were on the table. The yellow plastic radio, sitting atop a rickety metal end table, played at low volume. Charlie had all but glued his ear to the audio grating, rarely shifting his body so much as an inch. Sometimes I thought Charlie kept the volume low because he didn't want anyone to hear a personal message from God or one of his past tormentors. Now and then when Mama opened Charlie's door, he would be napping. He would wake with a start and grope for the volume dial, as if he were missing the explanation of his life. In a few seconds, Charlie's bloodshot eyes opened wide and blinked at the somber room. He patted the tobacco pouch in his shirt pocket and, as usual, bolted upright to do my mother's bidding.

Sometime in April, Papa finally informed Charlie that the Szuster family was moving to Israel, and that he would have to make other arrangements. In his last month on the farm, Charlie showed no trace of anxiety about the future. I wanted to talk to him. I wanted to ask him about Perel's death. Maybe he had pulled the curtain aside when Sheiye barreled through the lawn. He would have seen me signal Sheiye to avoid the blanket. But Charlie displayed no need to speak with any of the Szusters. He didn't meet my eye over Mama's boiled chicken, nor did he wave at me anymore on his way to the slaughterhouse. He had no wise words about justice—southern, northern, mortal, or divine.

One day near the end of my junior year in high school, Charlie was gone. Not temporarily disappeared, like the one time Sheiye found him drunk near Atsion, but permanently gone, back to Camden to live with his two maiden sisters. He had taken only his clothes, his playing cards, and the yellow radio. The girlie calendar was still nailed to the wall above the sink—several, in fact, one on top of the other, dating back as far as 1963. *National Enquirer*s lay strewn at the foot of his bed. A pair of worn black socks was stuffed under the pillow, a sign of negligence or protest. His mud-caked boots stood under the cot; a razor, still wet, leaned against a cloudy glass; a tobacco pouch with a few flecks of tobacco inside plugged the sink drain. Under a curling floor tile lay a buffalo-head nickel. It was dusty and looked like an old bottle cap at first. I picked it up and slipped it in my shoe. I would save it until Charlie returned. Certainly he would come for the rest of his belongings. But he didn't. No one ever mentioned Charlie again, though we went on referring to the shambling annex as Charlie's Room. I heard nothing more about him until I spoke to Sheiye fifteen years later.

22

🌿 MY PARENTS RELENTED ABOUT ISRAEL in late May. Their sudden trust in me to live with a family in Long-a-coming and not run wild with boys had no precedent. Of course they insisted on certain guarantees: that I not miss a day of school except when I was sick; that I *daven* every Shabbos and read the weekly portion of the Torah; that I write them a letter once a week; etc. They knew I was unscrupulous enough to make false promises, and I made them. I wasn't interested in their reasons for this uncharacteristic leniency. Not then. All I could think was, *Brantzche, you're free at last, thank God Almighty, you're free at last.*

I believed Mama and Papa were joking when they told me I would live on another chicken farm. Was the whole world a chicken farm? I would stay with Sonia and Laybl Kichner. Although they were survivors too, I had never heard of them before; my parents never socialized with Long-a-coming's two other survivors, never even mentioned their names. The Kichners would draw on a bank account funded by my parents, to which I would have no direct access. That way, I couldn't drop out of school and abscond with the money. If the Kichners needed my help in the coops, I was to do as told. Incidentally, the Kichners had a son, Gabriel, Sheiye's age, whose name I recognized from school. I hadn't known Gabriel Kichner was a Jew. I bet no one at school knew, either. Were they still in hiding too?

Mama and Papa wanted to be in Israel by the high holidays, which gave them four months to sew up their American lives. This included a visit to Perel's grave in Woodbridge, New Jersey, off limits to Sheiye and me, just as the funeral and unveiling had been off limits to us. What with the inconclusive decision to leave the property fallow, Papa planned to return within the year to try once more to interest housing developers in buying it. In the meantime, Sheiye, they decreed, would stay on the farm to protect it from vandals or, if he chose, would find tenants to rent the house. Bolero got to stay as well. Two peas in a pod.

Those four months were intolerable. As the anniversary of Perel's death approached, Mama started sobbing all over again. She pored over school pictures of Perel amidst her classmates, and over home photos of Perel surrounded by kittens and yard chickens. From her mahogany bureau, Mama retrieved Perel's report cards and awards of academic achievement, studying the predictions for success that grammar school teachers had written throughout the sixties. The yellowed newspaper clippings with Perel's name in a list for the academic honor roll Mama wrapped in cellophane. All these she filed carefully inside the brown leather purse with the broken clasp, leaguing Perel with the dead relatives and identification papers from the Bindermichel displaced persons camp. She fingered Perel's clothing, untouched for almost a year, and searched for traces of her daughter in all the corners of the house, just as she searched for bread crumbs at Passover. She complained to Papa, mumbling to herself that she had spent her adult life thousands of miles from her parents' graves, and now she would spend the rest of her life thousands of miles from her daughter's.

Papa's response to the first anniversary was more contemplative. He rested his elbows on the kitchen table, supported his forehead in his palm, and studied from the pages of over-sized purple books full of commentaries and parables in Hebrew and Yiddish. My parents had not stopped slaughtering chickens, and after a late night in the slaughterhouse, Papa, and sometimes Mr. Berg, interpreted the texts, rocking back and forth in their seats to cradle their rue. I suspect that Papa's attention to those commentaries was less a simplistic faith in an all-corrective God than it was a desperate attempt to keep believing. He must have asked the questions that intelligent men of faith ask: "Why did I lose my daughter, an innocent child? Wasn't it enough to lose my father, mother, sisters, brothers, aunts, uncles, cousins, and friends? Did I sin to deserve this punishment? Maybe we suffer for the sins of the world, and without suffering the Messiah will not come."

As dawn broke, Papa covered his eyes, as if to fortify himself with Job's lament: "Yea, though He slay me, in Him I will trust." My father yawned and rubbed his shoulder, his dead-end reflections having prickled the old bullet wound. The squeal of brakes in the driveway called him back to more temporal matters. In the early blue light, a butcher parked his truck in front of the slaughterhouse. "Mr. Berg," Papa said. "It's morning. You can get a ride to Camden with Horovitz." Sighing, Papa marked his place in the purple book with a yellow plastic chicken tie, wondering, perhaps, if all the commentaries were simply a more sophisticated state of ignorance.

When Horovitz the butcher knocked on the door, Papa and Mr. Berg were rocking back and forth, rasping a final cantorial melody in a minor key. Papa and Berg drew out two and three notes for every Ashkenazic syllable, sucking on the music like bees sucking nectar from a rose: *"Eli, Eli, Lomo asawtoni?"* My God, my God, why have You forsaken me? Their plaint was not a challenge to God's motives, but rather a comfort to their limited understanding, sorrow waltzing in time to their song.

The last time I saw Mama and Papa, they looked shrunken, reduced by their dated fancy clothes once more to cast-off refugees. They would never look like ordinary citizens, lulled into complacency by defensible borders, the longevity of genealogical lines, and the tacit approval of divine providence. No matter where they lived, they would look like wayfarers whose code of conduct prepared them only for crisis. Again I was embarrassed by their fragility, but this time my pride would not let me declare that I was communing with it.

That last day, as Mama busied herself with luggage locks and Papa confirmed airport limousine reservations, I didn't know how or what to feel. I concentrated on the set of my mother's lips and the single-mindedness of my father's walk, wondering if I was like either one of them. I had never had the security of mutual understanding with them that I had with Perel. How could I have? To my mind, they were indestructible: Even Nazis couldn't kill them. Lesser tragedies could vanquish me. We were made of different stuff and lived in different times. Why couldn't I just let it go at that?

Mama sat down on a box marked "Pictures." She exhaled all the air of her nineteen years on the farm, inspected her fingernails, and corralled a loose curl that had eluded her hair spray. Soon she and Papa would be shepherded through Customs in Philadelphia, two bewildered, middle-aged immigrants, rubbernecking at Hare Krishna groupies and businessmen in the waiting room, worried lest their luggage be stolen, Papa overly respectful to a bored clerk, Mama opening the clasp of her handbag to feel for the passports. I thought how futile their struggle for survival had been, what with Sheiye, me, and a ditched chicken farm as the reward.

Although I had imagined my leavetaking as a solitary walk along the White Horse Pike to the Kichners' farm, my farewell parting was actually much less romantic than that. Papa loaded the boxes of my clothing, books, and sheet music into the blue Chevy—Sheiye's blue Chevy now. Mama did not move from the box full of pictures. She turned her head to the kitchen window facing onto the backyard, brooding, perhaps, about the chain of events that had begun with her return from Buena Vista a year ago and would end who knew where. The memory made her bite her lower lip and check for her passport again.

I walked out to the doghouse. I stooped next to Bolero, trying to convey the significance of that hot August morning by staring intently into his eyes. He pointed his open mouth at my face and lapped my nose. I felt I had reached an understanding with him at last, and I regretted abandoning my pet to Sheiye's protection. Even Bolero, his eyes brown like Perel's, had already become part of my past life, because I could not bear running into Sheiye for the sake of seeing my dog. I kissed Bolero on the nose and then stood up to take one final look around the farm.

Papa called my name. His voice, which no longer had to compete with crowing roosters, the truck's engine, and the buzz of the slaughterhouse freezer, sounded louder than usual. Late summer cicadas jabbered in the trees, a chorus to Papa's command.

I opened the car door, got in, and placed my pocketbook on my lap, waiting for Papa to pull out of the driveway. *"Gezeygn zekh mit der mame,"* he said. Say goodbye to Mama. I marveled at the expression *gezeygn zekh.* No one on the farm had ever bid anyone else farewell, so I had never heard it before. *"Nu, gey shoyn!* Go!" said Papa. I didn't move. "Is this what you want Mama to remember about you?" He shifted into drive without waiting for my answer. I stared at the squished bugs on the windshield and wrapped the seatbelt around me. From the corner of my eye, the gray house reminded me of an old woman, her stockings bunched at the ankles.

Papa and I drove the mile and a half to the Kichners' farm in silence. I hadn't met the Kichners yet. They could have been ogres, but I was desperate enough to take a chance with them. In five minutes Papa parked the Chevy on Old Sawmill Road. "Can you handle the boxes yourself?" he asked.

I still could not bring myself to talk.

Speaking as if it incurred no strain on him—as if we would meet each other again in a few hours—Papa said, "Laybl Kichner doesn't want to see me on his property." Nervously, he began transporting the boxes from the trunk of the Chevy to the Kichners' porch.

Papa scanned the farm for a sign of Laybl Kichner. All we heard was an undercurrent of chickens' clucking, and an intermittent squawk from an offended hen. Papa walked around to the passenger-side door and opened it. A mustache of perspiration sprouted over his upper lip as he reached for another box. We avoided helping each other, Papa carrying the heavy items, I the light ones.

My father slapped his hands together. His face was now shiny with sweat. Hurriedly, he rubbed his large white handkerchief across his mouth and forehead. Forming beneath my stubbornness was the realization that I might never see Papa alive again, and a shudder of panic prompted me to speak.

"What about college?" I asked. I stared at my shoes. One day that summer, Mama and I had driven to Robert Hall's Department Store to buy new shoes and twice my usual fall wardrobe. A few times she had explained that she was spending Perel's share on me. Since then, I had been careful not to mention my future plans, not wanting to hear Mama rail at me for a future Perel didn't have.

"We'll talk about that later," Papa said. "In the letters."

"I'll be writing, like we agreed." I had tried to sound a little more affectionate, yet this cold comment was all I could muster.

"Brantzche," Papa said, narrowing his eyes at me. *"Di mame* was crying because you wouldn't say goodbye. I'll drive you home and back here again if you'll say goodbye to Mama."

I wondered whether my response would affect my college plans. But I couldn't move. Papa's hands extended towards me as I backed into my boxes.

"Say goodbye already!" a crotchety male voice yelled from the house. On top of my dread was bewilderment about Mr. Kichner's hostility towards Papa. What on earth was I getting into?

"Kichner!" Papa called out. Silence. Papa coughed. He seemed to want to say something, an apology, a thank you, but settled for "My daughter is here!"

Papa jerked his head back a few times to make me laugh, a last-minute attempt at reconciliation. If he wanted to patch up the insults and accusations of the past year with a wink, though, I wasn't game. What was I supposed to do? Throw myself into his arms and agree that Perel was dead because of my carelessness? Without meeting Papa's eye again, I knocked on Kichner's door. The tires of the blue Chevy crunched gravel as Papa pulled onto Old Sawmill Road. I wondered what his face looked like.

"We're starting a new life together," I said in Pop's voice. The sound of Perel's caricature startled me; it was like hearing a voice from the grave. Everything that would happen to me now would be the consequence of Perel's death, including my happiness. *We* weren't starting anything. Just me. And I would have to remember not to be too happy about my long-awaited liberation.

The elephantine Laybl Kichner appeared and pressed his nose against the screen door. He pointed his round head towards my boxes, signaling that he had no intention of carrying a single one. When I made my way to the door, a carton balanced on my hip, Kichner was gone. Thus, my welcome.

Book Two

1

⚹ HEAT WAVE 1983 IS AS OPPRESSIVE as heat wave 1968. As I awake in my Village apartment, south Jersey August seeps out of my hips and settles in the small of my back. The two houseplants on my east windowsill lean into the sun, yet their presence is more irksome than calming. From some unquestioned store of knowledge, I know it is unhealthy, even wrong, to wake up as I do, damning nature and craving unconsciousness. Sometimes I can't help it; I wince as I remember who I am, because every morning reminds me that I am a fragment, a piece of invisible code disconnected from love and family. And as my eyes reacquaint themselves with the props of my life—a few framed prints, a stack of paperback novels, the oscillating fan, and, of course, my piano—I recall how much of my life in Manhattan has been a cover.

Turning onto my side, I realize my legs are wet and sticky. I pull away the sheets to let Greenwich Village summer dry south Jersey from my body. Hoping to salvage another few seconds of oblivion, I close my eyes. But then I see the blanket molded to the monsterish contour of Perel's body. Although fifteen years have passed since my sister's death, I am still afraid that her soul has nowhere to go; afraid that my future will be dense with alibis, self-accusation, anger at Perel for hiding one time too many. Mostly I am afraid of the loneliness that surfaces up through my casual friendships, love affairs, and piano playing. It is a feeling so akin to grief that

I remember the morning after Perel's death, when I awoke dressed in blood down to my ankles. Finally, finally, I cried.

In my senior year of high school, my parents agreed to finance four years of my education at the Manhattan School of Music. Though we continued to have only the barest communication—mostly my acknowledgments of the weekly Torah portion and their bland exhortations to help out the Kichners—they were explicit in their disapproval of my course of study. They preferred either a standard liberal arts education at Rutgers in Camden or some vocational training that would assure me of a steady office job. I was furious at their low expectations, especially because they had once mapped out more glamorous careers for their children: Sheiye was to be a dentist, Perel a heart surgeon, and I a shrewd trial lawyer. Now, they seemed to imply, I had proved myself a failure, and they did not want to invest more than minimally necessary in "setting me up," especially in a career as frivolous and insecure as music. On the other hand, they did not want any more confrontation, and through the Kichners, my parents and I negotiated a contract: Mama and Papa would pay my room, board, and some expenses for four years, wherever I chose to go. During the summers, I could either stay with the Kichners or find a job. Beyond that, I was on my own.

I was probably too young and too inexperienced to realize the risk I ran. I had a lot of natural musical ability, but less than one year of serious training; and at the Manhattan School, I found that nearly everyone else was more advanced than I in repertory and music theory. In a way, my ignorance suited me fine, for I had a perfect excuse to channel all my thought and energy into my musical studies. Now I had license to disparage intellectual and literary pastimes, a convenient stance, I eventually saw, which spared me the trouble of contemplation. Luckily for me, my gift for improvisation and imitation carried the day, and by my junior year I was able to find part-time work in piano bars and cafés. My lack of ambition was an oddity in the business, for a lot of the other musicians I knew would have killed for the jobs I got. While I was relieved to have hit upon an easy way to support myself, I was bored, and even felt cheap for sliding into work and an environment that didn't interest me. Ironically, my education had given me the prosaic vocation my parents had predicted. Sometimes I think failure would have served me better. It might have reoriented my thinking or, more accurately, resurrected it from the far corner of painful memory where it lay slumbering.

Three years or so into my career, when I was twenty-four, I witnessed an incident that forced me to reconsider the life I had chosen to lead.

I was with Melissa, a flute-playing friend, waiting in a Far Rockaway bagel restaurant for a booth. The afternoon sun and the antics of bathing-suited teenagers had put me in a dissatisfied mood, and I was wondering who I would have been had I grown up among their older brothers and sisters. Gazing about the room distractedly, I noticed some commotion in one of the aisles. A little girl, maybe eleven years old, was sitting in an aluminum wheelchair, guarded by her middle-aged parents and her younger sister. The mother reached for the quilt comforter covering the girl's legs, for it had gotten caught in one of the wheels; and then, stroking the girl's blond hair, she asked if her daughter was all right. Suddenly, the child began flailing her arms, striking at her mother, and then at her father, who had tried sympathetically to intervene. One or two elderly restaurant patrons attempted to soothe the girl, and to their alarm she yelled, "Leave me alone! Just leave me alone!" Humiliated by the unwanted attention, the girl placed her elbows on the armrests and hid her pretty face in her hands. Groping for her little sister but not looking at anyone, she commanded her parents to wheel her out of the restaurant.

After the child and her family left, I couldn't stop reliving that scene. To say the least, my Saturday outing to the beach was ruined. After an hour of feigned interest in popular music, bar studs, and Melissa's strident political opinions, I begged off, pleading a headache, and took the subway back to the Village.

Traveling on the train, I felt the simplicity of that child's agony cut through all my pretenses. My relationship to memory, intellect, Perel's death, and my so-called musicianship disgusted me. Everything I did and thought was fake. By the time the train pulled into West Fourth Street, I was brimming over with self-chastisement. Why did my brooding never lead me to wisdom? Why had I shut myself off from my childhood curiosity? Why was I in a career I considered small? And given the tragedy that had disfigured most of my adulthood, what could still matter in life? And in this frame of mind, I entered my apartment lobby, opened my mailbox, and found the envelope of Mama and Papa's tape recordings, Lalke's return address in the upper left-hand corner.

Upstairs, I fumbled for my tape recorder, lying under a stack of sheet music, clicked a cassette into place, and heard my mother's voice for the first time since 1969. To my surprise, she sounded jolly, as if she did not take herself or the oral history project seriously. She liked the interviewer and began speaking to her in a singsong manner, as if telling a fairy tale. But by the time she got to the murders of her father and two sisters, Mama was practically chanting a dirge. Papa, audible in the background till now, had stopped teasing my mother in English to "smile, you're on *Candid Camera.*" When his turn came, he argued a good ten minutes with the interviewer that he disliked tape recorders; and when he finally agreed to talk, his stories were spare. Listening to the tapes, I was thrown into unappeasable despair because, I realized, I had never understood anything. Certainly, I had never known who Rukhl and Yankl Szuster were.

Afterwards, in tears, I dredged up some of the assumptions I had held about life, even during my years of self-imposed numbness. One was that, to me, living meant dying. If life consisted only of school studies, shopping, moviegoing, working, loving, and breeding, you weren't really living. In order to count for anything, I believed you had to undergo a trial by fire. The crippled child and my parents' tape recordings brought that futile credo home to me again.

Another assumption I cherished was that with the loss of my sister, I had become like Mama and Papa, bereaved and ignored witnesses of murder. And, perversely, I even enjoyed this picture of myself. I came to think that my life should be a sad story, like theirs. They didn't have family; I shouldn't have family. Their families died violently; mine should too. Life after the war hadn't mattered to them; life without Perel didn't matter to me.

With these disturbing insights, I saw how conveniently my piano-bar playing had provided a screen against my memories of the Szusters. After that Saturday in my twenty-fourth year, the screen began to wear thin. Frequently, at the piano in the middle of a tune, some seemingly irrelevant image foisted itself upon my concentration. Once, while playing "If I Fell," I saw myself as a five-year-old girl. I had just come home from kindergarten and was pulling off my black leotards. Mama entered the gray house from the slaughterhouse to find me half undressed. With an exasperated *neyn, neyn,* she covered her eye and cheek with one hand. She hoisted me up onto the kitchen table and kissed my crotch. Delirious with pleasure, I was slipped back into the black leotards, informed that I had to return to school to participate in the Christmas program. Why hadn't someone told me? Maybe someone did. I didn't know much English yet, and I was terrified of Yiddish, the language no one at school spoke or understood. I remember how the teacher had once instructed us, "I want you to know all the numbers from one through ten backwards and forwards." I wrote the numbers on wide-ruled yellow paper, literally backwards and forwards. You could only read them in a mirror.

In my more charitable moods towards myself, I wondered if I had chosen an environment that elicited my despair, not only over people but also over their situations. Some nights my head reeled from stories marinated in Jack Daniel's. The story of Lois, pickled every night I played, whose Rumanian cabdriver boyfriend loved her tenderly for six months, and then wrote from Rumania that he was married and had two children. The story of Rhonda, a lapsed Orthodox Jew, divorced after a ten-year marriage because her Orthodox husband came home one day and, unprovoked, beat her into next week. The story of Paul, born in an Austrian DP camp, who lamented that he had gotten his fantasies out of his mind and into his system. The story of Howard, a diagnosed manic-depressive, who told me in fluent Yiddish that he would commit himself to a job and a woman if he could sit in one place for ten minutes. The story of Bobby, an Armenian and a Trotskyite, who joined the Socialist Workers Party and planned a move to Milwaukee, where he would foment a workers' revolution.

Too often I saw men Papa's age wander into the piano bars where I played. I didn't look for my father, but I saw him everywhere in Manhattan—not so much in the face of a religious Jew walking to *shil* on Shabbos, hands clasped behind his back, or in the face of a wealthy realtor, although I hear Papa is a successful building contractor in Israel today. Instead, I saw Papa in the face of a Central Park groundskeeper stabbing flyaway candy wrappers with a long pointed stick; in the man, jacket open to the winter wind, delivering a pizza to a rich college girl's dorm; in the middle-aged man wearing a denim jacket stained with engine lubricator grease. In all these men I saw Papa's almond-shaped eyes and yellow smile saying, "I am aging and I don't understand anything that has happened to me—not my successes, not my failures, not my rewards, not my punishments. God only knows how, but I am still alive, with my memories of war, slave labor, prosperous Nazis on public buses, and devout rabbis. And today I sit in a green-carpeted condominium that overlooks an alley where the Sephardim air wedding dresses in windows. I wait for news of my granddaughter Perele, the only one who gives us *nakhes* now. Here I sit thinking about all we had to endure, and how these land deals never make the big killing they're supposed to. The *alte* Rukhl and Yankl, we sit here and think how our children should have been, and now all we have to do with our lives is wait." A face is personal, yet you can't hide it.

All this is not to say that I suddenly knew how to act on my revelations. But in the course of a year, my life started to change: I was less afraid to be the Brantzche Szuster of my childhood years—less afraid to be Perel's sister. I spent more and more time alone, returned to the books that Perel and I had read as children, and contemplated going back to school for a degree in literature. Naturally, this meant keeping at my piano-bar jobs, because I wasn't equipped to earn my living in any other way. After a year of classes at City College, I enrolled as a full-time student, studying by day, playing piano by night as infrequently as my finances allowed. By twenty-eight, I had written a thesis on Ellen Glasgow and acquired a master's degree in American literature; and despite the lower wages I would draw as a teacher or writer, I felt truer to myself, if not absolutely happy, with my decision. Between literature and my parents' oral histories, I have come to accept one truth about my past and future: I am not that different from Mama and Papa. Like them, I live without hope of settling scores yet love life unreasonably, and will until the day I die—even though I cannot reclaim what I have lost. And while I still have difficult August mornings, I do not flog myself endlessly with the judgment that I have no right to satisfaction because I should have died in 1968 too.

I saw no point in sacrificing the next four years to a doctorate. For one thing, I had no intention of hiding out in a university any more than in darkened piano bars. And for another, my professors' obsession with the novel as a "text" to pick apart and overrationalize bored me as much as my gigs, for it proposed formulaic thinking for an enterprise occasionally more eclectic and certainly more desperate than literary criticism. My ambition now, inspired by my parents' openness about the past, was to carve a place for myself in the world. It had taken me almost until thirty to believe that I had a right to exist. Little by little, the interests which I had forbidden myself became permissible. If I wanted, I could end my piano career and teach literature; I could travel to Poland and meet the few people who had sheltered my parents during the Nazi occupation; and terrifying though it was, I could have a child. At long last, I had to undo the damage of my parents' judgment on me. If I failed, Perel's death would never be more than a weapon to indulge my bent for personal punishment.

Now that I had adopted this fearless rhetoric, I had to put

it to the test. This meant one thing: renewing contact with the three people I still wanted to avoid. For the time being, I could not imagine going that far, and retreated once more into my personal Jake's Poultry Farm.

Steven Szuster, 1515 Blatherwick Avenue, Margate, New Jersey. A few years ago, Lalke mailed me an aerogram with Sheiye's address, and after noting which city he had settled in, I threw it away. I got Sheiye's phone number from one telephone operator, and a third or fourth reluctantly offered me his address. My hand shook and my heart pounded as I scribbled the information down. Judging by the state of my nerves, I knew I wasn't ready to talk to him or hear his voice. What if he was still accusative? Or, worse, nonchalant? But I couldn't procrastinate anymore. I mailed my brother a note saying, "Sheiye, I want to talk. Please. Brantzche."

Thanks to me, Sheiye and I had had no communication all those years. He did call me once or twice at the Kichners', but when I refused to talk to him, he never tried to contact me again. Incredibly, during my music school days, I had barely thought about Sheiye—even as I mourned Perel. His character, I believed, was not affected by conscience, self-reflection, or remorse; so why bother thinking about the incorrigible? Even after that incident in Far Rockaway, and after listening to my parents' tape recordings, I still refused to consider Sheiye as a grown man. It was as if all my waking thoughts and impressions walked respectfully around some immovable stone marker planted in the middle of my mind. Only this urgent desire to see my family had begun to dislodge it.

A month after I sent the note to Sheiye, I found a shiny "Greetings from the Boardwalk" postcard in my mailbox. On the back, in childishly mixed upper- and lowercase letters, it said, "B, Will meet yOu at AtLAntic City TeRmiNal, ARc-tIc AveNue eXit, Monday, AuGust 22, 1983. 8:30 A.M. If No GooD, write AgAin. S." But my brother knew me well: What other plans would I have made for the fifteenth anniversary of Perel's death?

2

FOURTEEN YEARS AGO, as I stood on the Kichners' porch vowing never to see Sheiye and my parents again, Sonia Kichner dashed towards me from a chicken coop. Her kindness was so spontaneous that I wanted to burst into tears. Although she suspected that her husband's curmudgeonly greeting had contributed to my troubles, she did not press me for details, and instead began helping me transport my belongings into the spare bedroom upstairs. Within a half hour, Sonia had me slicing Jersey cucumbers and tomatoes for lunch. More than anything else, I was shaken by the simplicity with which I had moved into a new life. Was this all it took to separate myself from my loveless family?

I wasn't at the Kichner farm many months when I learned the kind of information my parents had always sought to keep from me: namely, that Sonia had wanted a daughter in addition to Gabriel, but Laybl had refused to bring more children into "this rotten world," as he put it. I had never imagined that a married couple could be divided over a decision like childbearing; to all appearances, my parents were always united in thought and deed. By winter 1970, when Sonia had all but adopted me, I saw just how unwilling my parents had been to confide anything meaningful or controversial about themselves. This realization hurt and embittered me all the more, and I was determined to view Sonia as my real mother.

Sonia herself, living a kind of quarantine on the farm, reveled in our companionship, and used it to unburden herself of her childhood memories. Sonia Kichner, née Sonnenberg, was twelve when she entered Auschwitz. Somewhere along the line she graduated to Mauthausen, and finished her "schooling" at sixteen in Bergen-Belsen. That's how Sonia spoke of the camps—as academies of barbarism. The Nazis had put her small fingers to use making bombs in a munitions factory, "on-the-job training," as she dryly described it, an experience that serves her tangentially today in her work as an electronics technician for the Shulman Electronics Laboratory in Pennsauken, New Jersey.

As a girl, Sonia had worshiped her father, choirmaster of the Cracow Opera House, who had introduced her to every kind of music: Schubert lieder, cantorials, opera, even Spanish Civil War songs. Thirty years later, after a day cleaning chicken coops, Sonia would collapse in the living room armchair, sewing needle and torn underwear in her lap, and sing me tangos in Polish. She sparkled when she sang, her eyes shifting up and down, side to side, as if watching her father's baton. "The memory of my father got me through the days in Auschwitz," Sonia told me one night. "On days when the Nazis smashed babies into walls, I conjured up the beautiful concerts he had taken me to hear. One morning I heard every note of the 'Pastorale,' and instead of building bombs in Auschwitz, I was listening to Beethoven in Cracow with my father."

The real Sonia Sonnenberg, she said, died in the camps. Because of her brutal, unashamed honesty, I was moved during my abject brooding to see Sonia Kichner as the only person I have ever loved without hating at the same time.

Laybl Kichner was twenty-seven years older than his wife. They met after the war, in the British zone of the Bergen-Belsen displaced persons camp, when Sonia was sixteen and Laybl forty-three. Laybl had had a wife and two children, who had died in the crematoria. Before Sonia could even get her weight up to a hundred pounds, Laybl asked her to marry him. After a few years in DP camps, Laybl moved his wife and one-year-old Gabriel to New York, then Minneapolis, then Chicago, camp followers, so to speak, of Sonia's sister, originally believed dead, but, in fact, a survivor of Auschwitz. When Sonia's sister and her husband moved to Los Angeles, Laybl put his foot down. "I'm not moving to another American city," he said, whereupon he, Sonia, and Gabriel settled on an egg-breeding farm in Long-a-coming, New Jersey. Sonia always told me she liked Minneapolis best.

"Your father tried to undersell me!" Laybl would rant at me in Yiddish a dozen times a week. Alone with Sonia in the coop, I asked if it was true that my father had tried to drive Laybl out of business.

"Is that what Laybl told you?" she asked sweetly. Not even the chicken coop, choked with the dust of flapping hens and chicken feed, detracted from Sonia's loveliness. She was tiny, maybe four foot ten, with auburn hair. I always regarded her lips as Czechoslovakian, thinking, probably, of her fixed smile when she spoke of Auschwitz. She would blow up about the Germans, the Poles, all of Europe "soaked with Jewish blood," and even what she called "men's contempt for women." But she never once got angry at me, Laybl, or Gabriel.

Sonia brushed a chicken feather out of my hair and smiled. "One day, when Gabriel was ten or eleven, your father was supposed to pick him and your brother up from public school and drive them both to Hebrew school—"

"My parents never mentioned Gabriel to us," I said. "Neither did Sheiye."

Sonia wrinkled her brow. "Gabriel waited in front of the Long-a-coming Elementary School for an hour. When he didn't see Mr. Szuster, he walked home. Laybl considered it an insult to *me* that your father left Gabriel behind. He drove to your farm and threatened him with a broken pipe."

"But did Mr. Szuster—" Sonia never called my father by his first name, and sometimes I fell into her habit. "Did my father know he was supposed to take Gabriel?" I asked. "Papa always insisted he was a man of his word." I shrugged. "At least with strangers."

Sonia put her arm around my waist. I looked at the wedding band on her ring finger and thought, *A wasted life.* Darting her eyes towards the coop door, Sonia whispered, "My Laybl can't bear the thought of me talking to another man. Do you know what he told me when he met Mr. Szuster in 1950?" Sonia laughed. She looked at the door again and whispered, "Laybl said, 'Szuster's a religious man. All the religious men take the most beautiful women for themselves.' When Laybl saw your mother, Brantzchele, and how beautiful she was—don't look so astonished! You've seen her photographs. Rukhl! Dark eyes so innocent you couldn't believe the horrors she lived through. When Laybl saw your mother, he came home and told me, 'I don't trust Szuster as far as I can see him.' "

"You mean Laybl thought Papa was after you?" I asked. I pictured my father in tight jeans, shirt unbuttoned to the waist, gold chain around his neck, and a *yarmulke* on his head. He made a dubious philanderer.

"Shh!" Sonia put an index finger to her Czechoslovakian lips and hugged me so tight I grunted. "Brantzchele," she said. "You can stay with us as long as you like!"

Laybl was always sick. He had problems with his kidneys, his lungs, his prostate. He couldn't sleep. At four in the morning, he would crunch sand on the kitchen linoleum with his open-backed slippers and drink milk of magnesia from a teaspoon. It was hard to pity him, though, for his adoration of Sonia had reduced his store of love for anyone else, including his son. I tried to be sympathetic. Saturday afternoons Sonia carted out family photographs, just as Mama had, and I stared at a picture of Laybl, all wedge and angle in striped camp pajamas. From a barracks window, three other living human skeletons hung over Laybl's shoulder. Laybl had yanked up his pants to expose legs fragile as a grasshopper's. The photograph had a lithographic quality, black shadows cast deep into eye sockets, protruding jawbones and jagged teeth. I was too afraid of Laybl to ask him if he had volunteered that pose or if the photographer had requested it. Had I been younger, I would have asked if the photo was real.

The camps took a toll on Laybl's health, that was clear. But I thought his possessive love had also poisoned his system, completing the damage that malnutrition and overwork had started. Laybl blamed his chicken farm too, but he would have been just as sick had he become a stockbroker.

Sonia was enslaved by Laybl's glance, a wink, a diamond ring he bought her and replaced when Sonia lost the original in a movie house sink. Shopping with me at Humble's Supermarket in town, Sonia confided, "One smile from Laybl gives me the strength to do the work of two grown men." With Gabriel at Dartmouth and Laybl so frail that he was never able to work a full year on the farm, that's exactly what Sonia did, and with never a word of resentment.

I met Gabriel at Thanksgiving in 1969. He wore jeans and a faded blue turtleneck, conscious measures, perhaps, to neutralize his protesting red hair. Before he even dropped his knapsack on a kitchen chair, he called out, "Where's the orphan?" I walked into the kitchen, to see Sonia wrapped around Gabriel's waist and Laybl massaging his dyspepsia until the handshaking was over with. From Sonia's glowing reports of her son, I had already decided to marry Gabriel, even though I would have preferred that he look like my black-haired cemetery boy. I said, "You're less pasty-looking than most redheads." We shook hands.

At dinner Gabriel talked only about Vietnam. He spoke about rain forests as if he had sailed the South China Sea and slogged through them himself. He said "imperialism" several times while Sonia beamed. The greater part of his monologue was taken up by the mass protest marches and antiwar committees he participated in, with descriptions of the naked blond Yippie who presented Henry Kissinger with a pig's head, the Irish Maoist who dug only Oriental women, and the walleyed black woman who read about Jewish martyrdom in her spare time. I found these scenarios romantic and wanted to be part of them. Observing Gabriel's excitement as he spoke, I surmised that the drama exhilarated him more than the political rhetoric did. Galling him a bit, I said, "Gabriel, you don't care a fig about Vietnam. You're in it for the good time."

"I do too care a fig," Gabriel said without malice. He helped himself to the turkey I had seen gobbling in the Kichners' pen the day before. "Just wait till you leave south Jersey, hayseed!"

Laybl harrumphed. "You don't know people," he said to his son, reaching over Gabriel's elbow for the cranberry sauce. Laybl's hand shook and a few berries fell onto Gabriel's lap, and Sonia leapt up to get another napkin. Gabriel didn't say a word to his father the rest of the meal.

Later, in a grove of pine trees behind the largest coop, Gabriel took my hand, limiting from the outset the possibilities for our friendship. We sat down on a log, and he laughed.

He was suddenly so good-natured I couldn't believe Laybl Kichner was his father.

"Your hand!" Gabriel said. "It's small."

I withdrew my hand and held it before my eyes. "Yeah, it's riotously funny. I can barely contain myself," I said.

Remember the trees, Brantzche, I told myself, *and the smell of gasoline mixed with pine. Don't forget the pop of hunters' guns and the ant crawling through mulch, paying for his lone jaunt with expulsion from the colony. Remember Gabriel's unworked palms.* I wanted to shabbosify the moment, sabotaging time's passage so I would know one happy moment without memory of my sister's death.

Gabriel reached for my hand again and pressed it into his knee. "Talk to me," he said. That's how strangers introduced themselves to each other in the sixties—by probing for the personal tragedy beneath the ritual commonplaces. My hand covered a daisy-printed flannel patch from a girl's nightgown. I envied his membership in the world of proud, ripped knees, and I felt jealousy about the flannel patch's origin.

I told Gabriel about Perel's death, and how she invented comic characters when she was alive. Sheiye, I said, was a beast and never would be too soon to see him. My parents were zookeepers who kept chickens and children for their sadistic entertainment. In short, I tried to paint a rueful picture of myself so Gabriel would fall in love with me. For emphasis, I returned to the theme of my loneliness on this earth without Perel, and could almost hear her wheezing disapproval whistling past my earlobe: "You ah lowdown!"

Perel, my exploitation of your death was to no avail. Gabriel didn't view my waifdom as romantic. Instead of drawing my head to his chest, he squeezed my wrist and delivered a lecture. "Brenda—I prefer Brenda to Brantzche, don't you? Brantzche sounds like my father clearing his throat."

I laughed. "Perel used to say it sounded like our dog Bolero throwing up."

Gabriel leaned his skinny body towards me. He was as tall as Laybl and looked like a matchstick. "Brenda, listen. You're not the only one who suffers."

"I know. Vietnam, right?"

"Don't be glib. You're more likable when you laugh at yourself."

"You're more likable when you're not self-righteous."

"Cease fire!" He shook my hand. Didn't he know he could explore the body connected to it? Gabriel persisted in his serious tone, and I began to feel duped. "Brenda, I don't know what your plans are. Ma says, and I quote, 'She plays piano like an angel.' I told her angels play harp."

"I'm not ready for heaven," I said. "Besides, it's only pop tunes."

Gabriel reared his head and laughed. I hadn't said anything funny, so I sensed the gesture was calculated. I waited for him to kiss me. But he only outlined the flannel patch with my fingertip and said, "Brenda, leave Long-a-coming after you graduate. Split, skidoo, crawl, but blow this joint. I know you're attached to my mother, but don't be obliged to repay her with another year of your life."

"Gabriel, I love your mother. I love working knee-high in chicken shit with her. But I'm an ingrate." Defiant, I announced, "I'm going to get a job in New York City and study piano."

"You don't have to be so defiant." Gabriel laughed, throwing his head back again. "Just do it. Ma and I will always provide moral support."

"You should decide how often you want to do that," I

said, throwing my head back in imitation. "After a while it looks phony."

His self-consciousness uncovered, Gabriel ignored me for a few seconds, during which time I considered it preferable in situations like this one to be a man instead of a woman.

"One more thing," he said. Gabriel stood up and pulled me with him. "Brenda, make peace with your family."

"They're monsters," I protested.

He tickled my arm with a pine cone. "They're not."

"You wouldn't know, would you?"

Gabriel dropped my hand. "Brenda, you've entered yourself in a no-win sweepstakes. I thought I knew the definition of monstrosity till I went to college."

"Vietnam again," I sighed.

"Vietnam and then some," Gabriel said.

"Will I be as cryptic as you when I go to college?" I asked. I wanted Gabriel to grouse about his father, but he only inhaled with exaggerated patience. Yoga-style, he closed his eyes and rolled his head in a circle. Sometimes I doubted Gabriel Kichner's sincerity sentence to sentence, movement to movement.

Seeing as he wouldn't kiss me, I said, "Too bad you're not my brother."

"That would only limit—" Gabriel searched for the right word but came up only with "things." To my surprise, I wasn't flattered. Despite my lack of experience with men outside my family, I realized that he was the type who used coquetry to keep his options open. Yet as a great fan of the sly in my own way, I thrilled to his chicanery. I wanted him. But all he did on his rare visits home was hold my hand, instruct me to flee Long-a-coming, and insist that I make peace with my family.

After Gabriel graduated from Dartmouth he never returned to Long-a-coming, and he never held my hand again. He was married to an Irish girl a year and a half before he told his parents. Sonia cried to me over the phone, saying every pore of her body was Jewish, and she didn't understand what Gabriel meant by being a "world citizen." Today, with Laybl dead, Gabriel separated from his wife and two children, and Sonia working for Shulman Electronics, Gabriel no longer mentions Vietnam or lectures me about making peace with my family. Now he tells me how Jews can only be his sisters, not his lovers.

3

FEW OTHER PASSENGERS were making the 6:00 A.M. journey to Atlantic City. The casinos didn't open until ten, so I missed the typical NYC to AC crowd of blacks, Hispanics, Israelis, Chinatown Chinese, and elderly Jewish widows. Downstairs in the Port Authority, the bus driver stood at the Domenico Bus gate, taking tickets and drinking coffee from a Have a Nice Day paper cup. Sweat hunkered in his laugh lines. He winked at me in a way part avuncular, part lecherous. "Gonna take a gamble on love, hon?" he asked. Oh yes, I laughed.

In the bus, I sat down behind a woman with a blond beehive hairdo. With her frizzy yellow hair and her black-and-white-striped dress, she looked disturbingly like a bumblebee. Before the driver turned the ignition key, the woman faced me and said with a smile, "I'll look after you." I smiled awkwardly in response and pulled out my compact from a carryall to check my makeup. At thirty, I still look like a sixteen-year-old runaway. The beehive turned around again and saw me perusing the *New York Times* metropolitan section. She raised an eyebrow and considered stinging. Playing grownup, eh, little girl? Her look was simultaneously maternal and seductive, and it occurred to me that she was a Jersey shore madam. Maybe I would have to outrun her and her swarm of drones in the Atlantic City bus station. I hoped so.

On the other aisle, a few seats up, sat a young man with a long wispy beard and legs so stumpy they reminded me of my father's thumb. He wore a blue polyester suit gone shiny from overuse, white athletic socks, and a pair of black lace-up shoes. Crushing his tongue into the corner of his mouth, he fidgeted with a tape recorder on his lap. Suddenly, frantic, he leapt out of his seat and cried, "Sinners, two years ago I was one of you!" Before the driver could still him, the bearded young man sermonized that God had spared his life in a pickup truck accident, and during his year as a bedridden cripple, he was saved through the love of Jesus Christ.

Glowering at the lay preacher through the rearview mirror, the driver announced into the bus microphone, "Ladies and gentlemen, thank you for riding Domenico Bus Lines. There is no smoking on this coach in the state of New Jersey . . . restroom-equipped . . . approximate time of arrival in Atlantic City is 8:30 A.M. . . . pleasant trip." The driver warned the preacher not to play his tape recorder without earphones and then turned on the bus headlights as we entered the Lincoln Tunnel.

The presence of the madam and the lay preacher had put me into a semitrance, and I searched dreamily for prophetic meaning in both of them. But by the time we passed Weehawken, New Jersey, the lay preacher was immersed in a notebook of biblical quotations, and the sound of a distant lawnmower rose from the madam's throat as she slept. I stared out the window, expecting to see rain but finding only the chemical brown isolation of north Jersey.

As the bus lumbered down the turnpike, I tried to imagine what Sheiye and I would say to each other. My efforts were stymied as I pictured my brother as a thirty-three-year-old man. Was he the same person I had known as a child? Would I finally hear him confess that he had killed Perel, whether by accident or after a moment's deliberation?

Hazily, the lyrics to a song I had played the previous

night at Sir Ivory's returned to me: "There's a time I would go to my brother; I've asked my brother, will you help me please; he turned me down and I asked my little mother; I said, 'Mother, I'm down on my knees. . . .'" By the time Absecon Bay sparkled outside my window, those lines had bothered me into a realization. I had fled Sheiye and my parents not because I hated them, but because they had denied me an audience. Why should I have backed off from them? I knew I didn't kill Perel. I began to wonder if I should have pursued Mama and Papa to Israel, or even pleaded with them to stay. Hectoring them with my version of events had set them against me; perhaps a readiness to stand by them until their delirium was defused would have salvaged us as a family. Maybe because he was a little older, Sheiye had understood this and he had won.

Several times Papa had told us that a child must meet his parents more than halfway; that, eventually, a child must be more mature than his parents. I don't know why, but the burden of reconciliation had always lain on me. It was almost impossible for me to accept, almost more impossible to act on, but in view of all the damage done in their lives, Mama and Papa needed my love more than I needed theirs. Of course, in a way that matters to me more than analysis or charity, I know I cannot fully forgive my parents. And I also believe that my empathy belongs to a topsy-turvy universe in which children must be supernaturally sympathetic to their parents' frustrations. Yet my intelligence teaches me that the hate and vengeance appropriate at fifteen are, by themselves, shallow at thirty.

But even as the bus pulled into the Arctic Avenue station, I still could not be philosophical about Sheiye.

The beehive madam waited for me to leave my seat. Standing so close I could feel her breath muss my hair, she placed her moist hand on my shoulder and hummed, "Follow me." I had heard that rapists and molesters cringe at the sight of overt insanity and dislike references to bodily functions. I couldn't imagine picking my nose or scratching my crotch in the Atlantic City bus terminal, so, opting for insult, I drew myself up and told her, "You snore." Her lips parted, and just like in the movies, she called me a "hussy" and skirred into the terminal building. My insolence told her that I wasn't a malleable castabout from Ames, Iowa, ripe for bordello work, after all.

I had fifteen minutes to kill before meeting Sheiye. I had expected him to be there early, and when I didn't see him, I was certain he had stood me up. Sheiye had good reason to welch on our plans. For all he knew, I would make a scene or quietly insist on a confession before leaving Atlantic City. I positioned myself and my carryall bag against a supporting column. The madam, apparently having forgotten me, burrowed through the honeycomb of tourists and commuters for fresh girls. Near the door opposite me stood half a dozen redcaps, wiping their heavy-lidded eyes with boardwalk-embossed handkerchiefs and resting their feet on somebody's luggage. They looked me up and down with enough contempt to suggest that I had crossed them personally, and lucky for me, their gaze implied, the public eye kept them from roughhousing me in the storage room. The dome-shaped bus station was so humid with suspicion I could hear it pant.

Into this steamy rotunda walked my brother. He hadn't changed that much. He still wore blue jeans, but now they were new and pressed, not faded and patched. Although he had more of a gut, his full head of curly hair saved him from looking like a man tumbling towards middle age. His face seemed puffy, and he had grown a mustache. But I recognized him at once. I wanted to hide, because I was afraid, but also because I wanted to observe him. Sheiye searched left and right, sifting through commuters and redcaps to find me. He had chosen to stay behind in south Jersey, and did not look out of place here, as I fancied I did. The roar of mufflerless souped-up cars outside did not rile him, nor did the twang of the Philly/Baltimore accents. Nonetheless, Sheiye struck me as a naïf blundering into vulture territory, and I saw that the years had knocked the stuffing out of my brother.

Sheiye looked towards the pillar but did not appear to see the slender thirty-year-old woman dressed in white draw-string jeans and a yellow rayon blouse, her long blond hair pulled back into a single braid. He headed towards me as if to greet me, but then turned away. I slung my carryall over my shoulder, inhaled, exhaled, and walked towards Sheiye Szuster. Chin downturned, eyes straining to identify his sole living sister, Sheiye stopped and swayed, letting the hot air currents decide in which direction he would blow. It was absurd to expect Sheiye to take my bag or shake my hand or kiss me hello the way other people do in bus stations. Sheiye fastened his thumbs behind his belt. I was relieved he didn't touch me.

"I didn't recognize you," Sheiye said. Only four words, and any linguist worth his salt could peg the accent as south Jersey. Sheiye laughed, but it was so embarrassed it made me think of children studying each other's genitals.

It's been fifteen years, I could have said. I'm thirty now, I could have said. I'm not so different. Everything sounded trivializing, as if Sheiye and I had gotten together after his stint in the army simply to chat. Without the impetus of hatred, I was speechless.

One of the redcaps approached us. Tapping his cloth red cap, he asked Sheiye, "Need any help, suh?" Though it was obvious that I could manage my carryall alone, Sheiye began to offer my bag, looked at me, changed his mind, and then began to offer it again. He knew neither the etiquette nor the alibi for this situation or, I gathered, for many others, either. For a second, I was sitting alongside the olive-skinned Officer Lemons, listening to him say, "Nice guy, Steve. A little on the shy side." I remember thinking how uninsightful a stranger can be about the monsters you know so well. Now I had to scuttle a belief I had held for years. Sheiye had become a stranger whose name and parents I happened to know. Although I had seen this timid soul who was my brother hide from egg customers and from the slaughterhouse, I had always viewed him through the mist of loathing. I had chosen to see him as a shark, because I knew he could destroy me through his weakness. I speculated about the brother whom I met that day: Can a person go through a murderous phase in his life, just as he goes through adolescence or passion, only to pass out becalmed on the other side?

"Thank you, I can handle it myself," I told the redcap.

Just then Sheiye dropped his car keys and we both bent down to retrieve them. "It's all right," he said. "I got them."

"The car is this way," he told me, establishing some mastery over the situation and looking smaller for the attempt. We passed the blond madam on her dozenth whirl around the station. When she saw me, she spun away, looking for sweeter nectar. I smiled at how easily she bruised and then realized she could send a flotilla of thugs to settle scores with me.

Outside, the lay preacher leaned against the wall of the bus terminal, distributing pamphlets with radiant candles on the cover. "Jesus loves you," he intoned to Sheiye and me, handing us two pamphlets, which we accepted politely.

"Did you see that fat blonde?" Sheiye asked as we walked up to his green Pacer. "She recruits prostitutes."

"I know," I said, the first word I'd addressed to my brother.

"She come on to you?" Sheiye asked, his eyes flaring wide. Maybe he remembered his prophecy that I would become a Jew whore. He stared at my breasts.

"Yeah, but I decided to see you, anyway," I said.

Sheiye raised his stare. I cocked my head and he laughed. "Oh, a joke. I thought you were serious for a second." Sheiye's past viciousness had lent him a certain intelligence, and without it he seemed dim.

My brother opened the door for me because I was a stranger. He rearranged fishing tackle in the back so it wouldn't poke out my eye. A sun-faded *Mad* magazine lay on the passenger side, and Sheiye told me to throw it under my seat. My brother walked around the front of the car, got in, and placed his hands on the steering wheel. Mutely, he stared ahead at the lay preacher. I focused on my thighs. *I remember another time when you looked like this, Sheiye. You looked more determined then, that's the only difference. You didn't look vacant.*

"Where do you want to go?" Sheiye asked, still looking through the windshield.

What was this, a lovers' tryst? How about your place? "How about your place?" I asked, knowing instinctively Sheiye didn't want to take me there. Be more demanding, Brantzche. You are here to test the waters of the past. "What's wrong with your apartment?"

"My house," Sheiye corrected. I had been thinking of Sheiye as something of a Winnebago-camper man and was feeling sorry for him. Confused, I was glad that this man unsure of how to act with redcaps had a house.

"Well, then, your house," I suggested.

Sheiye said, "No."

"Okay, how about the boardwalk? We can sit on a bench and talk."

"Someone might see us," he said to the windshield.

"It's no crime to sit on a public bench and talk to your sister," I grumbled. Of course it was a crime. Sheiye and I were bush-league criminals—I still felt that way around him. Maybe a cop would finally clamp handcuffs on our wrists and drag us away to justice. Our case would make the "Crime" section of *Time*.

Sheiye rifled through a ringful of keys and inserted one into the ignition. "We can go to the house after eleven," he said. "For now, we'll drive to a beach in Ventnor."

My brother and I drove past the pompous monument near Atlantic City High School, which I had always pictured as Bert Parks on a horse, and away from Atlantic City's pink guesthouses and hoagie shops, to Ventnor's private homes and hyacinths. Profound revelation had not yet throttled me by the neck as I had expected it would on my seeing Sheiye. In my old childlike way, I still waited for an object or a person to reveal its dungeon secret to me, and thus expose a pervasive truth underlying all of life. Sitting beside my brother, I felt myself still believing that, even though I already knew Sheiye's secret. Yet I suspected that a real secret must lie further behind his crime, for his reticence implied he was holding something back from me. By the end of the day, I decided, I would know it.

"Isn't there a big pink elephant somewhere on the beach around here?" I asked. Sheiye answered that it had been dismantled years earlier, but did not elaborate. He finally parked the Pacer on a Ventnor side street, behind a bug extermination van whose motto on the back double doors advised, "Don't Tolerate—Exterminate." In an oddly cheerful tone, he said, "Everybody out!" Walking to the boardwalk, I noticed that

Sheiye's right shoe sole was worn down unevenly, and I could not resist the wave of pity that swept through me.

"You know what's funny?" I asked. Sheiye and I stopped to sit on a bench facing the Atlantic. Seagulls jetted over the water, and pigeons begged for crumbs. Ancient Jews in white vinyl shoes and sunscreen on their noses shuffled along the wooden planks and told each other where they had been born. "What's funny," I said, "is that I'm wearing my bathing suit under my clothes."

Sheiye watched two suntanned Philadelphia girls strut by. From his shirt pocket he withdrew a pair of sunglasses. He put them on and said, "Brantzche, if you're leading up to something, tell me outright. Why'd you want to see me?"

"I have to say why?"

"Say why," Sheiye said. "Say why and get it over with."

I opened my carryall and fished for my own sunglasses. "You know," I insisted.

Turning to me, he asked, "What do I know?"

"We're here to talk about Perel, okay?"

Sheiye took a deep breath. "Okay." He looked out at the ocean and said, "You know, Brantzche, sometimes whole days go by when I don't think about . . . about all that. Sometimes even a week."

"I don't believe it," I said.

"I don't know why not."

"If you could rewrite the script," I said. "If it could have been me . . ."

"Jesus, Brantzche, what difference does it make? I wish it had been Bolero. Or a pile of rags. That's what I wish!"

Sheiye gave no sign that he was about to storm off. I didn't want him to, and I didn't want to sit and accuse him, either. I just wanted to know who he had become. Perel, forgive me, but I can't ask for anything more.

Baring my neck to the sun, I said, "Sometimes I try to imagine what all the people I used to know are doing now. Mama, Papa, Charlie, kids from school. It's been fifteen years. It's hard to make it through fifteen years, and I can't believe they've all made it."

"They haven't."

My face flushed. I thought Sheiye was going to tell me one of my parents had died. But Lalke would have notified me, I'm sure.

"Charlie's dead," Sheiye said, and became almost lively, exhuming some of that ghastly mirth which had been such a dominant part of his character. "Yeah, you'll never guess how I found out. Five, six years ago, I'm depositing a check at the bank, and I vaguely see this black guy in the line next to me. I don't pay much attention to him but he notices me, and he comes up beside me and I think, uh oh, the guy's gonna hit me up for a loan. But it's Charlie and he shakes my hand."

"Charlie voluntarily shook your hand?" I asked. "I can't believe it."

"Believe, sister!" Sheiye said in black dialect. "He told me he had a job at the Atlantic City Salvation Army. He was sorting clothes in their laundromat. Living in Atlantic City and sorting clothes."

"And then he died?"

"Don't rush me!" Sheiye was in good spirits now. "Charlie made a bundle working in that laundromat, and I don't mean clothes. One day he's sorting and a ten-dollar bill floats out of some *shmate*. Charlie sticks his hand in and finds loads more. I guess the Salvation Army was his salvation, huh?" Sheiye laughed. But he realized he had been talking freely as he did when we were children and, biting his nail, censured himself.

"Strange," I mused. "You know, Sheiye, I used to think there was something messianic about you. A story like that coming from you, somehow it doesn't surprise me."

"Messianic?" Sheiye repeated. "I'm not bitter." I didn't know if Sheiye had misunderstood, or if he wanted to change the subject. He reached into his shirt pocket again and pulled out a Mounds bar, breaking off a piece for me. "I hate coconut," I said. Sheiye shrugged a "suit yourself" as if I had made a decade of wrong decisions, this last being the culmination, and he ate the bar in three bites. He made a movement with his hand like he was leaning down on a car horn, a gesture of approval I had seen in second- and third-generation American Jews. I thought, *He's beginning to look like a city Jew.*

Licking his teeth clean of chocolate, Sheiye said, "How'd he die? Howdy Doody!" Laugh. "It didn't have nothing to do with the Salvation Army. Charlie got drowned. You'll never guess where." Before I could wager a guess, Sheiye blurted out, "Atsion." He poked his index finger against his bottom molars and said, "They fished him out of the lake dead drunk, but really dead. He had a wad of wet cash in his pocket."

"How do you know it was Charlie? And if it happened at Atsion, how did you hear about it?"

"It was in the *Atlantic City Record,*" Sheiye said. "An article and a picture of Charlie bending over a washing machine at the Salvation Army."

"But what was he doing at Atsion?"

The baritone gargle of a prop plane overhead broke into our conversation. A long vinyl streamer from its tail advertised a comedy act at one of the casinos. There weren't many other people at the beach, and I was amused that the advertising addressed someone as morbid as I am. Instead of expecting Sheiye to explicate mysteries, I should have asked him directly if Charlie had mentioned anything about Perel. But I thought it best to leave Charlie floating in Atsion Lake for now. I pointed to the streamer. "Is that where you work?" I asked.

"How do you know I work in a casino?" Sheiye narrowed his eyes, trying to appear mean, I suppose, but merely looking as if he were about to sneeze.

"Lalke," I answered. "Lalke keeps me up to date on the life and times of the Szuster family. She said you work in a casino and live with a male lover."

"My lover is a wife." Sheiye bit his lower lip. Lalke had told me nothing of Sheiye's private life. I had surmised that homosexuality was the path Sheiye had followed.

"A wife," I said. "And how long has this been going on?"

"I shouldn't have said anything," Sheiye replied, and he might as well have told me, "I shouldn't have put butter on my roll"; he sounded that unperturbed.

"Because she doesn't know much about me, I assume. Or Perel."

"Brantzche, I didn't have to see you. I'm happy with my life."

"In other words, your wife doesn't know about Perel," I said.

Folding the Mounds wrapper lengthwise, Sheiye said, "I had a sister named Perel who died of leukemia when she was almost thirteen. That's the story everybody knows."

"Everybody," I said.

"My wife. Friends." Sheiye paused. All these years he had constructed an armory of secrets with the hope that one day he would lob each one at me—or whomever—to prove that life meant not only survival but happiness at any cost. The sadism that I thought had atrophied into mediocrity had revealed itself, cowering inside the provident folds of secrecy. If Sheiye took pleasure in his secrets from me, no doubt he took equal pleasure in the secrets he kept from his wife. His secrets were his only successes. I wondered if Sheiye had reintroduced me into his life as a dash of cayenne in a dull marriage. Perhaps he took delight in the sight of my face, slack with the realization that I had been erased, as he would take delight in seeing his wife wear a similar expression of the betrayed. In any case, Sheiye had learned pacing, a strategy essential to effective power. "And Mama and Papa know too," he said.

"How cozy. Do Mama and Papa remember the real story, at least?"

"Mama and Papa adjusted to reality," Sheiye answered.

"And I didn't. Well, you've all fixed things up swimmingly for yourselves. Congratulations." I extended my hand to Sheiye. He didn't want to shake it, but, as always, anybody's stronger conviction bowled him into submission. He briefly gave me his hand and then pressed it hard against his ankle, propped on his knee.

"What's the point of talking?" Sheiye said. "I'm only hurting you."

"I can't figure it out," I said. "Not for the life of me. All I did was witness. I lived to tell, the way they did."

"I gave them a grandchild," Sheiye said.

"Have any more bombshells? Go ahead, shoot. I'm in control of my biorhythms."

"Her name is Perel," Sheiye said.

"I hope you're enjoying yourself," I said.

Sheiye scraped his cuticles with the folded edge of the candy wrapper. "I told you I liked my life," he said. I thought of the affairs I had had with married men, and how they tell you about the wife, but they don't tell the wife about you, not unless they want to ditch her, which they do for someone else, not you, or for you when it's too late, or because they think being a bachelor is exciting, which it isn't, because the laundry doesn't get done. I learned about Sheiye's wife, but she wouldn't learn about me because she mattered more.

"You brought it all on yourself, Brantzche," Sheiye said. "I told you that a long time ago."

I jumped up from the bench, and Sheiye's shoulders flinched. "I'm fucking drowning in conscience!" I cried. Two seagulls flapped away in cawing protest. "I don't understand why you're happy. Do you at least cheat on your wife? Beat your kid? What right do you have to be happy?"

"Sit down or I won't talk to you," Sheiye whispered. "You're embarrassing me."

I thought I could keep screaming the same five words the rest of my life in Ventnor, New Jersey. If I didn't calm down, Sheiye would leave me there, I knew that. He had too much at risk. I felt for the bench and sat down. "I'm fucking drowning in conscience," I repeated, softer, to show that rage had nothing to do with my sentiment.

"Brantzche, sometimes I hear Germans talk their Kraut on the beach. They *shmir* themselves with suntan oil and listen to golden oldies on the radio. You think they feel guilty? No. They're on vacation. They're happy. And they have more reason to feel bad than me. What they did, they did on purpose. Me . . . us . . . it was an accident."

"I don't believe in accidents."

"Well, I do, and that's why I'm in better shape than you."

"If you believe in accidents, why don't you tell your wife the real story? How come you and Mama and Papa cooked up this stew about Perel and leukemia?"

"Brantzche, I can't discuss this with you. You're hysterical. Why aren't you married? Why do you have to piss in your beer about things done with?"

"Piss in my beer," I said. "That's a good one. I'll have to use that on the lushes at work. And by the way," I added, "I am not hysterical." I wasn't. I felt tired and had no interest in getting back to New York in time for my gig.

"You work with drunks?" Sheiye's eyes opened wide like Mendl's. "Oh, you mean like social work?"

"I mean like in a bar. I play piano in a bar. I'm surprised Lalke didn't tell you." Ah, Mama and Papa were ashamed of my work.

"That's good, Brantzche. You did something with your gift."

"My gift. It's more like a door prize," I said. I remembered Sammy Davis, Jr., a trumpet player on the downbeat in *A Man Called Adam,* whining, "It's no good anymore," and loping into the night with a raincoat sliding off his right shoulder. That movie upset me so much I turned it off in the middle.

"Why aren't you married?" Sheiye asked. "You must be thirty now. You still look young. You could find someone."

"Why don't I have a heart-to-heart with your wife? Maybe she can give me some tips on finding a good man," I said, and immediately regretted having exposed my bitterness.

Sheiye looked at his watch. "You haven't changed much, Brantzche."

"I have. I've forgotten a lot, and I'm sorry about that."

"That's your mistake," he said. "Forgetting is good."

Feel privileged, Brantzche. Everybody knows the facts of Sheiye's present life, but you are among the few who know the real story, one of them, anyway; who doesn't participate in the lies. For heaven's sake, I wonder if I can ever trust any person: He can have murder in his background and treat it like a little white lie.

Sheiye and I sat on the bench, sunglasses in place, our noses turning red, with nothing more to say to each other. The blood in our veins was the same, but we didn't belong in each other's lives. Still, I didn't want to leave him yet, and I think he wanted me to stay. At eleven, with Sheiye's wife at her blackjack table and the little Perel at day camp, Sheiye and I drove to his house in Margate, for some lunch, Sheiye said. But I believed my forbidden walk in his wife's shadow made my frightened brother feel strong.

Still imagining gore, I anticipated finding a bloody X brush-stroked on the door of Sheiye's weather-beaten house. But we pulled up in front of a pink three-bedroom bungalow with white shutters, a modest home, its ankles nestled in the bank of Margate Bay. The street was small-townish, lined on either side with marigolds and Detroit-model cars. Except for the post office around the corner, there was no sign of commerce. Several steps away from Sheiye's house lay a wooden dock, a spot so peacefully romantic that, for a moment, I imagined that Sheiye could not be guilty of all I had accused him of.

The front door opened into a sitting room furnished with a convertible couch, an old-time radio in an oakwood cabinet, a spinet piano, a maplewood grandfather clock, and a bookcase. The interior design expressed all the comforts of a small-town home of the American 1930s, an ambience that stood awkwardly at odds with Sheiye's actual past.

"Make yourself at home," Sheiye said. In this setting, Sheiye had become relaxed, treating me as an old friend passing through Margate. My brother busied himself in the kitchen, adjusting the air conditioning and fixing us bagels and lox. In the sitting room, I stared at Sheiye's framed wedding picture —gold script announced the marriage of "Steve and Frieda

Szuster, June 27, 1977"—and a Sears Studio portrait of little Perel Szuster. While the reborn Perele was thinner and blonder than the original, the disbelieving brown eyes were the same. Overcome by longing, I recalled one day in the 1950s when I stood in the kitchen of our yawning house, rocking Perel in her cavernous buggy. I remembered the buggy and its gray canvas, me at the helm, and my mother peeling potatoes at the kitchen sink, smiling. But I don't remember the baby inside, not its flesh, not what it would become.

The walls of Sheiye's fairy-tale cottage began to disintegrate. If I tried, I would be able to touch the sun dust that streamed around me like the thousands of dots in a Seurat painting. Only my vision and the young Perel's picture existed in the world now. I knew that when I blinked, Perel's eyes blinked too. I tried to hold my eyes open, so I could catch Perel blinking, but something tickled my lower lashes and I shut them. Behind my lids, I see my sister's body lying on earth disclosing its blood and leaving uncovered its slain. I don't scream, I don't cry; no conventional release is left to me. I reopen my eyes and the walls, seamed and cool, provide shelter again, evidence that Sheiye lives while I remember uselessly. I did not want Sheiye to catch me in mid-reverie, and moved to the bookcase.

The top shelf held hardbound college texts, all introductions, to biology, chemistry, general accounting principles, music theory. Each of the covers was green, as if the color were the thread unifying these disparate fields of study. I imagined Sheiye and his classmates at Glassboro skimming through *Introduction to Biology,* finishing the semester with a third of the chapters unread. These books were cousins to the gears and screws in Sheiye's childhood bureau that led nowhere in and of themselves, but might have generated a spark if plugged into an appropriate conductor. I fretted awhile that the introductory texts implied a lifetime of unfinished business, and that seeing me might be Sheiye's attempt to conclude at least one thing in his life.

Huddled beneath the weight of the textbooks like civilians arrested in wartime were the paperbacks: Harlequin romances, an Asimov trilogy, and one or two porn titles, awed into modest submission by the shadow of organized thought cast from above. The one anomalous title on the paperback shelf was *The Holy Scriptures.* The fake leather-bound, fake gilt-edged Bible might have been better placed on the top shelf, with the other introductory texts: It had introduced the Szusters to the torturous, eternal tension between our bestial and civilized natures. I turned to page one of Genesis, as I do with every Bible I pick up: "In the beginning God created the heaven and the earth," and, as always, I was taken aback that all our sorrows could have begun so simply, so beautifully. Arbitrarily, I turned to Isaiah, for the lay preacher had quoted him to a barefooted vagabond in the bus station. Though I distrusted Isaiah's pedagogical zeal and manic lamentations on the preacher's lips, I found that the prophet had foreseen my family's history: "Come, my people, enter thou into thy chambers, and shut thy doors about thee: hide thyself for a little moment, until the indignation be overpast." How long is a little moment, and whose indignation is more fierce—God's or Mama and Papa's?

"You still read *Khimish,* Sheiye?" I called out. I felt something muss my hair and turned around expecting to see Sheiye behind me. But my brother was somewhere in the house, in the bathroom or his bedroom, and nothing but discomfort stirred the hairs on my neck. I tucked the Bible back into its place and rubbed the goose bumps flat on my arms. I blamed the air conditioner for making me cold and for buzzing so I couldn't hear the bay water lapping, the occasional honk of a car horn, or the clomp of Sheiye's feet throughout the house. Blowing on my fingertips, I walked into the kitchen and sat down at the table. The last time I had eaten bagels and lox was at Perel's *shive*. Thence, the sight of that food had made me lose my appetite.

Sheiye entered the kitchen from the bedroom. Contrary to his ruffian childhood self, Sheiye was now a bit fastidious and had changed into a fresh shirt and jeans. "I thought you might want to see this," he said and, handing me a clipping from the *Atlantic City Record,* dove into the food. The *Record* article, actually a two-inch news brief, was dated August 2, 1980, and confirmed the death of Charles Dixon, employee of the Atlantic City Salvation Army. Local bathers had discovered Charlie lying face down in south Jersey's Atsion Lake with twenty-five wet tens in his pants pocket. As a result, the police had ruled out "foul play." The story mentioned nothing about Charlie's serendipitous windfall, nothing about his two surviving maiden sisters in Camden, nothing about his birthplace, nothing about his migration from Alabama to south Jersey.

"Why'd you tell me Charlie was bending over a washing machine?" I asked, startled by the accompanying photograph.

Swallowing a sliver of lox, Sheiye leaned across the table to squint at the picture. "Huh," he said, without much interest. "I must be thinking of some other picture. Oh, yeah, Charlie showed me a picture of himself at work. That day in the bank."

The newspaper photo was a frontal view of Russell's Funeral Parlor in Long-a-coming. Two dark-suited men, hands at their sides, posed at the entrance. A sloping, boldface caption read: "Residents near Atsion Lake transported the body of Charles Dixon, 57, to Russell's Funeral Parlor, above. Pictured are proprietor Willy Russell and Coroner Jack Millington, both of Long-a-coming, New Jersey."

"What rotten luck," I said.

"Yeah, he probably didn't know how to swim," Sheiye said. "Knowing our Charlie, *er hot zekh git ungeshikert.*" Sheiye's Yiddish threw me. Yiddish registered deep inside me, and despite my best efforts, I could never forget it. I heard the language of my parents only when I spoke to Sonia Kichner, and thought of it as the language of the wounded, the vanishing stubborn. Sheiye's Yiddish explanation that Charlie boozed it up allied him with my parents' sympathies. No wonder Mama and Papa couldn't condemn him: In every way, Sheiye spoke their language.

"I mean what rotten luck that Charlie ended up in Millington's hands," I said. "Russell's Funeral Parlor. People used to say it was stomping grounds for the Klan."

"Oh, yeah? I never heard that." Sheiye spread cream cheese on a second bagel.

"You must have," I told him, and then hesitated. "You knew Millington."

Sheiye looked across the table at me. "Brantzche, you sure you're getting enough sleep? You tell me I know some stranger in a picture I happened to have cut out of a newspaper. If you didn't have a steady job, I'd say you were going off the deep end."

"I saw you and Millington at the Assumption Parish carnival that summer . . . Perel's summer," I said.

"Who remembers?" Sheiye said. "Brantzche, maybe it's true that I was at some carnival in 1968, and maybe I did see someone by the name of Millington. But who can remember such trivia? I have enough trouble remembering my wife's birthday."

"I saw you, Sheiye. A priest talked to you and Milling-ton, this guy. Now do you remember?"

Sheiye swallowed and shook his head. "I don't remember what you remember, Brantzche. I don't dwell on the past, I really don't." He was lying about Millington. That photo-graph was still in his phylactery purse, and if it wasn't, he had had to throw it out, consciously eradicating a memory or an idea that no longer served him. Perhaps through an act of will, Sheiye no longer had clear recall of Millington's maleficence. My brother's lies gave me hope.

"How about the newspaper clippings in Charlie's room?" I asked. "Did you know Charlie hid some clippings inside the comic books? Remember the comic books in Charlie's room?"

"I remember the comic books," Sheiye said. "Yeah, there was *Archie* and *Superman,* I think, and *Spiderman.*"

"Once Perel and I snooped in his room, and I found some clippings in a comic book that said Charlie was acquitted of raping a white girl. You didn't know?"

Sheiye didn't appear at all surprised. "You have these clippings?" he asked.

"Mama burned them. Perel burned them. I don't know," I said.

"Maybe you saw an advertisement for something," Sheiye said. "Maybe you dreamed it up."

"I didn't. Afterwards, I wrote down everything I remem-bered. I still have that paper."

"Well, then, that piece of paper and a forty-five-caliber pistol are all that's left of Charlie," Sheiye said.

"A forty-five-caliber pistol?" I asked. "Okay, let's hear this one."

"A couple years after Mama and Papa moved to Israel, they came back to Long-a-coming to rent out the house. Some Puerto Ricans moved in. They wanted to fix up Charlie's room for a kid to live in. We didn't care, and the PRs went halves with us on materials. One day I'm helping them pull up the linoleum in Charlie's room and one of the older sons sees something black and shiny poking through the tile. I don't know why I didn't see it till then. It was so obvious what it was, poking through the tile a quarter exposed. It's a good thing Mama and Papa didn't stick around to see that. They'd have freaked." Sheiye got up from the table, went into the spare bedroom, and retrieved the gun. Moving the centerpiece of dried flowers to the counter, he laid it down on the table. "Let's face it," Sheiye said. "Charlie's elevator didn't go all the way to the top floor. We're lucky that—" Sheiye stopped.

I don't know why I never looked under Charlie's bed. The gun . . . Perel must have seen the gun under Charlie's cot. Is that why she hid under her sheets and then under the blanket a few months later? The sight of the gun coerced Perel to exercise the hiding reflex—the social contract between the Szusters and the world. Her denying brown eyes trained on the pistol, Perel set about forgetting. Yet Charlie's possession of the gun wasn't the forbidden action: Perel's seeing was. She didn't blame Charlie or the gun for existing. She blamed me and herself for implicating ourselves in Charlie's secret, his danger, his illegality, his blackness. Taboo as Jesus, the forty-five was no subject for discussion, not with me, not with Mama, not with herself. She wreaked revenge on the mystery inside the comic books, which threatened to implicate her further still in Charlie's black treachery. And in mine.

Charlie owned a gun, but I don't know if real menace backed up his occasional fits of insolence. I don't know if Charlie's elevator didn't go all the way to the top floor. I don't know if his enemy followed him north from Senior, Alabama. Yet Charlie left the forty-five in Long-a-coming. Can you forget to pack something like a gun? I don't think so. Weary of defending himself and the oath the gun signified, maybe Charlie decided to risk his fate without it. A fine bequest you two left me, Perel and Charlie; all these unanswered questions and untestable hypotheses you left me. And with each day's passing, your lives and deaths make less and less sense.

I ran my fingers over the gun and said, "You tell me Charlie had a gun and Mama and Papa were here. No one ever told me they came back to the United States."

"Just for a visit," Sheiye said. "A couple times to see their grandchild."

"To see you too," I said. "Why didn't anyone tell me?" Did Lalke know? She must have. And Sonia Kichner too?

"Brantzche, you're the one who cut ties, not them. You wouldn't kiss Mama goodbye."

"Oh, come on. You know that's an excuse. It's a straw man. They want to believe what they believe. They need a male heir to carry on the good Szuster name. They need an inheritor. And if I may make a suggestion, change the *z* to an *h,* like I did. Your daughter will thank you someday."

"If you wanted, you could see them again," Sheiye said. "What do you think? They come here and curse you out all day long?"

"No," I said. "I think they don't mention my name."

"There's no law that says they can't talk about you," Sheiye said.

"No law; just custom."

"They really suffer, Brantzche. They've been through a lot. You could be more understanding."

"I don't like them," I said. "I never did and I can't help that. I wish they hadn't suffered and I wish I didn't feel like a Nazi. Listen. I have sat through hundreds of evenings listening to their voices on my tape recorder. Nights after listening to every drunken heartbreak story in Manhattan, I've listened to them. Did Mama and Papa tell you they'll live forever in Yad Vashem?"

"I've heard some of the tapes," Sheiye said.

"Do you know I am insanely jealous of Yaffa Simontov, their oral historian? This nobody draws real personalities out of these people named Rukhl and Yankl. They are people who make me cry. I want to get to know them, and then it hits me, they're Mama and Papa. I like them. But the people I knew were deranged. They talked about dead people and a forest. They flew around like demons and slaughtered chickens. One of them prayed three times a day and the other one gave lectures. They are the people who passed this lunatic judgment on me! I survived something horrible, like they did. Do they pass judgment on themselves?"

"Probably."

"Why don't they blame you?" I asked.

"Because, for the tenth time, it was an accident." Sheiye drummed his oily fingers on the table. He picked up the gun and took it back to the bedroom. Why do they keep it in a bedroom?

"Why wasn't it an accident for me?" I called after him. Half to myself, I said, "They can't blame you. I don't know why, but they can't. And all along you knew they would clear you."

Sheiye returned to the kitchen. He washed his hands of the gun or the lox. "You haven't touched your bagel and lox," he said. "Eat up so I can drive you to the bus station."

I picked up a half bagel. "That's it?" I asked. "That's the mystery explained? I came to set things straight in my mind, but I'm more mixed up than ever."

"Contact them," Sheiye said. "I think they're ready."

My eyes felt tired. I was hungry, but the food reminded me of the *shive* day Mama caught me half swallowing, half choking on the lox. With my hunger stymied by memory, I felt confused about the wave of nostalgia sinking its teeth into me. I didn't know if I was missing Perel or if I wanted that gun.

"What are you doing the rest of the day?" I asked.

"I'm going fishing," Sheiye said.

"So late in the day?"

Without leaving his seat, Sheiye opened the refrigerator door. "I told my wife that's what I was doing today, so I have to catch some fish." He guzzled orange juice from the container and belched. "Excuse me," he said.

Sheiye stacked the dishes in the sink while I struggled with half a bagel and cream cheese. "That's how you commemorate her death?" I asked.

Sheiye turned off the faucet and wiped his hands on his jeans. "Brantzche, I want to be alone," he said. "I always told myself I'd see you as soon as you made the first move, no matter how inconvenient. Today of all days it was hard to see you, but I did. Now I want to be alone."

The fifteenth anniversary of Perel Szuster's death had stirred up old coals without heating that perpetual ache or illuminating how to proceed in this life. I ate my bagel and Sheiye shooed a persistent yellow jacket out the front door. On the way to the bus station, Sheiye said, oh yeah, Mr. Berg the *shoykhet* and Bolero were dead now too, the *shoykhet* of old age, and Bolero, well, a car on the Pike hit him when he was off his leash. Before I could respond, Sheiye changed the subject, realizing as he spoke that he didn't want to discuss any more automobile accidents. He asked me where New York began. I said I didn't understand. Manhattan, he said. I had used the word Manhattan. Where did Manhattan begin, he wanted to know. Did it begin in New Jersey? We made no plans to meet again.

4

BACK IN THE BUS STATION, the distorted voice of the public address system called my bus and gate number. Half an hour later, I was still sitting on the blue plastic seat, knowing I had yet more unfinished business in south Jersey. I got some change at a newsstand, telephoned the manager of Sir Ivory's to say I couldn't play that night, and bought a ticket to Long-a-coming.

I had forgotten many of the landmarks between Atlantic City and Jake's Poultry Farm: the gigantic white horse at the entrance to Old MacDonald's Vegetable Farm, the Territo Family Winery, the busloads of black and Puerto Rican blueberry pickers, still too poor to buy the cassette bargains at the Long-a-coming Farmer's Market and Auction. But on the surface, at least, a lot had changed. New seafood restaurants, gas stations, and construction companies had sprung up in my absence. Grocery stores and savings-and-loans had given way to Wawa supermarkets and employee credit unions. Even so, I expected to find the farm intact, our victories and misfortunes preserved for centuries in the land and buildings.

The bus stopped alongside the old white shelter, and as I stepped off, I looked around me with alarm. Sheiye had not prepared me for the ravages the farm had undergone. Only the gray house remained standing, its shingles chipped and lopsided, its cellar door smashed in. Charlie's room, never the sturdiest structure, looked as if an earthquake had shaken it half off the dilapidated main frame. Despite the need for more basic repairs, the current tenants had installed an air conditioner in the living room. And outside, several feet away from the ground where Sheiye killed our sister, hung four life jackets drying on the backyard clothesline.

The rest of the property was just as dramatically disfigured. Everywhere red earth was piled high in clusters, like giant ant hills, and orange earth movers waited idly to begin gouging again. In the right field, real estate developers had razed the coop and turkey pen and built half a dozen high-income condominiums—harbingers of the fate of my old eyesore house. Not one relic remained from the farm—not a chicken bone, not a crate, no feed sack, no doghouse.

The most appalling desecration, however, was the well-trafficked convenience minimart on the former site of the slaughterhouse. The land on which Mama and Papa had hauled chicken crates and slaughtered thousands of broilers, pullets, fryers, and roasters was a recently paved parking lot, and the store itself sat atop an old cesspool cover. As I walked across the hot tarmac, I thought of the classic science fiction scenario in which a long-familiar homestead changes in the blink of an eye into some new, ordinary, but jeering landscape; and nobody for miles around except for one eccentric old codger remembers the chicken-farm dwellers. In childhood I had loathed the poultry business with all my heart, and had judged it a bizarre occupation for my war-obsessed parents. Now the minimart and condos struck me as even more perverse. Gone was all evidence of struggle: to live, to produce, to improve. Qualities like Mama and Papa's fortitude and patience were dispensable values here, like memory—outdated and ineffective in an age of time-saving, convenience commodities. Where did Perel's death and my parents' war experiences fit in? There was no place for them in this new order of south Jersey civilization, and I felt old and displaced.

Gingerly, I made my way through the field to the railroad tracks, my progress hindered by the encroaching pine trees and gravel pits. An hour later, at the tracks, I had neither the energy nor the courage to search out that old game rack; the earth's upheaval had uprooted the forest animals or made them bolder, and I had already startled a snake across my path. I sat down on a rug of moss and caught myself praying to God as I had fifteen years earlier for one last opportunity to see my sister.

"Oh, Brantzche, I thought you were past all that," Perel responded. Her tone was chivying, like an adoring mother's, but she would always look thirteen.

"Perel!" I cried. "You know I need you more than ever!"

I looked up at a sassafras tree and imagined my sister crammed in between the lower branches like a wood sprite. Embarrassed by my emotion, she said dryly, "Well, you've got me now, just like you always wanted."

"But why sound resentful?" I asked, perplexed and hurt. "Don't you want me to remember you?"

"Oh, I guess I'm envious, that's all," she said. "I didn't make it to the finish line."

"Thanks to Sheiye!" I yelled, feeling the wide swath of hatred claw inside me. But even here, in the woods, where Sheiye and I had faced each other down, I could not sustain the rage, and it passed. A bit deflated, I explained, "I've just come from him."

"Oh, how is he?" Perel asked in a remote voice.

"Don't you know?" I was stupefied. I thought the dead knew everything. "Perel, don't you want to be avenged?"

My sister sighed. "You see things differently from my perspective. Don't be shocked, Brantzche. The dead mature too."

"Oh, Perel!" I cried out, overcome with love and frustration. "Why did you always have to hide? It was your fault for hiding!"

"Don't blame me, Brantzche," Perel said sharply. "Children hide from everything. They're allowed to." After a pause, she continued more wistfully, "I can assure you, our brother will regret that hour till his dying day. Not that that does me any good." This last Perel spoke demurely, like a pupil conjugating French verbs for her governess.

"What do I do about Mama and Papa?" I asked. "I'm afraid to see them."

Perel made some kind of clicking sound. "You think waiting another fifteen years will make it easier?" She looked at me knowingly. "They must have been impossible to deal with, huh?" Once more I felt a stab of loneliness, for only Perel could have appreciated the grim comedy of our parents' relentless judgments. My old impetus to turn Perel against our mother reasserted itself and I charged, "Do you know I caught Mama snooping in your room once?"

"Really!" Perel exclaimed, but her tone lacked outrage. As if appeasing me, she encouraged, "Tell me, I want to know."

One afternoon I had run up the stairs to get Perel, and I found Mama reading from a sheet of paper, pronouncing vowels and tocking consonants as if she were speaking Polish. Her English pronunciation used to grate on me. If the Poles wanted to mouth every letter in their language, fine. But English is a language of silent, vestigial letters, and the ideas they represent are turreted in beautiful, baroque *gh*'s, *tion*'s and *e*'s whose presence determines the music of a word. Mama didn't hear me on the stairs as I prepared to hound her for Policizing my language. Meaning floated up to her through the English phonetics and Mama suppressed a laugh.

"Find anything interesting?" I asked, arms folded, foot tapping outside the bedroom door.

Mama was still chuckling. "Matter of fact," she said in her clipped and monosyllabic English, "I did." Holding the paper out to me, Mama laughed outright, waiting for me to agree that youth is deluded, not to chide her for trespassing. Written on the page in carefully printed letters were seven plaintive words: "The problem is, children outgrow their parents."

"Perele forgot to put it with her other poems," Mama said.

"With what other poems?" I should have pretended Perel and I were co-conspirators against Mama and Papa, compiling anthologies of their injustices against us. Instead, Mama and I competed for the copyright to Perel's imagination. I felt cross with my sister for not telling me she wrote poetry. How were we supposed to beat Mama and Papa if Perel hid things from me?

"Perele writes poems," Mama said in her computer English.

"And she shows them to you? Or is *this* how you know?"

"A mother has a right to look through her child's drawers."

"Do I have a right to look at your diaphragm? Or does Papa use condoms?" A sure low blow, and Mama blushed.

"Brantzchele, you and Perele belong to me," Mama declared. She cocked her head at an angle and said, "It's biology. You were all part of me one time."

"Murderers were part of their mothers' bodies once," I said. "Does that mean the mother and child have something in common with each other? Besides, we left your body. We didn't need it anymore."

"No, no, no," Mama insisted, retying each child's umbilical cord with each no. "You will always belong to me. Even when you're eighty and I'm a hundred and five."

"When I'm eighty and you're a hundred and five, we won't know each other," I said.

Mama refused to be insulted, knowing that her patience exasperated me most of all. "You write poems too?" she asked.

"Yeah, hundreds of pages, novels, about how I can't wait to leave this dump," I said.

"Good. Save them and show them to your children." Mama turned the page face down, said something that sounded like "la la la," and went into the bathroom.

"Brantzche," Perel began faintly, ignoring my story and receding into an aching, though less accessible, recess of my memory. "You don't have to come back here anymore. There's nothing for either one of us."

The leaves overhead rustled just loudly enough to interrupt my reverie. My contemplation dispelled, I jumped up and pleaded, "How will I find you again?"

I waited to hear my sister's answer but heard only the distant whistle of an eastbound train. An aura of solemnity hovered in the humid air, prompting me to pronounce the blessings for wine, bread, and Shabbos candles, the only prayers I could recall just then. Brushing the twigs from my carryall, I walked alongside the tracks towards the Assumption Parish, where Perel and I had watched Sheiye and Millington at the carnival so long ago. As the train rumbled past, stacked double-decker with new Fords, the engineer blew the whistle again and I waved at him. Twenty minutes later I stood inside the phone booth in front of Humble's Supermarket, sweating and gritty from the dust that had swirled in the train's wake.

Although I had a set of keys to Sonia Kichner's house, I called her on the off chance that she might be home. A male voice answered the telephone. It wasn't Laybl; he had died three years earlier at seventy-eight from prostate cancer. "Gabriel," I said, surprised. "What are you doing home?"

"Well, I'll be damned!" he said like a true dyed-in-the-wool American. "It's the orphan! Where you calling from?"

"I'm in Long-a-coming, at Humble's. Come get me."

My tendency to see intention instead of coincidence in Gabriel's visit got me dreaming about the reason for his homecoming. As far as I knew, he had not been to Long-a-coming in years, and saw his mother only when he invited her to stay with him in Milwaukee. I rebuked myself for thinking of Gabriel in soap opera terms, for hoping that his marriage was, in fact, over, and that his sisterly affection for me would turn passionate. After I hung up the receiver, I studied my reflection in the booth glass, dabbing at a patch of soot on my cheek and wishing I had brought a more feminine change of clothing with me. As I squinted through the glass, I noticed that Marnie's Five-and-Ten no longer existed and in its place stood the Ask Josephine Travel Agency. As a child, I had viewed travel as the need to seek refuge, as emigration. But the posters in the plate glass advertised Caribbean cruises and European package tours for two weeks of "excitement" or "relaxation" or "culture," and this remodeled storefront, too, hinted at a different, more suburbanized clientele.

Wryly, I thought that even with these changes, I still did not fit in Long-a-coming. Walking out to Long Avenue, taking in the fire station, the new municipal building, where the grammar school had stood for forty years, the public library, where Perel and I had tried to decipher Freud, I was weighed down by that oppressive feeling of not belonging in this town, and wanting to, but still dreaming of flight. I remembered how on my trips to Marnie's every Saturday night with Papa to buy the *Philadelphia Inquirer,* I watched the volunteer firemen set up card tables in front of the open firehouse, the engines candy red and gleaming as the men drank beer and threw their cards down with a mix of privilege and defeat. I always begged Papa to let me purchase the Sunday paper while he kept the Chevy running outside. As I entered the store, I looked about for my schoolmates who might see me and report to each other that Brenda had been "out" Saturday night, a sighting, I believed, that would increase my prestige; for just setting foot in Long-a-coming was a sign that the town accepted you. Nothing momentous ever happened inside Marnie's, and we returned to the farm, Papa rendering "Get Me a Ticket for an Aeroplane" with a Yiddish flair, my few minutes in town an induction ceremony with no guarantee of membership.

I did not know what to do as I waited for Gabriel. I felt conspicuous, scared that someone might recognize me as the Szuster girl, and offended when they didn't. Heading back towards Humble's, embarrassed by my dirty white jeans, I stopped in front of the Ask Josephine Travel Agency and smiled to think that all my running—from family, from reconciliation—had merely brought me full circle to Long-a-coming. Would I find myself here in another fifteen years, an aging orphan with no ties to anything but my memory of Perel? Finally, I acknowledged the faded poster of Holy Land Tours in the upper corner of the window, set apart from the sleek couples cavorting on tropical beaches. By no stretch of the imagination did I belong to the pious, either, but before it was too late, I had to see Mama and Papa again on their turf, or risk becoming the poor wayfaring stranger forever.

As I gazed through the window, full of all the worship and dread that the thought of my parents conjured in me, Gabriel pulled into Humble's parking lot in a beige van with sliding doors, reunited with his wife and two redheaded sons. Already I felt the words assemble inside me, like a choral refrain, as much a consolation as a torment. Maybe nobody else would ever know or much care, but at will, I could resurrect the picture of a little girl standing on tiptoes, peering through the window of a chicken slaughterhouse, repeating to herself, *"Gedenk.* . . . Remember. . . ."